Francis Claudius Armstrong

The Pirates of the Foam

Francis Claudius Armstrong

The Pirates of the Foam

ISBN/EAN: 9783337044367

Printed in Europe, USA, Canada, Australia, Japan

Cover: Foto ©Andreas Hilbeck / pixelio.de

More available books at **www.hansebooks.com**

THE
PIRATES OF THE FOAM
BY
CAPT. ARMSTRONG

MISS BRADDON'S NOVELS.

Thoroughly Revised and in parts re-written, with Frontispiece and Vignette, handsomely printed and strongly bound in cloth, gilt, crown 8vo, price 6s.

LADY AUDLEY'S SECRET.	ONLY A CLOD.
AURORA FLOYD.	LADY LISLE.
ELEANOR'S VICTORY.	THE TRAIL OF THE SERPENT.
SIR JASPER'S TENANT.	THE LADY'S MILE.
JOH…	…TURE.
HEN…	
THE…	
CHA…	

PAR…   …VELS.
In t…   …page on
    to   …each.
THE…   …s require-
Bradd…   …nnounce a
every   …'s Novels,
in the   …le, printed
per w   …asily-read
Two   …gilt back,
Bradd   …n interme-
of pu   …erned, but
ceden   …he neatest,
Trade   …ks that the
well   …n procure.
press…   …w Edition
exper   …lume con-
legibl

LADY…   …'s WIFE.
HEN…   …D.

C…   …VELS.

LADY…   …SERPENT.
HEN…   …ILE.
ELE…
AUR…   …HE VUL-
THE…

…KS.
…ch.

1. F…   …e Best Way
…Col. Plate.
…w to Cook,
…What to do
2. T…   …Coloured

…st Way to
…Coloured

3. I…   with Bills of Fare for all the Year to   8. VEGETABLES… how they should be
Please Everybody; together with the   Cooked and Served Up; with General
Best Recipes for Sauces, Pickles,   Observations on Bread and Biscuit
Gravies, and Forcemeats.   Baking, the Dairy, &c.

4. POULTRY AND GAME; How to Cook   9. PRESERVES AND CONFECTIONERY.
and Carve, with General Observations   How to Make Ices, Jellies, Creams,
when In and when Out of Season.   Jams, Omelettes, Custards, &c. Co-
Coloured Plate.   loured Plate.

London: WARD, LOCK, & TYLER, Warwick House, Paternoster Row.

THE

PIRATES OF "THE FOAM.

A Novel.

BY

CAPT. C. F ARMSTRONG,

AUTHOR OF "THE CRUISE OF THE DARING," "SAILOR HERO,"
"PERILS BY SEA AND LAND," ETC. ETC.

LONDON:
WARD, LOCK, & TYLER, 158, FLEET STREET
AND 107, DORSET STREET, SALISBURY SQUARE.

LONDON:
PRINTED BY WOODFALL AND KINDER,
MILFORD LANE, STRAND, W.C.

LONDON:
PRINTED BY WOODFALL AND KINDER,
MILFORD LANE, STRAND, W.C.

PIRATES OF "THE FOAM."

CHAPTER I.

Mr. Skelton was sitting in his parlour with his wife and two daughters, when a letter, bearing the Ramsgate postmark, was placed in his hands. Hurriedly breaking the seal and reading a line or two, he turned alternately pale and red, exclaiming, " Dead !—how sudden ! "

" Dead ! " repeated Mrs. Skelton, startled. " Dear me ! who is dead, John ? "

" Why, Mrs. Morton, of Ramsgate," replied the schoolmaster, in a very serious accent, changing to a tone of vexation as he added, " and within a fortnight of the next quarter's payment becoming due."

The lady looked sad, as she said, feelingly, " Poor Arthur will feel this sudden bereavement deeply. What will he do ? "

" That's exactly what I want to know," answered the husband sharply. " I wonder if she has made a will, and has left anything to this castaway."

Mrs. Skelton's countenance was sorrowful as she murmured, " Poor young man ! I trust he will be provided with a situation at all events."

" Fiddlestick ! " muttered the husband; " let us think of ourselves, not of that proud upstart, who will find his level now. But I shall be in time for the one o'clock train. Lucky it is vacation. I will start at once for Ramsgate. Mrs. Morton has been dead nearly a week. When you see young Bolton, just tell him the old woman is no more ; you can continue to be civil to him till I hear or see how the land lies." And off went the schoolmaster.

" What can papa mean ? " exclaimed Anne Skelton to her thoughtful mother. " Surely he does not intend to be unkind to Arthur."

" Why. my dear," replied the mother evasively, " what

can your father do? We are far from rich. You cannot expect him to support Arthur Bolton?"

"No, mamma," returned the young girl almost reproachfully; "but he could show that he felt for his unprotected situation. He is quite fit to take the usher's vacant place. You know papa is anxiously looking for one to replace young Mr. Gleg—— "

"Unfortunately, my dear child, your papa has a great dislike to Mr. Bolton. Why, I cannot surmise, for the young man is endowed with fine talents, and is kind and attentive to every one."

During this conversation between mother and daughter, Arthur Bolton was in the garden assisting John Burton, the gardener, to fasten up plants, and trim and arrange Miss Anne Skelton's own especial flower-garden.

Whilst thus employed, intent on pleasing one who for many years had been to him as a most cherished sister, and unconscious of the great change impending, we will introduce our hero more fully to the reader, and explain why, at twenty, he was still studying in Mr. Skelton's school, and also tell why, with all his indefatigable industry, high principles, and submission to just discipline, he was an object of dislike to the gentleman who was hailed as master by a large number of pupils.

When Arthur, at the age of nine, was placed as pupil with Mr. Skelton, that gentleman regarded him as an orphan of good family, the *protégé* of a widow lady, a relative, whose name was Morton, reputed rich, and who resided at Ramsgate. Of her wishes there could be no doubt, for she paid most liberally for the child's education each quarter in advance, though she never saw him.

After a few months, rumour carried some report into the school, and Mr. Skelton, who worshipped wealth and power, and hated everything plebeian, questioned his pupil, and was disgusted to discover that he knew nothing respecting his parents, and had no recollection of any home but that of a shrimp-catcher, whose daughter had shown him the care and affection of a mother, and whose name he bore. He had been placed in that humble home by Mrs. Morton, who had saved him from drowning on the beach, and whose age prevented any scandal being attached to her charitable action. Beyond the mere act of saving the child's life, and the certainty that its infancy and early childhood were fostered and properly attended to, she seemed to ignore his existence, till suddenly she remembered, that having performed an act of Christian kindness towards the little foundling, duties were entailed which she resolved to fulfil. The first was to give him a good education ; and liberal payment was offered Mr. Skelton to make the boy clever. Kindness with learning might also have been advantageously bargained for, but Mrs. Morton knew nothing of kindness, and gave no apparent thought to what the poor helpless child might suffer in leaving his humble home to go among associates of a grade superior to that he had hitherto been accustomed to.

Fortunately he had been well trained. If he had been treated as a little prince in the shrimp-catcher's cottage, he had been taught self-denial, and to feel for those around him. His manners, if wanting in polish, were without vulgarity, and very soon he won his way to the affection of his young companions, though he made no progress in gaining an interest in Mr. Skelton's heart. That gentleman, with his predilection for birth and station, was jealous that a nameless castaway should distance more high-born competitors. In the schoolroom little Bolton, as he was at first styled, studied steadily, was so attentive to rules that the master had but few opportunities of punishing.

In the early part of his career at school, our young hero formed a strict friendship with a lad named Hugh Dormer, the son of a Hampshire baronet, and this friendship presented a great barrier against any unjust attack from the master, who saw his despised pupil climb every impediment thrown in his way, in his great thirst for knowledge, and advance in the love and esteem of all save himself. Some indeed would sometmes, in the heat of passion or envy, call him a shrimp, an then the indignant boy would prove he was about the worst kind of shrimp they ever handled, and discovered his claws had more of the lobster in their grip than the shrimp.

Little in reality did Arthur Bolton care, either for the sneers of the mean-spirited few, or the unjust dislike of Mr. Skelton ; the greater number of his companions loved him, and Mrs. Skelton had compassion on the orphan, and strove to be a mother in attention and affection. Her children were first his playfellows in the holidays, afterwards his companions, and by little kindnesses atoned for the conduct of the father, and thus rendered his life not unhappy, if deprived of all those ties so delightful to the young, viz., the loving smile of a mother,—a father's glance of proud satisfaction, as the hard-earned prize-book is given to his hand,—a sister's kiss of congratulation,—a brother's warm grasp. To all these feelings Arthur Bolton was an alien, but he steadily pursued his course of study, and had his reward in the consciousness of his own talents.

The greatest sorrow during these years was the departure of Hugh Dormer from school ; a departure soothed by promises of enduring affection and a constant correspondence, and the hope of future intercourse.

Two years before this tale commences, Mr. Skelton was informed that his despised pupil would, as soon as possible, be placed in a government office, and the young man was requested to prepare himself for its duties. These duties were not defined, but Arthur wanted no incentive to study, which formed his only occupation, almost his only amusement. He should be placed in the world, he was told—to rise, to shine. To make a position in that world he knew depended on himself ; and with a strong resolution, aided by health and spirit, he resolved to attain his wish. The contempt of Mr. Skelton—his lonely situation—the various little trials and disagreeables in his life—were unnoticed, almost unheeded ; the coming struggle was coolly thought of ; all was merged in future success, which must be gained by knowledge—experience, only time could give—but Arthur resolved to go to the battle of existence armed at all points—prepared for any emergency. He was now in his twentieth year, and the battle was about to begin.

As Mrs. Skelton and her daughter Anne entered the garden, Arthur Bolton put down his spade, and advanced to meet them ; he thought both were looking serious, if not sad, so much so that he said, for he greatly esteemed Mrs. Skelton,—

"I hope nothing unpleasant has occurred, Mrs. Skelton."

"In truth, Arthur," returned the lady, "I am very sad, and it is on your account. Mr. Skelton has just heard that your kind protectress, Mrs. Morton, has died suddenly."

"Indeed!" exclaimed Arthur, with visible emotion. "Poor, dear lady ; this is sad intelligence. To her I owe life, and next to life, the education that will, I trust, enable me honestly to pursue my career through life."

"I trust so, indeed," said Mrs. Skelton, with a sigh, as she thought how he would have to struggle with the world. "No doubt," she added, "Mrs. Morton has left some will or document stating her wishes respecting you."

"If I never receive more than the blessing of education her noble heart has bestowed upon me, I shall honour her generosity to the last hour of my life," answered Arthur emphatically.

Conversing on this sad and unexpected event, they left the garden and walked towards the house. Anne expressing all her kind, gentle heart dictated, to soothe and calm the emotion Arthur Bolton evidently experienced.

Mr. Skelton returned late the following night; all were anxious for his arrival, but Arthur had retired to his chamber, perfectly aware how much the schoolmaster disliked him, and had made up his mind to leave his house at a moment's notice.

Mrs. Skelton was waiting up for her husband, who looked, when he came in, agitated and annoyed.

"This is a bad business for Bolton," he exclaimed, throwing himself into a chair as his wife mixed a tumbler of negus for him. "We must get rid of him as soon as possible; it won't do to have to feed a great overgrown youth without the smallest chance of being repaid; he has not a fraction to look forward to."

"Good heavens!—how distressing," responded Mrs. Skelton, feelingly.

"Distressing, indeed!" snappishly returned her husband; "distressing to us, I think, if I had not secured payment in advance."

"But did Mrs. Morton die without a will, without any document, settling——"

"Tut! settling, indeed," interrupted Mr. Skelton, "she has not left a shilling; her income of seven hundred a year was derived from an annuity which reverts to a younger brother, no one ever heard of till after her death; and this brother turns out to be Sir Richard Morton, of Morton Manor, Derbyshire, a harsh, haughty, aristocratic-looking personage, who was telegraphed for by a solicitor of Ramsgate; he was aware who she was at all events."

"Was this baronet in Ramsgate when you arrived?" questioned Mrs. Skelton, greatly surprised.

"No; he arrived late last night, and I had an interview with him this morning. I was received with haughty coldness, and when I mentioned that I had a pupil in my academy, for whom the late Mrs. Morton paid, he interrupted me sharply, saying, 'I am aware of that circumstance, sir. But I have nothing to do with my late sister's eccentric acts. I find your demands in full are paid up to the first of next month; therefore, you, sir, can have no claim upon my late sister, or on me; and as to the youth brought up so handsomely through her eccentric charity, he may think himself (the child probably of some cunning vagrant), extremely fortunate in having received an education.'

"'Then I am to conclude, Sir Richard Morton, that

you refuse to contribute any further to his maintenance or education ? '

" ' Certainly ; if he is industrious, and has benefited by your instruction, I consider any further help unnecessary ; ' and with a cold, haughty bow from Sir Richard, our interview ended."

" What a proud, unfeeling man !" said Mrs. Skelton, disgusted.

" Nevertheless," returned the schoolmaster coldly, " he was quite right. Bolton must fight his own way in the world, so away from here he goes to-morrow. That old fool, Mrs. Morton, I heard, was to be put into a leaden coffin and carried into Derbyshire to be buried in the family vault."

" How very strange that Mrs. Morton should be sister to a baronet, when no one in Ramsgate knew anything about it till after her death."

" There is some mystery about the old lady, certainly— family differences, probably. However there is no mystery respecting her and this Bolton ; she was more than fifty years old when she snatched the bundle in which the child was wrapt out of the sea, just as the tide was carrying it away—an action witnessed by more than twenty persons. Now let us to bed; to-morrow I will let Bolton know that he must seek a home elsewhere, for here he shall not stay twenty-four hours—a child of shame no doubt."

" Oh, Charles," said Mrs. Skelton reproachfully, " do not add insult to unmerited misfortune. Arthur Bolton will make his way in the world, depend on it."

" Then the sooner he sets about it the better," observed the husband with a sneer.

Arthur Bolton passed a restless night ; he felt sincerely grieved at the death of his benefactress. He also very well imagined that if left helpless and unprovided for, his residence under Mr. Skelton's roof, which then sheltered him, was at an end ; he possessed a few pounds, saved from the generous allowance Mrs. Morton had made him the last four years ; this would carry him to London, and keep him for a month till he procured employment. He would write to Hugh Dormer, who he felt sure through his father's interest would be able to obtain him a Government situation.

The next day, immediately after breakfast, Mr. Skelton requested his pupil to attend him in his study.

Mr. Skelton, besides being mean and avaricious, was a harsh, unkind man by nature, and he delighted in humbling any one he disliked.

As Arthur entered the study, the master of the house looked up from his desk, at which he was sitting, and let his keen, malicious grey eyes rest upon the fine intellectual features of his pupil.

" I have to tell you, Mr. Bolton, that Mrs. Morton has died without making any provision for you whatever. Her brother, Sir Richard Morton, a Derbyshire baronet, with whom I had an interview, declares he knew nothing about you ; that his sister's eccentric conduct in petting up a child, brutally exposed by some tramp——"

" Take care, sir," interrupted Arthur, his dark eyes flashing, and stepping close up to the startled schoolmaster, " how you add insult to meanness. If the brother of my kind benefactress uttered the words you now make use of, his title to be called a gentleman is slight indeed ; if you possessed any human feeling in your breast, you would have scorned to repeat such words. Whatever my birth may be, neither you nor the baronet can know anything about it. You have been well paid for my tuition up to this hour, and I now leave your house, trusting it may never again be my misfortune to cross your path in my journey through life ;" and casting upon the abashed preceptor a look of scorn, the young man turned upon his heel and left the room.

Livid with rage, Mr. Skelton sprang from his seat and turned into the parlour, where his wife and daughter were sitting. " There's a young vagrant—a perfect firebrand. I am not sure that my life is not in danger. I always said he was a disgrace to my establishment."

Mrs. Skelton looked confounded. Anne and her sister frightened. Nevertheless Anne rose up and quitted the room ; there were tears in the affectionate girl's eyes, for she knew in her heart that Arthur, unless undeservedly treated or provoked, would never have uttered a word to insult or irritate her father.

" What has caused your anger, my dear ? " asked Mrs. Skelton, in a soothing tone. " What did you say to Arthur ? "

" Say to the cur ! " repeated the furious schoolmaster ; " I only repeated what Sir Richard said : that he was not going to extend his charity to the child of a tramp or vagrant."

" Oh, heavens ! you did not surely say those words, Charles," exclaimed the wife, a tear stealing down her cheek.

" Come, none of this trash," rejoined Mr. Skelton savagely ; " I'm not going to be bullied by a mere boy, and twitted by my wife, and all because the fellow has a fine figure and a handsome face.   Where is your sister gone, miss?" he added, turning to Emily ; "go and call her back directly.   No one in my house shall bid the young scamp farewell."

Whilst Emily was absent in search of her sister, Mrs. Skelton did all she could, exerting her utmost eloquence, to quell her husband's passion, and prevent his doing so harsh and cruel an act as driving young Bolton from their house, but all in vain ; his only answer was—" Out of my house he shall go, and that before night."

After half an hour Emily returned to the room, her face and eyes red from weeping.

" Where is your sister, miss?" exclaimed her father.

" She has gone to her room, papa, and Arthur Bolton has left.   John Burton has taken his things in the wheel-barrow to the station."

" The old scoundrel!" exclaimed Mr. Skelton, "to leave my work and use my wheel-barrow without my permission ; he shall not be paid for this day's work, and it's doubtful if ever he gets another here again."

There was quite a commotion in the schoolmaster's house that day.   The servants cared little for their master's anger, and showed how sorry they were for the departed handsome pupil, who was loved and admired by many in Canterbury besides the inmates of Skelton Academy.

Previous to his departure, Anne contrived to see him for a few minutes, giving him a letter from her mother, telling him to take great care of it, and expressing how deeply they deplored the unhappy deprivation that occasioned the interview with her father and its results.

It was not without emotion that Arthur kissed Anne's cheek, and bade her farewell, wished her every happiness, and entreated her to tell her mother his strong feeling of affection and gratitude to her for years of uniform kindness and attention.   Thus he left the house—his home for the last nine years, little conjecturing the struggle in which he must take his part—the strange events in which he must become an actor.

CHAPTER II.

Arthur Bolton, after quitting Skelton Academy, proceeded to the Railway Station, and took a second-class ticket for London.

The train was soon seen approaching, and on reaching the platform he entered an empty box, to be at liberty to give free vent to his thoughts ; but just as the train was moving, a man threw open the door, and had just time to take his place as the carriages moved on.

"Gad, I was nearly too late," said the stranger, seating himself opposite the young man, who looked up at his companion, and wished him away. He was not much attracted by his appearance, though he was respectably dressed. He appeared about thirty-five or six years of age, and carried a small leathern case in his hand, which he placed carefully beside him, and, after a few minutes' silence, commenced a conversation, saying—

"Pray, sir, are you bound for the great city? "

"Yes," returned our hero, "I am."

"Well acquainted with town, sir? "

"I cannot say that I am," returned Arthur.

"Neither am I, sir," observed the stranger, "but I dare say you have heard of the great establishment of Rimmell, the perfumer."

"I have used his soap, certainly, and very good soap it is," replied Arthur.

"Well, sir," continued the stranger, in a tone of great confidence, "I will tell you my business in town."

Our hero did not want to know his business, but before he could make any observation to that effect, his companion went on:

"I have invented one of the most delicious perfumes, and I feel satisfied, when brought out under Rimmell's name and patronage, it will make my fortune ; but pardon me ; you shall judge," and producing a carefully folded packet from his breast-pocket, he unrolled and exposed to view a small bottle. Taking out the stopper, he held it towards Arthur Bolton's nose, in a manner that he could scarcely avoid drawing in the perfume ; the moment he did so, he fell back a little bewildered ; the man with the perfume again held the bottle close to his nostrils, and in a moment he became insensible.

"Ah," said the stranger, corking the bottle quietly, "he is a strong youth," and he began to carefully inspect our hero's pockets ; he drew out his purse, just cast a look into it, and transferred it to his own keeping ; he then took several other articles, and was on the point of searching an inner breast-pocket, in which was Anne Skelton's letter, when the whistle sounded, the steam was turned off, and the train, reduced in speed, proceeded along the platform of ——— station.

"Ah, so soon," said the man, "three or four minutes more would have answered better ; as it is, I have left him no tin;" and opening the door he jumped out just as the train stopped.

Arthur looked as if he were in a deep sleep; the fact was, he had had administered a dose of powerful chloroform. No one entered the carriage at this station, and the train rolled on—the slight concussion of the carriages in getting into motion caused our hero to lose his upright position; this roused him—he opened his eyes, felt dizzy and confused, and his recollections mystified; but with a great effort he shook this feeling off, and rapidly recovered his senses.

"I have been the dupe of that villain of a pretended perfumer," he muttered, as he perceived that he was alone in the carriage, "and no doubt he has robbed me, and got out whilst I lay insensible."

A feeling of dismay pervaded his mind; he put his hand into his pocket—every fraction he possessed in the world was gone, even his keys. "Ah," said he, "how fortunate my packing up my gold watch and chain (the gift of Hugh Dormer's father, when he saved his schoolfellow's life), it is worth fifty guineas. I can get a supply upon that; but to arrive in London without a single shilling to defray the most trifling expense is embarrassing." It was night when the train drew up at the platform of -——— station. The place was crowded. Approaching the luggage van, which the porters were rapidly unloading, he examined the trunks, valises, portmanteaus, and all the parcels of luggage thrown out on the platform. At length the van was emptied. Still Arthur Bolton saw none of his luggage—consisting of two trunks.

"I do not see my luggage," he remarked to the porters.

"Where from, sir?" demanded the porter.

"Canterbury," returned our hero anxiously.

"This is all the luggage that came from that station," aid the porter.

The guard coming up inquired civilly:

"Have you lost anything, sir?"

"Yes," returned Bolton; "my two trunks are not here, and I saw them myself put in at the Canterbury station."

"What name, sir?" asked the guard, looking at the luggage left on the platform.

"Arthur Bolton, London."

The guard started and looked vexed.

"I fear you have been robbed, sir," he said. "I remember very well a person got out at -——— station and ordered the porter to take out his trunks;

he would proceed no further, though he had a ticket for London, going at the same time to the ticket porter, and adding, 'My business can be done here. You will find my luggage labelled Mr. A. Bolton, London.' The porter took out the luggage. I was passing by at the time, and saw the two trunks taken up and placed on a truck, but I had no idea there was anything wrong."

"The rascal!" said our hero, with a flush on his cheek at being so easily plundered.

"You had better see our superintendent, sir," said a policeman standing by—"acting promptly may recover them. He is in his private office ; you can see him now."

"Thank you," returned our hero ; "I will take your advice."

The policeman led the way off the platform, and along a row of offices, and pushed open a door, saying : "First door to the right, sir. Mr. Baldwin is our superintendent's name."

On entering the room Arthur beheld a middle-aged gentleman sitting at a table, busily examining a large bundle of papers ; as he raised his head, a side-door opened, and a youth entered the room, giving the superintendent a slip of paper: "Telegraph message, sir."

Mr. Baldwin ran his eyes over the paper ; and then looking up at our hero, said, "What can I do, sir, for you?"

Arthur stated his case briefly, but clearly. The superintendent smiled, and looking again at the paper, said, "I congratulate you, Mr. Bolton ; your luggage is recovered and is now safe under the charge of one of my officers at

———. I am sorry to say that the rascals that were so nearly getting off with it have as yet escaped. Of course I have no particulars ; this message merely says, "Luggage marked, A. Bolton, London—supposed stolen —safe under my charge—thief escaped—passenger, no doubt, in last train."

"So, you see, young gentleman, no time has been lost. Still," continued the superintendent, "I wish to ask you a few questions ; therefore, be so kind as to sit down. I will have your luggage here to-morrow morning."

"I am greatly obliged to your officer for his promptness in detecting the rascal that so skilfully plundered me," replied onr hero ; "like you, sir, I think there is a great deal of obscurity about the robbery ; for how the fellow knew my name, puzzles me."

"Oh ! I think I can guess that," said Mr. Baldwin. "We have to do with so many of these kind of affairs, that our wits are always on the alert. That fellow, no doubt, was looking for some one to prey upon, and whilst on the platform observed you putting your luggage in the train and remarked the name ; saw you enter an empty carriage, and planned his scheme on the moment. But I have to beg of you to let me know a few particulars respecting yourself, which, you will see, is quite necessary before I can deliver the trunks to you to-morrow."

"Certainly, any question you please to put," said our hero, "I will answer as far as I possibly can."

"I am quite satisfied from your appearance and manner, Mr. Bolton," said the superintendent, "that there is no deception whatever in your statement ; but I wish, if possible, to trace that fellow that plundered you of your purse, &c.   It strikes me, the more I think of it, that something was premeditated against you, even before you made your appearance on the platform at Canterbury, for your being alone in the carriage was a mere chance.   Where, may I ask, did you come from to Canterbury ? "

"Only from Mr. Skelton's academy," said Arthur. "Ah !" he added, " I forgot," and putting his hand into his breast-pocket, he pulled out the letter given him by Anne Skelton, and which most fortunately escaped the thief. "This letter, no doubt, will prove my identity to you, sir," and he broke the seal. As he unfolded it, he perceived it contained a locket and a bank-note for twenty pounds. The colour flew to his cheeks and temples ; putting the note and locket in his pocket, whilst his voice trembled with emotion, he said, turning to Mr. Baldwin, who was looking into the youth's face, watching its varying expression, " This letter, thank goodness, escaped the thief;" and holding it over to the superintendent, he showed him that it began, "My dear Arthur," and was signed, " Anne Skelton."

Mr. Baldwin merely cast his eyes upon the signature, took down Mr. Skelton's address, and then said, " I am exceedingly glad that the letter and its contents escaped that rascal. Now leave me your address in town, in case we catch this fellow and his associates ; and to-morrow I have no doubt I shall be able to let you know how Sergeant Maul regained your luggage."

" Could you recommend me a quiet, reasonable hotel, Mr. Baldwin ?   I shall feel greatly obliged, as I am a perfect stranger in London."

" I am glad you asked me," answered Mr. Baldwin ; and taking up a sheet of paper, he wrote a few lines, and signed it ; directing it to ' Mrs. Hartley, Crown Hotel, Cavendish Square.' "There, Mr. Bolton, go there._The landlady is my aunt. She will take all possible care of you, and not tax your purse too much. Oh, by-the-bye, you were robbed of your purse, and it's not likely you will get your note changed this time of the night ; you will want to pay a cab and porter ; let me furnish you with a little change till I see you to-morrow, say twelve o'clock ; I shall be here."

Thanking the really kind-hearted superintendent, Arthur left the office, and calling a cab outside the Station, he told him to drive him to the Crown Hotel, Cavendish Square.

On arriving, he entered a very nice, quiet, private hotel, and seeing an elderly woman and two young females in the bar, he gave Mr. Baldwin's note to the elderly woman, who having read it, said :

"Ah, so my nephew sent you to me, young gentleman, and says you have been robbed of your luggage, but luckily it will be recovered. Ah, he is a very smart man, is Mr. Baldwin, and you may depend I will make any one comfortable he recommends." She then showed him into the coffee-room, saying she would send him tea, &c., in a few minutes.

"Come," thought our hero to himself, "I am, thank goodness, out of this my first scrape in my struggle through life. Thanks to dear, kind-hearted Anne ;" and finding himself alone, he took out her letter, and eagerly perused it.

"MY DEAR ARTHUR,

"Do not fear to make use of the bank-note enclosed ; it is a trifling gift from my dear mother. The moment she heard of Mrs. Morton's death, she said to me : 'It is very possible, Anne, that Arthur may have to seek and make his own way in the world ; if so, he cannot be burdened with gold, poor fellow. Enclose this note in a letter, and express to him my kind feelings and wishes for his welfare and his happiness, and that a merciful Providence may assist his honest endeavours.' And now, my dear brother, for such I shall always consider you (for have we not grown up from childhood together ?), use this little sum without scruple, for it is my mother's own money, part of a legacy from a dear sister. And now farewell! Accept the enclosed locket from your affectionate and loving sister, and dear friend,

"ANNE SKELTON."

"Yes, dear Anne, I will use this money," soliloquized Arthur ; "because I know what you say is truth ; and I trust in God the time may come when I can repay both the money and the affection that caused its bestowal."

The next day, at twelve o'clock, he was on the platform of the —————— station, and proceeded to the superintendent's office. Mr. Baldwin received him very kindly, and stated that his trunks had arrived. "I will tell you how it happened that the thieves failed in their attempt to rob them of their contents:

"It chanced, just after the departure of the train from —————— station, that Sergeant Maul, a very keen, observing officer, who was walking up at the time to the platform from the goods station, saw two men crossing the line to a by-lane on the other side. One was wheeling a barrow, with something in it. This is not allowed, because down that lane there is a small alehouse which bears a very bad repute, and by order of the Company the gate of passage across the line has been taken away. Sergeant Maul called out to them, and walked on towards them. One of the men looked round, and then hastened on, crossed the railway, and proceeded rapidly down the lane ; the other man was getting the barrow over the rails when the sergeant overtook him, calling out: 'I say, my man, you know this is not allowed. You can read the notice that is up.'

" 'No, indeed I cannot,' returned the man.

" 'Whose luggage is this, and where are you taking it to ? ' questioned Maul.

" 'To the Railway Tavern down the lane, sir.'

" 'But whose luggage is it ? ' continued the sergeant ; seeing that it could scarcely belong to the class of people frequenting the little alehouse. The man seemed confused, and was trying, the sergeant perceived, to get a glimpse of the labels on the trunks.

So catching the man by the arm, he said coolly—

" 'Come, take this luggage back to the station ; I don't know you ; there's something wrong here. If I am wrong, I will pay you for your double labour ; but this luggage shall not go, till I see or hear who is the owner.'

" 'Curse me, if I take it ! you may do it yourself,' said the man, and he walked off, jumped over the rails, and ran down the lane.

" The sergeant looked round for some one to take charge of the luggage, that he might pursue the man, but no one was sufficiently near ; so he quietly took up the barrow, and wheeled it to the station, and sent one of the policemen on duty to see who was at the Railway Tavern. Just at that moment a guard of the train, who had stopped at the station, and the very man you spoke to about your luggage, came up, and looking at the labels on the trunks, said :

"' Why, these are the very trunks the gentleman from Canterbury was robbed of.'

"'That's lucky,' said Sergeant Maul. 'Just telegraph to our superintendent that the luggage is safe, and I'll go and have a look after these gentry.'

" Thus, by a mere chance, Mr. Bolton, your trunks were recovered ; for if they had reached the Railway Tavern, you may be sure they would instantly have been rifled. However, Sergeant Maul could gain no trace of the parties. He found only an old woman and a girl in the tavern ; the old woman either deaf, or pretending to be so, and the young one saucy."

Arthur Bolton returned Mr. Baldwin his sincere thanks for his kindness, and wished to send a donation to Sergeant Maul, but the superintendent would permit only the expense of telegraph, &c., to be paid, and then they parted, mutually pleased with each other, Mr. Baldwin promising to call and see him at the hotel in the evening, as he wished to have half an hour's conversation with him, when he had time.

Arthur, quite elated at his good fortune, returned to the hotel with his recovered trunks ; and that evening wrote a long letter to Hugh Dormer, giving him all the news of himself, and telling him he was just beginning his trials.

Till he received an answer to his letter he resolved to remain quiet and not seek for any situation. He had plenty to amuse his mind, in visiting the various sights the mighty Babylon afforded.

He also wrote a long and affectionate letter to Anne Skelton, enclosing one for her mother, sending both under cover to his old favourite and humble friend John Burton, to whom he sent a post-office order for a sovereign ; for John had promised to deliver carefully any letters Arthur might write to the ladies of the Skelton family.

One evening Mr. Baldwin came to see him ; they supped together with the landlady and her two pretty nieces ; the former had taken a great liking to her lodger, and as the old lady was pleased with him, it may be presumed the young ladies were so also.

When the gentlemen were alone discussing a bottle of port, Mr. Baldwin began the conversation, saying,—

" I have received a letter from Mr. Skelton, to whom I wrote, for I confess there is some mystery, more than mere robbing, in the extracting of your money and stealing your trunks. Mr. Skelton's letter is a miserable production, a compound of meanness, selfishness, and pomposity. He states that he was imposed upon, and received you into his

academy as a pupil, supposing you to be the *protégé* of a
wealthy lady, and of respectable birth."

Arthur coloured slightly, but remained quite calm. Mr.
Baldwin laid his hand kindly on his shoulder, saying,—

" I think I can judge your disposition, and I venture thus
to make free with you, feeling for you, I assure you, a sincere esteem. I am actuated by motives I cannot now exactly
explain; but I think you knew a Mr. Jackson, of Canterbury, a gentleman of independent means, did you not? "

" Oh, yes," replied our hero, a little surprised ; " he had
a nephew at Mr. Skelton's, and he himself often passed an
evening at our academy. I used to play chess with him ;
he was a member of the —— chess club, and often invited
me to his house, and a kind, amiable family he had. He
is a retired merchant."

" Exactly," said Mr. Baldwin. " How strange things
happen ! he is a very old friend of mine ; we passed years
of our early life together ; we were clerks in the same
counting-house. Now, it is very odd, but I actually knew
you before I saw you. I constantly correspond with my
old friend ; I am a chess-player myself, and a member of
the same club. In one of his letters lately he said, refer-
ring to a match between our club and the Maidstone, ' I
know a fine young man at our academy here who would
beat your best man all to chalks ; he's got a checkmate that
would puzzle your wits. Next time you come this way I'll
introduce him to you, he's as fine a young fellow as ever
you saw.' Now I see," added Mr. Baldwin, with a smile,
" that the world has not contaminated you, for you blush
like a girl of sixteen. But I have lost sight of Mr. Skelton and his letter. In it he said you had left his house
after grievously insulting him, and that he wished never to
hear your name mentioned : in fact, that you had no name,
for you were picked up on the sands at Ramsgate by a
foolish old woman, who, when she died, neither mentioned
your name nor left you a shilling ; and her brother, Sir
Richard Morton, grossly insulted him, because he ventured
to speak of you to him, thinking he might pay the quarter
due for your board and education. This and a good deal
more formed the subject of his letter. Now, in my voca-
tion as superintendent of police, many strange events come
to my knowledge. I wish you to let me hear all you know
of yourself, especially as to dates."

" I will willingly, my dear sir," said our hero, " give you
all the particulars of my short life, and such dates as I may
be able to recollect. But allow me first to observe that
Mr. Skelton has made a most incorrect statement. There

was not a fraction due at the time of my noble-hearted benefactress's death. She paid Mr. Skelton £80 a year quarterly, and in advance, and she died a few days or weeks before the expiration of the quarter already paid. Instead of insulting him, he meanly made use of terms, such as ' child of a vagrant or tramp,' shielding himself under the pretence that Sir Richard Morton had used those terms in speaking of me. I quitted his house on the instant in disgust; but, let me add, that during the years I spent under his roof nothing could exceed the kindness or attention that I received from Mrs. Skelton and her amiable daughters."

Mr. Baldwin shook our hero by the hand, saying warmly,—

" I believe every word you utter, and I say you acted perfectly right. Although it is getting somewhat late, just answer me a few questions, for I am about to leave town for some days ; when I come back, I hope to introduce you to my wife and family ; they live at Brompton. In the first place, have you any recollection of the year in which you were picked up on the sands in Margate ? "

" Oh, yes," returned Arthur. " I was placed to nurse with one of the kindest-hearted women in the world, though of humble birth and station. Mary Bolton was her name ; she was the grandchild of an old shrimp-catcher ; her husband was a sailor. She was as fond of me as of her own son, and used to say that she was sure that I was the son of a gentleman. She made me go to school in Broadstairs when five years old. Her old grandfather, however, would always have me out with him in his sailing-boat ; in fact, before I was eight years old I could swim and dive like a duck, and manage any kind of boat. When Mrs. Morton sent me to Mr. Skelton's, Mary Bolton gave me a little book, in which was written the day of the week, the month, and year in which I was picked up, and also stated what I had on, which in truth only consisted of a shirt without mark of any kind. I have the book in my trunk, but the date is Tuesday, the 14th of August, 1826."

Mr. Baldwin wrote that down in his memorandum book, and then asked whether Mary Bolton was still alive, and where she resided.

" Oh, far away from here," replied our hero. " Four years after my leaving her she came to take leave of me. Her old grandfather was dead, and she and her husband were going to Australia, and there they went. She promised to write to me, and cried bitterly when she bade me farewell, but I have never had a line from her since her departure."

" Well, my young friend, I must bid you farewell now,"
said Mr. Baldwin.   "Do not engage in any situation till I
come back, in a week at farthest.   I have a good deal of
interest one way or another, so take a little time before you
decide on a profession ;" and shaking our hero most kindly
by the hand, Mr. Baldwin departed.

CHAPTER III.

ON returning to dinner at the hotel, on the sixth day
of his residence, the waiter handed Arthur a letter ; the
first glance showed him it was not the long-expected one
from his old schoolfellow, Hugh Dormer.   It was directed
Mr. Arthur Bolton, Crown Hotel, Cavendish Square, and
had no post-mark.   Breaking the seal, he began reading,
wondering who his correspondent could be, and almost immediately his attention became engaged by the following
contents :—

" SIR,

      " Circumstances have made me acquainted with
several important matters connected with your birth.   I
can account to you why you were left on the sands in Ramsgate, in the year 1826, and the true reason why you were
adopted by the late Mrs. Morton.   If, therefore, you will
grant me an interview, it will be for your advantage ; but
I am not going to do you this service for nothing ; if I gain
you position and fortune, I shall expect to be rewarded ;
not till then, for I know when you left Skelton School you
had but very little money, and that was stolen from you.
If you will call this evening, at seven o'clock, at No. 4,
Bridge Street, near Thames Street, I will give you every
satisfaction, and make it worth your while to engage to pay
me One Thousand Pounds when you come into possession
of a property now held by the very person that caused you
to be exposed on the sands.

                     " Your humble servant,
                          " GEORGE REYNOLDS."

" I do not know what to think of this," thought our hero,
as he perused the letter a second time.   " Whoever the
writer is, he certainly has gained some very accurate knowledge of my early life.   It can do no harm to hear what
he says."

As the waiter was taking away the dinner, Arthur inquired his way to Bridge Street, near Thames Street.

" Oh, it's a long distance—almost as far as the Tower.
You must first go to London Bridge, and then any one
will show you the way. It is a bad neighbourhood, sir."

" Who brought the letter you gave me, James ?"

" A boy, sir."

Shortly after five o'clock our young hero started from the hotel and made his way to London Bridge, taking only a few shillings in his pocket, and leaving his watch in his portmanteau. Having adopted these cautious measures, and feeling secure since he had nothing of value about him, he entered Bridge Street, just as it was getting dusk, on a rather gloomy evening, in the latter end of September, and found himself in a poor, narrow, and thinly inhabited street, consisting principally of old dilapidated warehouses, the backs of which opened on the Thames. There were very few people passing, but No. 4 was soon found, being large and lofty, with the upper windows half smashed in; whilst the lower, with their dirty shutters up, looked as if they and the door of entrance had not received a brush of paint for half a century.

" Well," muttered our hero, " this is certainly not an inviting locality; but since I am here, I will even try and get in ;" and taking hold of an old piece of iron that served for a bell-handle, he rang. After the delay of a few minutes he heard a bolt drawn back, and then the door was partly opened, and a woman's head, with a very dirty crop of uncombed hair, and a remarkably filthy cap, presented itself.

" Well," said she, looking up at her visitor, " what's the matter ?"

" Not much," returned our hero, by no means captivated with the head or the cap. " I came here to inquire after a person calling himself George Reynolds."

" Oh, all right; show the gentleman in," uttered a voice from the inside.

Thus addressed, the woman opened the door a little wider, and Arthur entered a large hall. The door was closed by the female with a bang, leaving him in the dark. Not a ray of light could be seen, but before he had time for a moment's thought, or to repent his rashness in coming, he felt his arms seized from behind, and himself impelled forward. But Arthur was by no means inclined to submit to any such mode of treatment; he knew by the grip on his arms that it was not the grasp of the female, so with a violent jerk he freed his arms and grasped some male figure by the throat, exclaiming : " Rascal ! what is all this for ?"

" Hit him over the head, Jem, or this devil will choke me," exclaimed the man our hero held.

A flash of light was thrown on the scene from a lantern, and the entrapped young man was seized by another assailant, whom he received with a violent blow on the face, but the same instant a stunning blow on the head from some loaded instrument laid him senseless on the floor.

How long our hero lay in that state he could not say; but when he opened his eyes, and had in some slight degree recovered from the confusion of his ideas, he perceived that he was stretched upon an old mattress, laid upon benches, and, in attempting to move, discovered that his legs and arms were bound; he looked round his prison, and at once perceived that he was not alone. Directly facing him were two men seated at an old kitchen-table, who were conversing eagerly ; a tallow candle throwing but a faint light on their faces and over the dilapidated room, the walls of which were soaking with moisture. Arthur Bolton, without having his recollection perfectly restored, gazed at these two men, who were drinking out of mugs some mixture from a large black bottle on the table ; a loaf of bread and a large lump of beef on a plate appeared to comprise their supper.

On attentively regarding the men, he recognized in one of them the person of the celebrated perfumer. The other was a very powerful-looking fellow, with strongly marked features, but very coarse ; he was attired as a seaman, and had one of his eyes swollen and half closed—the effects of the blow he had received in the scuffle. These worthies conversed in a very low tone till, turning round, our hero caused the bench to creak, then both looked up and over at their prisoner.

" Ah," said the man with the black eye, " I thought my young cove would not be long before he'd wake up ; though, blow me, if he hasn't bunged up my eye and no mistake."

" Yes," returned the other, who was a middle-sized slight man, " and deuced near throttling me ; he's mighty pugnacious."

The speaker got up, and taking a knife from the table came over to our hero, and very quietly cut the cord that bound his hands, saying, " There, now you will be more comfortable ; you brought this treatment on yourself. Only be quiet, and you will come to no harm ; but be rough, and you'll get rough treatment."

Arthur Bolton made no immediate reply, but stooping down cast loose the cord that held his legs ; as he did so, the *ci-devant* perfumer pulled out a four-barrelled revolver from his pocket, and stepped back a pace, saying, " Faith, my lad, you take it coolly ; but don't tempt my barkers."

His companion at the table, who was helping himself to

the whisky in the black bottle, said, " Let him be, George ; he is not quite such a fool as to get his brains blown out."

Arthur stood up and looked at the two men attentively. We have stated that he was remarkably strong and active, and accustomed to all kinds of athletic exercises, in which few could excel him ; though gentle and kind in disposition, he was most resolute when attacked, and utterly fearless. He would not have hesitated to have grappled both men, had they been without firearms, and would have felt confident of success ; but one holding a revolver, and the other a long sharp-pointed knife, were antagonists deserving of consideration. He put his hand to the back of his head, as he sat down, and perceived that all the harm he had received was a pretty considerable bump, that might have puzzled phrenologists.

" Now," he commenced, looking the ex-perfumer steadily in the face, " what are your motives in treating me in this way ? What do you expect to get ? I recognize you. You are the man that used the chloroform in the railway carriage, and afterwards attempted to rob me of my luggage ; in this theft, however, you failed."

" Yes," returned the man, sitting down and helping himself to whisky, whilst keeping his revolver by his hand—" Yes, you are quite right, I am the inventor of the magnificent perfume ; you see it was too powerful for you to ——"

" Come, none of your jaw, George. We didn't come here to be spinning yarns," interrupted the other. " The tide's rising."

" All right, Jem," answered George ; " I only meant to convince this young man that we are acting for his good."

" Good !" repeated Arthur, " do you call knocking me over like a bullock acting for my good ? Come, be quick ; let me hear what you want. I have no more plunder for you, if that's your object."

" No, I am not seeking plunder ; I know very well that you are cleaned out, though you did get your luggage back, through the bungling of the rascal I employed. Now I'll tell you what's wanted of you. Your friends want you to leave this country, and I and others are employed to put you afloat. If you are only quiet and manageable, no hurt will come to you, but—" and the man spoke and looked savagely at his victim—" but if you give us trouble and attempt resistance, I'll use this weapon," and he cocked the revolver, " and bury your body in the vaults of this old house."

" You infernal rascal !" exclaimed Arthur passionately, " if you had not that weapon in your hands, I would knock your rascally head against the wall."

" Yes, I know that," replied the other coolly, " and no mistake. Just tell me, will you give us your word of honour not to offer any resistance, and we will neither bind nor hurt you, but take you quickly to your destination ?"

" No, I will not pass my word to such rascals," said Arthur fiercely; and he turned to look for some kind of weapon, but both men rushed at him, seized him, and Reynolds placed the muzzle of the pistol close to his temple, and swore a fearful oath that at the first struggle he would pull the trigger.

Arthur, though angry, was calm, and felt sure the villain uttered no mere threat; so he yielded to necessity.

" There," said the man called 'Jem, putting a pair of handcuffs on his prisoner's hands, " let us have no more jaw or bother; you shouldn't have let him free, George; if you really want to get rid of him, let us pitch him into the river, and not go blazing away with pistols and making a noise. The boat is at the steps now."

Having secured his hands, they not only put a gag into his mouth, but fastened a cloth over his eyes, and then made him sit down for a moment; then each taking him by the arm led him from the room, one of the men calling out :

" Bet, hold the light, you lazy baggage! I've left you whisky enough to make you sleep for a week."

Though unable to utter a word, the captive could think; and strange to say he felt a singular sensation of satisfaction come over him, notwithstanding the pain of the gag. Even in his then strange and doubtful position, it struck him that he could be no nameless outcast, or why should any one trouble about him, and seek to drive him from his native land, unless some weighty reasons existed for doing so. Some one must have urgent motives for such conduct, and he resolved to take events quietly, and trust in Providence and his own exertions to unravel the mystery.

The fresh breeze blowing in his face, as he was led along, convinced him he was going towards the river, and soon he heard the sound of many voices, and the noise of moving oars, &c., in a boat, and then a louder voice said :

" Come, be quick, men, the tide's falling."

" Ay, ay," returned the man Jem, " here we are, all right;" and then they led him down some steps and laid him in the bottom of the boat, suffering considerable pain from the bandage across his mouth, but resolved to be quiet and watch.

The men seized their oars, and after a few whispered words, the boat was pushed off and pulled rapidly down the river.

" I think you might take the gag from his mouth," said a strange voice, " and let him have the use of his peepers. The mad fit is off him by this time."

Our hero knew not what to make of these words ; but he felt the blade of a knife press against his cheek, and the gag fell to the bottom of the boat. Then the handkerchief was removed, and as he sat up on the stern sheets he perceived the boat was pulled by four men, and on each side of him sat Reynolds and the man Jem—the latter steering.

" Utter one word," whispered Reynolds, " and I use my revolver."

Had Arthur's hands been free, his answer would have sent Reynolds into the river. It was blowing fresh, and a rather thick fog lay upon the stream, so as to hide the shore on each side. It was also very dark.

As they progressed steadily down the river, when they neared a vessel or were hailed, Arthur felt the muzzle of the revolver pressed close to his head by Reynolds.

In this manner they proceeded some five or six miles, and then the man in the bows stood up, and opening a dark lantern showed a red light, which shone brightly on the water for some distance. Almost immediately after, a vivid red light was seen a short distance ahead.

" All right !" cried the man steering, " give way, my lads, we are close aboard," and a few seconds after the boat shot up alongside a very large brig.

" All right !" exclaimed a voice from the deck, swinging a lantern over the side and then a rope-ladder.

" Now jump up, Mr. Bolton," said Reynolds, in a respectful voice ; " I am glad to see you so quiet," and he slipped the handcuffs from his wrists.

Bolton would have turned and seized Reynolds by the throat, but the four men in the boat suddenly caught him in their arms and landed him on the deck.

" Now hand up Mr. Bolton's traps—and be quick ; there is no time to lose, the tide has turned this hour," said a voice from the deck.

Our hero eyed the speaker by the light of the ship's lantern. The captain of the brig, for such he was, also keenly scanned our hero's countenance, and then sang out " Steward !"

"Here, sir," replied a small, slight, respectable-looking man, coming forward.

"Just show Mr. Bolton his berth, and if he requires anything, pray get it for him immediately."

Though rather astounded by the manner and the words of the captain, Arthur was not going to be carried away from his native land without making another effort to regain his liberty.

"Are you the captain of this vessel, sir?" he said, addressing the quiet gentlemanly man giving orders to his men.

"Yes, Mr. Bolton, I am," he replied, calmly and courteously.

"Well, then, sir, may I ask why such violence was used to bring me on board, and why I am to be detained here?"

"All right now, sir," exclaimed a voice from the boat below, as a great sea-chest was hauled up and placed upon the deck.

"All right," answered the captain.

"Good night, sir," called out the voice of Reynolds, "a quick and pleasant voyage to you!"

The oars fell upon the water, and the boat pulled rapidly away, whilst some of the crew of the brig began to heave at the capstan, others letting fall the topsails.

"My dear sir," said the captain, turning to our astonished hero, "just follow the steward into the cabin; we shall have plenty of time to-morrow to converse on any subject you like. Now I must see to the navigation of my ship."

"But really, sir," remonstrated our hero, getting angry, and feeling his face flush with vexation, "this is a monstrous proceeding altogether. I am entrapped by two ruffians, gagged, bound, and brought by brute force on board this vessel; and you, the captain of a British ship, receive me from the hands of those ruffians, thus leaguing yourself with scoundrels and subjecting yourself to severe penalties and punishment for illegally detaining me, in order to convey me I know not where."

"I am bound to Jamaica, Mr. Bolton," returned the captain quietly. "What is done is done; a voyage to Jamaica cannot injure you. You are my passenger, and will be treated as such, though I beg you to take things quietly. To-morrow, as I said before, we will talk this affair over. I am going to take up passengers at Ramsgate."

"Ramsgate!" repeated our hero involuntarily.

"Ah! you remember Ramsgate," said the captain, with a start.

"Yes, I should think I do. I was left an infant to perish in the sands there, and——"

"Ah, by Jove! it is the fact then," said the captain, hurriedly, and turning away he called to his mate and gave some orders, for the anchor was up.

The unwilling passenger was left standing, his mind in a state of bewildered confusion, till roused by feeling some one touch his shoulder. Looking round, he beheld the little steward with a lantern in his hand.

"Will you please to come below, sir?" he said, stepping back a pace or two.

"Well, upon my honour," observed Arthur, half angry, half amused, "all this is very extraordinary. However, we shall see what occurs to-morrow;" and placing his hand on the steward's shoulder, he added, "Very well, show me my berth, my good friend."

The man led the way down the companion into the very large and handsomely fitted-up cabin of the brig, lighted by a handsome swinging lamp. Opening a door the steward passed into a neatly fitted-up private cabin, and lighting a lamp said, holding the door in his hand:

"Do you wish for anything to drink, Mr. Bolton?"

"Yes," returned our hero, "I will take a glass of brandy and water, and I should like to wash my hands and face. Those ruffians used their gag mercilessly, and my wrists are cut by their handcuffs."

"Good God!" exclaimed the little steward, turning pale, "were you so badly used as all that?" and then he took up a can and poured some water into a basin, conveniently placed in a corner of the cabin.

"What do you mean by saying 'were you as badly used as all that?'" inquired our hero. "I hope you do not imagine that I am a madman?" and in spite of his vexation he burst into a laugh.

Arthur Bolton might laugh—and they say laughing is contagious—but the little steward, on the contrary, turned pale, and looked startled, but did not answer the question, though he watched the young man closely as he bathed his mouth, washed his face and temples and the back of his head, which had bled a little, and then stripping himself very quietly got into his berth ; and, such is youth, in ten minutes was fast asleep.

CHAPTER IV

WHEN our hero awoke in the morning at a late hour, he judged by the motion of the vessel that they were out of

he river. His sleep had refreshed both body and mind,
and as he calmly revolved the events of the past night and
viewed his present situation, the prospect did not appear
so gloomy. True, he was taken by force from England,
but had he remained, what would have been his fate?
Daily drudgery as a clerk, years of toil to go through ere
promotion would place him in a situation to enjoy domestic
happiness. Passion must be subdued, feelings curbed,
constant self-denial exercised; he must become a machine,
wound up for duty in the morning, to relax at night only
when too tired for enjoyment.

How could he, with eyes dazzled by long rows of figures,
and a head aching from calculations, entries, invoices, and
discounts, sit to his beloved books and studies? No, he
liked a life of excitement, and he might perhaps enter the
merchant service and see other countries. He resolved to
be cheerful, and not, if he could possibly avoid it, question
or rebel, but submit.

With this resolve he jumped up as the steward entered
the cabin, and looking into his face the little man said:

"You have had a long sleep, sir, and it has done you
good. I suppose you can eat some breakfast now?"

"Yes, I will thank you for a cup of coffee, or anything
that is ready," replied Arthur. "Whereabouts are we now,
for I know we have run out of the river?"

"You are right, Mister Bolton," replied the steward;
"we are nearly off Ramsgate, with a fresh breeze on our
quarter."

"Ah, Ramsgate!" repeated Arthur, with a thoughtful
expression of countenance, "a place I have not seen for
twelve years. I must have a look at the spot where my
infant life was so nearly terminated."

"Humph!" muttered the steward, and then in a low
voice added, "he will have another attack, I fear; he's a
powerful youth, so I'll get out of the way."

The young man did not hear the words, but the exit of the
steward was so sudden that he looked after him in surprise.

As he finished dressing he heard the captain's voice, as
he came out from the main cabin, and the next moment he
threw open the door of the steward's berth, and seeing
Arthur dressed, he said:

"Good morning, Mr. Bolton; you and I have had a
good nap; will you come to breakfast? By-the-bye, here
is the key of your sea-chest. You will, I dare say, find
some garments there better suited for a ship's deck and a
long voyage than those you have on."

"Thank you," answered our hero, very quietly taking

the key; "I will very willingly join you at breakfast, but the steward tells me we are off Ramsgate, and I should like to have a look at the old place before we run it out of sight."

"Oh, you can eat your breakfast first," remarked Captain Courtney, looking into his face with a scrutinizing glance, "we are lying-to off Ramsgate, and shall probably do so till evening, as I take up some people here."

"Oh, very well, then I will eat my breakfast first," and Arthur followed Captain Courtney into the cabin.

It was exceedingly roomy and handsome, tastefully fitted up, with two private cabins for passengers leading from it.

A substantial breakfast was on the table, and Arthur, notwithstanding his strange situation, and the cruel treatment he had received the night before, did ample justice to it.

"By-the-bye," said Captain Courtney, "you do not seem troubled by sea-sickness. There is not much motion, to be sure, for a seaman to perceive, but quite enough to upset a landsman's good temper and feeding."

"I never was sea-sick," said Arthur; "I commenced my acquaintance with salt water very early. My first immersion nearly cost me my life. My next acquaintance with it was from the deck of a shrimp-boat. I then learned to swim and dive like a duck. So in the five or six early years of my life I got remarkably well seasoned, and certainly feel no sort of inclination to be sick."

Whilst he was speaking he was very scientifically carving a roast fowl, a leg and wing of which he transferred to his own plate, with a fair allowance of ham, the captain all the time leaning his two elbows on the table, with his knife and fork suspended from both, and his eyes fixed upon him. Our hero, without taking the slightest notice of the captain's fixed attention, continued to demolish his eatables with great relish.

"Ha!" said Captain Courtney, drawing his breath, "devilish extraordinary!" and then he attacked his plate of cold beef with determined energy.

Arthur appeared unconscious of the scrutiny of the captain, but he had his own thoughts; and when he had finished his fowl, he turned to his companion, and very quietly said:

"Pray, Captain Courtney, in what light am I considered on board this vessel? Am I a passenger, or am I to work as a sailor, or otherwise? for, from the strange manner in which I was brought here, I might be induced to believe I am considered as a lunatic, or half madman."

Captain Courtney immediately said, his bronzed countenance showing a flush on its surface:

" You are a passenger, Mr. Bolton, to Jamaica, and your passage-money, a handsomē sum, has been paid.   Once in Jamaica, you are perfectly at liberty to quit my ship. Indeed, I am led to understand that you will find full instructions how to act, in a letter in your sea-chest.   You have, I confess, knocked me into a heap.   I'm like a ship in irons, all adrift.   I should have given you one of the berths in this cabin ; but—but—you see—in the first place, I have a lady and her two fair daughters and servants, as passengers, going out to Jamaica ; they have taken my private cabin and berths ; so you will not be so very lonely. I trust this voyage will completely restore you ; I know your friends are most anxious it should."

Still further mystified, Arthur rose, and taking the captain by the hand said :

" I thank you, at all events, for your kindness and good wishes.   I feel no dislike whatever to this voyage ; on the contrary, it suits my inclination and wishes ; for I have neither relations nor friends, nor profession, nor means of support, beyond a small sum of money, which with my luggage is left at the Crown Hotel, where my extraordinary disappearance will create both anxiety and inquiry. This voyage and what it may lead to, I may call a fortunate event ; but why such exceeding cruelty and brutality were made use of to bring me on board this vessel amazes me ; and one of your own crew actually wanted to take my life."

" One of my crew !" exclaimed the skipper, looking rather serious ; " you must mistake ; I certainly sent my jolly-boat and four hands to St. Catherine's dock by agreement ; but these men are ordinary seamen—all old hands. Do you know the man who threatened you?   Did you hear him called by name ?

" Yes, captain, I did ; his name was Jem Hopeley."

" Ah," said the captain, " I thought he could not be amongst my crew ; that Hopeley, and a man called Reynolds, were the two men who had the charge of you, but neither of them are on board this vessel now."

At that moment a voice down the companion hailed the captain, saying a shore-boat was alongside, and a person in her wanted to see him.

" Well, Mr. Bolton," said the skipper, shaking his hand heartily, " be of good heart, this voyage at your age can do you no harm ; I'm somewhat puzzled and mystified, I confess.   I am paid, however, handsomely for your voyage out, and I promise you if we reach Jamaica, and you do not like to remain there, vou shall return to old England with me, free of all expense—so now make yourself happy. I like you. Go and examine your chest and rig yourself ship-shape. By Jove! I'll make a thorough sailor of you before this voyage is over." Thus speaking, Captain Courtney hurried on deck.

Arthur felt pleased. "After all," thought he to himself, "if I were requested to select a profession, I would say, let me try a seafaring life for a couple of years; anything sooner than standing behind a counter, or leaning over a desk, for twelve hours in the day. I think Captain Courtney has been deceived, and he is beginning to think so too. There is one thing I am truly glad of, and that is that I am not on board the same ship with that ruffian Jem Hopeley. It is also very clear to me that there must be some powerful reason for wishing me to be carried from the soil of England into so distant a land as the West Indies."

He then proceeded to his cabin, and examined the chest. On its lid was painted, in white letters—"Mr. Arthur Bolton, ship 'Foam.'"

Opening the box, he perceived it contained a tolerably large collection of garments. On the top of them lay a letter, directed to himself. With no little curiosity he broke the seal, and opening it, read as follows :—

"You are now placed, Arthur Bolton, in a situation that may lead to fortune—do not, from wilfulness, or from wrong conceptions, cast away a certain good to struggle with fortune, unassisted.

"At the bottom of your sea-chest you will find a letter directed to Mr. Henderson, Jamaica. He is one of the richest British merchants there. You have had an excellent education, therefore you will be appointed to a situation in his service, at a good salary, which will rapidly increase if your talents and industry render you deserving of promotion. Thus, in a few years, you may attain independence. What had you to expect if you remained in England?—A frightful struggle, unassisted and friendless—therefore take the advice now given you—be patient and hopeful. Let Captain Courtney imagine you are a passenger confided to his care for certain reasons, and under certain circumstances, and make no effort to undeceive him. He is handsomely paid, and is a man of well-known kindness as a seaman, and a skilful navigator. At any time you can return to England, but I emphatically recommend you not to do so till your fortune is made. In your chest you will find an ample outfit of clothes, and a cheque upon a mercantile house in Jamaica in a purse.

"I now conclude, and sign myself, whatever you may think to the contrary,

"Your firm friend,

"＿＿＿"

"Well," exclaimed Arthur, as he finished the letter, "I am more puzzled now than ever. I am apparently placed in the road to fortune, well provided, an introduction to a wealthy merchant in Jamaica, a cheque for an unknown sum, my passage paid. What on earth could I desire more?" But if all this had been offered me by a stranger openly, I would have said he was one of the most generous of mortals, and I would have gratefully thanked and blessed him for his generosity. Instead of being so treated, I am first robbed by a rascally pretended perfumer, then enticed into a low locality, brutally treated by two ruffians, through the very rascal who first robbed me, and brought aboard this brig in a cruel manner, and passed upon her captain no doubt as a person of weak intellect, sometimes so deranged as to require a gag and a strait waistcoat. Now, this treatment is scarcely to be borne with patience. No doubt, if I showed this letter to the captain, and explained circumstances as they occurred, he would permit me to land, and I might return to London. Well, suppose I were once more at the Crown Hotel, what could I do? My friend and school-fellow is evidently abroad. How, thus unassisted, can I hope to prosper? My mind is made up. I shall go with the stream, though I confess I would sacrifice anything to gain the slightest clue to my infant history. I should like to belong to some one, no matter how humble or poor; but I have not even a name."

He paused; his cheek became flushed, and he felt a sensation of sadness stealing over him: with an effort he shook it off, and then continued the examination of his chest. He found a sailor's jacket, heavy pea-coat for bad weather, and a few light garments of all sorts for hot climates. Nothing was omitted necessary for a young gentleman's outfit, even supposing he belonged to parents of high respectability, for everything in the chest was of the best quality. A large pocket-book lay at the bottom; in opening it he found the letter addressed to Mr. Henderson, with a large seal with simply the initial letters C. B. A purse, containing the cheque, which he perceived was for a hundred pounds, payable to Arthur Bolton, only.

"Well, all this is very strange; there must be some powerful reason for thus bestowing on a nameless castaway so fine a chance of fortune."

Attiring himself in a simple jacket and trousers, which fitted him as if his measure had been taken, and in which his tall fine figure looked to great advantage, he ascended upon deck, the vessel for the last half-hour or so lying as if in a mill-pond.

On gaining the deck, he beheld a very animated and beautiful scene.

The " Foam " was lying-to under her topsails only, her fore-topsail aback, and her mainsail hauled up, and only one jib set. The " Foam " was a clipper ship, remarkably long, though with fine beam ; her masts were very taut, and raked aft, more like a clipper schooner than a brig. They were scarcely two miles from Ramsgate pier. The wind was blowing off the shore, NNE., and the flood tide had ceased and the ebb commenced, which rendered the water smooth, though the wind was very fresh, with a fine clear sky.

Numbers of vessels and steamers were to be seen on every side, some making for the Thames, others leaving it. Some vessels of war were making sail from the Downs, taking advantage of such a fine breeze down Channel. Some were tacking into Ramsgate, and some running out. It was a lively, animated scene, and one so faithfully represented by the pencil of Turner.

The shore boat, with two persons in the stern sheets, had just left the brig, Captain Courtney waving his hat to them, and they returning the compliment.

Arthur's eyes immediately sought the well-remembered cliff, where the old shrimper's cottage once stood, but it was no longer there. A very pretty villa had replaced the humble cottage, and the little garden, some twenty yards square, was converted into a platform, on which a tall rigged mast was erected, and on which flags were hoisted on certain occasions by the owner, a retired naval officer, who had purchased the piece of land after the death of the old shrimper, and erected a handsome marine villa upon it.

" We are losing a fine spanking breeze, Mr. Bolton," said the captain of the " Foam," joining our hero on the deck. " This wind would drive us down Channel at the rate of ten knots."

" You will not be detained long, I suppose," answered our hero. " It certainly is a fine breeze for clearing the Channel."

" Why, no, I hope not ; though ladies are rather slow in their movements. Mrs. Marchmont and her two daughters are going out to join Mr. Marchmont, a very wealthy

merchant, who has lived in Jamaica for many years. Mrs.
Marchmont is of a very aristocratic family, and her daughters, born and educated in England, I am told are very
beautiful girls."

"Do you know much about Ramsgate, Captain Courtney?" questioned our hero.

"I cannot say that I do, though my wife and family are
natives of yonder town. The boat you saw leaving the
ship carried my wife's brother, who is a large ship builder
and owner. Ramsgate is a pleasant place for a retired
seaman; always something to be seen pleasing to a seaman's eye."

"Do you know who built yonder marine villa, with the
flag flying over the little battery?"

"Oh, yes," returned the captain, turning his glass upon
it. "An old post captain bought the land, about as much
as the mainsail of a three-decker would cover. The old
commodore, you see, has mounted two eight-pounders on
his little platform, and blazes away on every Royal birth-
day or naval victory."

"Many an hour, Captain Courtney," said Arthur Bolton, to the attentive captain, "have I spent on the spot
where that battery is erected; at that time only a very
humble cottage was there, with a few yards of garden,
excavated out of the cliff, having a zigzag path leading
down to the sands; and on those sands I was left, to be
washed away by the receding tide. At that time, too, an
old watercourse made its way to the beach. I see no such
stream now."

Captain Courtney looked seriously into the fine, handsome, intellectual features of the young man beside him,
who was thinking, "Why was I, a helpless infant, cast
into the tide's way, to be drowned like a blind kitten?
Was I the child of shame or of crime, that such means
were taken to destroy my infant life?"

"You certainly, Mr. Bolton," remarked the captain,
very thoughtfully, "seem to know every inch of the spot
before us; it is very strange. If this be a delusion, it is
very like reality."

"It is no dream or hallucination, Captain Courtney, but
truth. Moreover, I will tell you a fact you may have
heard from your brother-in-law. I was about eight years
old when a fine ship ran ashore in a dense fog, under the
cliff where stood the shrimp-catcher's cottage. She had
scarcely run aground when the wind shifted into the north-
east and blew a perfect hurricane."

' Why, bless my soul!" interrupted Captain Courtney,

"you are speaking of the barque called the 'Brothers,' which was built and owned by my brother-in-law. The shift of wind saved the craft, and she was got off safely the following spring-tide. You quite bewilder me; all you have stated proves to me that I have been imposed upon, and that the story of your being picked up on the sands and adopted by an old lady named Morton, is fact, and not a delusion of your own brain. But here is the steam-tug coming. Now, in my opinion, you had better go out with me to Jamaica. I have no clue to give you, to enable you to discover the gentleman who actually persuaded me that you were his only son, unhappily labouring under a melancholy delusion, from the period of your recovery from a fever, whilst in a school in Canterbury. He said the delusion no doubt arose from being in the same room with a school-fellow, to whom you were much attached, and who was, in fact, the boy picked up on the sands. You were both ill, your pretended father said, at the same time, and the physicians who were consulted said it was a strange hallucination; that no doubt you fancied yourself your comrade, and that the delusion would pass off with change of scene and occupation. We will talk over this matter again."

That Arthur Bolton was amazed, we need hardly say. That there was an object in all this well and cleverly arranged deception, he could not doubt. But he banished further thought upon the subject, and turned his attention to the steam-tug, which rapidly approached, bringing the passengers.

Presently it came alongside, and the gangway being opened, the ladies could step on board without any apparent difficulty.

"I fear, captain," said a tall, elegant looking woman, not more than forty, throwing back her veil, "that we have kept you longer than you liked, with this fine wind blowing. But you know, I dare say, that we women are very tedious in packing up our finery."

The captain assured his fair passengers that the delay was not of the slightest consequence; he was too happy in having such passengers to heed any delay.

Arthur Bolton stood at a little distance, regarding the party getting on board with some curiosity: he observed that Mrs. Marchmont was a very elegant and graceful woman, and that her two daughters were very beautiful, especially the youngest—a graceful lively girl, not more than seventeen years old, the eldest probably being nineteen. Two female servants, one a staid matron, the other a very pretty girl, about the age of the youngest sister. A gentlemanly-looking man about forty also stepped on deck.

After a vast heap of luggage and baggage, including a piano and a harp, had been put on board, and all pre-liminaries settled, the steam-tug cast off, the roar of her steam ceased, and the topsails of the brig braced round. The two vessels separated, the tug returning to the harbour, and the " Foam," like a steed released from the bit, dashing through the sparkling waters with a nine-knot breeze filling her lofty canvas.

The ladies having gone below with the gentleman to arrange their luggage and settle their cabins, our hero walked forward to look at the crew of the " Foam," which consisted of eleven men and two boys, two mates included.

The mates were tall men in the prime of life, swarthy and fierce-looking, with unshaven beards, and necks like buffaloes. As he passed one of them, the man looked very hard indeed into our hero's face, his large fierce dark eyes fixed full upon him. Our hero started, for his first im-pression was that he saw Jim Hopcley, the ruffian who assisted Reynolds in bringing him on board ; he was won-derfully like, but a second glance satisfied him that he was mistaken. The sailor before him was marked by the small-pox ; Hopcley was not.

" Do you think, young man, you ever saw me before ? " said the man, staring impudently into Arthur Bolton's face, and leaning his huge hand on his hip.

Our hero was surprised at the man's tone, which was almost insolent, but he merely answered,—

" I thought so when I first saw you, but my thinking so is no reason you should be insolent," and without waiting for a reply he moved on towards the stern of the brig.

He heard the man swear and mutter something, but did not hear the words. He never saw a worse set of men, as far as looks went, than the crew of the " Foam ; " one of the boys, an Irish lad about seventeen, looked a fine, clean, lively lad, but the other appeared sickly.

Meeting Captain Courtney, he said : " I have been taking a look over the vessel, and a glance at your crew."

" And I dare say," answered the captain, with a smile, " like myself, you do not much admire them, though they are good sailors every one ; but they are a rough lot. I did not select them ; my owners did. I found them on board when I arrived to take the command, and was assured they were first-rate seamen. My two mates are powerful fellows, at all events."

"Yes, they are," returned our hero, "what are their names?"

"John Jackson," said the captain, "is first mate, William Saunders second. That's a fine boy, Joseph Malone; I will put him to attend in the cabin. By the way, I have got another passenger, but only as far as Madeira—a naval surgeon, a native of Ramsgate. My brother-in-law begged me to give him a passage; he is a very gentlemanly man. Tell me, how do you like the ladies? You must take care of your heart, Mr. Bolton. By Jove! the mother and daughters are remarkably handsome—one of the girls positively lovely. You will have to guard your heart well; women are dangerous creatures on board ship."

"There is no fear of a nameless outcast," observed Bolton, "troubling himself with affairs of the heart to make his fate more miserable."

"Come, come," replied Captain Courtney kindly, laying his hand on his shoulder, "you must make a name, and be prouder of it than if it was bestowed by the loftiest ancestry."

"You are right, Captain Courtney," cried Arthur, speaking cheerfully. "I sometimes give way to despondency, but not often; the bright side of the picture is the fairest to gaze at."

Just then the male passenger came upon deck, and Captain Courtney introduced our hero to him. He gave a slight start and looked a little surprised when he heard the name of Bolton, but immediately the captain turned to give some direction to the man at the wheel, he entered into conversation with our hero, pleasantly and with animation.

"Is this your first voyage, Mr. Bolton?" inquired the surgeon; "I see you seem perfectly indifferent to the motion of the vessel."

"Yes, my first voyage certainly," returned our hero, "out of sight of the shores of old England. But I am accustomed to the sea, having passed some years of my life knocking about this very shore we are leaving."

"You have a fine fast craft under you," said Mr. Cunningham, "and her commander, by all accounts, a most kind-hearted man. I almost regret quitting this vessel at Madeira, for, to judge by the appearance of our fair *compagnons de voyage*, time will pass pleasantly."

Captain Courtney now summoned the two gentlemen to dinner. It wanted an hour to sunset; and though the "Foam" was running before a strong breeze, there was scarcely any motion.

On entering the cabin, Captain Courtney introduced all his passengers to one another. Mrs. Marchmont was very gracious, looked evidently with surprise at Arthur, who took his seat next the youngest daughter, whose name was Alice; the eldest was called Eliza.

There was a most excellent dinner put upon the table, well cooked and served. Joe, the Irish lad, and the steward attended.

"I am quite pleased," observed Captain Courtney, "to see that none of my passengers appear to feel any inconvenience from the motion of the vessel. I was afraid the young ladies, not being seasoned—"

"Oh, then you are quite out, Captain Courtney," interrupted Alice Marchmont, laughing. "If you think to save your provisions, you are mistaken. I made two voyages to Dublin with my sister last year, in the Adelaide steamer, and for three days it blew, the captain said, the heaviest gale he had experienced for years, with what all the sailors called a tremendous sea. Neither my sister nor myself had even a head-ache; so woe betide your good things if you reckon on our absence from meals during bad weather."

"I am rejoiced to hear you say so, Miss Alice," said the captain, with a smile. "Nothing annoys me more than to see my passengers suffer. Mr. Bolton, will you be so good as to help your fair neighbour to a glass of sherry?"

The conversation after the removal of the dinner became general, and, though all were previously strangers to each other, time passed exceedingly pleasantly.

To some observation of Arthur Bolton's, Miss Alice Marchmont said, letting her beautiful eyes rest upon his for an instant,—

"Then you never were in Jamaica; like ourselves—that is my sister and self—all will be new to you. Mamma has visited it thrice; and about the time we shall arrive the island will be very healthy."

"Do you know any one in the island, Mr. Bolton?" inquired Mrs. Marchmont, whilst the surgeon and Captain Courtney had a debate about the merits and sailing qualities of a ship of war both knew.

"Not a soul, madam," returned our hero. "I have a letter of introduction to a merchant of the name of Henderson, residing at Kingstown."

"Oh!" cried Mrs. Marchmont—"I know Mr. Henderson and his charming family quite intimately; he is one of the first merchants on the island, and has a most extensive plantation adjoining my husband's; they are very old friends."

"I should very much like," said Alice Marchmont to her sister, "to take a turn on deck, to see the sun go down and have one more glimpse of old England; to-morrow morning probably it may be scarcely visible."

"You will be close in shore to-morrow morning," returned Captain Courtney, turning round. "I touch at Falmouth, to put letters ashore; so if you wish to write a few lines to friends, to let them know you have got so far in safety, you can do so."

"I shall gladly avail myself of the opportunity," said Mrs. Marchmont and her daughters; "and now let us go for a turn on deck."

Whilst the captain and surgeon continued their conversation and finished their wine, our hero accompanied the ladies on deck.

The sun had just dipped half its glorious orb in the western wave; there was a bright clear sky, without even a speck to dim its setting glories; they were passing through the straits of Dover, not more than three miles from the shore.

"What a beautiful scene!" said Miss Marchmont to her mother. "What variety! and what animation!"

The waters were covered with crafts of every description,—steamers, ships, boats, yachts, vessels of war,—some scudding before the breeze, others sailing under reduced canvas, working to the eastward and plunging into the short seas, which dashed the white foam over their bows.

The "Foam" ran past every vessel they came up with, —her motion steady and easy, her great beam giving her great stability. Whilst those upon deck were enjoying the beauty of the scene around them, seen to advantage on an unusually fine evening, the captain and surgeon remained conversing earnestly below. To the subject of their conversation we must refer our readers in our next chapter.

CHAPTER V

"May I ask you a question or two, Captain Courtney?" said Mr. Cunningham to the commander of the "Foam," as they sat finishing their wine, after the departure of the ladies on deck. "I refer to that remarkably fine young man, Mr. Bolton. I am not actuated by mere curiosity, I assure you; but when you introduced him I was struck by his name. Not that Bolton is at all an uncommon one; but recent circumstances with reference to that name struck a chord in my memory, and the appearance and manner, and some words he chanced to drop in conversation, have interested me greatly."

"He is certainly a most promising and prepossessing young man," returned the captain, "and already I take a great interest in him; not only from the strange manner I have become acquainted with him, but from his own open, fine spirit and disposition."

"May I ask what is his Christian name?"

"Arthur."

"So far that corresponds," returned Mr. Cunningham, with animation. "So does his age. Now, can you tell me, without breaking any confidence, did he ever speak to you about his early life? Was his childhood passed in Ramsgate? Or do you know was he ever at school at Canterbury?"

"By Jove, you have awakened my curiosity now, Mr. Cunningham; and as the young man has not the slightest reserve or wish to hide his early history, but, on the contrary, speaks openly of the events of his childhood, and of his having been picked up on the sands at Ramsgate, and his adoption by an old and noble-hearted woman, residing there, of the name of Morton——"

"Ah, exactly," said the surgeon, filling his glass. "I am quite right. Now then, Captain Courtney, if we are not interrupted, I will give you a brief account of my acquaintance with the name of Bolton, and what I state to you I will also state to Mr. Bolton, for it may materially affect his after destiny :—

"About six or eight weeks ago I came to Ramsgate on family matters; I am a native of that town. One morning I was passing along Bay View Terrace, when a young woman, pale, and apparently terrified, rushed down the steps from a house door, exclaiming—'Oh, my God, my mistress is in a frightful fit,' and she ran on to seek a doctor.

"Thinking I might be of assistance till a doctor was procured—and I knew that there was not one very near—I hastened up the steps and entered the hall. Hearing a voice of lamentation in a room above, I ascended the stairs, and, guided by the sound, entered a drawing-room, and beheld an old lady, struggling in a severe fit on the floor, and an elderly attendant clapping her hands, and uttering sundry ejaculations. I pulled out a lancet—I always carry one—bared the old lady's arm, and told the woman to get a basin and hold the arm.

"'Oh, my God! I can't, sir,' she exclaimed. 'I can't

bear the sight of blood; I'll go for assistance,' and the stupid fool rushed from the room. However, I seized a vase on the table with flowers, threw them out, and opened a vein. All of a sudden the old lady ceased to struggle, opened her eyes, and fixed them full upon me.

" 'I am dying,' she said, with an effort. 'Listen, whoever you are.' I did listen, struck with the anxious, agonized expression of the old dame's features. Heaving a deep sigh, she continued, in a low intensely earnest voice :—

" 'In Canterbury school there is a young man—he's twenty years old.' She paused; I saw the fit was coming again. She grasped my hand, and, raising her head, she gasped out—'His name is Arthur Bolton; he is my nephew, the son of—' the head fell back, the eyes closed, and a shudder shook her whole frame. At that moment Dr. Hart entered the room, with the two servants and an assistant. He was the old lady's medical attendant: I knew him very well, so delivered up to him the care of the lady, who soon went into a second fit.

" I did not think a great deal of the broken sentences she had uttered. I did not exactly imagine she would die just then, so I went about my own affairs. When I returned home in the evening, my sister said,—

" 'Poor old Mrs. Morton is dead; she had another terrible fit, and died in it.'

" 'Who is Mrs. Morton?' I questioned, thinking of what had occurred in the morning.

" 'She was a very respectable old lady,' returned my sister, 'and in very comfortable circumstances, who has resided here for more than twenty years.'

" 'Any children or relatives?'

" 'None that ever I heard of; she was very charitable, but did some strange eccentric acts.'

" 'You are sure she never had or has a nephew? She spoke to me about a nephew, and told me he is at a school in Canterbury, and that his name is Arthur Bolton.'

" 'Oh,' returned my sister, 'she was no doubt raving about that child she picked up some nineteen or twenty years ago, on the sands. Ah, that was one of her eccentric acts. She put the child to nurse at an old shrimp-catcher's cottage, and never even, I am told, looked at him from the day she saved him from being carried away by the tide. Suddenly, when the boy was nine years old, she had him taken away and carried to a first-rate academy in Canterbury, and had him educated like the first gentleman's child in the land. Very strange, was it not? but it was very noble of her.'

" 'Who knows, after all, but that the child, or rather young man, may be her nephew in reality ? No doubt she has left a will, -and if she had ample means, as you say, and if she has any relatives, they will soon make their appearancc.'

" I had to leave that morning for London, and after a few days I found I had to make a voyage to Madeira. I returned to Ramsgate to bid my maiden sister farewell, and then your brother-in-law, an intimate friend of mine, told me that in a day or two a fine brig, bound to Jamaica, commanded by you, would touch at Ramsgate to take in some lady passengers; that you would stop at Madeira, and he would get me a passage out. I was rejoiced at this, so packed up and got ready. In the evening I said to Martha, ' Well, Martha, did any of old Mrs. Morton's relatives come to her funeral ? '

" ' Oh, she was not buried here. Bless you, she turncd out a great person after all. Hcr brother is a rich baronet, Sir Richard Morton, of Morton Hall, Derbyshire ; a fine, stately, aristocratic gentleman ; he had the old lady put into a lead coffin, and had her carried into Dcrbyshire, to bc buried in the family vault.'

" ' And what became of the young man, at thc school in Canterbury ? '

" ' Well, there are a number of reports ; indeed, I can't tell what to believe. It is said the boy's school-mastcr came to know what was to be done with the youth at his establishment ; that the baronet received him vcry haughtily ; said he knew nothing about him ; he was not accountable for his sister's eccentric acts. The boy had received a most expensive education ; his board and schooling bill all paid in advance ; thercfore the young man might consider himself very fortunate, and could push his way in the world as well as many less fortunately endowed.'

" ' Then,' said I, ' if this Sir Richard Morton acted in this way, and deserted his sister's *protégé*, without even providing him with temporary funds, he has acted very cruelly and unjustly.'

" I thought it very strange," continued Mr. Cunning-ham ; " for thc old lady knew she was dying. She called upon God that she spoke the truth ; that the young gentle-man was her nephew, and the son of ——. No doubt, she meant the son of her brother, Sir Richard Morton. Now, it strikes me," added the surgeon, " that he may be the illegitimate son of this Sir Richard Morton, and he wished to hide the fact. Having two or three days to spare, I wrote to a surgeon settled at Derby, and asked him if he knew anything of a Sir Richard Morton

" In reply, he said :

" Sir Richard Morton was of a very old Derbyshire family, a man of rank and station, and much liked. That his wife was the daughter of Lord Pintire, a very hand-some and amiable lady. Had a son about eighteen, and two very beautiful daughters. They were residing at Morton Hall. He stated he was professionally employed by Sir Richard; he also informed me that the baronet had an only sister, unmarried, and many years, I think nearly twenty, his senior—a most eccentric lady, lately deceased; he never heard of any other relative. As I did not say why I made the inquiries, he stated nothing further.

" This is all I know, and this much leads me to suppose this young man to be his illegitimate son, born previous to Sir Richard Morton's marriage with his present wife."

" Your conclusion, Mr. Cunningham," said Captain Courtney, " appears natural enough; still I do not think such to be the case. I will tell you all that occurred to me, and the young man will tell you his own history. Ah, here come the ladies; we must leave it to another time."

The wind slacking during the night, and drawing more to the northward, the " Foam" did not reach the entrance to Falmouth harbour till the morning of the second day after leaving Ramsgate. Here Captain Courtney received a considerable amount in gold, consigned to a firm in Jamaica; letters were sent ashore, and before night the vessel was again under way, with a light wind from the east.

Mrs. Marchmont and her daughters appeared extremely pleased with our hero's manner and conversation. He had read a great deal, was eminently talented, and spoke well and fluently. He played chess scientifically; in fact, few could check-mate him; and Mrs. Marchmont and her youngest daughter delighted in that fascinating game. Then the harp was brought out. Alice was a delightful performer, and Arthur, who was exceedingly fond of music and played the flute well, borrowed Captain Courtney's instrument, and accompanied her. Altogether, though their progress was slow, owing to light and trifling winds, time passed delightfully with the young people.

Mr. Cunningham and our hero had a long conference; the former told his story, communicating the incidents just as he had done to Captain Courtney.

Arthur was greatly surprised. What to suppose he knew not, but he resolved, when he returned to England, to try and unravel the mystery of his birth if possible.

From Captain Courtney he had the following account of how he came to be deceived, and to imagine that he had been sent a voyage to Jamaica to be cured of a singular delusion or hallucination :—

" The person called Reynolds, the man with the magnificent perfume, when properly attired, was very respectable-looking. Some days before the 'Foam' sailed from the river Reynolds came aboard and requested to see me ; he introduced himself as the steward of a gentleman of fortune, named Bolton. One of the gentleman's sons was labouring under a strange delusion, fancying himself another person ; but in everything else perfectly consistent. Mr. Bolton wished to place his son under my care, for a voyage to Jamaica. He was willing to pay a large sum for his passage out, provided I would take charge of him; appointing a meeting at the Bath Hotel, Piccadilly, to introduce me to Mr. Bolton and his son.

" I called the next day, and on inquiring for Mr. Bolton I was shown up into the drawing-room; there I saw a most gentlemanly looking man, about forty-five or forty-six years of age, who, after some few questions concerning the 'Foam' and the voyage out, explained the delusion under which his son laboured, and, ringing the bell, he desired the waiter who answered to tell young Mr. Bolton he was wanted. The waiter returned, stating that Mr. Bolton and his sisters had just gone out.

" ' Two years ago,' said Mr. Bolton, addressing me, ' my son was attacked with this delusion, after a brain fever ; he has recovered perfectly his health and strength, but to my intense sorrow he no longer considers me his father—only his benefactor ; and thinks himself a poor cast-away, left on the sands at Ramsgate, to be washed away by the tide. He is most amiable and affectionate, highly accomplished, and gentle and inoffensive. Eminent physicians advise a long voyage, with change of scene and occupation. I am going, therefore, to consign him to the care of a merchant in Jamaica, who will, to all appearance, take him as a clerk and give him employment. I am sorry he is not at home. No one in the hotel has the slightest idea that my son labours under any infirmity. He goes anywhere he pleases, and is like any other young man in manners and ideas. Now, Captain Courtney, if you think £150 will pay you for taking my son out, and seeing him consigned to the care of the gentleman I will name in a letter my son will take to you, I will provide him with a chest of garments, and every comfort necessary for the voyage.'

" I felt quite satisfied, being handsomely paid—all the passage money being my own perquisites; and I bade Mr. Bolton adieu for the time.

" The ' Foam' dropped down as far as Greenwich to take in some small goods and receive my young passenger. The day before sailing I received a very kind note from Mr. Bolton, stating that his son would be sent aboard that night, and begging me to send my boat to St. Catharine's wharf; the fact was, his physician had made a last effort to overcome his delusion, which had so excited and irritated him that he refused to go on board the 'Foam' of his own free will; he would send his steward and another person with him, and his chest would be there also. Now, I firmly believe," said Captain Courtney, after stating the above to our hero, " that the Mr. Bolton I saw at the Bath Hotel was no other than Sir Richard Morton, and if I live to get back to England I will find that out. There is some powerful motive in Sir Richard Morton's mind for getting you out of England."

" Probably," observed our hero, with a flush on his cheek, " he wished to get rid of and provide for me, as an illegitimate child, in a far-off land."

" No, I do not think that; Mrs. Morton or rather Miss Morton—for she was a maiden lady—declared to Mr. Cunningham that she was dying, and that she spoke God's truth, saying that you were her nephew, her lawful nephew. At such a moment, such assertions, if untrue, are rarely made. It is possible you may be Sir Richard Morton's nephew; he may have had another sister or brother, though Mr. Cunningham's friend at Derby knew it not."

" We can only conjecture; so for the present," said Arthur Bolton, " let the subject rest; unless by any chance Mrs. Marchmont might inquire who and what I am,—then I prefer facts to any other statement."

Two days after quitting Falmouth they encountered very bad weather, with heavy gales from the westward. Captain Courtney by no means admired his crew; they were sullen, and, though they did their duty, evidently they did it grudgingly.

Arthur had observed the conduct and manner of the men, and particularly that of the second mate. He caught him often with his eyes fixed upon himself with a fierce, malicious expression, quite uncalled for. Being fond of the sea, he personally exerted himself, and did duty often at the wheel, besides taking instructions from Captain Courtney in navigation and all nautical matters.

One evening, Alice and her pretty attendant, Mary, came

on deck to breathe a little fresh air; the night and previous day—the gale was so heavy and the sea so high—the meal could not be partaken of by the ladies in the chief saloon, so they confined themselves to their private state rooms. The brig was under double reefed topsails, the wind still a smart gale, and the sea exceedingly rough, at times breaking over the fore part of the vessel and deluging the decks to the mainmast.

" Ah, Mr. Bolton," said Alice Marchmont, holding on by the companion, and her attendant looking very pale, " this is a grand scene, though I shall not be able to bear it long ; the heat below is very great, so ten minutes of this breeze will be a relief."

Arthur fastened the young girl's cloak about her, for the gusts of wind were violent, and, placing a bench, secured to the deck by bolts, she sat down, and desired Mary, the maid, to go below and tell her eldest sister to come up in her stead. The second mate, Saunders, was at the wheel, steering.

As Arthur Bolton looked round, he could perceive this man's eyes following all his movements, at times regarding the Miss Marchmonts with a strange expression of countenance.

" This is a very different kind of sea, Miss Alice," said our hero, " to that you witnessed in the Irish Channel."

" Oh, very different indeed. Here the huge waves look like mimic mountains, and roll towards you as if going to overwhelm you. But what is that man doing? What a dangerous position he is in."

Arthur turned and beheld Jackson, the first mate, standing on the bulwarks, holding the fore shroud, and leaning over to catch a topsail sheet, or some rope that had broken adrift. The same moment the brig gave a tremendous pitch, and Jackson, either through carelessness or self-confidence, lost his hold, and was flung into the troubled sea to leeward.

Alice saw the accident and uttered a cry of terror, but the next moment she hardly breathed, felt faint and sick; for Bolton no sooner saw the accident than he seized the end of a long coil of rope lying on the deck, kicked off his shoes, put the end of the rope round his body, and leaped overboard.

The sisters were horror-struck. The cry of a man overboard—that cry of horror on board ship—brought the captain and surgeon on deck. Seizing the wheel, the captain brought the brig to the wind, and threw her topsails aback ; and Joe Malone, with singular presence of mind, knotted a second coil of rope to the one Arthur had seized, just as it was on the point of being run out.

Strange to say Jackson, the mate, could not swim ; but our hero, being an excellent swimmer, had reached the mate as he was about to sink the second time. Luckily the man's senses were nearly gone, so that he made no attempt to grasp his preserver, who laid hold of him by the collar of his jacket and held him up, and then called out, amidst the roar of the gale and the splash of the breaking billows, " Haul in !"

The two girls stood gazing out upon the scene with breathless anxiety. Alice for the first time in her life felt an overpowering interest, and a sensation unknown to herself.

" My God! he will perish !" she exclaimed, in a low voice to Mr. Cunningham, as she grasped his arm to steady herself.

" No, no. Please God, my dear young lady, he will be saved by that brave, gallant young man. See, he holds him up ! "

" All right," joyfully exclaimed the captain, " the rope is fast to him. Haul in gently, my men—haul in gently."

" Curse him !" hissed a voice close to Alice Marchmont's ear ; "I wish Jackson could be hauled in without him."

Alice trembled and looked round, but saw only the back of a man, who was walking rapidly forward.

" I cannot have heard aright," she thought to herself, as she strained her eyes, watching Arthur Bolton and the mate dragged through the broken seas.

" They are saved !" shouted the captain joyfully.

None of the crew echoed the cry. Alice dropped Mr. Cunningham's arm. How she contrived to get down the companion she knew not, but she reached her own berth, and threw herself, agitated and trembling, upon the bed. In a few minutes her sister joined her.

" They are quite safe, Alice dear," she said, kissing her sister's cheek. " It was a frightful scene,—too much for one so young to witness."

Three days after this incident the " Foam " anchored in Funchal roads. Here the ladies landed, Mr. Cunningham procuring them a residence for the three or four days Captain Courtney intended staying.

Those three days were the happiest of Arthur Bolton's life. He rambled with the mother and sisters through the romantic scenery of Madeira, and gathered plants and flowers for their collection ; in fact, love was sporting with the young hearts of Alice Marchmont and our hero unknown to themselves.

The day arrived for sailing. Mr. Cunningham had an hour's conversation with our hero before the departure of the "Foam."

" I shall return to England," said the surgeon, " before the autumn, where you can write to me. I feel great interest in you, and will do anything in my power to assist you in any inquiries you may be inclined to make. There is one thing strikes me as strange ; I have observed it, though I did not think it exactly worthy of naming. You have a bad set of men in the ' Foam.' Captain Courtney is aware of it, but he cannot help himself. One in particular, Saunders, the second mate, seems to regard you with some kind of malice. Did you ever offend the man, or see him before you came on board the ' Foam ' ?"

" No," replied Arthur, " I never saw the man before I met him in this vessel. But I have observed his sinister looks."

" Keep a strict eye on that man; I fear he means mischief. Have you remarked how sullen and dogged the first mate has been since you saved his life ? He never thanked you, or expressed the least gratitude. One word more—and forgive me if I trespass on the privilege of so short an acquaintance—but I really feel as if I had known you from your childhood."

Arthur Bolton pressed the kind-hearted surgeon's hand, who continued fixing his eyes upon the ingenuous countenance of his companion.

" You have given your heart into the keeping of that young and lovely girl, Alice Marchmont."

" I have never spoken one word of love," replied our hero calmly ; " but I love her with my whole soul,"—and his eyes sparkled, and his voice trembled with emotion, as he spoke.

" I could see that, and so does her mother. Now listen," continued the surgeon. " I have told Mrs. Marchmont all about you ; omitted nothing. A fond mother watches her offspring with wonderful instinct. She sees what others might not see, even with the most vigilant attention. Mrs. Marchmont is full of the milk of human kindness. She adores her children ; but she has a husband, who is a kind, indulgent, and fond husband and father ; but he is nevertheless proud of his daughters, proud of his wealth, and lives in the hope that when he returns to England, in two years, his daughters will form high and wealthy alliances. The mother, though herself the daughter of a baronet, and the niece of an earl, having married for love, cares only for the happiness of her children. Strange to say, the eldest has given her heart to a young officer, a lieutenant in an infantry regiment, of the name of Danvers, but who does not possess a shilling beyond his pay. His regiment is under orders for Jamaica. They have plighted their troth, and the mother says she has nothing to say against their love, for the young man is of good family, handsome, high-spirited, and amiable. And now, supposing her beloved Alice, secretly the pride of her heart, should feel a pre-possession in your favour, and the father remain opposed to your union, what prospect of future happiness have you in nourishing the passion you now feel?"

"You are quite right, my dear sir. I shall guard well my actions and my attentions during the remainder of the voyage. I would bear any sufferings myself to shield her gentle heart from a single pang."

The "Foam" sailed with a fair breeze, and soon the lowly, but beautiful, little island of Madeira was lost in the distance.

After leaving the island the conduct of the crew became almost unbearable; they would only obey, with any degree of willingness, the first mate. Captain Courtney was forced to use harsh measures, and for mutinous behaviour he put the second mate in irons for twenty-four hours, and at another time two of the men underwent the same punishment.

Heavy weather came on, and so mutinous were all hands that Captain Courtney, our hero, and the little steward, always kept arms at hand. Not to alarm his female passengers, the conduct of the crew was kept secret; but the two girls were quick of penetration, and they perceived that the government of the vessel was not going on smoothly, though they would not alarm their mother by stating what they observed.

CHAPTER VI.

WITH a favourable wind, the "Foam" was, on the ninth day after leaving Madeira, drawing near her destination. The crew worked better, and Captain Courtney hoped to finish his voyage without any further disturbance.

Sitting one night after the ladies had retired to the captain's private cabin, our hero and the skipper were enjoying a bottle of Madeira and the captain his pipe, when a sudden crash was heard, followed by a wild shriek; the next moment the trampling of feet was heard, and as the captain and Arthur Bolton sprang to their feet, the cabin door was violently burst open, and Bill Saunders, with a drawn cutlass in one hand and a pistol in the other, rushed in, followed by several of the men, who came crowding down the stairs armed with knives and hatchets.

The occupiers of the cabin rushed to seize the revolvers hanging up by the side of the couch, but before the skipper could move a step Bill Saunders seized him by the throat, at the same time firing his pistol full in the face of Arthur Bolton, the powder half-blinding him ; but fortunately the ball only just grazed his forehead. Two of the men then tried to kill him with their knives, as Saunders dragged the unfortunate captain from the cabin ; but Jackson, the first mate, thrust them aside, swearing with a frightful oath—saying, "Let him be, anyhow—a life for a life ;" and, suddenly grasping our hero round the waist, he and another man, after a desperate struggle, thrust him back into the cabin, one of the crew striking him over Jackson's shoulder with a heavy marlinspike, which knocked him, partly stunned, on the floor. The door was then shut and locked outside. Meanwhile the other ruffians had dragged Captain Courtney on deck, having previously disposed of the unfortunate steward.

Rousing himself from the stupor caused by the blow of the marlinspike, and wiping the blood from his face and eyes, our hero groped about till he found the captain's revolver ; then with a blow or two of his foot he dashed open the cabin door, and rushed upon deck, determined to die in defence of the captain : but before he reached the deck the ill-fated Captain Courtney, with an exulting yell from the mutineers, had been cast overboard, and the murderers were proceeding forward when Arthur, a revolver in each hand, appeared before them.

"Cut him down !" roared Saunders, flourishing his cutlass.

Our hero fired, and Saunders fell, but almost immediately regained his feet, and staggered up against the companion. The other men threw themselves upon our hero, and but for Jackson his death would have been inevitable. He beat the men off, saying,

"I told you I have bargained for his life—let him be, or by——"

After a struggle, however, they disarmed him, and then Jackson said,—

"If you are wise, go below, and tell the women they will not be hurt if they keep quiet. If you sacrifice your life by opposing us it will be worse for them."

He ended by pushing Arthur down the companion, ordering his companions to put on the slide and batten him down.

Horrified and appalled, Arthur sat down on the stairs and buried his face in his hands. The fate of the captain and steward was dreadful; but he must think how best to save the lives of the helpless women, whose cries and lamentations reached his ears.

"This is horrible—horrible!" he exclaimed aloud. "My God! if these demons drink, woe to the unprotected women."

This thought roused him from his stupor. He saw there was a light in the steward's pantry, and, descending the stairs, he looked in and perceived that it had been ransacked, and the wine and spirits carried away, and decanters and glasses all smashed, the cutlasses and pistols all gone. Taking the light, he proceeded to the chief cabin, the doors of which were locked, with the key on the outside. He heard the sounds of voices within, and he knocked, saying,—

"It is I, Arthur Bolton, who knocks."

A wild cry of joy was heard within, and the pile of tables and furniture which the terrified females had raised against the door, hoping that such frail articles could prevent the murderers from entering, was removed. The women had been spared, but how long that mercy would be extended to them was a question none could answer.

When the door was opened Arthur entered, forgetting that his face, neck, and garments were covered with blood. An exclamation of dismay and terror escaped all present. But Alice betrayed the secret feelings of her heart; she turned very pale, and sank, half fainting, beside her mother, upon whom the elder sister and Mrs. Morris, her own personal attendant, were bestowing their attention. The sight of Arthur Bolton roused Mrs. Marchmont into action; a gleam of hope shot through her mind; she had thought him murdered, but he was alive, and to him they could look for protection.

Mary Pearson, the young attendant of the daughters, a devoted and high-spirited girl, was again beginning to pile the furniture against the door, but our hero stopped her, saying it could not be of the slighest avail if they had a wall of iron there, as the cabin was accessible from the skylight above.

"Oh! Mr. Bolton," cried Mary, "wash the blood from your face and neck; it makes us all shudder."

"I trust you are not seriously hurt, Mr. Bolton," exclaimed Mrs. Marchmont anxiously, as he turned round to leave the cabin to do as Mary Pearson requested.

" No, Mrs. Marchmont, not much ; I will return in a few minutes."

Entering the steward's cabin, he washed his face and neck ; he then changed his coat in his own cabin, and, putting a brace of loaded revolvers in his breast pocket, returned to the main cabin, where could be heard the sounds of footsteps on deck, and even the voices of the mutineers as if in angry contention.

" I wish," he thought, " they would quarrel and fight ; we might then be able to defend ourselves against the survivors."

Alice Marchmont shuddered as she looked up into the face of our hero, and saw the wound upon his forehead. Alice was far from being a weak-minded, or even a timid girl. Death she could meet with resignation, but there was something appalling in their present situation that awed the spirit and mind of a woman ; there was, apparently, no help but in God !

Arthur sat down beside the mother, whose tears were falling fast. He took her hand, and, kissing it with the devotion of a son, said,—

" Courage, dear lady, courage ! Hope never dies in the human heart, and the Almighty will yet deliver you and your beloved children from this horrible peril. Whilst life is left me no hand shall injure any here."

" Alas ! my dear Mr. Bolton, what can one brave spirit do against the many? Why we have been spared, even till now, amazes me. I heard one villain say, as they dragged the poor captain up the stairs—'Kill him ; knock him on the head.' 'No, no,' said another wretch, with a fearful laugh—'Let us pitch him overboard—he swims like a duck—he'll have plenty of room.' Ah ! my God ! I shall never forget our horror last night when we were roused by the crash of breaking in a door, followed by a shriek of pain from the unfortunate steward. We hurried on some clothes, and then Mary began piling the things against the door. We listened to the struggle in your cabin—heard your voice and the pistol-shot." The mother looked at Alice as she continued—" We thought you were killed or wounded, and we could do nothing to help or save you— expecting every moment to see the door dashed open ; for we at once guessed that the crew of the brig had mutinied."

" What an hour of fearful suspense you must have assed !" observed our hero. " I think and trust the villains will commit no further outrage; they evidently have mutinied for the sake of the large amount of gold and bullion in this vessel, and will probably run ashore upon some part of the American coast, divide their booty, and escape into the interior. This is mere supposition, but it appears likely."

"But how were you saved?" said Alice anxiously. "Or were the men ignorant of your being alive?"

"Oh, they know I am alive," returned our hero, looking affectionately into the pale features of the young girl. "They would certainly have killed me but for the interference of the man Jackson, the first mate, whom I saved from drowning. He swore they should not harm me. He is evidently the leader, and the others fear him; otherwise that terrible ruffian Saunders, who is the most powerful man I ever saw, and who seems to have a particular hatred to me, would decidedly have slain me. I shot at the wretch, and hoped I had killed him, but I only slightly stunned him, the ball glancing along his temples."

"God protect us! our only hope is in Him," sighed Mrs. Marchmont.

"Oh, Mr. Bolton," said Alice, with a firm, steady voice; "give me a pistol; I will die before any one of those wretches shall lay a hand on me."

"They must kill me first," returned Arthur, "but I still hope that they will confine themselves to sharing the gold on board. They may possibly put us into a boat, when in sight of land."

"That would be a blessing, to being obliged to remain on board at their mercy," said Mrs. Marchmont. "If they get at the spirits, our doom is sealed."

"There are two nine-gallon casks of spirits under the floor of the steward's pantry," said our hero; "I will go this moment and let it all run off."

"Do not attempt it, Mr. Bolton," pleaded Alice; "in their frenzy of disappointment they would assuredly destroy you."

"Alice is right," said the mother thoughtfully. "Hark! there is a strong breeze rising."

"I thought," cried Arthur, "the sky looked very threatening. I would advise, dear madam, that you and the young ladies should take a few hours' rest. There is no immediate prospect of further mischief, for it is decidedly coming on to blow a gale, and that will keep all hands employed. I will keep watch here."

After some few more words on a subject so important to

all, the mother and daughters, with sad hearts, retired to their private cabins.

"Do, Mr. Bolton," said Mary Pearson, "give me a loaded pistol. I am not afraid; and I will help you if necessary, and risk my life cheerfully for my young ladies."

"You are a good, brave girl, Mary, and I will get all the arms I can find in the poor captain's cabin. I know there are two or three brace of small pistols in one of the chests. But, hark! the gale is increasing. I will try and get on deck."

Placing his pistols in his pea-coat, which he put on, he proceeded up the cabin stairs, and then paused to listen. The wind blew in fearful gusts, and the sea was rapidly rising. He could hear Jackson's voice calling out to the men to come aft, and cursing them for drunken rascals. "If you don't secure this mainsail it will be split to ribbons."

The roar of the sudden storm through the rigging and sails was like thunder, every moment adding to its violence, dashing the waves furiously over the decks, whilst the intense darkness augmented the danger. By the noise and thundering reports, our hero judged the great mainsail had broken loose. Determined to see what was going on, Arthur placed his shoulder against the companion door, and with a strong and resolute push burst it open, and, stepping out, stood upon the deck. The scene was startling: the wind blew a perfect hurricane, sending the spray over the brig in unceasing showers; whilst the breaking billows at times flooded the deck. Caught under a press of sail, with half the crew intoxicated, and the rest little better, the ship was near foundering in the furious hurricane that had so suddenly burst upon them. The mainsail was split in two; the fore-topmast had been carried away under the topgallant cross-trees; the fore and main topsail were split, and the jib flying in ribbons.

The sky was obscured by a dense mass of black clouds, and as our hero came on deck, flash after flash of lightning illumined the storm-tossed deep; whilst the peals of thunder that followed each flash sounded like the crash of doom.

Several of the crew lay helplessly drunk in the lee scuppers; Jackson and two of the men were dragging down the mainsail; and Saunders, with two others and one of the boys, trying to brail up the main topsail. At that moment the electric fluid struck the foremast, and a storm-gust, appalling in its violence, and shifting several points, struck the brig. Away went the foremast, and then followed the mainmast; the next instant the whole was swept over the side, crashing the bulwarks, and sweeping every soul on deck over the side into the foaming deep.

Bolton, by a miraculous effort, escaped the crash of the masts; but, being struck by one of the yards, he was hurled against the companion, which, being shivered by the yards into pieces, dashed him down the stairs, completely insensible, bruised and bleeding it is true, but preserved from the fate of the mutineers.

As he recovered recollection and opened his eyes, he found he was lying on the floor of the cabin, the vessel rolling fearfully and the sea sweeping over her; and at times a quantity of water poured with violence down the cabin stairs, flooding the passage, the pantry, and captain's cabin. The main cabin was reached by a couple of steps, which saved it from the rush of the sea down the stairs. It was daylight, but the skylight being partially covered by a tarpaulin lashed over, rendered objects indistinct. His eyes first rested upon the pale, terrified face of Alice, who was kneeling by his side and holding a cup to his lips, and near him, bathing his temples, was Mary Pearson. Mrs. Marchmont, her eldest daughter, and her own attendant, were holding on to the sofa in a state of terror; the tables and chairs now dashed against the sides of the cabin; and at every roll or pitch the unfortunate brig gave, the passengers with difficulty kept their feet The thunder still roared over head, but more distant; but the gusts of wind were still terrific.

" Ah, thank God !" murmured Alice, in her gentle voice, " he is alive ;" and the tears she could not control rolled down her cheeks.

Arthur raised himself on his elbow, and, with a look of devotion and love into Alice's sweet face, said,—

" Thank God ! you are now in His hands alone. Every soul on board this vessel, except poor Joe, the sick lad, has been washed overboard.

Mrs. Marchmont shuddered, but her old and faithful attendant exclaimed, clasping her hands,—

" The Lord be thanked ! those brutal murderers have only met the doom they richly deserved !"

" We were driven from our couches," observed Mrs. Marchmont, tears of thankfulness running down her cheeks, " by the fearful pitching of the ship ; and then came that frightful crash. We thought the vessel had struck, and that all was over; then we heard something driven down the companion stairs, and hurled against the cabin door with violence. Mary ran to see what it was, and, opening the door, she gave a great cry of fear, for she saw it was you; she thought they had murdered you, and thrown you down the stairs. My two daughters and Mary lifted you in here; and then we saw you were not dead, but only insensible. But, Mr. Bolton, how were the mutineers all carried off the ship?"

"By the masts and yards sweeping the deck," said Arthur, "and carrying away the boats and every possible thing that obstructed their progress. The vessel was struck by the lightning, and it is a mercy of Providence that the squall, or rather tempest, carried away mast, rigging, &c. The deluge of rain will, no doubt, shift the wind and lull the hurricane."

"You must be terribly hurt and bruised," observed Alice anxiously, seeing by the expression of our hero's features that he suffered considerable pain.

"Bruised and sore I am, Miss Alice; but, thank God, no bones are broken : in a little while I shall be able to go on deck, and see in what condition the hurricane has left us."

After a short rest Arthur proceeded to his own cabin, changed his garments, and, as well as he could, attended to his own hurts, for there was scarcely a part of his body that was not sorely bruised. A glass of brandy, however, taken internally, and cold water,—the only outward remedy he could apply,—relieved him greatly; whilst as he made his hasty toilette he listened to the rain as it came down in tremendous torrents. Then the wind began gradually to lull, though the violence of the sea continued with but little diminution. He was particularly anxious to reach the fore-cabin, where Joe, their favourite attendant, had been lying ill for several days past.

Entering the cabin, he found Mary Pearson endeavouring to light the fire in the stove, in order to make her mistress some coffee, and on inquiring for the ladies was told that, being quite overcome with fatigue and anxiety, they had retired to rest. After assisting Mary to get a few requisites from the steward's pantry, Arthur went on deck. The rain was still falling heavily, and a thick heavy atmosphere lay upon the surface of the troubled ocean ; the brig was a perfect wreck; the masts had broken off by the deck, and, when swept over the side, had carried away every plank and stanchion. On the lee side of the vessel there was not a vestige of anything left, beyond short pieces of shrouds, the anchors, and the stump of the bowsprit; the wheel was dashed to pieces, also the handsome binnacle; luckily the skylight had escaped, the companion having borne the brunt of the shock.

As he stood gazing along the deck of the ship, he suddenly beheld an object rise up on the lee side, and to his amazement he saw it was a man. Astonishment held him spell-bound, whilst the half-drowned creature raised himself, seemingly terribly exhausted, over the shattered bulwark, and then fell over on the deck. By the size of the body, Arthur Bolton conjectured it was either Jackson or Saunders; but the long dark hair hung matted and dripping over the face, and as the brig rolled tremendously, and immense waves rushed across the deck, it was not easy to go forward. Nevertheless, anxious to ascertain who it was that had contrived to save himself, probably by clinging to some rope or spar, he watched for an opportunity to cross the deck, and as he did so the figure raised itself up, and, dashing back the tangled mass of hair which had concealed the face, revealed the features of Bill Saunders, the second mate. He glared wildly at Arthur, who was unarmed. Strong, active, and powerful as Bolton was, victory in a contest with so Herculean a man as Saunders would be doubtful. Still, he advanced; but Saunders, holding up his clenched hand, with a frightful imprecation, said,—

"Ha! you see I'm alive, and likely to cut your throat yet;" and, turning round just as the forehatch was gently lifted up, he tore it off, and, with a shove of his foot beat down the lad Joe, who was making an effort to get out, and leaped into the cabin after him, cursing and abusing him fearfully.

The cry of pain uttered by Joe irritated Arthur; but to attempt to descend while Saunders was waiting for him was too hazardous. So, instantly returning to the cabin, he took one of his revolvers, put on a fresh cap, and hurried across the brig to the forehatch. He paused, hearing the voice of the villain, Saunders, uttering threats and imprecations, and Joseph imploring his pity.

"You have already beat me till my body is covered with sores," said the lad.

"Yes, you whelp. You wanted to betray us; curse ye. I'll make a jelly of you if you don't do as I bid you. Only wait till I gain strength, after hanging on for hours under water, and I'll cut that fellow Bolton's throat; he shan't live to inform on me."

" You murderous villain," cried our hero, " let that boy come up ;" and, stooping over the hatch, he could just see that Saunders had removed the steps, and that he stood holding a long-pointed knife ; a candle was burning on a locker, and crouching in a corner was the lad Joseph.

" Ah, you come down: only let me get my hand on your throat, I'll make short work of you.　You nearly did for me some hours back, but I'll pay you off."

" You infernal murderer, I should be justified in blowing your brains out where you stand ;" and he held the pistol pointed at him.　"Put the steps up, Joseph ; and if Saunders lays a finger on you, I'll shoot him, as sure as he stands there."

Saunders showered a torrent of abuse at our hero and Joseph, but the pistol followed him wherever he turned. Joseph put up the ladder and joyously rushed up.

" Now, hark ye," said Saunders, choking with passion. " You have the best of it.　You are a coward ; but I'll live to trample on you and cut your throat afterwards.　Fasten that hatch on," and he swore a terrible oath, "and I'll fire the ship ; there are five barrels of gunpowder the other side of this bulkhead ; if you don't let me have provisions and drink, I'll fire the ship, and send you all to ——."

"I should be justified in killing this murderer," thought our hero ; " still I cannot bring myself to do it till he attacks me ; I cannot shoot him as he stands.　We must only carefully watch him, till we are seen by some passing ship.　When this weather clears, we shall be seen at once ; besides, we cannot be far from land."

A wild mocking laugh came up from the forehatch, and then Saunders's head appeared over the combings—" Oh, you'll watch me, will you?　You think you'll hand me over to be hung in chains?　Ho, ho, ho! we shall see. I'll watch you ; and woe to you if I catch you sleeping. I'll cut the throat of every woman aboard." Exasperated, our hero raised his pistol, but Saunders disappeared below.

" Bedad, why didn't you shoot him, sir?" said Joe.　"I can hardly stand from the beating the villain gave me."

" We all thought you were ill, Joe, and many nice things were sent from the cabin for you."

"I was not ill at all, sir, except from the beatings they gave me.　That villain Saunders held my mouth to drown my cries, and kept a knife to my throat besides.　I found out the plot, sir.　They intended, after they had murdered the captain, the steward, and you, sir, to run the ship on the Musquito coast, toss up for the unfortunate ladies, and then go with the gold into the wild country on that coast, and get amongst the Mexicans. But they are all drowned, sir, except this terrible Saunders, the worst of them all."

"The wretches deserved a far worse death, Joe," returned our hero. "We shall have to keep a sharp look-out on that villain Saunders, till we fall in with some craft, which we must do when this weather clears. But come below, Joe ; the cabin must be put in order. The fearful death of our kind-hearted commander has had an awful effect upon the females ; we were too careless in our watch upon them."

As they descended into the cabin they met Mary Pearson, who exclaimed,—

"Oh, sir ! my mistress and the young ladies are again alarmed. One of the murderers has been saved."

"Yes, Mary, the greatest villain of them all has contrived to save himself by holding on to some ropes or spar fast to the vessel; but one ruffian, let him be ever so powerful, is easily dealt with."

"How singular," observed Mrs. Marchmont, "that this man should have been preserved, and all the rest, with the exception of the poor boy, who I feel satisfied had no hand in the mutiny, should be drowned."

"Joseph says he had no hand or share in the mutiny."

"I am so glad he is able to leave his sick bed," said Miss Marchmont; "we missed him very much. He will be a great assistance to you, Mr. Bolton. Alice tells us that the fog is very thick ; she could not see, she said, one hundred yards from the ship."

"It may clear up by sunset," replied Arthur, "and I sincerely trust it will, for we are nothing more than a mere log on the water, quite at the mercy of whatever wind may blow. I do not think that we can be more than a day's run from the land ; but where that land lies I cannot yet say."

"What a dreadful fate our poor captain has met !" observed Mrs. Marchmont. "What a tale for his poor dear wife and children to hear ! Oh, my God ! the memory of this voyage will cling to me for life."

Thus conversing, all were busily engaged in restoring the cabin to some kind of order. The broken table, chairs, and other articles were removed, and Joe, who knew where all the provisions and articles in use for the cabin were stowed, was very busy in preparing, with Mary Pearson's assistance, some food for the ladies.

The caboose on deck was carried away, so that everything they required must be cooked in the cabin. But Mrs. Marchmont entreated our hero not to trouble himself about them ; anything with a cup of tea—a biscuit—would keep them well enough till some vessel came in sight. In fact, Mr. Bolton was very little able to exert himself, for, although he was silent on the subject, he was severely hurt, though several times he caught Alice's eyes fixed anxiously upon him when he unconsciously betrayed signs of pain in moving anything.

"Mr. Bolton," said Alice, "you must be very careful; that is a horrible man whose life is saved."

"But how did you know he was saved before I came back to the cabin to tell you, Miss Alice?"

"When you went on deck," replied the young girl, with a little increase of colour, "I had a great desire to see how our poor ship looked. So I got up the stairs and held on by the broken companion, and, looking after you as you made the dangerous passage across, I beheld, to my utter amazement and terror, the huge figure of a man rise over the side and fall apparently exhausted on the deck. When he regained his feet and looked at you, I recognised him at once. I have often noticed that man's malicious looks and manner, and never passed near him, strange to say, without a shudder."

"Do not be uneasy, Miss Alice, about him; he is comparatively harmless. Wretch as he is, I cannot shoot him in cold blood; but the first time he attempts any annoyance, he is doomed to die a death far too honourable for a cowardly murderer like him."

CHAPTER VII.

ARTHUR BOLTON's feelings were a strange mixture as he paced the deck of the dismasted "Foam," of which he was now commander; whilst Joe—the injured Joe—comprised his crew. Proud of being the sole protector of five females he certainly felt; his resolution to take them in safety to the father and husband was firm and strong—firm and strong as his love for the fair Alice. Peril had forged a link to connect these two young beings; and though no words of love had been uttered, each knew the sentiments of the other. The mother looked on without disapproval, and surely the father would let services rendered, and the happiness of a child, weigh down the scale balanced only by ambition. These hopes came bright and cheering to the anxious walker on that deck, strengthening his resolution, rising up to lighten his responsibilities. Difficulties surrounded him, but beyond was a bright reward, to be his when those difficulties had been trampled down; each one subdued would bring him nearer the desired haven. It is true he stood on a dark abyss, filled with dangers that at any step might cause destruction ; but the landscape was bright beyond, and could only be reached by passing through the perils. Alone he would calmly have encountered all ; but others depended on him and his exertions for their safety, and he well might be somewhat appalled at the labyrinth he had to thread. But it must be done. The first struggle had come, and he would be the victor. With the smile of anticipated triumph on his lip, he ceased his walk, and, seating himself on the stump of the mainmast, watched the increasing darkness, listened to the mournful sighing of the breeze, as it swept over the mastless hull, as if in mockery of its helplessness, till a dreamy insensibility to surrounding objects gradually came over him, from which he was aroused by an exclamation of alarm from the companion stairs, and the voice of Alice bidding him be on his guard. Looking round, he saw Saunders stealthily approaching, his unsheathed knife in his hand. Another moment and he would have sprung upon his intended victim.

" Ha ! detestable villain !" cried Arthur Bolton, drawing his revolver and cocking it ; " did you think to commit another murder ?"

" Yes," answered the infuriated mate ; " yes, curse you, I would have had my knife in your throat now but for that love-sick girl. Curse ye both. Fire, if you want to kill me ; but if you miss me—" and he laughed in hideous mockery, as he stood within six paces of our hero, glaring at him with savage ferocity, but not moving a step. Bolton lowered his pistol. " I might," he thought, " miss ; and I am not strong enough now for a personal contest with that giant ruffian."

Joe, hearing Alice's cry of alarm, came running up from the cabin, and held his pistol in his hand, ready to aid our hero.

" You won't fire, then ?" retorted Saunders mockingly. " Well, I tell you what. I'll murder you, or die in the struggle. Don't think I am going to wait till some ship overhauls us ; before twenty-four hours are over, you or I will die ;" and, deliberately turning round, he walked back to the fore cabin and went below.

" Oh, sir, why did you not shoot the villain," said Joe, " or let me ?"

" His punishment will come," replied Arthur, more indignant at the insulting words addressed to Alice than at the intended attack on himself.

" If my right arm was only well, so that I had my usual

strength, I would try that wretch's power, and master him ; but I must run no hazard, nor must I risk the safety of Mrs. Marchmont and her daughters."

On joining the ladies at the evening meal prepared by Mary and Joe, Alice met him with her usual sweet smile of welcome, saying: "You must not, Mr. Bolton, sit dreaming on deck, with such a wretch watching you as Saunders. We all admire you for resisting the impulse you must naturally feel to shoot him ; still, it is better, if possible, not to have even that wretch's blood on your hands, unless in a positive struggle for life."

"I think Alice is right, Mr. Bolton," observed Mrs. Marchmont sadly.

"Well, I differ with you both," cried Miss Marchmont. "I do not advocate the shedding even of that monster's blood. Still, so many lives are at stake, so much of danger to others exists, whilst he remains alive, that the first opportunity, if he attacks you, or even threatens, I would not spare him were I in your place."

"He would not be alive now, Miss Marchmont," said our hero, with a flush upon his cheek, "but from the fact that I have little or no power in my right arm ; the blow I received—"

"Ah !" interrupted Alice, speaking with sweet emotion, "I thought something was the matter with your arm, by the manner you used your hand. Why have you suffered so long without letting Mathews see it ? there is an excellent medicine chest on board, and she is a very clever nurse."

"It will be better in a day or two," said our hero, "now I have Joe's assistance ; but you see a pistol may miss, and, if it did, that man would overpower me, and you would be left at his mercy."

"That is too true, indeed," returned Miss Marchmont sadly, "and I beg your pardon for giving an opinion. We know your resolution and courage, when you risked your life to save our lamented captain's. We may entreat you, however, to be constantly on your guard ; for that man will watch like a lynx to take your life."

That night, it was agreed that our hero should keep the first watch ; Joe the second, whilst he rested on the sofa in the cabin. The next day perhaps the weather would be clear, and some ship come in sight and release them from their painful situation.

Joe went to sleep in the steward's berth, and Arthur proceeded to his watch on deck, vainly trying to discern some object in the dense fog that covered the water through which the hull of the brig was sailing at the rate of three knots per hour.

His watch expired, Joe got up, and our hero, who had in reality not rested since the murder of Captain Courtney, lay down, and was in a sound sleep in a few minutes. Joe unfortunately felt so intensely drowsy from weakness that he could not keep his eyes open. There was a light in the cabin, and Mary Pearson, who strongly suspected Joe's capabilities of being a good watchman, crept softly out of her young mistress's state room and entered the main cabin. As she expected, our hero was sound asleep, and Joe in the same state.

" My young mistress was right," thought Mary, " but I will let them both sleep. That wretch Saunders cannot come in without displacing the furniture ; " so Mary sat down and watched.

After a time she fancied she heard a slight sound above. She listened ; Bolton lay directly under the skylight. Her eyes presently became fixed upon the grating ; she herself was seated in the obscurity of the cabin, the lamp throwing but a faint light beneath ; and that light fell full upon our hero's upturned face. His throat was bare, and his right arm hanging over the sofa. Presently Mary beheld the grating slide slowly back, and then the point of a sharp knife protruded through the aperture. She sprang like a startled doe from her seat, seized Arthur Bolton by the arm, and dragged him on to the floor of the cabin just as the knife, fastened to a strong staff, was driven by a powerful hand from above into the sofa.

A volley of curses followed the failure just as our hero recovered his feet, and he and Joe seized their pistols.

One word from Mary explained.

" Then I will spare the wretch no longer," said Arthur, and taking away the fastenings of the door, pistol in hand, he rushed upon deck, merely saying to Mary: " Do not disturb the ladies—I owe you a life—I will never forget it."

But when our hero reached the deck Saunders had disappeared below in the fore-cabin. As Arthur was in the act of springing down, Joe caught him by the coat:

" Don't, sir, don't ; before you could see him he would stick you with that knife ; there's no light below."

" Then put on the hatch, and let us keep the villain down."

" Oh, do ! " roared Saunders, " I'd like to see you do it. I will fire the ship in five minutes, and——"

But Arthur Bolton considered this but an empty threat,

and without more words he and Joe put on the hatch, and placed the strong iron bar across it—Saunders foaming and raging below like a maniac, uttering the most fearful threats.

"He's sure to fire the vessel, sir," said Joe.

"The villain has not the slightest ambition for a fiery martyrdom," replied Arthur; "but I will take it off in the morning, and if the wretch comes up and menaces me, I will shoot him!"

No more rest for the young man, who continued to watch the falling breeze, and the gradual calming of the sea, till daylight.

At breakfast he found the family below, who all looked pale and anxious; Mrs. Marchmont had heard the noise on deck, and thought also that she distinguished the voice of Saunders.

Alice gazed anxiously in Arthur's face, who, smiling at her in return, said :—

"Suppose you were to come on deck, Mrs. Marchmont, and the young ladies also ; a little fresh air would do you good. I have that villain Saunders fastened down in the fore-cabin."

"Then something did happen during last night!" exclaimed both the sisters.

"Now it is over I may tell you; I owe my life to Mary Pearson's watchfulness."

Alice shuddered, and he went on and told the particulars of the occurrence ; and looking at the sofa on which he had been lying the previous night, a deep rent was observable where the knife had penetrated.

"Oh God, help us!" exclaimed Mrs. Marchmont, becoming fearfully pale. "Had that wretch succeeded, we should have been lost."

Joe's voice from above calling out :—

"We are near land, bedad, I hear breakers," caused Arthur to rush upon deck, and all in the cabin hastened to follow with intense anxiety, to know their fate.

The sound of breakers was distinctly heard to the right ; but immediately after, the same sound was heard to the left denoting the nearness to land, but the water looked deep and green ; nothing could be distinguished through the fog. Anxious and excited, each of the six beings on the deck of the vessel gazed around to discover something to show them where they were, or give some sign to guide them in their movements.

The sound of the surf was on every side ; but, strange to say, as the brig moved slowly on with a strong current more than with the light wind that blew, the ground swell became less, and in half an hour there was scarcely any swell at all, whilst the sea gently breaking on rocks sounded behind them.

" We must be entering some sheltered bay or river," said our hero, watching Saunders, who during the night had contrived to break the iron band fastening the hatch, and coolly taken his seat on the combings, gazing earnestly around on every side, as if seeking his opportunity for vengeance.

" Land !" exclaimed Alice, and almost at the same moment the brig took the ground with a gentle shock; when through the mists and fog they could make out land on both sides of them.

" Where are we, I wonder," cried the ladies, astonished at the little motion of the vessel as the gentle ground-swell ran past them, and broke upon a sandy beach some three hundred yards off.

" We will go below," observed Mrs. Marchmont, " and pack up some things ; but do you, Mr. Bolton and Joe, keep a careful watch upon that man ; he is glaring at us like a wild beast."

It was nearly three o'clock.

Arthur Bolton, after the retirement of the ladies, kept an anxious watch upon Saunders, and also upon the land, wondering where they could possibly have run ashore, whether upon the main land or an island, and whether, when the mist should clear away the situation of the vessel would be seen by persons ashore.

Joe had gone below to assist and get some things ready, when Saunders getting up walked coolly along the deck till he reached within five or six yards of our hero, who with his pistol cocked kept his attention fixed upon the villain, determined to shoot him the moment he attempted the slightest advance further towards him. Saunders stood with his arms folded, looking, with a terrible expression on his massive features, at his opponent.

" I tell you what, Arthur Bolton, as you call yourself," he began, " though that's not your name, the best thing you can do is to let bygones be bygones, and become friends. There's gold enough in this ship to make us both rich. You may take that young girl you hanker after, and——"

" Villain ! " exclaimed our hero, enraged that the ruffian should so coolly make such an infamous proposition to him. Raising his pistol, he added : " Go forward, then. Why I do not shoot you, murderer as you are, puzzles me!"

" Then here goes, curse you !" exclaimed the seaman, with a ferocious cry or howl of rage, as he sprang with one bound upon Arthur.

The young man was prepared, and levelling the pistol within a yard of his head, he pulled the trigger. The hammer fell upon the cap, but no explosion followed. He had neglected to put a fresh cap on for the last two days, and the damp fog had destroyed the powder.

With a yell of exultation Saunders threw out his arms, but quick as thought our hero grasped the barrel and struck his enemy direct in the right eye, destroying the sight for ever. Nevertheless, with a horrible oath, regardless of his torture, he grasped Bolton with his left arm and tore his bowie knife from his breast. By this time the noise and wild yell of Saunders startled those in the cabin, and all rushed up the cabin stairs, Joe cocking his pistol, and Mary Pearson seizing a knife. As they reached the deck Alice Marchmont, who was first, beheld the termination of a horrible struggle, for at that moment Arthur Bolton, making a superhuman effort, after receiving two or three stabs from the knife, hurled his half blinded antagonist from him, and with such force that he rolled over the unprotected side of the brig into the sea, whilst our hero sank, apparently insensible and utterly exhausted by the effort, prostrate on the deck.

Alice did not attempt to control her emotion, and with a cry of grief and despair that struck a chill to the heart, she threw herself beside him she loved so well. She saw his face and neck covered with the blood from Saunders's wounds, and she thought him slain. Mrs. Marchmont thought so too, as she knelt beside her daughter and raised his head.

But Arthur was only overcome by the frightful struggle he had had. He heard Alice's sobs, and, instantly raising himself, he caught the fair hand that wiped the blood from his face, and, kissing it, said, heedless of her mother's presence,—

" I am not hurt, dear Alice ; I would risk a thousand deaths for this moment of happiness !" Continuing, as he raised himself up, "I heard a pistol fired—I heard it, though almost insensible. Where is Saunders ?"

" I fired at the villain, sir," said Joe, " but missed him. He has swum ashore, and gone out of sight in the fog."

"My dear madam," said Arthur, addressing Mrs. Marchmont, and taking the tumbler of wine Mary Pearson had brought him, " I regret to have caused you such terror.

My pistol missed fire, and that wretch nearly overpowered me, for my right arm is still weak. But the horror of your situation, should he kill me, gave me strength I could not otherwise have possessed."

" Oh, thank Heaven!" said Mrs. Marchmont, " you have escaped. I really thought the blood that disfigured your face was your own. What a providential escape we have all had! How much we owe you! a debt that can never be repaid !"

" It has been paid a hundredfold," replied our hero, with a look of fond affection at Alice, who, still pale as death, timidly stood resting against the companion.

" I understand you, Mr. Bolton," returned the mother, with a kind and affectionate look and accent. " I have not been blind to your mutual attachment; it has my approval at all events, but another time we will talk of this. Do pray go and get the wounds you have received dressed by Mrs. Mathews."

" Oh! they are nothing," answered our hero, giving Alice a look of intense happiness, whilst the young girl said, in her gentle sweet voice,—

" Oh! do as mamma wishes. Your jacket is cut in several places, and even now you are bleeding from the arm," and she shuddered as she beheld the stains on the deck from two rather deep gashes in the arm, and one in the neck.

Alice, when she entered the cabin with her mother, threw herself into her arms and wept unrestrainedly.

The fond parent kissed her child's cheek, and seeing how overstrained her nerves and feelings were—how much she had suffered from the dreadful night when Captain Courtney and the steward had been so cruelly murdered, she strove all in her power to soothe and console her.

" You are not angry then, dear mother—that—that " —and she buried her burning cheeks in her mother's embrace.

The mother understood her fully. "No, my beloved child, I am not, for I understand your feelings. It could scarcely be otherwise. Your brave preserver deserves your love, and I trust in God, when we are all restored to your dear father's arms, that he as well as myself will approve of the brave young man to whom you have disposed of your affectionate and loving heart."

Whilst mother and daughter were thus communing, Arthur, convinced of Alice's love, and of her mother's approval, was undergoing at the hands of the skilful Mrs. Mathews, a rather painful operation with the most stoical indifference. His thoughts were of Alice. and Mrs. Mathews looked up several times into his face, wondering to see how coolly he took her proceedings—for one wound was a deep one, and by some means a piece of cloth had been drawn into the cut made by the knife, and the gash in his neck had to be sown up.

" The Lord bless us! sir," said Mrs. Mathews, as she finished, "you had a wonderful escape. If the knife had not struck this button on your collar first, and turned aside, it would have gone into your neck up to the hilt. Bless us! what a frightful wretch that man is."

" Yes, Mrs. Mathews, he is indeed; I only wish I had shot him. My own negligence might have cost us all dear —I shudder to think of it."

" Well, it is to be hoped we are rid of him now, sir; he will not attempt to come on board again, I think."

"If he does, Mrs. Mathews, I must be more careful of my fire-arms."

On entering the cabin, our hero found that Joe had managed to get up a tolerable repast. The brig sat perfectly upright. Mrs. Marchmont and her daughters, considerably relieved from the fact of having escaped two terrible misfortunes—the relief from Saunders and the escape from shipwreck—were all three attentively studying a large chart of the West Indies, but turned as Arthur entered, and looked anxiously into his face, and made many inquiries concerning his wounds.

Alice's beautiful eyes met his, and a flush came over her pale cheek, but the expression of her sweet features showed him how happy she felt at seeing him so well after his terrible struggle for life.

He sat down beside Alice, who said, " We are looking over this map; mamma fancies that we may be stranded somewhere on this line of coast,"—laying her finger on the chart. " It's called the Musquito Coast."

" I have been thinking the same," replied Arthur. "I know we were, when we lost our poor captain, more to the westward of Jamaica than he intended. We have certainly got into some sheltered estuary, or wide river, and I see several large rivers marked on the chart, and numerous islands off the Musquito Coast."

" My husband," observed Mrs. Marchmont, "has been twice to Bluefields, on the Musquito Coast, and I remember his giving me a long account of it. He told me that it is chiefly inhabited by negroes and Indian tribes; some fierce and wicked, others kind and hospitable, but the negroes are a sad wicked, drunken race. This Musquito Coast is also infested with Mexican desperadoes, half savages

and bandits; descrters from the Mexican navy and army.
Altogether, if we are on the Musquito Coast, our situation
is not the most agreeable ; but if we can get to Bluefields,
we shall be safe, as there is always an English resident
there, who has communication with Jamaica."

" I will now go on deck," said our hero, " it is so intensely warm here, and see if the fog is clearing."

" We will go with you," cried the two sisters. " We
are so anxious to see what kind of a place we are cast
upon."

On ascending to the deck they perceived that the sea-
breeze which had risen was rapidly dispersing the fog, and
that the sun was setting brilliantly.

" Oh, it is clearing delightfully," cried Alice ; " look, Mr.
Bolton, I see a great wooded hill rising out of the mist, to
our right."

" But you must not call me Mr. Bolton now, dear Alice,"
whispered our hero, contriving to gain possession of the
little hand that trembled in his.

" Well, I think," answered the young girl, with a sweet
smile, " I may call you Arthur."

A pressure of that hand was a sufficient answer, as Miss
Marchmont, with a quiet smile, turned to them, saying,—

" Now that you have established an amicable arrangement, which I think very justifiable, and one I will myself
adopt, just look round, Arthur, and tell us what you think
of this beautiful bay. We have not long to look at it, for
the sun is setting, and you know in the tropics we have no
twilight."

Our hero, delighted with the kind, sisterly familiarity of
Miss Marchmont, turned his attention to the surrounding
scenery. The brig had drifted full three or four miles from
the spot where she first took the ground. As the fog cleared
off the waters, the party on deck were surprised at the
scene before them. They were stranded about three hundred yards off a bold bluff headland, crowned with timber,
whilst the water was covered with innumerable birds.
Ducks, teal, and immense flocks of the white ibis ; the
river or estuary was full three miles wide ; the opposite
shore appeared flat and marshy, and covered with the luxu-
riant growth of a tropical climate. They could not see the
sea, for another abrupt headland blocked up the view.
The tide had turned, and was running down rapidly.

Our hero did not know that this tide was the last of a
remarkably high spring tide, and that the " Foam," now
hard and fast, would not float again for a fortnight, if
then.

He made Joe sound with some twine, and then calculated that the brig would have six or seven feet of water round her at low water.

" I scarcely think," observed Alice, " that there are any natives along this wild shore, or we should have been seen. Where can that horrid man, Saunders, have gone ?"

" Where we first struck," said Bolton, " was on a sandy shore, and he got safely to land, for Joe saw him wade on to the dry sands, and then lost sight of him in the fog. I am certainly inclined to think we must be up one of the rivers on the Musquito Coast. This brig has a most valuable cargo, besides a large amount in gold and silver. If assistance could be procured from Bluefields, she could be got off quite safely, and her cargo preserved from plunderers."

" Alas ! poor Captain Courtney," said Alice, with deep feeling. " What a fate was his ; and the poor ship he was so proud of, what a wreck it is here ! Can we be extricated from our present situation, Arthur ?"

" Oh, it would not be difficult, if materials could be procured from Bluefields, to rig up jurymasts, and with a few hands, to run us safely to Jamaica."

The sun had set in all the glories of a tropical climate, and soon the whole scene became lost to view in the gloom of night ; there was no moon, but the stars shone with surpassing brilliancy.

" Ours is a very strange situation, Arthur," remarked Alice, as her sister descended into the cabin; "thus stranded and helpless on an unknown shore; hundreds of miles, perhaps, from Christian help, surrounded, may-be, with savage tribes of Indians."

" And yet, my own Alice," returned her lover, " I never before felt so happy. God has protected us and shielded us amidst fearful perils, and let us trust that the same divine eye watches over us still."

" You are right, Arthur," answered Alice, in a low voice, " I feel no fear, but I can never forget the peril we have gone through. Come, let us join mamma."

Pressing the gentle girl to his heart, and kissing her fair brow with a pure and holy love, he said,—

" My life, Alice, shall be devoted to you; to save that gentle heart one pang, I would suffer a thousand deaths."

That night our hero kept watch on the deck of the " Foam," his worst enemies were the mosquitoes, and they were in truth an enemy not to be despised. As the night set in, the calls of innumerable aquatic birds, the plunging of some huge animals in the water, the howling of various others on shore, formed altogether a medley of sounds far from harmonious. The deck of the " Foam" was by no means a place where a lover could enjoy a delicious reverie; therefore, leaving Arthur Bolton to continue his lonely watch, we beg our readers to excuse our return to the shores of Old England in the next chapter.

CHAPTER VIII.

WITHIN a few miles of the village of Chatsworth, and the banks of the Derwent, stands the fine old family mansion of Sir Richard Morton. The baronet was a married man, with a family consisting of one son and two daughters.

Morton Chase was a fine and picturesque property, extending for three miles along the banks of the Derwent. The mansion, though of considerable extent, retained, at the period of this narrative, but little of its original Elizabethan form, each different owner having pulled down or added, according to the taste of the time, or his own peculiar fancy.

Sir Richard Morton's estates were totally unencumbered, producing a rental of nearly eight thousand a year. Lady Morton was a handsome, amiable woman, greatly attached to her husband, and devoted to her children. She was the youngest daughter of a high patrician family, and possessed a handsome fortune in her own right.

The heir to the estates, a fine spirited youth of about eighteen or nineteen, was at Oxford; the daughters, of the respective ages of fifteen and seventeen, were both handsome and accomplished.

Sir Richard himself was a tall, noble-looking man, prepossessing in manner, and well educated; but at times subject to moments of profound gloom and disquietude, which surprised his family, and pained his affectionate wife, who could discover no reason for these frequently recurring fits of despondency.

In his youth he was said to have lived a wild, irregular life; but from the period of his marriage with the Honourable Miss Dacre, his conduct underwent a complete change. It is during one of these times of depression, and about four days after the departure of the " Foam" from Ramsgate Harbour, that Sir Richard comes as an actor on the stage of our life drama, the scene the library at Morton Hall, where the master was seated at a table, reading a letter, the contents of which seemed to add to the dejected expression of his countenance, and to plunge him into deep thought, from which he was aroused by a slight knock at the door, followed by the entrance of his own personal attendant, saying,—

"There is a man in the hall, Sir Richard, who desires to see you. He said you would grant his request instantly if you read this paper.

Sir Richard opened the folded paper presented to him, slightly changed colour, and then said—

"Show the man in, Wilkinson; I know the individual. I promised to get him a situation."

The man was shortly after shown into the library, and Wilkinson having retired and closed the door, the baronet looked up, and regarded the stranger with a somewhat troubled look. We need not describe the new comer; we have met him before, in the train, when he introduced himself to Arthur Bolton as the inventor of a new perfume.

"I expected to have heard from you two days ago," remarked the baronet, first breaking the silence that followed his scrutiny; "what has caused the delay? why come yourself? is anything wrong?"

George Reynolds, the *ci-devant* perfumer, cast a strange look of mingled cunning and dissimulation at the baronet, and, after a short hesitation, replied,—

"No, Sir Richard, there is nothing wrong: the vessel has sailed, and the young man has sailed in her; but there was some difficulty in getting him on board. We had to use force, but Captain Courtney, believing the story of the delusion, thought us quite justified in our conduct."

"I am sorry for the violence," said Sir Richard, "though I wished him out of the kingdom for a time. I think I have placed him where his talents will win him fortune. It is not the young man's fault that he was born out of the pale of matrimony. Your father acted an incomprehensible part in placing him where he did."

"Well, Sir Richard," returned Reynolds, "I have heard my father say he did not know that the charitable Mrs. Morton, of Ramsgate, was your sister. But I am thinking, Sir Richard, you are somewhat mistaken when you say that your son was born out of the pale of matrimony, which is, I suppose, that you consider him illegitimate."

"What do you mean, man?" exclaimed the baronet, turning deadly pale. "What are you up to now? some fresh scheme of extortion and villany."

A dark frown gathered on the man's face, as the baronet uttered those words, and he sulkily answered,—

"It is time, Sir Richard Morton, that we should more fully understand each other——"

"Speak out then, and to the purpose," fiercely interrupted the baronet ; "let me hear what you mean, and from what motive you are playing this deceptive game."

"Well, Sir Richard, you shall understand my motive. What I am going to tell you may astonish and annoy you, and you may not believe me, but I have about me abundant proof of its truth. When you, Sir Richard, went through the ceremony of marriage with Grace Manning, you positively believed that the man, Jay Pearson, was an abandoned profligate, and not a clergyman, and therefore that the ceremony was a mere nothing, whereas Jay Pearson was, beyond a doubt, a real clergyman, and at that very period actually curate of S——. That this man was a disgrace to his cloth no one can doubt. He deceived my father as well as you, and he was afterwards found out and disgraced, and fled from England to avoid the doom of a forger."

"Villain !" interrupted the baronet, half suffocated with rage and amazement. "What infernal project can be in your head to induce you to utter so monstrous a falsehood, when you must know that Grace Manning died nearly two years previous to my marriage with the present Lady Morton."

"No, Sir Richard," returned George Reynolds—or, rather, George Mason, which was his real name—"no ; I can prove it. Grace Manning, or rather"—and he looked the baronet, who was exceedingly pale, steadily in the face—"the real Lady Morton, did not die ; my sister, who wonderfully resembled her, did die at that time, and it was she you saw in her coffin. Grace Manning lay for four days in a kind of trance, and did not recover her reason for many months after."

Whilst George Mason was speaking, the baronet's eyes never left his face ; he gazed at him like one stupefied. But suddenly his eyes flashed, his cheeks flushed with passion as he exclaimed,—

"And so, wretch, you and your father have been concocting a frightful game of double villany. You say Grace Manning is alive. Where is she ? Where is Jay Pearson ? "

"Jay Pearson is dead—died in Delaware. Your first wife is with my father and family. I have Jay Pearson's confession, signed and witnessed by two most respectable citizens of Delaware.

"Villain ! I will see your proofs," and with a sudden spring the baronet caught the startled George Mason by

the throat, half strangling him.   " Now, reptile, show me
your proofs," almost shouted the excited Sir Richard.

George Mason, a man of ungovernable passion when
roused, struggled desperately. He became livid with rage.
" Proofs ? " he gasped out, " here ! " and thrusting his hand
into his breast, he suddenly drew a bowie knife from its
sheath, and struck Sir Richard a violent blow on the chest.

With a stifled gasp and groan, the baronet drew back,
staggered, and then fell, apparently dead, into the arm-
chair, before his gasp relaxed; Reynolds's waistcoat had
given way, and a small bundle of papers had fallen upon the
floor.   Aghast at his own act, Reynolds did not perceive
the fate of the papers, as he made a grasp at the baronet
to save him from falling heavily on the floor.

The look of the man, who believed himself a murderer,
was horrible, as he stood gazing at his victim. The perspiration poured down the assassin's cheeks ; but after a
moment he recovered, and casting his glance over the
table, instantly perceived a bundle of bank-notes lying
with a weight upon them, and beside them the baronet's
jewelled watch. The notes he seized and thrust into his
breast, buttoning his coat, and then, seizing his hat, he
dropped the knife by the baronet's hand, muttering, " It
may be thought he killed himself." Then, opening the
door, he stepped out into the long corridor leading from
the library to the hall. By the time he reached the
hall he had regained his composure ; just then, two young
ladies were crossing the hall, having just entered from the
lawn. Reynolds held his hat in his hand, and as he passed
them he bowed very low so as to hide his features.
The young ladies were Sir Richard's daughters. They
looked surprised, seeing a stranger leaving from that part
of the house, where their father's library and study was ;
but they passed on up the great staircase. The porter,
however, said to Reynolds, as he was hurrying out,—

" Is there any one with Sir Richard at present ? "

" No," returned Reynolds, in a sort of husky voice ;
then hastened through the door down the long flight of
steps, and almost ran towards the lodge gate.

" What the deuce is the matter with that fellow ? "
thought the porter, as he closed the door and rang his
bell ; he looks as pale as a ghost, and walks as if doing it
for a wager. One of the footmen answered the porter's
bell—" Tell my Lady that Sir Richard is now disengaged,"
said the porter ; " the man who was with him has left."

About a mile from Morton Chase stood one of those

small beer-houses frequently met with, by the side of a
rather frequented by-path leading from the main road to
a bridge that crossed the Derwent. At a hundred or two
yards from this alehouse were scattered ten or twelve
labourers' cottages, the inhabitants of which frequently
of an evening indulged in a pipe and a glass of beer;
sometimes, indeed, the number of glasses taken of an evening sadly interfered with the good wife's *ménage* for the
ensuing week, as the beer had to be paid for—no scoring
in chalk being allowed.

Sitting on a bench smoking a pipe, and at times dipping
into a quart mug of ale, on the morning of which I
write, was a tall, strong man, habited as a sailor. There
was no one in the house at this time but the landlady
and a young girl, both of them occupied washing in a
huge trough, and occasionally looking out of the window
at the sailor, who proved himself to be George Reynolds's
confederate in the house in Bridge Street, who, having
finished his beer, rose, and sauntered up the lane towards
the road that led to Sir Richard Morton's mansion.

Now, Jem Saunders, with all his acuteness, did not perceive that two men were quietly watching his movements
from behind a hedge, not fifty yards from the alehouse;
nor was he aware that as soon as he moved up the lane,
one of the men said to the other—

" He is going to meet his confederate, Reynolds, *alias*
Mason. You see, Dick, if we had secured him, the alarm
might have spread, and the other chap, who is the chief
object of our capture, might get off. Now, I wonder is it
to Sir Richard Morton's he is gone? I can't think what
$uch a rascal can have to say to such a gentleman as the
baronet."

" Well, Jim, it is odd if it is to his house he's gone, and
I am sure it is, for the man I questioned said ' he see'd
him,' and he described him exactly, ' go up to the lodge
gate,' and there's no other mansion or house near that he
could go to; and what brings him down here I can't
think."

" No, nor I, Dick; but it is quite certain we have tracked
the right men as carried off that young Mr. Bolton;
whether they killed him, or what they did with him, who
can say; but before night we shall have them."

" That fellow, Saunders, is a mortal strong chap," observed the man called Dick; " he won't give in without a
struggle, I guess."

" Ah!" said the other, " a brace of barkers within an
inch of his head will cool his courage. Now, do you, Dick,

go along that great field, and keep that 'ere chap in sight, whilst I keep my eyes on this pot-house; for there may be more ways than one to the baronet's mansion, and the fellow's been gone two or more hours, I calculate, from the time you accosted the workman ; that half-hour's delay at Redhill put us out, or we should have nabbed them both in this pot-house this morning."

Richard Blewit, the name of one of the detectives, then proceeded along the field, keeping a thick thorn hedge between him and his intended prize.

Thomas Chalders took out a short pipe, struck a light, began smoking, and resting his back against the hedge, fell into a reverie.

An hour passed over, when he was roused by the return of his comrade.

" Well, it is very odd," said Richard Blewit. " I see no sign of Reynolds returning from the baronet's. This fellow Saunders is coming back to the pot-house; I heard him growling and swearing loud enough for me to hear him, that his comrade was cursed long, and he'd see him hanged if he'd wait much longer."

" Well the fact is, then," said Thomas Chalders, " we must be stirring. Let us secure Saunders and handcuff him ;" I will then leave him in your charge, and I'll at once proceed to the baronet's, and learn what's become of Reynolds, if we cannot squeeze that information out of Saunders."

Both men looked to their pistols and their staves ; they were in plain clothes, and both were very powerful determined men.

They watched till they saw Saunders enter the little beer-house, then, making a circuit, one entered the front door, whilst the other went round to the back.

Thomas Chalders was first in the room, which served for kitchen and drinking room. Saunders was sitting at a table, preparing to demolish a large plateful of eggs and bacon, which the young woman had just placed before him, the old woman continuing the process of washing.

Saunders sprang to his feet—for persons in his situation have an instinctive knowledge, no matter how disguised a police officer may be, of their dreaded enemy—and gazed at Chalders with a fierce, savage glance, placing his hand in his breast-pocket. Just then the other policeman entered, and Saunders saw that he was trapped.

" Don't be a fool," said Chalders, seeing him draw his hand from his pocket with a pistol in it, " you are in for a trifle ; attempt to take life, and you'll hang."

With a ferocious laugh, and a frightful curse, Saunders fired full at Chalders's breast, and the next instant, amidst the screams of the women, he sprang through the window, smashing the frame, glass, &c., into a thousand atoms.

Police officers ought to have charmed lives, and, indeed, it frequently appears as if they had. The moment Saunders lifted his pistol to fire, Chalders made a spring, but, fortunately for him, slipped on the flags, falling on his face just as the trigger was pulled. Richard Blewit rushed out, and threw himself upon Saunders, whose foot striking a wooden bar outside the window, caused him to fall violently on the ground; and before he could rise, his face cut and bleeding from the glass, Blewit threw himself upon him. The next instant Chalders, with his nose double the proper size, and his neckcloth stained with the crimson fluid from that rather prominent feature of his face, which had come in contact with the edge of the table, joined him, and after a fierce struggle, which irrevocably ruined for that season the little flower patch under the window, secured and handcuffed their prey; whilst the women, perfectly bewildered, rushed out at the back of the house, and made the best of their way to the nearest cottages, all the females and urchins belonging to them rushing out at the uproar they made.

" What a cursed fool you have made of yourself," said Chalders, as he and his comrade followed Saunders into the house and into the kitchen.

" Why, curse you," returned Saunders, looking at his smashed plate and the eggs and bacon strewed about the floor—" Could not you wait till a fellow swallowed his dinner—what do you want with me ? "

" Oh, you will find that out time enough; there's the warrant for your apprehension—you're James Saunders, you do not deny that, I suppose ? "

By this time the two women had returned, several labourers from the field had collected, and a dozen or more of women and girls from the houses.

" Send one of these boys," said Chalders, addressing Blewit, "to Chatsworth for a couple of constables. Keep your eye on your prisoner; I must be off to the baronet and see after this Reynolds, or we shall lose him." So saying, Chalders made his way through the crowd, telling them they were police officers that had captured a man who had been guilty of several crimes; told them to go back to their houses and be quiet. He then gave a boy a shilling to show him the way to Sir Richard Morton's.

Thomas Chalders reached the front of the baronet's

mansion about the very period that the tragical event recorded in our last chapter occurred. He paused at the
lodge gates, which were closed, and then pulled the bell.
A woman with a baby in her arms, and two small children
holding on by her apron, made her appearance, opening a
small iron gate to admit the stranger.

" Pray, missus," asked Chalders, " would you be so
good as to tell me, did you see a man (describing Reynolds, *alias* Mason, very accurately indeed) go up to the
house about—let me see—nearly two hours ago."

" Yes, sure," returned the woman, " I did see a man ;
he's just like the person you describe, but he has not
returned ; not this way at least."

" Ah ! " said Chalders, " there's another way then from
the house, without passing this lodge ? "

" Why, yes, there is of course through the Park ; but
then no strangers go that way ; only the family and their
visitors drive through the Park."

Just then Chalders perceived, coming hastily down
the avenue, a man, who, though he was running, looked
every moment behind him.

" That's my man," said he, in a tone that startled the
woman.

"Close your gate," he continued ; " I am a police-officer,
and the man coming this way from the house I am going
to take into custody."

" The Lord save us ! " exclaimed the woman, " what's
the matter ? " and she hurriedly closed the gate and rushed
into the lodge ; the baby screaming, and the two children
roaring at being left with such haste.

Chalders stood just inside the door, and the next instant
George Mason made for the gate, his hand was on the key,
when Chalders sprung out ; but quick and active as he was,
and sure of his man, Mason was more active, for as the
police-officer made a grasp at him, he ducked his head and
plunged between the legs of his enemy, throwing him
over himself upon the walk.   In an instant both regained
their feet, but light and exceedingly active, and having life
at stake, Mason went away at full speed in the direction of
the Park, with Chalders full chase after him. As they
started off, to the wonder and amazement of the gate-
keeper's wife, and became lost to view in the thick shrubbery on each side of the lawn, a gentleman came cantering
up to the gate. The woman ran to open the lodge gate,
saying—"I beg pardon, Doctor Sharp, but indeed somehow something has stopped me all day in opening the gates,
and now this minute I've been frightened out of my wits."

" What has frightened you, Mrs. Vickers? you look pale," said surgeon Sharp, riding through. " Is Sir Richard at home ? I want to see him directly."

" Yes, doctor, he is sure to be, for no one has passed the gates to-day but that policeman and the man he is running after."

" What policeman ? What's going on—a poacher, eh? " inquired the doctor, checking his horse. But before the woman could reply, galloping was heard, and the next instant a groom came cantering up to the gate ; but seeing the doctor, stopped, saying in an agitated voice,—

" Quick, sir ! Thank God you are here ! I was going for you. The master is, I fear, dead ! "

The gate-keeper screamed with fright, whilst the doctor, without asking a question, galloped furiously up the avenue.

In the meantime Chalders, annoyed at being again baffled, pursued the fugitive through the shrubbery. He had his pistol cocked, determined to bring him down if he could get within a sure distance; but Mason ran for his life, and gradually distanced his pursuer, dodging in and out between the trees to avoid being shot at. He had no idea, however, how to get out of the grounds, for the river, broad and deep, lay on one side, and the open lawn on the other. Still he ran on, and, fortunately for him, not in view of any of the domestics about the house. Chalders, to his intense vexation, perceived he did not gain on his intended victim, so resolved on a shot the first time he got a clear view of him ; about twenty yards off, he fired. It was not a bad shot, for it knocked off Mason's hat, who only ran on the faster, and Chalders, who was a stout man, was getting blown.

They had gained the park, and Mason himself was beginning to slacken his speed, when he beheld a light skiff, used by the inmates of Morton Chase for crossing the river or fishing, fastened to a post on the river's bank. With an exclamation of joy, the fugitive reached the boat, cast off the chain, and snatching up a boathook, pushed off into the stream, and then taking an oar began to scull towards the opposite bank.

Chalders stamped and swore with rage and vexation; he was beat. In vain he loaded and again fired his pistol; Mason was beyond his reach. There was no bridge, he knew, on either side for several miles, and the nearest ferry was three. The fugitive reached the other bank in five minutes, leaped out, and fastened the boat, that it might not drift with the wind back to his enemy (for it blew pretty strong from his side of the stream); this done, he pursued his way across the country, broken in spirit and crushed by remorse, for, bad and wicked as he was, he never contemplated the crime he thought he had committed; but a slave to passion, and exasperated at the apparent failure of his scheme (and for the moment imagining Sir Richard really intended to choke him), he, in his fury, struck the baronet with the bowie knife he always carried concealed in his breast, and which opened with a spring.

Chalders, chagrined and annoyed, returned slowly to the lodge gate, where he found Mrs. Vickers, crying.

"Oh, Mr. Policeman!" she exclaimed, the moment she saw him, "here's terrible news."

"Why, what's the matter here?" exclaimed the detective, wiping the moisture from his dripping brows.

"Oh, the master, Sir Richard, is dead, I fear—has killed himself with a great knife."

The policeman started, exclaiming, "Good God! that man I pursued has murdered him; I have no doubt of it;" and without a word more he hurried off to the mansion, where he found the whole household in awful confusion and consternation. Having made himself known to the butler, he learned all the particulars. Lady Morton, it appeared, had entered the library after the departure of Mason, and on beholding the horrible spectacle of her husband lying insensible, with a pool of blood and the knife on the floor beside him, uttered a fearful shriek, and fell prostrate on the carpet. The shriek roused every one in the mansion, and a terrible scene ensued, in the midst of which, most providentially, Surgeon Sharpe galloped up to the door; and pushing aside the crowd of horrified and stupefied gazers, reached the side of the baronet, whom he had instantly placed on the bed in the nearest room, and examining his wound pronounced him not dead, and proceeded to stop the flow of blood. There being an excellent medicine chest in the house, he at once administered remedies to Lady Morton, who went from one hysterical fit into another, whilst her daughters, in their state of distraction, could be of little service.

At this time it was thought that the baronet himself had committed the rash act; but the two young ladies and the hall porter recalled the circumstance of seeing a man coming from the library and leaving the house as they entered; and they also recollected remarking to one another his singular paleness and even agitation; whilst the porter stated that he saw him run down the avenue, after quitting the house, and looking back several times.

"What kind of knife was it that was found?" demanded the policeman eagerly.

"A foreign kind of knife," said the butler. "Mr. Sharpe said it was a bowie knife."

"Ah! then by —— it was that man Mason who attempted the murder," said the detective. "Is there any hope of saving the baronet's life?"

"The doctor says he is alive, but he cannot say more at present."

"Well, I failed," said the detective, "in capturing the villain, but I will start after him again. I have a comrade with me, and I do not think he will escape out of this county before I lay my hand on him."

"But why," asked the butler, detaining him, "why do you say so positively that the man I mentioned committed the act?"

"Because I have information that this man Mason, *alias* Reynolds, always carries concealed in his breast a bowie knife that opens by touching a spring."

"That's precisely the kind of knife picked up at my poor master's feet," said the butler, "and it's one no one in the house ever saw before."

"I am quite satisfied," returned Chalders, "as to who committed this murder, or attempt at murder. I have captured his comrade at all events. He is in the care of my chum at the Red Cow alehouse, near here. I will now take and lodge him in gaol, and then set out in pursuit of Mason."

Chalders left, and proceeded to the alehouse.

But Chalders was destined to endure a second disappointment. As he left the lodge gates he met two or three countrymen heated and excited.

"Well, what's the matter now?" said Chalders.

"Be gummers, the chap you left at the Cow be off," answered one of the men. "He 'av broke your comrade's head wi' a blow of the iron handcuff, and he beat us all, and got off."

Chalders uttered an exclamation not very complimentary to his hearers, and hurried on to the beerhouse. There he found Blewit washing the blood from a wound in the head that had bled profusely; though, luckily, it was not a dangerous cut.

By his account, Saunders, by his submissive conduct and persuasive eloquence, in promising to reveal to him a secret respecting Mason that would make his fortune, as it concerned Sir Richard Morton, induced him to take off his handcuffs, that he might eat his meal comfortably; not having, he said, had any food for twenty-four hours. Blewit laid his loaded pistol on the table, and turned the key of the handcuffs; he had scarcely done so before Saunders, with an imprecation, dashed the irons upon his head, felling him to the floor, and snatching up the pistol, set every one in the inn to flight, and, finally, knocking over a countryman or two, made his escape.

Chalders was furious; but as soon as his comrade was sufficiently recovered from the blow, both left the Red Cow, determined to track the two ruffians till they had secured them.

CHAPTER IX.]

THE sixth day after the attempted assassination of Sir Richard Morton, the two eminent physicians, who had been telegraphed for to London, gave Lady Morton hopes of finally saving her husband's life. They considered the danger over; but before they left they strictly cautioned her ladyship not on any account to allow her patient to speak, excepting a few sentences at a time, and by no means to permit anything to excite or agitate him.

After the first terrible shock, Lady Morton recovered her nerves, and, with her son and daughters, were constant in their daily and nightly attendance upon the invalid. She had carefully examined the library, and was attracted by the papers dropped by George Mason in the struggle, when his vest was torn open by the grasp of the baronet. She felt convinced from the first that this man was the attempted assassin, and that there was some cause of enmity between her husband and him.

The notes were not missed, for the baronet had received them that morning from his banker in a letter, and intended remitting them to the very villain that had struck him down. His watch, and other valuable articles lying on the table, were untouched, which proved to Lady Morton that robbery was not the intention of the miscreant.

She took up the papers, and, without looking at them, locked them up in her own private cabinet. Though she did not examine them, she was struck by the words— "The confession of John Jay Pearson," written on a blank sheet, containing two or three other papers.

Of course the attempt to murder the baronet, and the escape of the assassin without robbery, created a great sensation and much talk, not only in the baronet's household, but also for many miles round, and various were the surmises, but all wide of the mark.

At the expiration of a fortnight, a great and beneficial change in the baronet's health took place, and it became evident that he would soon be able to move and to converse. That night Lady Morton, for the first time, retired to her own chamber. She had no inclination to sleep, and as she sat in quiet repose in her easy chair, she felt an intense desire to look over the papers she had locked up in her cabinet.

She could not resist this feeling ; therefore, unlocking her cabinet, she took them out, and unfolding the wrapper, her glance rested on the inner paper. On it was also written "The confession of John Jay Pearson." Surprised, but not alarmed, she read on, even to the end, and then a deadly pallor and sickness came over her, her hands trembled, and, gasping for breath, she dropped the papers, and clasping her hands in agony, cried aloud, "Oh, my God! pity! mercy!—my children!" and fell back upon the bed, insensible. At that moment the door softly opened, and a female entered the room. Lady Morton's maid—for she it was—advanced into the room, and the next instant her glance fell upon her mistress, lying back upon the chair, as if dead. She was about to alarm the house by a shriek of fear, when her glance fell upon the open papers at her mistress's feet. Curiosity conquered fear.

"She has only fainted," soliloquized Jane Heathcot, drawing her breath, and gazing at the papers. "There is some mystery going on in this house, I am sure there is ; " and Jane, a very shrewd and designing woman, who had hitherto completely disguised her real character, hastily advanced, and picked up the papers, read them through, glancing every moment at her mistress.

"Ah," said she, turning pale herself with astonishment, and the many thoughts that ran through her brain, " I have gained a great secret. If this does not make my fortune, I am a fool." Dropping the papers on the floor, she took some water, sprinkled her mistress's face, and applied salts to her nostrils.

With a heavy, prolonged sigh, Lady Morton began slowly to recover. As her eyes opened, they rested upon Jane Heathcot, her personal attendant, and then a violent shudder shook her whole frame. Slowly she rose up, and immediately her glance was directed to the floor. She saw the papers lying there. Her attendant at once began with great anxiety to inquire how she happened to faint without having time to ring her bell, which was close to her hand.

Lady Morton, who possessed, notwithstanding her having given way at the first shock, a strong and firm mind, looked Jane steadily in the face, saying,—

"Jane, you have read those papers," pointing with her finger to those on the floor.

Jane could not stand that calm, searching glance; she coloured as her lady's dark eyes rested on hers, and then grew pale; but at last said,—

"I did just look at them, my lady."

"Well," returned Lady Morton, with a sigh, "you have forfeited your integrity to satisfy an idle curiosity. What those papers state may or may not be truth. I suspect them to be false, or the wretch who held them would not have resorted to murder to gain his ends. But, true or false, it is my determination to sift the matter to its foundation. I want no secrets kept, or confidantes; you have broken my trust in you, and therefore you must seek another place; with me you cannot stay. You may now retire."

Confounded and abashed, Jane withdrew without a word—crestfallen—all her air-built castles had vanished. She knew her mistress too well to try and attempt to gloss over her act, and to express contrition. Jane had a mean, vengeful disposition; the very next day she packed up her trunks, and when she left, to the great amazement of the several domestics, who questioned her as to her sudden departure, she said: "She would no longer serve a lady who assumed the title of a wife, but who was in fact only the baronet's mistress!"

This daring assertion amazed her fellow-servants; they cried shame! She laughed scornfully, merely saying, "You will see by-and-by that I am right. I know too much to be retained."

The words of Jane Heathcot, strange and incredible as they appeared, created a great sensation amongst the domestics; but the old butler, who had witnessed the marriage of his master with his present lady, declared with much indignation, "That base woman shall be punished for her wicked slander!"

Sir Richard Morton was now only attended by his own physician; he could be lifted from one bed to another, and in a few days it was expected he would be able to sit in his easy chair. During the hours of extreme illness, Sir Richard Morton did not think at all; in fact, for the first two or three weeks he had only a very confused recollection of anything, past or present; but as he regained strength, he began to recall things to his mind, and his first thought was, what had become of the villain, George Mason. He soon learned that he had baffled all attempts to secure him, and had escaped out of the county. Then he began to recall all the villain had stated to him, and he shuddered when he thought it possible that his words and assertions were founded on facts. "And yet," he said to himself, "how is it possible that Grace Manning can be alive; and, if alive, why for so many years refrain from asserting her rights and the rights of her son, should it be true that John Jay Pearson was in holy orders? Ah! my God! I am justly punished. But my adored wife! my beloved children! Are they to be sacrificed for my sins?" As he regained strength, he observed that Lady Morton looked care-worn and sad. Could she possibly have gained any information of George Mason's business with him? He recollected that almost at the moment the assassin struck him with the knife, a small parcel of papers fell from his breast-pocket, but insensibility followed. He now asked himself, could those papers be the proofs George Mason spoke of, and, if so, had Lady Morton perused them?

One evening the baronet, feeling wonderfully better, was seated in his chair, watching Lady Morton, who was near him. Long and anxiously he gazed, and he could see that her eyes were suffused with tears. "She knows all," thought Sir Richard, and a low groan of agony escaped his lips. Lady Morton started, and became even more pale, and trembled as her husband laid his burning hand upon hers.

"Anne," said he, his voice trembling with deep emotion, "you know my fatal secret; why did you not let me die?"

The still fond and devoted woman sobbed, as she laid her head upon his shoulder. "Yes," she uttered, "I know all; but you did not, could not have known the wrong you committed."

"God bless you, Anne, for those words; as God will judge me, I did not; neither do I yet believe that I have wronged you. How have you obtained this cruel intelligence?"

"From papers dropped in the library by that wretch who so nearly murdered you," replied Lady Morton—a ray of hope causing her heart to throb.

"I am strong now, Anne; let me see them, for I still think I am the dupe of a detestable villain."

Lady Morton brought the papers. The baronet calmly and carefully perused them. The document purporting to be the confession of John Jay Pearson was a lengthy one ; the others were a marriage certificate signed by John Jay Pearson, Sir Richard Morton, John Mason, and Grace Manning, together with a letter from John Mason, then residing in Delaware.

"Now, Richard," said Lady Morton, calmly, "if this certificate is real—and your first wife lives—the die is cast. My children and myself are outcasts from the world."

"No, no, no," exclaimed the baronet, in intense agony of mind. "Not so; it is impossible; Grace Manning cannot be alive. My wife she may have been—for it now appears that they deceived me. I do not want to shield myself from guilt. God will be my judge, for I have been guilty, and the errors of my youth were great. But I still maintain that you, and you alone, are my lawful wife. Your son, alas! will no longer inherit my title and estates, if this marriage certificate is true ; the signatures are all genuine—I recognize them all ; but the question is, was that wretch, Jay Pearson, in holy orders at the time? In order that you may understand the matter clearly, I will relate the particulars of this crime as it really was committed. I will extenuate nothing. Jay Pearson's confession is confused ; and, observe, he declares he saw Grace Manning alive when he was on his death-bed, in Delaware, and he then repents his evil acts, and, as it appears, writes this confession in the presence of several witnesses, and dies. Now, the moment I receive strength and health, we will go abroad ; I will leave you in any continental city you please, whilst I proceed to America, and, in disguise, visit Delaware. There is some terrible mystery in all this. But that Grace Manning lives, is impossible ; I saw her dead, and followed her body to the grave, deeply repentant for the act I had committed. Her child, however, lives."

"And how did you dispose of the poor innocent boy? If this certificate of marriage is correct, he is your lawful son and heir."

"Yes," returned Sir Richard, "I fear he is."

"Do not fear it," cried Lady Morton. "Act firmly and honourably. Restore him to his birthright. I will be the first to welcome him, and make him forget the past. Where is he?"

Sir Richard's conscience pricked him sorely as he listened to the words uttered by his noble-minded wife. He answered, however, truthfully, and told Lady Morton all.

" Now," he continued, " listen to me ; I cannot rest till you know everything. At my father's death I was very young—master of wealth—wild—thoughtless, and, alas ! with very little principle ; my whole object in life pleasure, and the gratification of my passions—no matter at what cost. My father's agent and manager of the estate was a very respectable man in manner and appearance, but at heart of most extravagant and unprincipled habits. He had two daughters and one grown-up son ; his name was John Mason ; the son, George, was a profligate, reckless young man, and to a certain extent I made him a sort of companion.

" John Mason's family resided in a large house on the estate, the same now inhabited by Mr. Henderson. There was a school-fellow of his daughter called Grace Manning, an orphan, on a visit to his house ; she was young, very beautiful, well educated, and I became for the time greatly attached to her ; I never thought of marriage—but Grace, though she returned my passion, was virtuous ; she resisted any attempt I made to persuade her to be my mistress ; I confess I was infatuated. About this time I discovered that John Mason had forged my name to a document. It will suffice to say that he became my slave to save himself. He consented to procure a man who would personate a clergyman, and that the marriage ceremony should be gone through between me and Miss Manning. I was to give him a certain sum, to destroy the forged document, and he and his family were to proceed to America. He deceived me. This man, Jay Pearson, that he bribed, was, it now appears, a curate of some parish. But almost immediately after my marriage, for some gross forgery, I believe, he fled from England ; and John Mason could never trace him.

" Grace Manning never knew I had deceived her. She died in giving birth to a boy ; and, almost immediately after, the Masons left this country for America. The son, George, having committed several crimes, had fled some months before. Some time before John Mason left England, he had increased his family by two sons. After Grace Manning's death I went abroad for twelve months ; began to deeply regret my past life, and returned to England a wiser, and, I thought and hoped, a better man.

" To George Mason my infant son was intrusted, and a sum given him to place him where every care would be taken of him. There is much more to relate, but I can only now say the object of my life will be to discover the truth of this Jay Pearson's confession. By that confession it appears he fled to America, endured great privations and hardships, and when, shaken by mortal disease, he reached Delaware, had an interview with John Mason, who was living in a farm near that place, and then, it appears, he died."

"A ray of hope enters my breast," said Lady Morton, with a sigh. "It is just possible this unworthy man, Jay Pearson, may have been deceived on his death-bed through the cunning of your former bailiff. If Grace Manning was in reality your wife and lived, what possible reason could Mason have in keeping her existence for so many years secret?"

"You see, my dear Anne, this Jay Pearson got out of the way, and carried the certificate of marriage with him, and flying the country, baffled all Mason's search after him, whose own crimes and his son's forced them to leave England also. I now really believe my marriage with Grace Manning to be valid, but I will never believe she lives. Their plot appears to me to be this; knowing my love for you and our children, the Masons conceived that they could extort a large sum of money from me, by giving up the certificate ; and Pearson being dead, my first marriage could thus never be proved, or the rights of our son disturbed."

"Ah !" said Lady Morton fervently, " God forbid that son of mine should ever succeed to an inheritance acquired by crime. No, my beloved, for such you still are, and ever will be, seek the truth of this strange affair, write to your son, and restore him, not only to his rights, but to that love he has been so long deprived of—the love of a fond father."

"I will do so, dear Anne, so help me God ; and as long as I retain your love, and find that you are my lawful wife, and our children legitimate, every wish of my heart will be gratified ; and I trust, when I make atonement for the past, that God will forgive me the errors of my youth."

Lady Morton conversed for some little time longer with the baronet. She read over again the confession of Jay Pearson, and almost became convinced that he was a deceived party also, and that the dead body Sir Richard saw was in reality Grace Manning's, and not Eliza Mason's, as Pearson's narrative would have induced the baronet to believe.

Sir Richard began to take his wife's view of the case ; however, before she left him she calmed and toned down his agitation in a great measure.

"You have raised a gleam of hope in my heart, dear Anne," said Sir Richard, pressing his wife's hand; "I will do anything you wish, act under your guidance, do everything but—live without you."

With a faint smile Lady Morton kissed his cheek, and bade him good night, ringing the bell for his attendant.

"To-morrow," she said, as she left the room, "we shall be able to talk more calmly and dispassionately."

It was then about ten o'clock at night; Lady Morton, full of thought and reflection, and trusting to the mercy of Providence, proceeded to the drawing-room, where she had left her son and daughters.

As she entered, her youngest daughter, Ellen, said,—

"How is papa to-night? he looked so improved this morning, that we were in hopes a day or two more would enable him to join us again."

"He is, thank God!" replied the mother, "improving fast."

Alfred Morton laid down the book he was reading, and looking over at his mother, who was reclining on the sofa, said,—

"Dear mother, you have knocked yourself up completely."

"No, my dear boy. I only feel a little lassitude from the heat of these last few days; but we are advancing into September, and the cool breezes will do more to restore your father than anything else."

Alfred was at this time about nineteen years of age, tall, graceful, and manly, like his father; kind-hearted and generous in disposition—like his mother. His eyes and hair were dark; whilst his sisters, though very beautiful girls, had both blue eyes and light auburn hair. Alfred had distinguished himself at Oxford; he had acquired honours, and had kept himself free from many of the follies and indeed vices that characterized too many of his fellow-students.

The girls were educated at home, under a most accomplished governess, who devoted her whole time and talents to their improvement, having masters to assist her. At the time of the sad affair at Morton Manor, Miss Henderson, the governess, was on a visit in Yorkshire, with her family, and was not at all aware of the frightful event that had so nearly marred the happiness of the family she was so devotedly attached to.

"I think, mamma," observed Celia, the eldest daughter, who was engaged in writing when her mother entered the room, "now that papa is so very much recovered, I may write to Miss Henderson, and let her know the reason you did not wish her to return just yet. Her own father has been very ill, she says in her last letter."

"You may write to her, of course, my love," replied the mother, with a suppressed sigh ; "but still I would rather she did not return yet. Another fortnight will make a great difference."

"Do you know, dear mother," said Alfred Morton, "that I find it exceedingly difficult to answer the questions I am constantly asked respecting the miscreant who stabbed my father? I rode over to Chatsworth this morning, and met Colonel Wilton and his brother, who is a county magistrate. After many inquires about my father, Mr. Wilton said—'Has your father, Mr. Morton, been able to throw any light upon this abominable attempt at assassination? We have not gained the slightest clue that will lead to securing the villain who committed the act. We are waiting till your father's recovery enables him to give us some particulars as to what led to such an attempt. Your father is a very powerful man, and that ruffian Mason or Reynolds is a slight small one ; so, at least, the London detective, Chalders, told me.'

"'Indeed, Mr. Wilton,' I replied, 'we are all in the dark as yet. My father is still weak, and we wait till his recovery is more advanced.' Has my father given you any particulars, mother?"

"It is a very painful subject, Alfred," answered Lady Morton, with a sigh ; "but as far as I know, you shall hear. It appears that this villain Mason is the son of a man who was once your father's steward and bailiff, and in whom he placed great confidence. Many years ago he went and settled somewhere in America. It was not known for some time afterwards that he carried away with him papers most important ; and from time to time it seems he managed to extort certain sums of money from your father, on the plea of restoring the papers, which he never did. The son George had an interview with your father in the library, and your father, finding he was trifling with him, seized him by the collar, and threatened to hand him over to the law for an act he committed some years ago, if he did not give up the papers he stated he had about him. In his rage and disappointment he drew a bowie-knife and stabbed your father. This is the true state of the case, and you may make the same explanation to any inquiry made to you."

I wish to heaven that villain was taken !" cried Alfred Morton ; "and I cannot imagine how two men so remarkable as Mason and his confederate have continued to baffle the detectives."

Some four or five weeks after this conversation, it was announced that the baronet and his family were going abroad for a year or two, for the complete restoration of the former's health. Accordingly, having arranged everything for an absence of some time, the family set out on their journey. On the borders of the Lake of Geneva, Sir Richard rented a beautiful villa residence, and there he left his family, returning, after three months' residence, to England, whence he embarked for New York.

CHAPTER X.

WE left Arthur Bolton upon the solitary deck of the dismasted " Foam," keeping watch, during which myriads of mosquitoes permitted neither rest nor thought till the return of daylight, when a strong wind relieved him from his tormentors. Joe made his appearance on deck, and telling the lad to call him at high water, as the wind blew down the estuary, the brig would doubtlessly drift seaward, and, if so, they had better try and get an anchor overboard. All was quiet, the ladies no doubt fast asleep in the main cabin ; so he turned into his own berth, and was very soon insensible to everything around.

He slept long and well, till the sound of voices awoke him ; when, jumping up, he dressed himself and hastened on deck, where he found the whole party assembled, gazing curiously on the striking scene before them.

He cast one look at the tide, which was running out. The brig had not moved.

Greeting his fair Alice with an affectionate pressure of the hand, he said—

" I have made a rather long sleep of it, Alice ; I told Joe to call me at high water."

" Oh, Arthur, my sister and I were on deck just at high water, and Joe told us the tide did not near rise its height, for the brig would not float by two feet ; and that, therefore, he had better let you have a good sleep. To this we all agreed, so now come to breakfast. But is not this a grand scene, Arthur ? so wild, and yet so beautiful ! "

" It is a truly wild scene, dear Alice ; and yet it is very singular that no signs of canoes or of human beings of any kind are to be seen ; we must have run upon a very deserted part, if this is in reality what is called the Musquito Coast."

" If we have seen no natives," said Miss Marchmont,

" we have seen and felt mosquitoes. There was no possibility of getting rid of them. We must have some kinc
of gauze or muslin across our berths; poor Mary's eyes
were nearly closed by their stings, and Mrs. Mathews
declared she was nearly smothered, trying to save hersel
from being devoured."

" They are frightful pests," said our hero; " but they
are capital companions for keeping a sentinel wide awake
No fear of falling asleep on deck."

" Are those beautiful white birds yonder, in such flocks
the bird called the white Ibis ?" asked Alice—" and who
thousands of ducks ! "

" I should think they were, Alice; if I had a boat,
should try and kill a few for our use, it would be an agreeable change. You are recovering your spirits and colour,'
continued our hero, pressing the little hand he held as they
descended into the cabin.

" Ah, Arthur, to think of the mercy of Providence ii
preserving us, when our situation was so terrible—the
fearful anxiety we suffered those four days would, if they
had continued, have nearly killed us, and the fate o
kind Captain Courtney oppressed us with an unspeakabl
horror."

At breakfast, Mrs. Marchmont, whose spirits had als
greatly revived, had a long conversation with our hero, o1
their future proceedings. Having no boat, they could no
communicate with the shore.

" But surely," said Alice, who was present, " there mus
be natives ; we must soon be seen by some passing canoe o
vessel of some sort. This is a large fine river we are in.

" I agree with you, Alice," answered Arthur, " som
kind of craft must navigate this fine stream. At al
events, the brig will not float till the next spring tides
I could easily swim to land, but, from the appearanc
of the shore on both sides, there is no sign of inhabit
ants ; it all looks as if left to a state of nature fror
time immemorial."

The day passed over without any visible signs c
human beings on shore, and our hero and Joe began t
talk of building some kind of craft with the hatches an
spare spars in the hold. They cleaned and put in goo
order the late captain's double-barrelled fowling-piece
and another excellent gun, and found plenty of powde
and shot. But fresh provisions were becoming neces
sary ; the climate was intensely hot, and the air through
out the day sultry to a degree.

Towards sunset masses of thunder-like clouds rose t

the eastward, which in reality burst upon them in the early morning, with the terrific fury and grandeur peculiar to tropical climates. The thunder crashed over their heads with appalling uproar, and the vivid lightning seemed to play about the deck of the " Foam," and to linger on the anchor, and to seek every nook and cranny of the ship. Then came the roar of the storm-gust dashing the waters of the estuary in wreaths like snow-drifts. Upon the bare hull of the brig it did no mischief, she remained immovable. Before the sun was two hours high the storm had ceased, and a brilliant, dazzling sky, unobscured by a single cloud, was over them.

During the height of the storm, all the ladies had dressed and assembled in the cabin. It was the first time the Miss Marchmonts had heard or witnessed a tropical tempest so terrible in its violence and so short in its duration. A fine refreshing breeze, after it had passed, came in from the westward, and all went on deck to enjoy it, after the overpowering heat of the night.

On gaining the deck, Arthur Bolton exclaimed—" A vessel at last ! " Alice ran to his side, and both gazed down the estuary, and true enough, about five hundred yards from them, lay a small schooner, of about thirty tons. Arthur brought his glass and examined her. Her sails were all down, and furled, but no one appeared on deck.

" She is doubtless a Spanish schooner," he remarked, " and her crew are below, sleeping. She must have run in here just before the storm began. I see no boat in her or towing astern. Joe, bring me the gun, and I will rouse them. That schooner would just do to take you all to Bluefields, and there assistance could be got to save the valuable cargo in this brig."

" But surely, Arthur," said Alice eagerly, " you would come with us, you would not trust us with strangers ? "

" You know, my beloved, you are dearer to me than all the treasures of a dozen ships ! How we shall manage will depend on the character of those in yonder schooner, and the distance we are from Bluefields. All your luggage and valuables, and more than £20,000 in gold, are in this vessel, and to leave it at the mercy of plunderers would be cruel, and indeed dishonourable."

" Then I will tell you what to do—but excuse, dear Arthur, my giving you advice or counsel—we will all stay with you, and you can employ that schooner, or the crew that is in her, to go to Bluefields, or the nearest port to us, and bring back assistance. She could be towed by a steamer into Bluefields, if this is really the Musquito Coast we are upon."

"I will act upon your suggestion, Alice, and at once. I will rouse the crew of the schooner; they evidently do not see us, or the sight of a mastless hull would have attracted them;" and taking the gun, he fired several shots; but not a soul appeared on the deck of the schooner.

Mrs. Marchmont and all the females came up, wondering what the shots were for.

Arthur pointed to the schooner, saying, "I do really think that there is not a soul on board."

"Perhaps the crew have gone ashore in their boat," observed Mrs. Marchmont.

"I will swim with the current to her," observed our hero.

"I will go with you, sir," said Joe, "for if we find her deserted, we can bring her alongside."

"Do not run such a risk, Arthur," pleaded both girls at once, Alice, looking startled, adding, "How can you tell whether there are sharks here or not?"

"Oh, we should have seen them if there had been," returned our hero. "The schooner is scarcely five hundred yards off. I shall certainly swim to her, but Joe can remain."

"No, no," cried Mrs. Marchmont. "Let him go with you at all events, for you will require help if you find the schooner deserted, which would be very strange. Some one, at all events, must have put the anchor out."

"If they are ashore, they will soon be attracted by our getting her under weigh."

Our hero merely took off his jacket and shoes, the light cotton dress he wore would be no incumbrance, and jumping over the side, swam for the schooner, followed by Joe, who got down by a rope.

Alice and the rest of the little party watched their progress with great anxiety; but, with the tide running down to the schooner, it took them but a very short time to reach her. Arthur got on deck, and assisted Joe, who was very nearly carried past by the force of the current. By this time it had become dead calm, and extremely hot, with a strange brilliancy in the sky over the land.

There was not a soul on board, but every evidence of there having been a crew very lately. Seeing no boat along shore, our hero began inspecting the craft, resolved to wait till the turn of the tide should enable them to get her under weigh. She was not more than thirty tons, had hatchways fore and aft, and a forecastle. She smelt strongly of fish, unpleasantly so. She evidently was employed in the turtle fishery, for, lifting one of the hatches, he perceived a heap of shells, and all the requisite materials for fishing and turning turtles.

"I tell you what I think, Joe," remarked our hero, " this little schooner must have drifted up here from some anchorage further down, during the storm of last night. The tide will turn directly: we will drop her up alongside the brig, and anchor her. That will bring her owners after her, and thus we shall know correctly where we are, and, no doubt, get them to go to some port and send us assistance."

When the tide slacked, they proceeded to get the anchor a-peak, and, having done this, Joe went to take a pull at the foresail haulyards, to hoist it, for there was a light air in their favour ; but as our hero came to lift the anchor, he found it so embedded in the mud at the bottom, that their united efforts could not move it.

" There's a hatchet on a bench in the forecastle," said Joe ; " cut it."

" No, that would not be right, there's no other on board ; give me that log of wood, and I'll fasten it to it, and slip the cable, which is a very short one."

All this time they paid no attention to the peculiarity of the clouds hanging over the spot where the brig lay. The sky was of singular brilliancy ; the omen of a tropical hurricane, a storm-gust that so often follows a tempest from one quarter by a violent rush of wind from the opposite. Scarcely had they dropped the cable and set the foresail, when, looking towards the "Foam," our hero, to his amazement, beheld between him and the brig a vast sea-drift, like a snow wreath.

"Lower the foresail, Joe!" he shouted out, "and hold on."

But before the words were spoken, the storm-gust had reached them ; the foresail disappeared in ribbons, and a shower of spray passed over them, blinding them in its fury.

Joe threw himself flat, and our hero catching the tiller, the schooner spun round, and dashed off before the hurricane like a scared sea-bird.

The whole estuary became a sheet of foam ; to have attempted to turn the schooner either to port or starboard would have ensured its destruction. Joe made his way aft.

" Faix, sir," he cried out, " we shall be blown on the rocky islands at the mouth of this river, or out to sea."

" It may not last beyond a few hours," replied our hero, " we can then beat back again. The ladies will be terribly alarmed. Keep a keen look-out, Joe. Lie down for'ad, and sing out if you see rocks ; though, in truth, this blinding spray blocks the view."

Joe went forward, and putting his head over the bow, tried to make out where they were running, with the speed of a racehorse. On drove the little schooner, skimming the curling waves; the sky brilliant and clear to windward, with a thick haze to seaward. In less than three-quarters of an hour they came close up with the islands blocking the mouth of the estuary. Some of the highest they could see, but there were ranges of rock just covered by the water. Our hero anxiously sought for a clear space through them.

"Starboard!" shouted Joe.

"Starboard it is!" and the schooner shot by a huge black rock, covered with spray, and only to be seen when close to it.

"Starboard!" again roared Joe. "Port! hard a-port!" he screamed the next instant.

It was a marvel to see the schooner twisting and driving through the scattered rocks, one moment buried in the spray, the next almost dashed against sharp-pointed rocks. Joe was in a fever and hoarse, whilst on drove the schooner, and destruction threatened on every side.

A vast mass of rock was seen right ahead. Arthur shifted his helm, another mass showed on the port side, there was no help for it; he steered boldly between the two, at the risk of being jammed. It was an anxious moment; with a slight shock, or rather a graze to the rock on the port side, the schooner glided through uninjured, and then the open sea was before them.

Arthur, with a deep-drawn breath of relief, exclaimed—"By Jove! Joe, that was running the gauntlet with a vengeance."

Joe crossed himself, and thanked all the saints in the calendar for their escape.

Still the squall, with unabated violence, drove them out to sea, till, just at sunset, it ceased as suddenly as it had commenced, leaving the sky to windward of a dull crimson.

The schooner, by this time, was fifteen or eighteen miles from the coast, which was not to be seen, for, as the wind ceased, the haze gradually drew off the land and settled on the sea.

After rolling uncomfortably till quite dark, a light westerly breeze came on, and then Arthur and Joe set the fore and aft canvas of the schooner, and made a tack for the land.

Our hero was exceedingly uneasy; he knew how fearful must be the situation of those on board the "Foam;" he knew, even if the breeze, which was not very favourable for making the land, stood steady, they could not expect to get back into the estuary before morning.

"Now, Joe, search the forecastle, and see if you can find any kind of garments, or food. Otherwise we must fast till morning."

"Faix, it was a bad job, sir, that squall didn't come ten minutes sooner; we would not have let go our anchor. Be dad, sir, I'm as hungry as a hawk, and, unless we can eat turtle-shells, I fear there's nothing here."

However, Joe found two or three canvas jackets, a jar of oil, two dried fish, and about two or three dozen bad biscuits.

"Try down under the hatches," said Bolton: "there must be some wine; these craft are never without water and wine."

After ten minutes' search, Joe made his appearance with a large jar of wine, and some salt meat, and said, with a glad smile,—

"There's a small fireplace for'ad, sir, and cooking-pots, and other things, and things like potatoes in the locker. I'll make a fire and cook this meat."

"Just give me a pull at the wine, Joe, first," said Arthur, who was steering. "I am exceedingly thirsty."

Joe brought a mug, and both had a draught of tolerably good wine.

"The schooner works very badly, Joe, without a foresail or jib. Have a second hunt under the hatches, there must be another foresail or a jib or two; there's no keeping her out of the wind."

Joe lighted a candle, and searched the lockers, and, after an active scrutiny, found some spare sails, ropes, blocks, &c.

Having picked out an old foresail, it was set up, and the schooner sailed all the better for it.

Joe having boiled the piece of salt meat, they made their breakfast off it, with some biscuits and a draught of wine, during which a fine fresh side wind carried them on rapidly for the land. Still, though they approached within a few miles of the coast, they could not recognize any opening like the mouth of a large river. The land looked flat, and the shore was bordered with sand-hills, whilst in the distance appeared a range of blue hills. To the south rose a faint vapour, as if from a steamer, and on the horizon, more faintly seen, several vessels.

"I cannot," said our hero uneasily, "perceive either the rocky island or the great gap between the two hills, up which the river, where the brig lies, runs. We have been swept away to the eastward by some strong current."

"Be dad, sir, there's a boat pulling round yonder point, and coming towards us."

"Ha! so there is—haul our fore sheet in, and I'll stand in for the boat; the water, apparently, is quite deep to the shore."

They were soon not more than a mile from the shore, when, hauling the fore sheet to windward, they waited for the boat to run alongside. It carried six men, dressed in red shirts and red caps, no doubt Spaniards or Mexicans, perhaps the owners of the schooner. Arthur, though a tolerable hand at French and Italian, could speak neither Spanish nor Portuguese.

As the boat neared them, he perceived that the men in her were a fierce, savage-looking lot, with long beards and mustachios. They came up to the side with great violence, and jumped on deck, vociferating something in Spanish, and, flourishing their long knives, made a furious attack upon Arthur and Joe.

A struggle ensued, in which Arthur and his companion, having no weapons but two turtle irons, stood at fearful odds against the six Spaniards; but Providence befriended the weak in the contest—Joe was knocked overboard, Arthur striking the nearest of his assailants to the deck with his iron, and following him.

Joe, who was a first-rate swimmer, diving to avoid a blow made at him, struck out for the shore.

Fortunately, during the fray, the schooner went on the other tack, and her boat broke loose, and before the crew could recover the boat and put about, the fugitives struck out vigorously for the shore, and shortly afterwards reached the sands.

"Well, Joe," said our hero, giving himself a shake, "we have had a providential escape from those rascally Spaniards or Mexicans. You are not much hurt, I hope?"

"Faix, sir, it was nearly up with us. I got a few blows, nothing to speak of; but what will we do without clothing?"

Our hero, washing the blood from a deep cut from a knife he had received, replied, "We must do as the natives do till we get back to the brig."

"What did they want to kill us for, sir? May be they thought we stole their craft."

"That's quite possible, Joe; yet it did not look as if we intended keeping her, as we waited for them. However, we had better seek shelter; this scorching sun on our bare backs and heads is trying."

The men who boarded the schooner had torn the red shirts from their backs, leaving them only their light cotton trowsers for clothing. Having traversed the sands and passed over a sand-hill, they obtained a view of a rather singular and striking extent of country; and behind they beheld the schooner making its way to the westward.

CHAPTER XI.

THE progress of Arthur and Joe, as they swam towards the schooner, was watched with anxiety by the party left in the vessel—an anxiety greatly relieved when they saw them climb on to the deck of the schooner without accident; or, as Alice feared, any pursuit by sharks. They watched them haul up the anchor and make all their preparations, and, thus engaged, saw nothing of the coming storm till it burst upon them in all its fury. It was quite a marvel, as it swept over the dismantled brig, that it did not hurl those anxious gazers into the foaming waters. With difficulty they all gained the cabin, and then Alice rushed to the cabin windows to look for the schooner, but the space between the two vessels was a sheet of foam and spray.

The remainder of the day was passed in restless anxiety; and when night came on, and neither Arthur nor Joe appeared, not one of those four lonely females closed their eyes in sleep. Several times Mary, at her young mistress's earnest request, stole up upon deck to see if she could discover the schooner; but the little vessel continued invisible.

At daybreak, the storm having ceased, Alice and Mary again went on deck. There was scarcely a ripple on the broad surface of the estuary; the wind had changed, and a light breeze blew in from the sea.

"Good gracious! Mary, where can Arthur have been blown to?" cried Alice, greatly agitated.

"The Lord save us!" suddenly exclaimed Mary, after gazing around. "Here are two canoes coming down the river—filled with Indians, I think."

Alice trembled as she turned to gaze at two large canoes paddling towards them. The alarm spread, and soon all the terrified females were on deck.

Miss Marchmont brought the telescope, and fixing it upon the canoes, cried out in an alarmed voice,—

"Oh, God help us! One of the canoes is full of Indians, the other of Europeans.

"Oh, mother!" exclaimed Alice; "if that wretch, Saunders, is amongst them, we are lost."

" I will kill the villain if he is," said Mary Pearson, her cheeks flushing, and, rushing down the cabin stairs, she went into Arthur Bolton's cabin, and secured a pistol which she knew was loaded.

" That villain, Saunders, is bringing those Indians to plunder the brig," said Miss Marchmont, greatly agitated.

Tears of apprehension, almost of despair, were in Mrs. Marchmont's eyes, as she looked at her daughters. Alice ran to the windows, and gazed eagerly down the stream, but no sign of the presence of the schooner could be discerned.

" It is no use," said Mrs. Marchmont to her attendants, "to barricade the doors ; they can force any defence we could make, and it would only irritate an enemy, and rouse their passions ; besides, the cabin can always be entered through the skylight."

The approach of the canoes was watched with feelings of alarm and dread. As Miss Marchmont had said, the men in the first canoe were all Indians ; the second contained four Indians paddling, and five Europeans, one of whom was Bill Saunders. As they neared the brig, the canoes separated, and prepared to advance nearer, with some degree of hesitation.

" Ah !" said Alice, with a flush in her cheek, " they think Arthur is here, and they know how brave and powerful he is, and that there are fire-arms in the ship. Oh! if he were, we might resist them, and put them to flight."

" If I could shoot that Saunders," observed Mary, " the rest might be content with plunder. But what vile-looking men those are in the boat with Saunders !"

After a short consultation, the two canoes made a sudden dash at the brig, with a shout of exultation ran alongside, and with a fiendish yell from the Indians scrambled up upon deck.

To describe the feelings of those in the cabin of the " Foam" would be scarcely possible. Only to think of their probable treatment from such a wretch as Saunders was horrible. There appeared no earthly chance of succour.

Still Mrs. Marchmont and her daughters summoned up all their energies, and, with a silent prayer to Heaven, awaited the result. Mary placed herself near her young mistress, with a revolver concealed under a mantle thrown over her shoulders.

Presently several heavy feet were heard descending the cabin stairs, and, pushing open the door, Bill Saunders, attended by two ruffians, entered the cabin.

Saunders held a cocked pistol in one hand, and a drawn

cutlass in the other, looking even more ferocious and horrible than usual. Glaring round the cabin with his one bloodshot eye, he seemed to seek some object upon which to wreak his vengeance.

" Come," he exclaimed, " you all look mighty pleased to see me ; I told you I should come back, and here I am. But, curse it, where is my enemy, Bolton ? If you don't say where he is hiding, then —— me if I don't cut all your throats. I must have his blood ; " and he stepped towards the table, and laid his hand upon it, whilst the Mexicans and blacks stood eyeing the females with savage ferocity, each, as it were, selecting a victim.

Mary's hand grasped the pistol convulsively ; the length of the table only was between her and their enemy, and she longed to rid the world of such a monster. Still a look at the fierce faces above paralyzed her arm ; for if she killed Saunders, those men would avenge his death.

Mrs. Marchmont, although almost overpowered by terror, said, in a firm voice,—

" Mr. Bolton is not on board this brig ; he swam to a schooner that was anchored below us, yesterday."

Saunders started, struck the table with a frightful oath, and, turning, to his comrades, by signs and bad Spanish told them what Mrs. Marchmont said.

" Caramba ! " exclaimed the men, " why lose time ? Make the women come on deck : the sooner we get at the gold the better ; the schooner was a guarda-costa probably, only driven out by the gale."

Mrs. Marchmont understood what the men said, and hope revived in her breast. The guarda-costa would surely return if Arthur Bolton was on board.

" Curse him ! " cried Saunders, " is it possible that he has escaped me ? But I know where the wind lies. I'll have a terrible revenge. Now go on deck," he said savagely, turning to the females, " if you don't want me to call the sailors to pull you up."

Mary whispered in Alice's ear—" Oh, miss, shall I shoot that wretch ? "

" No, no, the others would in their savage fury murder us all ; wait, I have a ray of hope stealing over me."

As the females were hurrying up the cabin stairs, the loud boom of a heavy gun struck their ears. The sailors on deck uttered a shout and a yell of rage, and Saunders rushed past the females with a terrible blasphemy on his lips. The whole party hurried on deck.

Eagerly Alice and the rest gazed down the river, and beheld a rakish-looking schooner coming under full sail

towards them, and not a mile off. A prayer of thanksgiving mingled with the furious curses of Saunders and
the Spaniards, as their eyes rested on the schooner.

" The guarda-costa !" they all exclaimed. " To the
boats ! or we're caught !"

The baffled Saunders stamped with rage. One moment
he hesitated as the rest rushed to the boats, and then, with
an oath, he exclaimed—" Now for my revenge !" and
with a bound he seized Alice Marchmont round the waist,
and bore her shrieking over the side. Mary frantically
followed ; the mother and sister strove to grasp Alice's
garments, but the wretch who held her sprang into the
large canoe, and Mary Pearson, seeing she could not
save her mistress, flung herself after her into the canoe.

" Curse the girl ! " said one of the Spaniards, " pitch
her overboard." But Alice tore herself from Saunders's
grasp, and held Mary, who in desperation drew the pistol
and fired in Saunders's face, dashing him back in the
canoe, blackened and scorched by the powder, but untouched by the ball, which passed within a hair's breadth
of his temple.

One of the men lifted his cutlass to strike the brave
girl, as the Indians paddled off into the deep water. But
Saunders shouted out :

"Let her be—curse her!—she nearly took my other eye
out; but I like her—she shall be my second wife,"—and the
wretch stooped and bathed his scorched face in the river.

" Caramba, the schooner's aground !" exclaimed the
Spaniard. " There goes a shot."

The ball from the gun struck the water close by the
leading canoe, which, with its companion, paddled in
shore, keeping the hull of the brig between them and the
enemy, and then continued their course up the river as
rapidly as possible.

Mrs. Marchmont—distracted, horrified, at the abduction of her daughter—went from one fainting fit to
another. Her daughter and her attendant carried her into
the cabin, and laid her on her couch, using every means
in their power to restore her.

As soon as she revived, she exclaimed :

" Oh, my God ! my child ! Oh, go see if they are out
of sight, and if the schooner is pursuing them."

Leaving her mother to the care of Mrs. Mathews, Miss
Marchmont, trembling in every limb, ran on deck. The
canoes had turned an abrupt point, and were out of
sight. The schooner was aground on the bar, and her
crew were clewing up her sails and launching a boat.

" Oh, Heavens! if they only made haste, Alice might be saved," cried Mrs. Marchmont. " Ah ! how little Arthur knows what misery is in store for him."

The Mexican schooner that had so unfortunately taken the ground on the bar was the " Maria Gloriosa," a guarda-costa, commanded by Capt. Juan Castinos Valagos, and had come from Nicaragua on a cruise to Cape Gracias.

On the day that Arthur Bolton and Joe were driven out to sea by the hurricane, the Maria Gloriosa was anchored in a deep bay, some miles to the westward of the river where the "Foam" lay. Just as the guarda-costa was getting under weigh, after the squall had blown itself out, a canoe with a single Indian in it paddled out to the schooner. The Indian did not understand Spanish, neither did Capt. Valagos understand the Indian.

" Send the black cook here," cried the captain, " till I know what this fellow wants."

The cook, a powerful negro, soon made his appearance.

" Ask that rascal what he's gabbling about, Cato."

The cook did as he was ordered.

" He says, sar," observed the negro, " that there is the hull of a large vessel, reported to be laden with valuable goods and a lot of gold, lying aground in the Punza Pulka river, and that a party of Sambos, with a half-dozen Mexican deserters, are gone down the river to plunder her."

" How does the Indian know of this vessel ? "

Cato questioned him.

" He says, sar, that he is from Quamwatta, and that he saw and heard the men speak of going to plunder the ship."

" Take the fellow aboard," said the captain to his solitary officer, a young lieutenant, " and hoist his canoe in. If the rascal is telling a lie, I'll strip his red hide off his back."

Whether the Indian understood the captain or not, we cannot say ; but, instead of letting himself and canoe be hoisted on board, he took his paddle and made for the shore.

" Caramba ! " exclaimed the captain, " the rascal is lying. Fire a shot after him."

A man with a musket let fly at the retreating Indian, but missed him.

" I should think," observed the first mate, " that there was some truth in that Indian's story. I cannot see any motive for a falsehood."

" Well, then, up anchor and let us go and see," said the captain.

And accordingly the Maria Gloriosa got under weigh, with a land breeze, which, however, changed to a sea breeze as they reached the islands. Running between two principal ones, they very shortly after sighted the hull of the "Foam," and again in a few minutes beheld the canoes pulling ahead.

"Ah!" exclaimed the captain, "there was some truth in the Indian's account. Fire one of our eight-pounders; it will frighten those rascals, who are going, no doubt, to plunder the wreck."

As he spoke, the schooner took the ground.

The water was smooth, and just the last run of the ebb; so, hauling down and furling their canvas, they put out their boat, having fired a shot at the retreating canoes.

As the tide made, they dropped up, and then let go their anchor close to the "Foam."

Captain Valagos then got into his boat, with Cato, who spoke English, as interpreter. He expected to find those on board were English, for, with his glass, he had seen the ladies on deck, as they stood watching his movements with painful curiosity. As the boat came up alongside, Mrs. Marchmont said—

"Now we shall have that villain pursued."

When Captain Valagos, therefore, entered the cabin, both mother and daughter were prepared to receive him.

The Spaniard paused, looking surprised. The cabin, with its elegancies and decorations, also attracted his attention. He saluted the ladies in his rough manner, and said something in Spanish. Mrs. Marchmont understood a little Spanish, but could not speak it to be understood, therefore she replied in French. Valagos shook his head and called out for Cato.

"Ask those ladies," said the captain, "what's the name of this vessel, where she comes from, and where bound to, and what's her cargo."

"Golly!" observed the negro, rubbing his huge head. "'Ere four questions all de same time."

"Do you speak English?" asked Mrs. Marchmont, addressing the black.

"I does, marm, speak de English; I once cook aboard man-of-war, English. I lub de English."

"Ah!" cried Mrs. Marchmont, "then tell your captain that some Spanish deserters and Sambos, and a sailor belonging to this vessel, have carried off my daughter and her maid in their canoes; but if he pursues them at once, they may, with God's mercy, be rescued."

Cato rubbed his woolly head, thought the speech a very

long one, but told the captain as much of it as he could get into his head.

"Tell the lady," returned the captain impatiently, "that I cannot pursue them up the river; there's no water for the schooner, and my boat could never catch Indians in their canoes. Ask her again the name of this vessel and where bound to."

Mrs. Marchmont shed tears of vexation as she comprehended what the Spaniard said, and saw that, as far as the recovery of her daughter depended on his exertion, she had little to hope. She perceived also that the Maria Gloriosa was not the schooner Arthur Bolton had swum to. She therefore, after much delay, made Valagos acquainted with their mishap, and requested to know if he would carry them to Bluefields, where she was sure to procure help.

When Castinos Valagos learned that the ship was so valuable, he became deeply interested.

"I will leave six of my men in this vessel," he said, "well armed, and will take you to Bluefields, which is only a few hours' sail from this river."

"But, good God!" exclaimed the lady, "what will become of my unfortunate child?"

Cato again rubbed his woolly head, and seemed to feel sorry for Mrs. Marchmont; and whilst the captain proceeded to give orders to warp the schooner alongside, he told Mrs. Marchmont that he knew the Sambo Indians well, had been amongst them, and knew their haunts. If she could prevail on the captain to let him go ashore, he would track them and the Mexican deserters to their haunts, pretend he had run away from the guarda-costa, get protection, and perhaps be able to send a friendly Indian to Bluefields.

Mrs. Marchmont eagerly grasped at this proposal. She knew, once at Bluefields, she could send word to her husband in Jamaica and also employ people to follow in the track the negro Cato would point out.

Captain Castinos was at first sulky, and unwilling to comply with her request; he swore the negro wanted to run away; but when Mrs. Marchmont bound herself to pay eight hundred dollars if the black did not return in a reasonable time, he consented, and Cato was equipped for his intended expedition—having a small amount of dollars and gold concealed about his person, so that, if necessary, he might bribe a friendly tribe of Indians to assist him. He was landed in the point round which the canoes had disappeared.

The unhappy Mrs. Marchmont and her sorrowing

daughter embarked on board the guarda-costa, which, before sunset, had passed the islands, and was standing along the shore for Bluefields.

CHAPTER XII.

FEW are the attractions found on the Musquito Coast, where our hero and his humble companion sought shelter from the violence of the Mexican desperadoes. No traveller in search of the picturesque would wish to linger in its precincts—whilst sailors ever shun its shores. The negro race inhabiting this narrow slip of land are a brutal, licentious race, always at variance with the Indian tribes dwelling farther inland, who are their superiors in every respect, and who show a never-ending hatred to the Sambos and the Mexican deserters who there find a home, and who, restrained by no law, indulge in every description of profligacy, commit the most horrible crimes without fear of punishment, and are a terror to the few vessels which chance or storms may send to the coast.

The only station along the shore that could boast of an English resident was Bluefields, and at this place resided that mockery of royalty, the Musquito King.

Our hero and Joe, who possessed, notwithstanding their misfortunes, excellent appetites, commenced searching for turtles' eggs. Having collected a considerable number, they again descended the bank, and looked down at the scene before them. Joe, who was an adept at mat-making, in which most sailors excel, whilst his master was regarding the country lying east and west of them, gathered a quantity of long grass, dried up by the scorching sun, and commenced platting it into a kind of covering for their backs and chests; it was a primitive manufacture, but our first parents commenced with less.

Looking from the height on which they stood, Arthur gazed down upon a noble sheet of water—one of the great lagoons that stretch along that coast communicating by numerous creek channels with the river. This lake extended two miles, and the shores on both sides were thickly wooded.

"There's a thin stream of smoke coming out from that tuft of trees close to that fine lake, Joe," said Arthur; "let us go towards it. I am most anxious to get information how to reach the river where we left the brig. Imagine the distress of Mrs. Marchmont and her daughters at our absence."

"Just put these two pieces of mat over your back and

chest, sir," returned Joe, presenting two square pieces neatly plaited ; "they will save you from being scorched, anyhow."

"Not bad, Joe," observed Arthur, tying the mats on with plaited bands. "Something of the same kind for a hat will do famously, for I confess the sun is hot."

They then proceeded towards the smoke, Joe carrying the turtle-eggs.

With a certain amount of pain, being without either shoes or stockings, our two castaways proceeded towards the thick tuft of brushwood and trees from whence issued the smoke.

Pushing their way through a mass of vegetable and long grass, they soon perceived an Indian hut, which had, apparently, been hastily constructed, and near to which was a small frail canoe, covered partly with huge leaves of plants, to protect it from the rays of the sun.

Our hero was not at all afraid of the Indian tribes being hostile ; he, therefore, advanced towards the entrance. As he did so—making some noise by breaking the dry branches they trod on—a young Indian girl, with a spear in her hand, rushed out; but after casting a glance at them, she seemed to recover from her alarm—for she paused and looked at them, without fear. Arthur also gazed at this first specimen of the Indian race he had yet beheld, and was astonished. She was young, not more than seventeen, tall, and well formed ; the only article of dress she wore was an exceedingly short skirt, like a Highlander's kilt, of red and white striped cotton, confined round the hips by a very ornamental belt. She had, however, mocassins on her feet, lacing up to the calf of the leg. She was not darker than a Creole, whilst her features were positively beautiful, with hair dark as the raven's wing, and confined by a narrow strip of hide, ornamented with gold beads. After looking at each other for a moment, the young girl came close to our hero, and said :—

"White man—Englis ? "

"Yes," returned Arthur, surprised at the young Indian uttering even these words, "we are English ;" and approaching close to the girl, who showed no fear, he continued : "Do you speak our language ?"

But she only shook her head.

"Now, this is very embarrassing," he observed to Joe, who stood gazing at the Indian with great curiosity.

The girl perceived that Joe carried some turtles' eggs, and she made signs with her hands and smiled, showing a row of teeth like ivory. Arthur Bolton determined to try what he could do by signs, and intimated that he was remarkably hungry and wanted to cook the eggs.

The maiden at once understood him, and with a light laugh she signalled them to follow her into the hut, Bolton wondering very much how she came to be alone. There was a wood fire smouldering on the ground ; the girl took a stick, raked the ashes together, and blew up a good fire.

"By the powers, sir! she's a tidy girl, and has as nice a foot and leg as you would wish to see on a fair day."

And Joe knelt down, saying, "Here are the eggs, my little beauty. I've eat eggs before now cooked in ashes ; but, faix, we don't grow turtles in ould Ireland."

The girl laughed at Joe, took the eggs and covered them up in the ashes, Arthur thanking her with his eyes. She smiled, and looked pleased as she took from a peg some pieces of meat that looked like dried beef. With her knife she cut it into strips, and broiled them over some sticks. Arthur sat down ; he was unmistakeably hungry, so he helped to turn the meat and take out the eggs, and roast some plantains, which the girl took from a heap in a corner of the hut.

When all was ready, she nodded her head ; and when the meal was finished, seeing that her guests were satisfied, made signs that she was going away, and got up. They followed her out of the hut to the spot where lay the small canoe, covered with leaves and branches. By signs she made her companions understand she would come back, and then they carried the canoe and placed it in the water. The girl sprang in, smiled, waved her hand, and seizing her paddle glided rapidly from the shore towards the opposite coast of the lagoon.

"That light bark," said our hero to Joseph, "would scarcely hold three, at least not safely, to cross the lake, or I should very much like to have gone with that young and interesting Indian girl. I wonder if all her tribe are as comely?"

"We had better stay here for the night at all events, sir," replied Joe ; "we can't travel without shoes. If I had only a knife, I would make a kind of a shoe out of the hide hanging up in the hut; we could keep them on with thongs."

"Not a bad idea, Joe," returned Arthur, who kept watching the canoe with its graceful occupant till it disappeared round some bluff on the opposite shore.

Our two solitary castaways then returned to the hut, and feeling exceedingly tired and heavy after all they had gone through since leaving the brig, they stretched themselves on the heap of dried leaves in a corner of the hut, and in a moment were buried in a most profound sleep.

CHAPTER XIII.

A LONG tropical day was drawing to its close, the sun was approaching its setting. In a few minutes it would be lost to sight in the bright glistening waters. The stillness of the lagoon and its placid surface became gently rippled by the evening breeze then rustling before the still leaves of the forest, and various sounds were heard amid its dark recesses, betokening the awakening to life of the various denizens, who, during the day, rarely move.

It was sunset, and Arthur Bolton and his young companion were still buried in a deep sleep. Just at this period three canoes came paddling up to the lagoon from the westward. Now this sheet of water had a direct communication with the broad stream of the Punza Pulka river, where the unfortunate brig, the "Foam," lay a-ground, by a narrow and in parts by a very rapid stream. In the leading canoe were six Sambo Indians; in the other Bill Saunders and the Mexican desperadoes. Driven from plundering the "Foam" by the unexpected appearance of the Maria Gloriosa, they had pulled up the river into the creek, and then made their way to the Sambo village of Quamwatta, the inhabitants of which were the most ferocious and brutal of the race.

The canoe containing our unfortunate heroine and her devoted attendant had been urged up another creek, which would take them direct to Quamwatta, where they were consigned by Saunders to the care of a party of Sambos, whilst he and his desperate associates towed their canoes through the creek into the inner lagoon, their purpose being to seek for the very men and the vessel from which our hero and Joe had so narrowly escaped with their lives.

As the canoes approached the shore, one of the Mexicans said to Will Saunders, " There's the hut," pointing to the one in which our hero slept, quite unconscious of the near approach of his most deadly enemy.

" Come, then," returned Saunders, " we will go in and wait till your comrades land from the schooner ; with their help we will manage yet to have the gold out of the brig ; we'll scuttle her by means of Jose, the diver, sooner than let the guarda-costa carry her off as a prize."

Here the Sambos in the first canoe, after a few words

with the Mexicans, pulled across to the opposite side of the lagoon, whilst Saunders and his four associates grounded their canoes just upon the spot where the Indian girl had started from some hours before, and where, notwithstanding the sounds of the men's voices, our hero and Joe slept.

Stepping out of the canoe, they pulled her up, took out a large kind of mat-basket, full of provisions, and then they all walked up to the hut, against which were piled large heaps of dried wood. Two of the Mexicans spoke broken English, and Saunders, who had been an adventurer on that coast before, could speak a little Spanish.

"Why, here's a goodly collection of firewood," said Saunders; "who's been here?"

"Some of the cursed Woolwa Indians," returned one of the Mexicans; "they often come to this part of the coast for turtle."

By this time the sun had set, and twilight there is none; therefore, when Saunders advanced, before striking a light, to examine the hut, it was quite dark.

So singularly sound did Arthur and Joe sleep, that not till Saunders gave a shout of exultation, when the light from the dry piece of wood he held flashed on their up-turned faces, did they awake.

The villain had recognized them at once. Starting up at the sound of his voice, Arthur at once saw his foe, whilst Joe lay shaking with terror, thinking it must be some frightful dream.

"So here you are!" exclaimed Saunders.

Arthur stood ready prepared for a deadly struggle, Saunders having drawn his long Mexican knife.

"Come out, Saunders, quick, quick!" exclaimed the Mexicans outside the hut. "Here's three canoes full of Woolwa Indians; our deadly enemies."

"Not," returned Saunders, with a frightful imprecation, "till I have dug this beggar's eye out—an eye for an eye!" —and dropping the torch, he sprang at our hero; but Arthur warded off the blow, getting only a deep gash on the left arm, and caught his antagonist by the throat, and, after a frightful struggle, both rolled over on the floor. Joe threw himself on Saunders's arm, grasping the hand that held the knife, and at that instant the hut became enveloped in flame.

Blinded and half suffocated by the smoke, the two powerful men relaxed their hold of each other, and rising together with Joe, staggered out of the blazing hut in time to see the Mexicans, aided by the light of the flames which showed all round them, and shone on the bosom of the lagoon, hastening towards the canoes.

The Indians in the canoes approaching the shore were shouting furiously, and paddling with might and main to reach the spot, and stay their flight.

Half blinded, burnt and furious, Saunders saw that both he and his associates were lost if they hesitated; with a fearful malediction, he shook his clenched hand at Arthur, who, scorched and choking, could not prevent his departure, joined the men, who seized their canoe, carried it over the sand-hill, and launching it in the sea beyond, instantly paddled along the coast out of reach of their enraged enemies, the Woolwas, who did not attempt to follow them.

Arthur and Joe, scorched as they were, and a little bewildered by the nearly fatal contest they had been engaged in, breathed freely when they beheld the flight of Saunders and his comrades, and saw the patpans of the Woolwas paddling swiftly ashore with comparative indifference.

Our hero knew that the Woolwas were the furious enemies of the Mexicans, and their loud shouts, and war-cries, and desperate gestures, he thought, might be directed against himself and Joe, as well as against the fugitives.

" Be gor! let us fly into the woods, sir," said Joe, gazing at the Indians in the canoes just touching the shore ; " faix, they'll murder us."

" We should make a bad race of it, Joe, against Indians," replied our hero.

The Indians, as soon as their canoes reached the shore, leaped out ; several, with spears in their hands, rushed over the sand-hills after Saunders and his comrades. To the fugitives' surprise, amongst some women who came ashore was the girl they had met in the hut. The women, and the young Indian girl, with three men, came towards Arthur Bolton ; the girl, by signs and smiles, giving him to understand that they were friends, and all exclaimed, " Englis, Englis!" as if pleased; but no other mode of communication existed. Joined by the other men, who soon returned from their fruitless pursuit after Saunders, all surrounded our hero, and examined him and Joe with great surprise. One old Indian, seeing they were scorched and burnt, went down to the canoes, and returned with a calabash, which he gave to the women.

Without any ceremony they insisted on pulling off their scorched clothes, and then anointed them all over with the contents of the calabash. This gave them immense relief;

but our hero, though he could not help a smile, felt exceedingly uncomfortable with the remarkably scanty clothing left him. The hut had been totally consumed; but the Indians drew up their canoes, and collecting branches and stakes, soon constructed two small huts, to hold their weapons, tools, &c., and to serve as shelter for their wives. The party had come to spend a few days, according to custom, turtle-hunting. Fire was kindled out of the *débris* of the hut, and preparations made for cooking supper.

These Indians, our hero thought, were a very fine comely race, and the women exceedingly good-looking. "I will remain with the party till to-morrow," he said to himself, " and then get one of them to guide me to the river where the brig is stranded."

The Indian girl, whose name he discovered was Achupa, informed him, by signs, that the men were going to hunt turtles on some small islands called Cays, three miles from the shore, and that they would not return to their village for eight days ; holding up her fingers, she touched them one by one.

Arthur Bolton so improved on making signs, that he made Achupa understand that he wanted a little more clothing.

The girl laughed merrily, and going to her mother, a very fine-looking woman, she spoke to her. The females all laughed ; but Achupa's mother went to one of the canoes and took out of a plantain basket a long roll of red and blue striped cotton, and made signs to him to dress as they did ; but our hero wonderfully objected to so primi- tive a costume, as it would expose him to the unmitigated attacks of the mosquitoes. He preferred the remnants of his cotton trowsers, but necessity is ingenious ; and, with the assistance of Achupa, he manufactured what he consi- dered a most excellent covering for his own and Joe's back and chest; with this addition to his attire, they felt consi- derably better.

Their supper consisted of maize, plantains, papayas, and stripes of manitas, broiled, and some fish caught in the lagoon.

The males of the party seemed very taciturn, spoke little, and looked serious. The women were quite the contrary.

All this time our hero felt intense uneasiness ; he could not banish from his mind the idea that Saunders would lead his desperate associates to plunder the brig. The situa- tion of the females, therefore, in their unprotected situation was too horrible to think of.

Knowing how uncomfortable a journey would be without shoes, Bolton determined to adopt the Indian moccassins; and again his good genius, Achupa, provided them with a pair each. Joe passed part of the night in manufacturing two hats out of the broad-leaved flaggers, and they answered the purpose admirably. With energy and perseverance man can accomplish much, and with very inadequate means.

When everything was cleared away, the women retired to their huts ; some of the men to the canoes ; two kept watch, whilst our hero and Joe passed the remainder of the night under two poles stretched across the canoes, with their light mat sails spread over them. Arthur did not expect or care to sleep, for he had much to occupy his thoughts. The oil applied to his burns had wonderfully relieved the pain ; in fact, he scarcely experienced any annoyance. Joe, having nothing particular to think of, and being free from pain, soon fell asleep. Towards morning our hero enjoyed two or three hours' repose, and only awoke hearing the voices of the women when they came to take some things out of the canoe.

CHAPTER XIV

The party of Woolwa Indians that arrived so opportunely to the assistance of Arthur Bolton and Joe, belonged to a tribe residing some distance from the seashore, and were now on their annual visit to the lagoons.

The Woolwas were particularly friendly with the settlers at Bluefields, and traded with the English residents there.

They knew the difference between the English and Spaniards and Mexicans ; they esteemed the first, but the latter they detested.

When our hero awoke in the morning, he found that all the men and women, excepting Achupa and her mother, had carried their canoes across the sands, and were gone turtle-hunting ; they had removed their canoes without waking them, by putting props under the poles.

Achupa's small canoe was the only one left. After making a hearty breakfast, prepared by the young Indian girl and her mother, Arthur, whose mind was bent upon reaching the Punzi Pulka river, which he now felt satisfied communicated by some creek or stream with the Tonza lagoon, commenced a conversation by signs with Achupa.

After a considerable amount of signs and drawing

figures on the sand of lagoons and rivers, he got the young girl to understand that he wanted to go to the Punza Pulka river.

When she thoroughly understood him, she pointed to her canoe, and then to the west, and with a stick very clearly showed him on the sand, that he must cross the lagoon and keep along shore to the setting sun; he would then see a broad creek running out of the lagoon into the Punza Pulka river, but it was in places a rapid dangerous stream, for it appeared that the lagoon partly emptied itself into the river where the "Foam" lay.

The next thing was to get Achupa to lend him the canoe. She understood him at length, and that there were English in a ship in the Punza Pulka. She spoke a long time with her mother, and then they both made signs to him to take the canoe; the young girl, with a serious face, taking his hand, and by various most significant signs making him promise to come back before eight days went by. This he sincerely promised to do, if alive.

Mother and daughter then put some provisions into a basket, together with a calabash of water, and assisted to carry the canoe to the water, where our hero and Joe joyfully embarked, after the most friendly leave-taking from mother and daughter ; indeed, Achupa felt inclined to accompany them, and looked quite sorrowful when our hero waved his hand in adieu.

"Faix, sir," said Joe, flourishing one of the paddles in a very doubtful manner, and thereby nearly upsetting the light bark they were in ; "faix, sir, it is dangerous to sneeze in this here craft; she's as ticklish as my father's ould mare, be gorra ; many's the toss the jade gave me, as I took the fruit to market."

"Then you were a bogtrotter, Joe, before you became a sailor," returned our hero, plying his paddle cautiously.

"Be dad, you're right, sir ; my father's cabin was in the middle of the great Bog of Allen, and many's the trot I and the ould mare have had over the soft turf."

"Do not put your paddle so far out, or so deep, Joe : with a little practice we shall get on ; we were nearly becoming Indians, as far as attire went, and if we have much to do in such crafts as these, we shall be able to join a tribe with some degree of credit, if left in this country."

"Be gor, sir, it's not a bad country at all, barring the mosquitoes ; the girls are very comely, only their skin is a bit too red and brown."

Just then Joe missed his stroke with the paddle, and

fell against our hero, nearly upsetting the canoe in the middle of the lake.

" Hallo, Joe ! you must leave the red and brown girls alone ; we should have a long swim, if our craft went over here."

" Faix, sir, I'm not thinking of the beauties at all ; I hopes to get back to ould Ireland some of these days, and I should not like to take my ould father a red wife."

In a short time they came up with the opposite shore, on which grew some noble trees, forming a dense forest to the eastward as far as the eye could trace ; they could by this time impel the canoe along with considerable swift-ness and steadiness, keeping near shore, and continuing west and north, where they at length caught sight of a tolerable wide creek running to the north.

Into this creek they urged the canoe, and discovered as it grew narrower that there was a considerable current ; after a short space the channel narrowed to twenty yards, and the stream increased in swiftness, running nearly six miles an hour, but so smooth and deep that their velocity was scarcely perceptible, except when regarding the shore on each side.

As our hero proceeded, his anxiety to reach the brig increased to a painful degree ; a thousand distracting thoughts flitted through his brain ; paramount amongst which was his anxiety whether Saunders had yet visited the brig, or whether he was projecting to do so.

As the canoe floated past the shores on each side of the inlet, the Englishmen were surprised at the wildness of the scenery ; apparently no human foot had traversed the land, and yet the scenery was magnificent ; the grass was of great height, great clumps of gum arabic bushes, knots of huge pine-trees, with here and there a magnificent palm-tree, grew luxuriantly. Beyond a great mango swamp, innumerable parrots chattered in the trees, screaming as they shot by them ; whilst the cotton-trees swarmed with them. Presently a sound like a fall of water fell upon their ears, and the canoe, only steered by a paddle, pro-ceeded with great swiftness.

" It will be hard work, Joe, to return by this stream ; but hark ! we are approaching a fall or a rapid ; sit steady, leave me to guide the craft."

The next instant the canoe shot down a rapid of con-siderable length, studded with huge rocks. Joe held his breath, and grasped both sides, for the rapid was an ex-ceedingly dangerous one ; but Arthur Bolton was cool and collected, and watching the rocks, he steered quite clear of

the dangers and even escaped the whirlpool at the bottom
by a few strokes of the paddle, and they were in still
water, with scarcely a perceptible run ; but a moment's
examination showed our hero that the tide reached to the
foot of the fall, and that along the shore on the eastern
side there was a kind of towing-path leading along the fall.

" Faix, I thought it was all over with us, sir," said
Joe, regaining his breath. " We can never ascend that
rapid."

" No," replied Arthur Bolton. " I see now that the
Indians carry their canoes past the fall. Yonder is a kind
of path trampled through the thickets. I am satisfied we
are all right ; the tide proves we shall run shortly into the
Punza Pulka."

After two hours' paddling they emerged from the creek
into the great stream of the Punza Pulka, the creek having
a great mango swamp on each side.

Arthur Bolton gazed anxiously down the stream, but a
projecting and thickly-wooded point from the opposite
shore shut out the broad estuary where the " Foam " lay
stranded.

Paddling across, they had just reached the point, when
they were hailed by a voice from the shore. Ceasing
paddling, our voyagers turned their attention to where the
sound came from, and beheld a negro pushing through the
bushes, and getting out on a projecting rock, hailed again.

" That's a black man," said Arthur Bolton, " in European clothing ; let us go to him."

Urging the canoe close into the rock, they looked at the
black particularly before they let the canoe touch the
rock. We need not describe him, for it was Cato, the
black cook of the Maria Gloriosa.

The black stared at them with much greater surprise.

" Holly, golly ! What ! you be no Indians ?"

" No," said Arthur Bolton, " we are English. Where
do you come from ?"

" Me cook to the guarda-costa, massa ; me come from
de brig. Pray, where you come from ? "

Arthur started, and pushing to the rock, he exclaimed,

" You come from the brig ? Are all the females well
aboard ? "

" Golly, massa ! they be gone to Bluefields, but the
young missy de dam Sambos and de Mexican thiefs 'ab
carried away."

A terrible feeling came over Arthur ; terror took possession of his mind and paralyzed him. The black looked
at him ; he saw the start and the change of countenance,

and though puzzled, he said, " Me now go look for missy ; but me can no cross the ribcr. You take me in canoe. Me sure find missy."

In a few minutes, Arthur Bolton, recovering the shock, pushed ashore, and heard all the particulars as well as Cato could explain them. His beautiful Alice was in the power of the Sambos, for she certainly was not with Saunders and his associates, and his mind was made up at once.

" Now, jump out, Joe. I will land this noble-hearted fellow on the other side of the creek ; he will follow in the track of the Sambos. I will come back for you, for the canoe will not hold three. We will proceed to the brig, resume our clothes, and, well-armed, follow Cato. No time must be lost. Jump out."

Joe wished the canoe would hold three; he did not much like the look of the place where he was to wait his master's return ; but Cato consoled him by stating, " No wild beasts eat you up till dark ; you quite safe for dat."

" Be gor, they shan't eat me by day or night," thought Joe.

And the moment the canoe pushed off, and was out of sight he climbed up a tree, and ensconced himself in the branches. But Joe was by no means aware that a very large monkey was seated above, eagerly watching his movements, and, as he did not look up, he suddenly received a sharp stroke from the beast's paw, the beast uttering a frightful scream at the same time, and jumping on a higher branch.

Joe was paralyzed, the perspiration literally poured from his forehead. He thought his hour was come, and in an agony of fright—though as brave a boy in affairs of actual life as could be—he roared, and implored the help of every saint in the Irish calendar. But the monkey beat him hollow in his ejaculations, screaming and chattering, and making hideous faces.

Joe, half dead with fright, at last looked up, and there beheld his enemy swinging by the tail to a branch, and uttering all kinds of cries, and twisting himself into every kind of shape ; and then, becoming quiet, showed his teeth, and spat like a cat at his enemy.

" Oh ! " said Joe, wiping the moisture from his forehead and eyes, " it's you, is it ? Be gor, I thought 'twas a bear. Faix, I'll pay you off for this ; the Lord save us ! I'm just as if I was hoisted out of the river."

He then got astride on a branch, and surveyed his enemy.

"A monkey! faix, he's a big ugly customer; but, be
dad, I'll have him out of that."

And he commenced breaking off a stout branch ; but as
he did so, he heard a great crash of branches below,
and looking down, to his inconceivable terror beheld a
huge beast breaking through the brushwood, and coming
towards the river.

It was what the natives call a tapir, not unlike a wild
boar, but very much larger, the back highly arched, with
a kind of proboscis hanging over its mouth, and which the
animal uses in the manner of the elephant. The skin is so
hard that it will resist a musket-ball. Now, though the
beast is so formidable to look at, it is perfectly harmless,
and lives on plants and roots, and can exist in the water
for a time.

As the beast came towards the tree on which sat the
stupefied Joe, the immense ape above him, which afterwards turned out to be a tame one escaped from a native
village, gave a scream, and sprang on Joe's shoulders.
Joe roared with fright, lost his hold, and fell, actually
pitching on the back of the tapir, which luckily broke his
fall. The astonishment of the beast was equal to Joe's
terror ; it bellowed with fear, and, crashing through the
trees, plunged into the stream, and swam out of sight.

"The Lord be merciful to us, he's gone!" muttered Joe,
venturing to rise ; "it's a mercy that every bone in my
carcass wasn't broke. Bad 'cess to the beast! its backbone
was like a rod of iron."

And carefully examining his limbs, and stretching out
his arms, he looked round for the ape, but he too had disappeared. He then scrambled out on the rock, and to his
infinite joy beheld Arthur Bolton returning.

"The saints be glorified!" ejaculated Joe. "I ain't a
coward, neither ; but, faix, with a monkey as big as a man
above you, and an elephant below, be gor it requires a
stout heart not to be frightened. I was not afeard of the
ape ; be dad, I'd have settled him in no time ; only the
brute was so infernally nimble, and hung so by his tail.
Faix, swinging by a tail ain't a bad thing at times, but
inconvenient with one's clothes on."

Arthur paddled to the rock, exclaiming—

"Jump in, Joe, we have no time to lose. The sun will
be down in an hour."

"Faix, Mr. Bolton, it's myself has had a great escape
entirely," said Joe, getting into the canoe. " Sure, I was
near drowned, sir, by an elephant and an ape."

"An elephant!" said Arthur Bolton, laughing, " why,

you're dreaming, Joe: there are neither apes nor elephants in this part of the world."

' Oh, be dad, then, they are out of their reckoning, and were cast ashore like ourselves, for I see'd or felt them both." And Joe described his adventure with the beasts.

Arthur laughed heartily.

"Your story surprises me ; but elephant it could not be, though it had what you call a trunk ; there are, I know, some strange animals in these forests ; but elephants there are none, and from your description the animal was more like a wild pig."

" Be dad," returned Joe, laughing, " he was a big pig, and had a mighty fine snout of his own for picking up the praties."

Just then they turned the point, and beheld the brig.

" What did you do with the negro, sir ? " asked Joe.

" I put him ashore on the far side of the creek. He is well armed, and has money, and says he will be sure to find out where those wretches have carried Miss Alice Marchmont. I promised to follow as soon as we had obtained clothing and arms. He strongly advised our return to the Woolwas, and to accompany them to their village. I should most likely find him there, and the Woolwas were sure to help us against the Sambos, in rescuing the young lady."

Paddling along as fast as they could, they soon reached the side of the brig. The Spaniards on board looked at them with great surprise. But Arthur, ascending the side, soon made the officer left in charge of the vessel understand him. Mrs. Marchmont, before her departure, had told Capt. Castinos all about our hero and his companion, Joe, in case they should return, and requested him to state the same to his mate, whom he had left on board ; therefore our hero experienced no difficulty in proving to the mate who he was, and in making him understand what he intended doing to rescue Miss Alice.

" You must be very cautious," said the mate. " Carrajo, those Mexican dogs are real cut-throats ; they have committed I don't know how many murders. They stole a schooner from Nicaragua, and killed the padrone and one man and a boy. As to the Sambos, they are a drunken, besotted race, capable of anything brutal and ferocious when indulging in what they call a ' big drunk.' Without Cato you will have no chance ; his advice to stay with the Woolwas was good."

Early the next morning, our hero resumed his usual attire, and concealing a considerable sum in dollars and gold in a belt fastened round the waist, he and Joe prepared to depart with the first of the flood. For arms Arthur had an excellent double-barrelled fowling-piece, and Joe a rifle, and a brace of pistols each. A basket of provisions, and some flasks of rum, and a jar of brandy for the Woolwas, was also put in the canoe. Taking leave of Juan Peraz, the mate, a remarkably kind, civil Spaniard, our hero and Joe entered the canoe, and pushed off from the brig.

As it was possible the brig might be taken to Bluefields before their return, the mate advised them to take Cato for a guide, and to cross the country to that place, as by so doing they would be sure to come across the party that Mrs. Marchmont would despatch from Bluefields.

Paddling up the river with the tide, our hero remarked to Joe that the weather, though then calm, looked anything but pleasant. The mate had also remarked it, and said that heavy thunder-storms and tremendous rains were very frequent at that period of the year.

" We shall barely reach the creek before we have a storm, Joe," said Arthur.

Joe looked up and saw that dense masses of clouds were advancing from the south, and that a brisk breeze was rising. He remembered his adventures the day before, and by no means relishing the idea of passing the night in the woods, he redoubled his exertions. An immense flock of the blue-winged teal passing within thirty yards, induced Arthur Bolton to load with shot, and try to bag a few. Fifteen teal he shot with both barrels, besides many wounded, which he would not pursue, for the breeze was increasing, and the sky threatening. Just as they gained the creek, and got within its waters, the storm burst, with thunder and lightning, and furious gusts of wind, but no rain. He urged on the canoe, so as to gain the foot of the falls, for when descending the rapid our hero observed that a lofty range of rock, pierced with several openings like caverns, stood exposed on the further shore. As the rain was sure to come down in torrents, Arthur was extremely anxious to reach this shelter before it began, for he saw it was quite impossible to carry the canoe past the rapid that day, as the rain and storm would no doubt last for hours. It was with exceeding difficulty they kept the canoe afloat. The gusts of wind threatened to force her out of the water, and the roar of the blast, as it swept through the trees, crushing and breaking the branches, and hurling them over the creek, almost equalled the thunder in uproar. Keeping close in under the bank, the storm swept over them, and just as some immense drops of rain began to fall they reached the foot of the rapid, almost breathless from their exertions.

"Now be quick, Joe," said our hero, jumping ashore; "there are the rocks, lay hold of the canoe, in five minutes we shall have a deluge."

Seizing the light canoe, they easily bore her to the rocks, and as the rain began to descend in a marvellous torrent, they gained shelter in a large and spacious cavern.

"Come, this is indeed fortunate," said our hero, as they placed the canoe on a gravelly bottom, and then turned to look at a tropical downpour of rain. The thunder rolled to a distance; the lightning, considering it was yet daylight, was brilliant and incessant, but soon ceased, for the storm passed on with great rapidity; the deluge of rain, however, ran by the mouth of the cave like a deep river, and this continued till nearly dusk, when the clouds broke.

"We are here for the night," said Arthur, "so let us make ourselves as comfortable as we can. Take out the basket, Joe, and we will sup—why, it's a perfect river running by the mouth of the cave. This stream from the summit of these rocks will make the fall very rapid to-morrow."

"Faix, sir, I hope none of those beasts I saw yesterday will take it into their heads to come and sleep here."

"Not much fear of that, Joe, with such a stream running by our door. I wish we had some wood; we could make a fire, and smother out these abominable mosquitoes, far worse enemies than the hog that frightened you."

"Be dad!" muttered Joe, "I never seed a hog with a probosus a yard long over his snout."

Having satisfied their appetites, they next sought out a dry spot on which to pass the night, and a long dismal one it was; but our voyagers, nevertheless, contrived to get a few hours' rest, though Joe felt exceedingly disinclined to sleep, for various strange sounds and hisses were distinctly heard coming from the forest and jungle round the cavern.

The morning broke fine and beautiful with a refreshing breeze, and the air cooled by the storm of the past night. The stream before the cavern had become a rill, and the parrots and parroquets were chattering and screaming with might and main.

Having breakfasted on the contents of the basket, they then rubbed and brushed up the guns and pistols, and loaded them with ball, excepting one barrel of the fowling-piece, which was kept loaded with shot for any kind of game that might come in their way,

They had to carry the canoe a full mile before launching her ; but Arthur had adopted an easy manner of carrying her, by suspending her on a light pliant pole, each supporting an end. It was very evident that the Indians who navigated this creek always carried their canoes past the rapid, when going to the lagoon of La Tonza, for a narrow path bordering the stream was visible, the thick brushwood being cut away and the branches cleared. Still, it was a rough and tiresome path. They had nearly accomplished their task, when the loud and peculiar whoop of Indians struck upon their ears.

They paused, and looking in the direction of the sound, to their surprise beheld a large canoe and a patpan just shooting the fall. The canoe was full of Indians ; the patpan, a broad, shallow flat boat, held Saunders and the Mexican despcradoes. Though they flitted by like a flash of lightning, Saunders had recognized them, and with a yell of exultation fired his musket at them, but without effect.

" Now then, Joe, our lives are at stake ; there's not a moment to be lost ; they will pursue us on foot the moment they reach the level."

Exerting themselves to the utmost, they reached the level and launched the canoe, and then commenced urging her up the stream towards the lagoon. Loud shouts shortly after were heard in the woods, proving that they were pursued. Arthur had loaded his second barrel with ball, determined to make a desperate resistance, and, if possible, put an end to the career of that villain, Saunders. If their pursuers were on foot and did not carry their canoes with them, they had every chance of escaping, as they could land on the opposite shore, and shelter themselves behind the immense trees on its banks.

CHAPTER XV.

IT was a very critical trial for our voyagers, for their enemies were numerous and vindictive, and their shouts and menaces, and howls of rage resounded through the woods. Presently they came into view, ten of them carrying the long Indian canoe.

"Now be steady and cool, Joe," said our hero to his young assistant ; " those Mexican scoundrels have fire-arms."

A shout of exultation broke from the Mexicans, and a yell of savage delight from the Sambos when they beheld those they hunted.

They were still musket-shot distant, but with six paddles

in their canoe they would soon gain on them. Joe was
but weak, and could not handle his paddle as well as Arthur
Bolton.

They could see two of the Mexicans standing up in the
canoe with muskets in their hands, watching, no doubt, till
near enough to fire. On flew the light canoe, but Joe's
power was not equal to the powerful strokes of Arthur
Bolton's paddle, so consequently he had to keep the craft
straight and to use only half his power.

The Indian canoe came rapidly up with them, and so
eager was Saunders for the blood of his intended victim,
that he fired the moment they were within a hundred yards;
the ball went through the side of the canoe, making poor
Joe's heart beat faster. Luckily the hole was two inches
above water.

Bolton's blood boiled ; checking his paddle, he seized his
gun. They were not more than eighty yards from the
Indians. Another shot, the ball whizzing close to Arthur's
cheek. He could distinguish Saunders and one of the Mexicans standing erect, whilst the Sambos urged on the canoe.
Saunders was reloading, when, taking a steady aim at the
wretch, he fired. With a yell of rage Saunders staggered
and fell on the side of the canoe, which instantly upset,
sending her entire crew into the creek. Joe gave a cheer
of genuine delight, and then both seized their paddles and
urged the canoe towards the lagoon.

"Faix, sir," said Joe, "the rascal's got it this time.
Thanks to the saints, it was right in his locker."

A bend in the creek shut those struggling in the water
from their sight. Ten minutes more and the canoe shot
into the lake.

"Thank God!" said our hero, "that was a fortunate
shot. The villain's fall overturned the canoe ; no doubt
they can all swim, but I think before they can right their
canoe and get ashore, and re-embark, we shall be too far
for pursuit. Just put a plug in that hole, for the lagoon
is rough, and the breeze is against us."

The wind blew so fresh that they were forced to keep
along shore, and for two hours made little or no progress,
till turning a point of land, they got some shelter. To
cross the lake till the breeze decreased was impossible ; so,
lifting the canoe upon the beach, they resolved to wait till
the sun set, when the breeze, as it was from the sea, would
most probably cease.

As Arthur conjectured, the sea-breeze slackened considerably, as the sun declined ; so, launching their canoe,
they paddled across the lagoon. Every hour's delay

appeared to Arthur an age; he was perpetually thinking of his beautiful Alice, exposed to all the horrors of a captivity amongst the brutal Sambos, and was selfish enough to rejoice that she had the companionship of her devoted attendant, Mary Pearson; and he hoped, too, that the Sambos only detained her to extort ransom. He was also buoyed up with the idea that he had killed Saunders; at all events, wounded him, which would for a time prevent him from committing further atrocities.

It was quite dusk before they reached the spot where they had left the Indians; but their approach was perceived, for our hero observed some women holding pine torches on the beach. As soon as the canoe touched the shore, and he leaped out, he was surrounded by the women, and welcomed with smiles by Achupa, who, waving her torch, gazed at our hero, considerably surprised by his and Joe's change of garment. Several of the men looked delighted at the fire-arms, and one tall fellow, taking up the jar full of rum put it to his nose, and then with a strange gesticulation, cut several singular antics, to show that the contents of the jar pleased him greatly. Still none of them touched the fire-arms, or attempted to appropriate anything in the canoe, only carried them up to the huts, of which there were now several; Achupa making signs to Arthur that their party was increased by eight or ten men. She also strove to make our hero understand that the new comers were great chiefs, and very friendly. As they reached the front of the huts, there came forth an Indian in a costume that somewhat astounded our hero, and so amused Joe that he could scarcely keep his countenance. He was a tall stately man, in the prime of life. He wore a very short check shirt, and an old naval uniform coat, with long tails, and a lieutenant's cocked hat; other garments he had none, if we except a pair of sandals or mocassins. The rest of the Indians assembled around him, showing him great respect. The Indian raised his cocked hat, and advancing, held out his hand, saying in English, "How do you do, sar? Very glad to see you, sar. Me chief of de Woolwas: and me name—Punka Bosswash Cookra Malagalpa Rama."

"Be St. Peter," muttered Joe, in a low voice, "there's a stinger of a name,—Punka Pigswash!—Holy Moses!" As the chief shook our hero cordially by the hand, he looked sharply at Joe, whose muttered sentence had evidently reached his ears. Arthur Bolton rejoiced to hear English spoken, and thanked the chief, saying he was most happy in making his acquaintance, and begged his acceptance of a jar of rum.

"Holly golly, sir! me very glad, drink your health;" and taking the jar, he removed the cork and took a steady pull.

"Faix, that's no Pigswash, anyhow," muttered Joe, as the Indian drew a long breath.

"De rum very good, and——" and making a sign, one of the Indians brought the half of a cocoa-nut shell, and all surrounded their chief, who gave each about a wine-glass full, and then, corking the jar, handed it to one of his wives to take care of.

Punka Bosswash, as we shall call him, then ordered our hero's effects to be carried to one of the huts which he intended for his sole use, and then said he would change his dress and visit him by-and-by. All hands began preparing a meal which served for their supper. Achupa seemed quite pleased and most anxious to be of use. She lighted a fire before their hut, and assisted Joe, who felt quite at home with the Indian girl, in toasting a couple of blue teal for supper. She brought them plenty of yams, and water in a gourd; and when all was ready, with a smile, left them to themselves.

"Gosh, sir, Mr. Pigswash knows how to suck the monkey first-rate."

"Punka Bosswash is the name, Joe," said Arthur Bolton, with a smile. "Indians are excessively sensitive of ridicule. This Indian chief speaks English tolerably well, and no doubt has passed many years of his life in Jamaica, or where English is spoken. I have now great hopes of being able to induce this chief to assist me in the search after Miss Alice Marchmont—and no time must be lost."

"I wonder, sir, has the black Cato come upon the track of the villains that carried her off. Faix, sir, I hope you have killed the desperate villain, Saunders, anyhow."

"I shall certainly not regret having done so."

Whilst conversing, and Joe having cleared away the remnants of their supper, Punka Bosswash entered the hut and sat down upon a log of wood. He had laid aside his costume of coat and cocked hat, and appeared like the rest of his tribe, saving that he wore a species of coronet round his head, in which was placed two very handsome feathers of some native bird.

"Me come have big talk wid you, sar," said the chief, filling his pipe with tobacco and then lighting it. "My daughter, Achupa, say you English, and me lub de English much—and me tell you how I came speak English, and den you tell where you come from, and what you do in this country, widout ship or much company."

Arthur Bolton had a small jar of brandy, and forthwith helped the chief to a glass, which he relished exceedingly; and having puffed at his pipe for a few moments, he gave our hero the following account of himself:

His father, he said, was a great chief; but when he was nine years old the Sambos made an attack on their village with a party of Mexican villains and plundered it, and carried him and some other boys and girls off from the squaws—for the men of the village were all out at a great hunting party. The Sambos took him and others to a place on the coast and sold them to an American trader. They were afterwards wrecked on the Island of Jamaica; but though the ship was lost, the crew and all on board were saved. The American captain sold him to an English planter, whose name he thought was Copeland. He was very ill-used for four or five years; but, after that, he fell into the hands of better masters, and finally, when grown up, and married, was sold, together with his little one, to a rich English merchant, named Marchmont. On the mention of this name, our hero started, and became much more interested.

The tale proved, as it proceeded, that Mr. Marchmont and his good wife were the best people in the world, and when the emancipation of the negroes took place, they restored him and his wife and family to their own country laden with presents. When he rejoined his countrymen, he was elected chief, his father having just died. He had recently visited Jamaica, and was just returned; he had seen his good master, Mr. Marchmont, who was expecting his wife and daughters from England. " And now, sar," continued the Woolwa chief, having finished his story, and two cocoa-nuts full of brandy, " what you here for? and what me can do for you, for I lub de whites, and de English much more——"

Arthur at once made Punka Bosswash acquainted with the state of affairs. He told him of the wreck of the "Foam," and of Miss Marchmont being in the hands of the Sambos and the Mexican desperadoes, headed by the villain who had murdered Captain Courtney. The astonishment of Punka Bosswash was great indeed; he became quite excited, muttered all kinds of Indian expressions, and finally told our hero, that he would break up the turtle expedition, and return at once to their settlement. He would then call a council, and, with a party, attack the Sambos of Quamwatta, where he felt sure Miss Alice Marchmont was held captive.

This determination of the chief greatly pleased our hero,

and when Punka Bosswash departed, he shook him most cordially by the hand.

The next morning all the turtle party were busy packing up. Achupa came, and by signs and words told our hero that he and Joe should keep her canoe for themselves; they would like it better than being in the larger canoes, with her countrymen.

This arrangement suited our hero's wishes, and he thanked the chief's daughter for all her kindness.

Having finished their morning meal, the canoes were launched, and, all being ready, the whole party pushed out into the lagoon. Arthur and Joe in their light craft kept up easily with the larger canoes. Passing across the lagoon, the little fleet kept away to the eastward, the chief's canoe leading. Arthur, now that he was positively on the track of his beloved Alice, became more calm and collected. He would sacrifice life or release her, and he confidently hoped, that though she must be in a fearful situation, she was free from the horrors of being in the power of Saunders. The Sambos, greedy of gain, no doubt joined in carrying her off for the sake of ransom, whilst Saunders's efforts were directed to the plunder of the brig.

The lagoon of La Tonza formed one of those singular lakes that, joining each other by narrow creeks and channels, continue along the Musquito coast as far as Cape Gracias, forming an immense inland navigation bordering the sea-coast, at times merely separated by a belt of sand. These lakes extend a distance of one hundred and sixty miles.

Having crossed the lagoon, they turned a bold point to the eastward, and entered a wide creek, which brought them to a long, narrow piece of water; paddling its entire length, they entered a narrow, and somewhat rapid channel, which ran in a westerly direction, and drawing up alongside an island, their fires were lighted, and their food prepared and eaten. Punka Bosswash informed our hero that they would reach their village the next day; that they would camp where they were, as they had to ascend a rapid river, which required daylight to accomplish.

On the spot where the Indians had cooked their meals vegetation flourished in the greatest luxuriance. Here, for the first time, Arthur beheld the graceful and gigantic ceiba, or silk-cotton-tree; it was then in bloom; on the summit of this beautiful tree was a crown of flowers, in rich profusion of various colours, but chiefly bright carnation. It was nearly eighty feet high, and almost five feet in diameter. The perfume was almost overpowering, whilst the ground beneath was covered with its gay blossoms.

The natives take the cotton from the pods, which succeed the flowers ; when ripe, they burst open, the inside being full of a silky fibre of soft light cotton. The Woolwa chief told Arthur Bolton that the chief use they made of the tree was for making canoes and dories, as it rarely splits from the heat of the sun, and is besides light and buoyant.

The next morning they started very early, and, after shooting two rapids, entered a broad, noble river, which our hero thought was the Punza Pulka River ; but he learned afterwards that it was the Rio Grande, that led by a creek into the Bosswash River.

The scenery, on entering the latter river, was diversified and beautiful. Two hours before sunset they came in sight of the great village of the Woolwa chief—a long range of huts on the right bank of the river. Around the village were extensive plantations of Cassava, and all kinds of fruit and vegetables were visible in abundance.

The appearance of the turtle fleet returning from their hunting expedition, brought out all the inhabitants, old and young, of the village. Our hero and his attendant were regarded with considerable surprise and curiosity. Their chief, in his quiet way, made them all acquainted as to who his guests were, and at once they ceased to be troublesome by crowding round them, eyeing their guns with eager scrutiny.

Achupa and her mother conducted them to a commodious hut, which was to be their exclusive abode, and an Indian girl and Achupa attended to their wants, providing them with food, fire, &c.

" Well, be dad, sir," said Joe, depositing the guns and pistols, after carefully wiping them, in a corner of the hut, which consisted of only one room, " they are a quiet, kind, comely people, and one soon gets accustomed to the rather scanty clothing they wear."

" Yes, Joe, they are kind and hospitable ; very different from the Sambo race. I shudder when I think of poor Miss Alice Marchmont, amongst such a most uncivilized, drunken, vicious race. I trust Punka Bosswash will not delay our expedition beyond to-morrow. Perhaps Cato may arrive either to-night or to-morrow, he could reach her by a shorter way than we came."

" May-be, sir, he is spying out where the villains keep the young lady and her attendant—that may delay him."

"Most likely, Joe—just keep up the smoke by putting on some damp wood; those confounded mosquitoes are bent upon mischief."

"Faix, sir, it's a hard case; we must either consent to be suffocated or murdered entirely by those beasts, bad 'cess to them. Be dad, if we were dressed after the fashion of Mr. Bogwash, they'd eat us entirely—our skins are more tender, I suppose?"

Having finished their supper and smoked out the mosquitoes, they retired to rest on the bundles of dried, scented leaves of some peculiar plants selected for that purpose, and with which Achupa and her attendant had well supplied the hut.

CHAPTER XVI.

WHEN Alice, with her devoted attendant Mary, was seized and carried off, her despair almost deprived her of existence. Mary, with tender affection and that total carelessness of self which distinguished her, supported her throbbing temples upon her breast, and, in whispered words, strove to encourage hope in her heart, when, alas! hope was almost dead within her own breast.

Saunders gazed upon his victims, as the Indians paddled up the river, with fiendish exultation :—

"So," said he, fixing his savage eye upon Mary, "you all thought you had done with William Saunders; but my turn is now come. I will have a terrible revenge on you all—an eye for an eye—I will gouge out that accursed Bolton's eye, as he did mine, and then put him to a death of torture!"

"Miserable wretch, whose hands are dyed with innocent blood, do you think there is no God hearing and watching you?" said Alice, raising her head and letting her eyes, for a moment, rest, with indignation, upon the hideous face of the miserable Saunders. "God will protect us still, and your own fate will yet be even more terrible than that your brutal imagination pictures for your victim."

Mary Pearson trembled all over; she feared her young mistress's words would rouse the furious passions of the wretch in whose power they were.

Saunders gazed, bewildered, for a moment at the excited maiden, whose steady gaze never quailed before the ruffian's glare. The spirit of the young girl, never before roused or tried, was visible in her beautiful features and dark, flashing eyes. Alice, from that moment, cast aside

the timidity of her nature, and resolved to face her destiny
with a firm reliance upon Providence.

"Well, curse me," muttered Saunders, "if you an't a
young vixen, and no mistake; blow me, but I think, after
all, that you'll make an excellent wife for a bold adventurer, and mine you shall be at all events;" and with a
horrid laugh he added—"and your pretty attendant there
will do for the second. My jolly friends, the Sambos,
allow a man two wives, so thank your stars you will not
be separated."

Alice, with a look of scorn and defiance, turned away,
and though her heart was throbbing with painful excitement, she made no reply.

The three boats proceeded rapidly up the river. Saunders and the Mexican desperado coolly conversing, in half
Spanish and broken English, of their plans, being fully
resolved to plunder and destroy the brig. In forty-eight
hours they fully expected to get sufficient help to overpower those left in the vessel by the guarda-costa.

Crossing the stream, the canoes stopped at the mouth of
the creek or channel leading into the Tonza lagoon, and
there a consultation took place between one of the Mexicans and the Sambos. Saunders and the Mexicans got
into a canoe with the Sambos, whilst several Sambos took
their place in the canoe with Alice Marchmont and her
attendant.

"I leave you in good hands," said Saunders, as he left
the boat; "don't fret after me. I'll be back with you in a
day or two; and if I'm lucky, I'll bring your fancy man,
Bolton, back to witness our wedding;" and with a horrid
laugh, he left them, and with his comrades paddled up the
channel leading to the Tonza lagoon.

"Thank God!" exclaimed Alice, clasping her hands,
"that wretch and his comrades are gone. Hideous as
these Sambos are, I feel a wonderful relief, even as their
prisoner."

"Ah, Miss Alice," said Mary, "there is a chance of
escape, depend on it, Mr. Bolton will get back to the brig;
and when he hears of your being carried off, no power or
persuasion will prevent him from pursuing our villanous
enemies."

Whilst Alice and Mary Pearson were conversing, the
Sambos in their canoe paddled up the stream for four or
five miles, and crossing to the west side, went up another
river or channel, and after an hour's paddling entered a
noble stream, down which they went at a rapid pace, pre-
ceded by the other canoe.

From this river they entered a lagoon just as the shades of night were covering the waters. They ran the canoes upon the beach before a large village of huts, with numerous dories, and patpans, and canoes hauled up before them.

A number of frightful-looking Sambos, men, women, and children, crowded to the water's edge. Many of the men were drunk, and some of the women not much better.

The two unfortunate captives were horrified at the crowd; some of the women carried lighted pieces of pine wood, steeped in a kind of gum, which they flared about in a wild and reckless manner. One of the Sambos in the canoe seemed to have authority over the rest, for he spoke fiercely to the crowd, and made them fall back. To the surprise of the captives he turned to them, and spoke in broken English. He told them they should not be hurt, and should have a hut to themselves, and food, and a woman to attend on them; but if they attempted to escape, they would be chained.

They were then helped ashore, and three or four women took charge of them, and talking and gesticulating, led them up the beach, followed by a lot of screaming children of both sexes, without a particle of clothing, till they came to a hut at some distance from the other huts, and into this miserable substitute for a dwelling they were forced to go.

The hut was tolerably large, neatly wattled at the sides, and the door made of canes. Rough blocks of wood served in the place of seats, and a curious kind of frame, about a foot from the floor, and on which was a heap of soft leaves and fine hay, served as a bed. The two women, after sticking a kind of torch in the floor, retired, but shortly returned with two baskets, one containing cakes of corn-meal, and some kind of broiled meat, and a calabash full of sweet wine, made from the palm, and not unpleasant to the taste. As the women placed those things before them, the Sambo who spoke English entered the hut, and, to the infinite disgust of Alice Marchmont, sat down on one of the logs of wood.

"Dat very good to eat," he said, pointing to the contents of the baskets; "no be afraid. To-morrow you will have cassava, squashes, and cocoa-nut, and plantains."

"If," said Alice, forcing herself to look at the very hideous Sambo before her, his head all frizzled, and his face disfigured by a disgusting disease—a kind of leprosy, "if you have taken me from my protectors for the sake of gaining a large sum of money, I faithfully promise you, if

you restore me to liberty, and conduct me either to Bluefields, or put me and my attendant on board the brig, you
shall be paid, without question, a thousand dollars."

The Sambo started, repeating—

"A thousand dollars! dat big moncy! who pay dat?"

"My father will pay it cheerfully," said Alice; "and
thank you for releasing me from that villain, Saunders, for
he alone committed this outrage. You would not have
done it but for him."

"Him debble, no doubt, missy," said the Sambo, shaking
his head. "He burn our huts, and kill us, if we let you
go."

"Are you such cowards," said Alice earnestly, "as to
let five men terrify you?"

"Ja, missy; de be twenty men, with gun and pistol.
De murder de women. De give me drink, and all go mad
together."

"But, surely," said Alice, still hoping, "there are
English in Bluefields?"

"Ja, ja; no, missy; no Englis. De white people die
in dis climate. No go, missy. De man English and de
oders say de hab you and de oda missy for wife, and de
Sambo do nothing." And giving a ghastly smile, the
Sambo chief left the hut.

"What a frightful wretch!" said Mary, with a shudder.
"Oh, if we could escape!"

"But where, Mary, could we go? We should die in
the forests and swamps, or be killed by wild beasts. We
do not know the country, nor how to cross the numerous
rivers and lagoons. We must depend on Mr. Bolton; and
no doubt my beloved mother will send persons in pursuit.
The men in the cutter may be on our track. I do not fear
the Sambos, though, by all accounts, they are a brutal,
drunken race; but they would do anything for drink or
money. It is that Saunders, and his vile associates, that
I fear."

The night passed without any disturbance, except the
howling of dogs, of which great numbers were kept in the
village. There was no window of any kind in the hut, but
a large hole in the cane-door, which did not open on the
village, but towards the lagoon.

The women attended to their wants, and thus two miserable days past. Hot as it was, they were obliged to keep
their doors shut, for sundry attacks to get in were made by
legions of pigs, whose grunts and screams, as a score of
half-starved dogs attacked them, distracted the ear. At
night, to keep the mosquitoes out, they were forced to

smother themselves till they were half suffocated. Still they kept up their spirits by hoping. What a blessing hope is!

On the third day, by the noise and confusion, pigs grunting, and dogs growling, and men shouting, and women screaming, our captives conjectured, and felt no little terror in doing so, that some kind of jollification was going on. About mid-day, the Sambo chief came into the hut, kicking and thumping three great hogs that wanted to rush in. Alice Marchmont's face flushed, for the brute was drunk, and had to support himself by leaning against the side of the hut.

"Well, missy," said the man, grinning, "how do you do dis morning? Grand feast for six days. Your English husband come dis night, he berry glad to see you; we have jollification for six days."

Alice gazed at Mary with a look of horror. "Good God! does this miserable wretch mean that the villain, Saunders, is coming?"

"Oh, ja," interrupted the Sambo maliciously, "dat is he; de all come; you hear fire gun—and de debbles big drunk." And with a horrible laugh, the Sambo reeled out of the hut, leaving the captives in a terrible state of anxiety.

"I will listen to your plan for escape now, Mary; even death in the woods would be better than to remain here, to become the victims of that vile wretch, Saunders, and his associates. Who can say what atrocities they may commit, when giving way to drink, and with such horrible wretches as these Sambos."

Mary Pearson was terrified.

"Yes, my beloved mistress, death would be preferable; they will be all drunk in this accursed village before dusk. Let us get into the woods and trust to God's providence."

The unfortunate maidens made up their minds to trust to the chances of escape through the woods, and get, if possible, to the sea-shore.

All day, the shouting, yelling, and frightful uproar continued, accompanied by the firing of guns—becoming more fast and furious as the sun set.

As soon as it was dark, Alice and Mary, with heavy hearts, opened the door of the hut and gazed forth. The noise and uproar was behind them—for the hut they occupied was some little distance from the cluster. The lagoon lay before them, some two hundred yards off; but to the right of the hut, and quite close, was a thick belt of

trees. None of the Sambos, men or women, watched the
hut , for the prospect of a big drunk, in which the women
always participated, drew the two females, who generally
kept watch, away, to join the revellers.

With no other protection to their persons than the
shawls they had on when carried away from the brig,
the fugitives crept cautiously from the hut. As Alice
gazed into the dark forest and listened to the hideous
noises, even then beginning, especially the howling
monkey, she and Mary hesitated. Looking back at the
village, they beheld huge fires, and the dark forms of the
drinking Sambos men and women dancing furiously, for
the strong glare of the fires revealed the figures and
actions distinctly, as they gazed. They clearly beheld
amongst them the figures of several Europeans, with guns,
firing them off, and exciting the Sambo women into frantic
dances. Suddenly Alice grasped Mary's arm, saying—

" Ah, there is that wretch Saunders—he is a head taller
than the others."

"We can hesitate no longer," said Mary ; " death will
be better than the touch of that monster and murderer."

And then rapidly gliding across the space between the
huts and the wood, they entered beneath the deep sombre
shade of the latter. Whether some of the Sambos caught
a glimpse of the fugitives, as they crossed the space, or
Saunders himself happened to be casting a glance towards
the hut, we cannot say ; but scarcely had they entered
beneath the trees before Saunders uttered a shout of alarm
that the English girls had gone out of the hut, and were
escaping into the forest.

Saunders, and two of his comrades, and three or four
drunken Sambos, with torches, started in pursuit. Not ten
yards from the spot where the maidens entered the wood,
stretched upon the ground, hidden by the shrubs, and
watching intently the proceedings of the revellers, was a
tall and powerful negro. This watcher was Cato, the
black cook of the guarda-costa.

Starting up, he rushed after the fugitives, calling upon
the maidens to stop, saying—

" I am Cato! a good friend ! "

Astounded, they hesitated, for they, of course, knew
not who Cato was. Nevertheless, they paused, and the
black stood beside them. In a few words he stated who
he was, begged them to go back to the hut, and, as he
now knew where they were, he would communicate with
Mr. Bolton, who, he told them, was with the friendly
Woolwa Indians. He told them to have no fear, but to

go back at once, for to escape by flying through the woods was impossible. As the black spoke, the shouts of their pursuers coming nearer was heard.

" In three or four days," said Cato hurriedly, " you shall be free," and darted off into the wood.

" Come, Mary, let us thank God for this good news. I have no fear now," said Alice, " Mr. Bolton is on our track."

Holding Mary by the arm, Alice and her companion walked calmly out of the wood towards the hut, as Saunders and one of his associates, half drunk, came, out of breath, upon them. Seeing them quietly returning, Saunders paused, uttering a terrible malediction.

" How is this!" he exclaimed. " What made you leave the hut—were you trying to escape ? "

"It does not look like it," said Alice haughtily. " You see us going back. Fresh air and a little exercise is requisite, if you do not want to murder us by confinement."

" Curse you, you won't gammon me that way," said Saunders, reeling, as he made a grasp at Mary Pearson's arm, and held her, by main force, despite her struggle. " Come, my beauty, I'll have you for a wife this night, at all events."

But Mary Pearson, frantic with passion, suddenly snatched the long Mexican knife he wore in his belt, and, with all her force, drove it right at his breast. The steel buckle turned the blow, but, nevertheless, inflicted so severe a gash across his right breast, that the ruffian staggered and fell, believing, at first, that he was mortally wounded.

By this time the maidens were surrounded by a crowd of drunken Sambos, both men and women. One of the Mexican desperadoes drew a pistol, and with a frightful imprecation, swore, if Mary did not throw down the knife, he would shoot her. Alice, pale but collected, whispered some words to Mary, who at once threw the knife away, just as Saunders staggered to his feet, and, pressing his hand to his chest, said—

" You thought to murder me, you vixen. You have only scratched me, however; but you shall live, both of you, long enough to curse your existence. Take them," he continued, addressing the crowd, " and confine them in the stone house, and manacle them with the chains. To-morrow I shall get over this scratch, and the schooner will be here, and then you will learn how William Saunders revenges himself on those he hates."

He became so weak from loss of blood that he sank

down on the ground, telling his comrades to get a bandage to stop the blood.

Six or eight Sambos then surrounded the two maidens, and seizing them by the arms, hurried them along towards the beach. At some distance from the huts stood a stone building, formerly belonging to some Prussians, who had settled on the Musquito Coast, but who had finally perished from the climate and the inhospitality and brutality of the Sambo negroes. This building was evidently used as a store—it had one strong iron-studded door, and a window twenty feet from the ground. At this time it was half unroofed by time and by storms—there was no kind of furniture in it—and into this miserable abode Alice and her unfortunate attendant were thrust, to pass the remainder of the night on the bare damp ground.

From a belt of trees Cato, the negro, was watching all that took place, and having seen them locked up in the building, he muttered,—

"Ah, ja, dat just do. Cuss him—dat berry fine gal—tam him, wish she had killed him!" and then, tightening his belt, he set out for the Woolwa Indian village.

Alice Marchmont, as soon as the door was closed and locked, and the vile rabble of men and women gone, threw herself into Mary's arms, and wept for several minutes unrestrainedly, the excitement of the last hour having completely overpowered her. Mary, equally excited, and tremblingly alive to the terrible scene they had gone through, still strove to soothe her mistress.

"Ah!" said she, "if I had only killed the wretch! Unfortunately, something broke or turned my blow; at all events, the monster has a wound that will keep him quiet for a few days, and, before long, we shall, please God, be rescued."

"Wretch as that Saunders is, dear Mary, I am glad you did not kill him; the thought of having shed his blood and slain him would have haunted you through life."

"No, no," said Mary resolutely, "to put out of the world such a monster could create no other feeling than thankfulness that God had given me the power to do so. But what a wretched place the villains have put us in."

The moon had risen, and its rays shed a light through the broken roof upon the shattered rafters and slates covering the stone floor. Seating themselves upon a block of stone, and leaning their backs against the wall, Alice, the child, we may say, of luxury, and her faithful attendant, passed the remaining hours of the night. Sleep was out of the question, for even within the dreary, bare, damp walls of the building the insatiable mosquitoes abounded, for that swampy shore was teeming with tropical insects of every description, whilst in the interior the Mexican lion, and various wild beasts, roamed the vast forests unmolested.

Leaving our unfortunate heroine in her miserable prison, with her devoted attendant, we will, in our next chapter, follow Mrs. Marchmont to Bluefields, and see what steps the fond mother took to rescue her lost daughter.

CHAPTER XVII.

Mrs. Marchmont, her daughter, and attendant, with most of their private effects, were embarked on board the guarda costa. In vain the fond mother strove to conceal the anguish of mind she experienced. In leaving the brig it appeared to her as if she were abandoning her child. Her daughter and old attached servant did and said all they could to cheer her, and persuade her that Alice would be restored to her safe and uninjured. Mrs. Marchmont was distressed, too, by the unaccountable disappearance of Arthur Bolton and Joseph, at a time when their services would have been so valuable in rescuing her daughter from her abductors.

She resolved, immediately on reaching Bluefields, to despatch some small vessel to Jamaica, with letters to her husband, entreating him to come to her, for to leave the Musquito Coast without positive intelligence of her daughter was out of the question.

The captain of the guarda-costa was civil and obliging enough, but understanding each other's language only imperfectly, little was said.

With a fair breeze, the Maria Gloriosa came in sight of Bluefields early on the following day. Mother and daughter were on deck, for the small ill-ventilated cabin of the guarda-costa was close and suffocating, and both gazed with a saddened feeling upon the long white line of sand dividing the lagoon, on whose shores Bluefields stands from the sea.

No scenery could be more monotonous or uninteresting. Here and there a solitary palm was to be seen, and a green belt of trees, and in the far distance the blue hills from which it takes its name.

As the guarda-costa tacked, so as to run in through the narrow entrance, they had a clear view of the lagoon, at the extremity of which the town—if a collection of miserable huts could be called a town—stood, some ten miles distant from the entrance. No vessel of any country was to be seen upon that solitary sea, and within the lagoon nought but patpans, and dories, and canoes were visible.

"What a wretched place," said Miss Marchmont to her mother, as the cutter ran swiftly up the lagoon, tacking here and there to avoid the many shoals scattered through its shallow waters.

"And yet," said the mother sadly, "Bluefields is called an imperial city, for that farce of a Musquito king resides here."

"Oh, my dear mother!" said Miss Marchmont incredulously. "A king—a black king—and his palace is yonder wretched place."

"Your father, my dear girl, has often amused me with stories of these people and their king. When he was here, there was an English resident—I forget his name, and the Musquito king resided with him. There was also a colony of Prussians, but somehow they all died, or vanished; indeed, your father said only five or six escaped out of a hundred or more. This climate and place is pestiferous, low, swampy, and intensely hot, subject to terrible storms and heavy rains; but see, the aspect of the town itself is picturesque;" for amongst the huts they could see many palms and plantain-trees, and stalks of the golden-fruited papayas. The entire shore seemed lined with dories, canoes, or patpans—many of the dories were from 50 to 60 feet long.

"But why are those people called Sambos?" questioned Miss Marchmont, "I thought they were all called Musquito Indians."

"There are Indian tribes in the interior," said Mrs. Marchmont, "some of them friendly, kind, and hospitable, but the race inhabiting the sea-coast are a miserably degenerate brutal tribe; in fact, negroes or mongrels, half Indian and half negro, called Sambos."

The anchor was now let go, and the cutter's sail furled. Numerous canoes and patpans kept paddling round the vessel. One of them came alongside with rather a singular person aboard—a hideous negro, dressed in a post-captain's old tattered uniform, and calling himself an admiral. This negro could speak English. The captain of the guarda-costa permitted him to come aboard, and held him in conversation for some minutes; he then approached Mrs. Marchmont, making a tremendous bow, saying, "Morning, mam."

Captain Castinos intimated to Mrs. Marchmont that

this man had the command of the town during the absence of the king and the English resident, who was daily expected to return from Jamaica—that he would order a hut to be prepared for him and his family, and recommended that she should bargain with him.

Mrs. Marchmont cared little about bargaining. She felt sorely depressed at hearing that the English resident was absent, and that there was not a single vessel of any description in the lagoon capable of going to Jamaica.

She told the admiral she wanted for herself and family the best accommodation the place afforded; the terms were indifferent to her, but she must have a residence completely to herself.

The negro admiral bowed profoundly, and said: "Madame should 'ab de king's palace till de king comes back, and den she should 'ab anoder." He then summoned a dorie, and having again had a conference with the captain of the Maria Gloriosa, Mrs. Marchmont's effects were brought on deck and lowered into the dorie, and then she and her daughter and attendants, after thanking Captain Castinos and distributing some dollars amongst the crew, entered the dorie, followed by the admiral, and four hideous negroes paddled them ashore.

On reaching the landing-place a great crowd attended, regarding our voyagers with much curiosity; but the admiral, who assumed airs of considerable importance, soon dispersed them, and, leading the way, ordered numerous negroes to carry the luggage.

The dwelling inhabited by the Musquito king and the English resident, was a small framed, plain-looking edifice, one story high, and divided into four chambers, most scantily supplied with very plain furniture. But Mrs. Marchmont and her daughter cared very little about their style of residence; they settled with the admiral to supply them with the best food the place afforded, and gave him some dollars to pay the negroes who carried their effects.

On talking to him about sending people in pursuit of the ruffians, who carried off her daughter, the admiral shook his woolly head, saying:

"The king and the English guvenor would be home in two or three days, and den he would do all he could in de business."

This was all the answer Mrs. Marchmont could get, and it left her in a state of intense uneasiness. Her sole hopes now rested on Arthur Bolton, should he return to the brig, and on the exertions of the black cook, Cato.

Day after day the fond and anxious mother and sister

watched for the English schooner from Jamaica; but not a sail threw a shadow on the still waters of the lagoon. They did not attempt to stir out of the hut, for the place was disgustingly filthy, and swarmed, like all Sambo villages, with naked children, pigs, and dogs.

On the tenth day of their residence, loud shouting, firing of guns, and sundry strange noises announced some event, and shortly after the admiral made his appearance, announcing that the English schooner, with the king and prime minister, was working up the lagoon.

Mrs. Marchmont, uttering the words, "Thank God, at last!" rushed to the window that looked down the lagoon, and beheld a handsome full-rigged schooner with all sails set, tacking up the river. As the vessel neared the anchorage, the negroes began firing old rusty muskets, and a dilapidated old four-pounder, mounted on a platform some eight feet square, just before the house, was loaded, and, after a variety of attempts, fired, amidst a tremendous noise, shouts, cries, &c. No gun was fired from the schooner, and no flag displayed beyond the simple ensign flying at the peak. So the admiral informed Mrs. Marchmont that the king could not be aboard, as his majesty delighted in making much noise with guns and cannons.

As soon as the schooner anchored, her sails were furled, and her boats launched from her deck.

"I trust," said Mrs. Marchmont to her anxious daughter, "that though the king is not on board, the English resident is."

"We shall soon see, dear mother," returned Eliza Marchmont, "for there are several persons getting into the boats; but it is too far to distinguish figures. They are Europeans, at all events. There are four in the first boat."

Nearly all the population of the place rushed down to the beach, and surrounded the persons landing, and shortly they were lost to view.

After a few minutes, both mother and daughter perceived a single gentleman advancing rapidly towards the house they occupied.

Mrs. Marchmont gazed intently at the approaching figure, and then uttered an exclamation of joy:—

"Oh, my child!" she exclaimed, clasping her hands, and tears streaming down her cheeks; "it is your father!"

Miss Marchmont rushed to the door; the next moment, mother and daughter were folded in the arms of

Mr. Marchmont. For some time not one of the party could speak, but gazed at each other with fond affection.

" Oh, William, my beloved husband! what an unexpected joy is this. Must I damp it by telling you——"

" Alas! I know all, my beloved Fanny. It was the first intelligence I heard on landing. I did not expect to find you and my child Eliza here. I only knew that the 'Foam' was wrecked, or supposed to be wrecked, somewhere on the coast. So I at once, in terrible anxiety of mind, embarked with Captain Courtney."

" Captain Courtney!" exclaimed mother and daughter in a tone of bewildered amazement. " Surely, not poor Captain Courtney?"

" Yes, dear Fanny; it is the worthy captain of the 'Foam' I mean—most providentially saved, when cast overboard by those atrocious mutineers. I would not allow him to come with me till I broke the intelligence to you both. We have just heard from the negro, Admiral Wellington, that the 'Foam' is safe, though dismasted, in the Punza Pulka river, and that the Maria Gloriosa is with her, getting up jury masts, &c. I will despatch twenty armed negroes and six English sailors, with the dawn, to scour the country for those villains who hold my daughter's person; and to-morrow I intend sailing in the schooner for the Punza Pulka river, and try and track them up that river. But where is Mr. Bolton? Captain Courtney is most anxious about him; Admiral Wellington knows nothing about him. But stay, I must go for Courtney, for he is very desirous to see you both."

" Oh, if our beloved Alice were but here," exclaimed Mrs. Marchmont, clasping her hands, " what joy would be mine!"

" God has been most merciful in his goodness," said Mr. Marchmont, with solemn earnestness, " may His mercy restore our child uninjured!"

Mr. Marchmont then hurried to the hut where he had left Captain Courtney.

" Oh, Eliza, I am so bewildered, so overpowered, and so thankful to Providence, that I scarcely know what I say or do."

" Only to think of Captain Courtney being alive! it appears incredible. There must have been some vessel near us on that dreadful night," said Miss Marchmont, " which picked him up."

" If that had been the case, my child, surely they would have pursued us; and besides, if so near, they must have heard the shouts and cries of the poor doomed steward, for he was not saved. But here comes your father and our dear good friend the captain, looking as well as ever."

Captain Courtney was flushed and excited as he clasped Mrs. Marchmont's hand in both his.

"I cannot tell you, my dear madam," he exclaimed with much emotion, "what joy this interview gives me, to see you and your daughters—for we will, please God, soon restore Miss Alice to your arms—safe. In the hour of my terrible trial, when death stared me in the face, I thought of you all, in the power of those remorseless ruffians."

Mrs. Marchmont shed a flood of tears; the memory of that hour, and the loss of her daughter, though hope was not dead in her heart, overpowered her. In the evening, when all were more calm and collected, and the heat of the day tempered by the cool breeze from the mountains, Captain Courtney gave the party assembled an account of his most providential escape from a terrible death. "On that fearful night," began the captain, "when Mr. Bolton and I were seated conversing in my private cabin, the door was suddenly burst open; and Saunders and the others, after a desperate resistance from that gallant gentleman, Mr. Bolton, who was knocked down senseless, and would instantly have been murdered, had not my first mate, whose life, you may remember, he saved, interfered, overpowered us, dragged me up the cabin stairs—two or three of the ruffians making every effort to stab me with their knives; but in the confusion and darkness I fortunately escaped their blows, and was finally hoisted overboard—the craft then going at eight knots, but not much sea. The poor steward had fallen a victim to their brutal fury before being thrown into the sea.

"My first thought was to recommend my soul to my Maker, and let myself sink, and thus end my misery. But I was always an excellent swimmer, and somehow, strange as it may appear, the love of life prevailed, and I rose to the surface, and got rid of my coat, waistcoat, and shoes, and then turned on my back, and began, even in that terrible situation, to think. I thought of you all left in the power of those terrible villains; I thought of my home, of my dear wife and children, and then I prayed, feeling that before long I must sink. It was a very dark night, and as I thus lay, rising and falling on the seas, my head came suddenly against something hard, and to save myself from sinking, as I was turned over on my face, I grasped at a mass of ropes in which I became entangled; and then I perceived, even in the deep gloom, that I was holding on by the rigging tossed over an immense mast, and above me

were the huge tops of a large ship. On to this mast I
scrambled, and then up into the tops, which floated quite
clear of the water. Here I paused to breathe, with a
thanksgiving to Providence. I was saved for the time.
Some ship might pass, might see me—there was a chance,
and when will not man hope against the most desperate
odds. I was now secure from drowning, for in the huge
tops of a large ship I was safe, even in a hurricane. Fastening myself round the waist, before morning I actually
dozed.

" As the dull light of a gloomy day broke over the heaving ocean, I eagerly gazed around me ; the weather fore-
told a storm, but no vessel was in sight. As I looked down,
floating amongst the rigging, and held to the tops by a
rope, I beheld the dead body of a man, a sailor by his
dress, but fearfully decomposed. I shuddered as I cast off
the rope to rid myself of a sight so sad. That poor wretch
no doubt held on till starvation sapped life ; several others
might have shared the same fate, and their fate, I thought,
might be mine.

" The day passed ; I lashed myself securely, for I saw
by the look of the heavens that a storm was at hand, and
that night it broke with surprising fury. It was only of a
few hours' duration, and for half the time I was under
water ; but with daylight came blessed hope, for scarcely
four miles from me, I beheld a large bark, under close-
reefed canvas, running right for the heaving mast. I was,
providentially, right in the ship's course. As the ship
neared me they perceived the mast, and standing up, I
waved my arm, and shouted till I was hoarse. I was seen,
and then it was that nature gave way, and, bursting into
tears, I became insensible.

" When I recovered, I was in the ship's boat, the gallant fellows, though it was a work of great peril, having
rescued me. The ship was Spanish, and bound to Cuba ;
the captain spoke French, and was most kind. He supplied
me with garments, and shared his cabin with me, when I told
him my story. A very heavy gale, in which he sprang his
fore-topmast, and also sprang a leak, forced him to run for
Jamaica, to my infinite joy, as I thought it possible some
British cruiser would be induced to search for the brig and
the mutineers ; for I had a very good idea as to where
they would run the 'Foam' to plunder her. I knew that
the second mate, Saunders, had once been on the Musquito
Coast, and had often heard him talk of his wild course
there, and how easy a fellow might lead a life of plunder,
with the jolly lot of Mexican adventurers who frequented

that coast ; but my first task, and that a most painful and
dreaded one, was to find out Mr. Marchmont, and make
him acquainted with my terrible story. I need not tell
you or speak of that painful interview ; you are now,
thank God, united.

"Imagine my delight, when, a few days after my arrival
in Jamaica, a schooner cast anchor in the harbour, and
reported that she spoke a Spanish guarda-costa off the
Punza Pulka river, on the Musquito Coast, the captain of
which stated that there was a large English brig ashore,
dismasted in that river, and that he was going to Bluefields
for assistance. The governor at once placed a small armed
schooner at Mr. Marchmont's service. We accordingly
embarked with the English resident of Bluefields, and put in
here to land him, intending to proceed to the Punza Pulka.
Imagine our joy when the negro admiral told us you were
here, but that one of your daughters had been carried off
by a party of Sambos and some Mexican desparadoes.
Such, my dear madam, is my brief narrative, which plainly
shows that even in the most desperate circumstances we
should never despair of the divine mercy and assistance of
Providence."

CHAPTER XVIII.

The following morning beheld the departure of the
schooner, with Mr. Marchmont, Captain Courtney, and a
strong, armed party, for the Punza Pulka river. It was
the most expeditious mode of proceeding. On reaching
the brig, Mr. Marchmont, with negro guides, and a dozen
well-armed sailors, and twenty armed negroes, sent by the
English resident of Bluefields, to assist, proceeded to visit
Quamwatta and all the Sambo villages on the different
lagoons, till they discovered Miss Alice Marchmont, and
rescued her.

They also took materials with them to complete the rigging of the "Foam," to enable them to take her to
Jamaica, calling off Bluefields for Mrs. Marchmont and
family.

Leaving them to prosecute their search, we return to
our hero, whom we left in the village of the Woolwa
Indians.

Arthur Bolton, in his intense desire to commence his
search for Alice Marchmont, was up with the dawn : but
the whole village was astir, and the chief, Punka Bosswash, was coming to his hut to rouse him, accompanied by
t egro, attired in European costume, in whom, to his in-

finite delight, our hero recognized Cato, the cook of the guarda-costa. ,

"Ah! my good friend," said Arthur, grasping the cook's hand, " have you any good news? Have you discovered where the young lady is ? "

" Yes, massa, me 'ab. Me good news and bad news."

Punka Bosswash then proposed that they should go inside the hut, and consult about what was best to be done.

Accordingly they all entered, and sat down on the logs of wood. Punka Bosswash lit his pipe and took a whiff, and Arthur Bolton, who knew that the Woolwas, though a sober race, loved a small allowance of brandy, produced his little jar, and handed a cup all round, and then begged Cato to tell his good news and bad.

Cato related how he thought he had tracked Miss Marchmont to Quamwatta ; but before entering the village he kept a secret watch upon what was going on, for he heard there was to be feasting for three days, and a big drunk on the last day."

Whilst watching in the wood, he beheld, to his great surprise, two females, white people, leave a hut, and run into the wood, close by where he lay concealed. He at once knew that they must be Miss Marchmont and her attendant ; he also knew it would be utterly impossible for them, even with his guidance, to escape through the forest, and across rapid streams, and their pursuers after them. So he advised them to go back, which they did, and then he continued his watch, and finally having seen Miss Marchmont and Mary forced into the stone house, which he described as a very strong place, with doors plated with iron ; but with a rope-ladder they could scale the walls, as half the roof was off.

Punka Bosswash listened to Cato's account with great attention, and, having finished his pipe, he said—"That's good," and then, nodding his head, told Cato to say what he thought it best to do.

Cato continued to say that, after quitting Quamwatta, he came up with two Sambos and two of their females ; that he easily persuaded them that he was a runaway from the Spanish guarda-costa, and was hiding in the forest till the schooner left the Punza Pulka. He had a full canteen of brandy, for, on an emergency, he reckoned much upon its efficacy. Having primed the two Sambos and their wives, who belonged to Quamwatta, they told him if he went to their village he would be safe, for they had twenty Mexican desperadoes well armed with them, and they

would kill the men of the guarda-costa if they came to
their village.   They also informed him that there was to be
a "big drunk" for three days, and that a great "Sukia"
(sorceress) was to be there, and that she was to defy fire,
and to foretell the fortunes of the Mexicans who would
come to the lagoon in their schooner, to take away their
white wives, and go to Cape Gracias, to where gold was to
be got, and where no power could touch them.

Arthur Bolton felt his cheeks flush as he heard this intelligence.

"Then," said he, "there is no time to be lost."

"No, massa, no time; cause to-morrow night last night
of big drunk and the Sukia woman; they will den be all
drunk, de men and de womens."

Punka Bosswash said he would collect twenty braves,
all of their village—there was no time to send and collect
more—but that before they tried force they should endeavour to get the women out over the walls of the great
stone house.   Every one would be sure to be collected
round the Sukia, to see her defy fire, and tell fortunes,
and all were sure to be dead drunk after seeing her.   They
could easily lie concealed in the thick jungle at the back of
the village.

This plan our hero approved, and forthwith Punka
Bosswash proceeded to collect his twenty braves, and to
have ladders of twisted grass made.   The whole party was
to set out at sunset, so as to reach Quamwatta by sunset
the following night.

Our hero and Joe set about cleaning and preparing their
arms.   To Cato was given the carbine, and Joe took the
cook's pistol.

By sunset three canoes were ready, and all the women
of the village came to see them depart.   Achupa was presented by Arthur Bolton with the only ornament he possessed, and that was a handsome gold ring.   Dollars she
refused, shaking her head, but the ring she hung round
her neck, fastened to an Indian necklace, and bade our
hero farewell with a somewhat sad smile.

It was our hero's intention to seize the Mexican schooner,
and, putting Miss Marchmont and Mary Pearson on board,
to sail for Bluefields, Cato knowing the coast well.   Punka
Bosswash was armed with an English musket, and his
braves with bows and spears.

Proceeding down the Bosswash river, they arrived, just
as it became intensely dark, at the Rio Grande, and, crossing it to the eastward, stopped on the opposite shore for
the remainder of the night.   Fires were lighted to smoke

away their bitterest enemies, the mosquitoes; but the frightful noises, particularly those of the howling monkeys that infested the great forest, quite banished sleep from Arthur Bolton's eyes. Besides, he felt such deep interest in the fate of Alice Marchmont and her faithful Mary, dreading lest Saunders and his villanous associates should carry them off before they could reach the stone house.

At this period the rainy season, always accompanied by storms, was expected ; and when it does rain on the Musquito Coast, it is a ceaseless down-pour for days. Then swamp fevers rage with violence.

"No doubt," thought Arthur Bolton, "those ruffians, the Mexicans, will depart from this coast as soon as possible, for none but the natives have a chance of escaping the fever."

Thus he lay thinking through the hours of the night, the fires, notwithstanding the heat, being kept up to scare the mosquitoes. Of wild beasts there was no fear, being so near the sea-coast.

As soon as daylight appeared, the Indians prepared their food, and hauled up their canoes, as the rest of the journey was over land and through thick forests, so as not to cross any open country till they came to the borders of the lagoon on whose shores was the Sambo village of Quamwatta.

Punka Bosswash came and sat down by Arthur Bolton to smoke his pipe before starting. Our hero was making his breakfast off a fine fowl Joe had skilfully broiled.

"We shall reach the forest that backs the Sambo town of Quamwatta by sunset," said Punka Bosswash, in his peculiar, but easily understood English ; "and there we must lie hid till the great drink begins, for our force is small, and we should fail if we attacked them and the Mexican robbers before they all get drunk. You understand, my son."

"Yes, chief, I do," returned our hero. "I think only of the whites, those Mexican ruffiaus. The Sambos are great cowards ; twenty brave Woolwas would drive into flight the whole village."

"The Woolwas are brave," returned the chief thoughtfully, "but they are prudent and wise. If the maidens can be carried off without surprising or alarming the Sambos or the Mexicans, so much the better."

To this our hero agreed. "But should cunning not succeed, would the Woolwas fight to gain their object?" asked Arthur.

"The Woolwas die," said the chief, proudly; "they never run; so be satisfied, we will free the maidens or fall."

Arthur pressed the chief's hand, and having finished his pipe, Punka Bosswash rose up, stating it was time to commence the journey. In ten minutes the Indians were all ready for the march, and our hero and Joe followed. Their way lay through a dense forest without any visible track; nevertheless the Indians knew well the direction to take, cutting through many obstacles and keeping steadily in one direction.

The overgrown and entangled vegetation under the deep shade of the trees was to our hero wonderful to look at. Cato amused him by telling him various stories of the Sambos, of their brutal love of intoxication, and the frightful excesses they committed when drunk; but even Cato, though many years a cook on board British ships, was a firm believer in the sorceries of the "Sukia," or fire woman. "De talk," said he, "and stand in de middle of a big wood fire till de cloth de hab round de loins do crisp and cut up, and de Sukia no feel de fire one bit."

"Well, Cato, that will not prove the miserable pretender, or sorceress, to be a witch, or able to work miracles. We have showmen and conjurors in England who can do the same for the small charge of one shilling. They wash their hands and feet or the whole body in the juice of some plants, or with some chemical preparation which resists fire; and I have no doubt your sorceress, the Sukia, does the same."

"Ja, ja, massa," returned Cato; "dat not so, de Sukia tell what come to-morrow. Cure de sick of de fever."

"I thoroughly suspect, Cato, that the cures are very few compared to the deaths, for notwithstanding your famous Sukias the race of the Sambos is yearly becoming less numerous and more sickly and weak."

"Ah, ja, massa, de drink till all blue—dat kill more den de fever, and we are not far from de rivers, and den come de fevers—de rivers rise—ten, twelve feet, and no possible pass across the country."

"If we can manage to get possession of the schooner, we can reach Bluefields much sooner and much easier than over land, so that if the rains do come on, they will not retard or interrupt our journey. You and I and Joe can easily work the little schooner to Bluefields."

"Ja, massy, easily. If we got over de bar at mouth of lagoon—it very bad bar—full of rocks and banks. De guarda costa nigh lost dere one fine night; if bad, night, she sure go pieces."

Arthur felt uneasy ; this was a contingency he had not taken into consideration, for even if they got the captives to the shelter of the schooner, and afterwards ran aground on the bar, the Sambos would surely pursue them in canoes and patpans ; and if recaptured, he shuddered to think what might be their fate.   During the journey, though his mind was preoccupied, still he could not but observe the wild and at times singularly picturesque scenery they passed through ; with his gun he could have killed abundance of game ; amid the dense coverts of the jungle bounded the antelope and the deer.   Numbers of gibionite and the cani-paca or pig-rabbit, scampered over the savanna, and here and there that magnificent bird, the crested carrassow, walking with stately step, showing but little fear at the approach of man ; innumerable quails also invited the sportsman, so little afraid were they of an enemy.   Night and morning also the air was filled with cries of the chattering of parrots and macaws.   Our hero felt a great wish to bring down a carrassow, its plumage so beautiful and as large as a turkey ; the rich dark brown of its feathers, except on the neck, where the colours became ash, and the breast a reddish brown.

On leaving the forest, they came to a most magnificent savannah, though of limited extent, through which ran a shallow river ; along the bank of this river the scenery was exceedingly beautiful.   Giant cestas, the feathery palm, and the singular trunks of the matapato, so much resembling snakes as to startle the traveller ; round these, hundreds of beautiful plants bound their slender tendrils, and here and there in clumps of gorgeous colours—flowering with a splendour known only in tropical climes—the astonishing variety of acacias, the fine-leaved gum arabic, palmathos ; and, mixed with them, dark groups of pines ; and though all so various in their colours and shades, nature had grouped them so harmoniously, that no disorder appeared in the arrangement.

" What a lovely spot—and what scenery ! " thought Arthur Bolton ; " and yet what a deadly climate—death and beauty hand-in-hand ! "

During the day's journey they saw many snakes, some very large, but only one poisonous ; and one of the Indians narrowly escaped its bite ; stooping to pick up a branch under which was coiled what the Musquitoes called the *pinta sura*, poison-snake, it struck at him, but by great good fortune missed its aim—he then killed it. This snake was not more than twenty-six inches long, and

not thicker than a man's thumb, with a somewhat large
flat head.   The Indians consider it one of the most deadly
under the tropics.

It wanted an hour of sunset, when the party entered the
dense wood that extended to the back of the Quamwatta
village, and still at some distance.

Avoiding all possible tracks made by the Sambos, they
pushed their way through almost impenetrable masses of
jungle and underwood, till, just as it drew dark, the party
halted ; by this time the howling monkey had commenced
his nocturnal music, and the noise was deafening.

" Cuss des customers," said Cato, as he joined our hero ;
" de make de debbles noise."

" What is to be done now, Cato ? " demanded our hero,
as Punka Bosswash sat down and was surrounded by his
braves.

" You come wid me, massa, and I take you to a place
where you will see what's going on in the village ; you
will see where missy is kept shut up ; and when all get
well drunk, we will carry off missy to the schooner, if she
is there."

To this our hero eagerly agreed, and Punka Bosswash
and his braves, after a short consultation with Arthur
Bolton, also proceeded to a place where they could inspect
the proceedings in the village.   They had scarcely traversed half a mile towards their intended place of concealment, when the shouts and cries of the Sambo village
reached their ears.   Cato led the way ; and presently the
light from the fires flashed through the trees.

They then separated, and our hero, with Cato and Joe,
crept up so close to the village that they could distinctly
observe the faces of those collected in crowds, and yet
remain perfectly concealed in the thick growth of low
shrubs that covered a ridge of sand, about two hundred
yards from the waters of the lagoon, and scarcely six from
the scene of the festivities.

We may readily imagine the feelings of our hero, as,
lying flat upon the ground, he gazed out from the thick
cover upon the scene before him.   The village of Quamwatta consisted of an irregular row of miserable huts,
on a slightly rising ground above the broad lagoon.   A
great crowd of Sambo men, women, and children were
collected together in groups, and shouting, dancing, and
vociferating furiously, the whole scene lighted up by
numerous torches stuck in the ground, and here and
there great fires.   The stone house Arthur Bolton eagerly

looked for, and Cato pointed it out to him. It was some distance from the village, and close to the borders of the lagoon.

Cato, in a low voice, said, " The schooner is at anchor. I see de masts."

Our hero looked, and at length made out the little vessel some three-quarters of a mile below the stone building.

Cato then pointed out the canoe where the great drink, the mushla, was prepared. This beverage is composed of pine apples, plantains, cassava, and maize. These compounds, being bruised, are thrown into a canoe, water added, and then Indian corn masticated by the chiefs' wives and daughters, and the whole stirred up with a big stick or one of their canoe paddles, and then the assembled crowd surround the canoe with shouts and cries and extraordinary gestures and contortions and antics, and dipping in their cocoa-nuts, drink till the scene becomes too disgusting to describe.

As our hero watched anxiously what was going on, he beheld a party of Mexicans come out of a large hut; all had fire-arms, and as they passed on into the crowd of women, he distinctly recognized Will Saunders. The cries and shouts became loud and furious, as men and women began imbibing the contents of the canoe, the Mexicans joining and firing off their guns, to the frantic delight of the Sambo women, who commenced dancing. Presently a great fire was made ; and when it blazed up, a crowd of women came forth from a hut, surrounding a woman with no other covering than a narrow long cloth. The Mexicans, with Saunders, also joined the group, and all ranged themselves in rows on three sides of the fire. Cato touched our hero, saying, " The Sukia woman ; after her performance, they will all get frightfully drunk. We must then break into the stone house, and as soon as we can release the prisoners, get to the schooner ; the wind blows out of the lagoon, but the weather looks bad."

Bolton was so intent watching the proceedings before the hut that he paid no attention to the weather, which looked dark and lowering over head. As the Sukia woman approached the fire, the Mexicans and Will Saunders handed her something which she laid on the ground. She then calmly and quietly stepped into the midst of the flaming pile ; there was no deception. Arthur Bolton certainly beheld her with exceeding surprise. She was a tall thin woman, straight and erect, and as she stood unmoved, the flames darted up and, encircled her above the waist, and even to the head. She was perfectly nude save the thin torrison. She appeared like a statue till the blaze fell. She broke a bamboo staff, and from it took a large Tamagasa snake, which she grasped, went through some ceremonies, which our hero could not distinctly see, and finally trampling out the flames, she walked up to the Mexicans, and waving her arms in a strange manner, no doubt predicted their future destinies, whatever they might be. Then commenced a scene of drinking and abominable orgies, till men and women fell down drunk, shouting furiously and beating drums, whilst every available noise a brutal population could make rent the air.

"Now, massa, let us go," said Cato ; "we break into de house. De chief and his young men watch and keep de drunken Sambos away if they see us."

Disgusted and eager to release his beloved Alice from her miserable prison, Arthur sprang to his feet, and he and Joe, looking to see that their arms were all right, followed Cato through the wood ; Punka Bosswash saying he and his young men would keep between them and the village, and keep back the Sambos till they saw them embark in the schooner. One of his young men, Punka Bosswash observed, had examined the schooner from the shore, and there were only two men on board.

Keeping a bank of bushes between them and the shore of the lagoon, our hero and his two attendants reached to within fifty yards of the stone building, when the noise of oars in the water startled them, and they paused, crouching down behind the bushes ; the night was exceedingly dark, but the lights from the scene of festivity flashed against the high walls of the old stone house. It was necessary in approaching the prison of Alice Marchmont to be quick in their movements, for should any of the revellers happen to look in that direction, they could easily distinguish them. The fall of the oars came nearer, and at length they perceived the schooner's small boat with two Mexican sailors pulling, run ashore close to the house. Two men landed, threw a grapnell out to secure the boat, and then approached the door of the house and paused, and both spoke in their own language for some moments. One man moved on towards the village, the other hesitated, but at length joined his comrade, and both proceeded towards the scene of festivity.

"Ah, ja, dis very good," said Cato ; " dere boat for go board schooner "

" What did they say, Cato ? " questioned Arthur.

" One say, massa, to the oder, 'you go tell them drinking that the tide soon turn de much sea on bar.' De oder say, ' Come, comrade, we have half an hour's lark,' and de both go."

" Then we must lose no more time, Cato. It's a dark night, and we must pass the bar. Have you the rope-ladders, Joe ?"

" Yes, sir, I have them." Then stooping as low as possible, they passed across the open space and reached the door of the house. A short examination convinced them of the impossibility of forcing the iron-bound doors. Passing round the house, Arthur examined the wall where the roof was broken in, and taking the rope prepared for the purpose, with a small grapnell at the end, he threw it over the wall, the hooks caught, and then, proving the strength, Joe, being the lightest, quickly ascended, and hauling up the rope-ladder, made it securely fast to a rafter, and then his master, with a beating heart, followed.

The noise, slight as it was, evidently alarmed those below, for a faint cry of alarm reached his ears as he threw down the ladder. Arthur quickly descended, saying in a low, clear voice : " Miss Marchmont—Alice—beloved Alice, it is I—Arthur Bolton."

An exclamation of joy burst from the lips of the over-joyed girl, as she rushed towards the sound of his voice; in the impulse of the moment he clasped her to his heart with a feeling of love and devotion.

"Oh, Arthur?" she exclaimed, as Mary Pearson, weeping with emotion joined them, " this moment of joy repays me for all my sufferings ; and my beloved mother and sister ? "

" All well, thank God," said our hero, pressing the hand of poor Mary, who was beside herself with joy. " No time must be lost, Alice ; you must try and mount this ladder."

As he said the words, Joe called out from above, "Make haste, sir ; Cato says the Indians have given the alarm, and I see dark figures moving out from the crowd and coming this way.

Placing two heavy stones on the ropes to steady the slight ladder, Arthur Bolton ascended, taking the precaution to pass a rope round Alice's waist, so as to steady her, and in case of accident, should she slip. With a beating heart, but firm nerve, the young girl safely gained the top of the wall, followed by Mary Pearson, and then as quickly they gained the ground.

By this time a crowd of intoxicated Sambos, carrying torches, were rushing, screaming, and shouting towards the house ; the Mexicans and Sambos, dreadfully intoxicated, staggering after. They caught sight of the fugitives as they ran towards the beach. Arthur Bolton, carrying Alice in his arms, and Cato catching up Mary like an infant, they made way rapidly for the boat. Suddenly Punka Bosswash and his braves, with the true Indian war-cry, rushed upon the drunken Sambos, and in a minute the terrified wretches fled back to their huts ; but Saunders and half a dozen Mexicans broke through, and had reached within fifty yards of the fugitives, who were then close to the boat. Saunders and the Mexicans paused and fired, but providentially they were too drunk to aim accurately, and the balls rattled harmlessly by.

Placing Alice in the boat, Arthur seized his gun, and, singling out Saunders, fired. The ruffian fell on his knees, but with a yell he regained his feet and ran on. By this time the boat was afloat, and Cato and Joe pulling out into the lagoon. Fortunately, in their haste and drunkenness, the Mexicans had forgotten their ammunition. Punka Bosswash and his braves, seeing the boat afloat, and the enemy baffled, gave a loud whoop of triumph and disappeared in the woods.

CHAPTER XIX.

WE have said in the preceding chapter that the weather towards the decline of day looked lowering and threatening. In fact, the temporale was daily expected—a period of storms and tremendous rain, though of short duration.

So absorbed, however, were our adventurers in their projects that they paid little if any heed to the aspect of the heavens ; but scarcely had our hero succeeded in getting Alice Marchmont and Mary into the boat and pulled out from the shore, than they were startled by a flash of vivid lightning, instantly followed by one of those tropical peals of thunder that must be heard to be appreciated, for the crash over their heads was more like the uprooting of a world than a thunder peal, so terrible, so prolonged did it appear.

Alice trembled and hid her face in her hands ; the boat appeared to rock under them. Cato and Joe pulled manfully, whilst Arthur steered for the schooner, revealed to them distinctly by the continued flashes of lightning.

" Massa," said Cato, " dis berry bad. Wind gone. De cursed Mexicans run back for canoes to pursue us."

" Ah, Arthur, we shall be overtaken, and you will be slain ! " cried Alice, in terror.

" Have no fear, dearest," whispered our hero ; " lay your head on Mary's lap. She is a brave girl, with a stout heart. You are mine now, and only with life shall they separate us. This storm comes from the east, and the wind will rise. Ha ! the schooner—lay in your oars."

A flash revealed, at that moment, every object distinctly for a long way. Our hero saw the schooner ; and Cato and Joe beheld a dozen canoes in pursuit.

Scarcely were they alongside, and Alice and Mary placed on board, ere the storm gust came sweeping down the lagoon, forcing the water from the surface and scattering it in drifts over the vessel, almost blinding those aboard, and, although the thunder ceased, down came the rain, with continuous blaze of lightning of the deepest blue, playing, as it were, over the surface of the lagoon, lingering upon the iron work of the schooner, and rendering every object as distinct and visible as open day.

Placing Alice and her attendant in the shelter of the little cabin—Cato and Joe began to cast off the lashings of the foresail, and to heave up the anchor—but a flash of vivid lightning revealed to our hero a dozen canoes and patpans within fifty yards of them.

" Cut away the cable, Cato," Bolton shouted to the black, " Joe, run up the foresail—the canoes are close alongside."

Up went the foresail, and the schooner swung round with the fierce squall, just as a large patpan, full of Sambos and two or three Mexicans, ran against her, and were sunk. Two Mexicans made an effort to cling to the rigging, but our hero, with a blow on the head with the butt of Joe's carbine, dashed one into the boiling sea, while Cato, with a turtle spear, disposed of the other. Away flew the schooner, Cato steering, by calling out to our hero at the helm, " starboard; and then port," as they flew by some rock or bank, seen by the lightning flash ; the shrieks and cries of the baffled Sambos and Mexicans, as they strove to regain the shore in the ruffled waters, were drowned in the whistling of the blast through the rigging. Fortunately, the wind blew right out ; still it required all Cato's watchfulness and knowledge to avoid the rocks that lay scattered over the entrance into the lagoon. The rain came down in a deluge, beating the decks of the little schooner like hail-drops, and the furious blasts driving it with remorseless fury in the faces of the anxious crew. As they reached the bar, the great heave of the sea was felt, but, being partly off the land, the little vessel was able to bear the close-reefed canvas. The open sea gained, Arthur proposed to the black cook to heave her to for the night, on account of the numerous keys (reefs) that lay some distance off from the land and extending for a considerable distance all along the Musquito Coast.

Having no great deal of sea to contend against, the schooner lay-to very well. The lightning shortly after ceased, and the gale moderated; but the rain fell in one continued down-pour. Shut up in the little suffocating cabin, the odour of turtle shells, stock-fish, and half-decayed gourds and melons, with which the lockers were stuffed, Alice Marchmont and Mary were nearly fainting, when Arthur Bolton removed the hatch to give them air, as the sea no longer washed over them, and a tarpaulin to windward protected them from rain.

It was by this time near early dawn, and the clouds showed symptoms of breaking, for the temporale on that coast had intervals of quiet, though, in general, the storms followed one another rapidly.

As the dawn made, Arthur anxiously gazed into the pale features of his beloved Alice.

"You have suffered, dear Alice," he said, pressing her small hand tenderly; "suffered much, I fear."

"Yes, Arthur," said the young girl. "We have both suffered; but our bodily sufferings were nothing compared to our mental tortures. If you had not rescued us last night, I shudder to think what I might have been tempted to do; for we know that wretch Saunders and his associates intended putting us aboard this vessel, and sail for some part of the coast, where we should perish a miserable death, for live to endure such degradation as was threatened us would be impossible; but for Mary's tenderness and devotion I should have given way to despair."

"And to think, after all," said Mary Pearson bitterly, "that the miserable wretch, Saunders, should escape."

"His time will come, Mary; he will not escape the punishment due to his crimes, depend on it. I struck him when I fired, but did not wound him seriously, for he was up in pursuit a moment after."

"Now tell me of my beloved mother and sister," said Alice; "they must have suffered severely?"

"I have not seen them, dear Alice, since the day I boarded this schooner, for this is the same I swam to from the 'Foam.'"

"Good heavens! is it possible?" exclaimed Alice, surprised. "Where have you been, and how came you so blessedly to our rescue?"

Arthur Bolton told her all, briefly stating his own adventures. By this time it was broad daylight; the rain had ceased, but the weather looked wild and stormy, with a shifting wind.

Cato came aft, and proposed their running into the Punza Pulka, where the "Foam" was sure to be, especially as he said there was not a morsel of food there that missy could eat; and he looked, besides, for a gale from the westward, against which they could never work to Bluefields.

Though Alice, pale, exhausted, and really unwell, anxiously desired to reach Bluefields, to join her mother and sister; yet she saw the necessity of following Cato's advice, for it began to blow hard, and the sea to rise; so, close reefing their sails, they began working to windward, and having an ebb tide in their favour, they made the mouth of the Punza Pulka in three hours, and running in between the islands to smooth water, permitted Alice and her attendant to dispense with the hatches.

"Holly, golly! massa!" exclaimed Cato, "dare be the ship in the river — the guarda-costa, and an English schooner."

All aboard the little vessel turned their eyes in the direction of the "Foam," and to Arthur Bolton's great surprise he beheld the brig with jurymasts up, and her rigging and yards, though on a very small scale, nearly ready. Close beside her was a large schooner, with the long pennant streaming in the breeze, and at a short distance the Maria Gloriosa was at anchor.

"Ah!" said Alice Marchmont, with a slight tinge of her former colour in her cheeks, and her fine eyes sparkling with pleasure, "there is the dear old brig with its masts up. Who can they be in that English vessel? Who do you think, Arthur?"

"Most likely she is from Bluefields, and come to help the guarda-costa to take the brig to Jamaica."

"Oh, if dear Captain Courtney and the poor little steward were alive, we could almost forget what we have gone through."

Cato got ready an anchor and cable as they ran up towards the "Foam;" their vessel was already perceived, and many persons were looking over the bulwarks, both of the brig and schooner; running up close to the cutter, Cato hauled down the sails, and Joe let go the anchor.

The schooner's boat, with an officer in the stern-sheets, and a couple of seamen pulling, came alongside the turtle schooner. The officer, jumping aboard, looked with exceeding surprise at Miss Marchmont, and then at our hero—raising his hat, he said, politely saluting Alice—"Miss Marchmont, I presume?"

Alice bowed, and then turning to Arthur Bolton, he said—
" I suppose, sir, you are Mr. Bolton, who was passenger in
the 'Foam,' reported missing?" On our hero's replying in
the affirmative, he continued—" You have been fortunate in
rescuing Miss Marchmont. I am sure her father will be most
rejoiced at your success, on his return."

" My father !" exclaimed Alice, clasping her hands, " has
he been here ?"

" Yes, Miss Marchmont, he has. He and Captain Courtney
of the 'Foam.' "

Alice turned pale, and fell back against the hatchway, her
dark eyes fixed on Lieutenant Staunton with a look of utter
amazement—whilst our hero, though mystified, said—

" Can you mean Captain Courtney, who left England as
the Captain of the ' Foam,' and whom I saw thrown into the
sea by his cowardly and mutinous seamen ?"

" The same, Mr. Bolton," returned the lieutenant; " he
was singularly preserved, and is at this moment, with Mr.
Marchmont and a strong party, gone into the Sambo district
to hunt out those rascally Mexican deserters. How you
managed, with only that black and the young lad there, to
rescue Miss Marchmont, appears to me marvellous."

" Oh, I had the assistance of a party of Woolwa Indians,"
returned our hero ; " but, Miss Marchmont, you and Mary had
better get on board the 'Foam,' and occupy your old quarters
till your father returns ; you will find abundance of provisions."

" Anything Miss Marchmont or you may require," said
Lieutenant Staunton, " you are welcome to out of my stores."

" You are very kind, sir," said Alice ; " we will go at once."

By this time the captain of the guarda-costa had reached
the side of the turtle schooner, and was receiving all the particulars of their seizing the craft, &c., from Cato.

Alice and her attendant were then put aboard the " Foam,"
by the cutter's boat, and, after leaving the turtle schooner as
a prize to the Maria Gloriosa, Arthur followed, promising
Lieutenant Staunton to spend the evening with him.

Joe returned to the brig, and Cato, highly pleased, and
sure of being well rewarded by Mr. Marchmont, went back to
the Maria Gloriosa.

Alice Marchmont found everything untouched in her own
and sister's private cabin, for Mrs. Marchmont had purposely
left everything she thought she might want when rescued
from the miscreants who carried her off. She felt both weary
and worn out from the suffering of mind and body she had
endured, and the miserable treatment she had received. The
two or three days passed in the damp, dismal, and totally un-

furnished stone house, with only a scanty supply of dried grass to lie upon, and wretched food which she could scarcely bring herself to eat, was beginning to tell upon her constitution. Mary, more robust, and able to bear hardship, struggled against the suffering, aided by her ardent love for her young mistress.

Having made a cup of coffee, and obtained some slight refreshment, Mary persuaded Alice to retire to rest, saying, " One hour's rest with a mind free from care, would be worth all the sleep she had had from the period she left the 'Foam.' "

Alice's mind, however, was not free from care, or relieved from painful thought, though she knew her mother approved of her having bestowed her affection upon Arthur Bolton, and herself admired and esteemed the young man for the sterling qualities he possessed. She knew her mother secretly dreaded an explanation with Mr. Marchmont, for, though a most kind husband and father, she was aware that he was a proud man, and ambitious of seeing his daughters well married. Wealth was not his object. Himself a younger branch of a noble family, and master of great wealth, he meditated, on his return to England, to mate his daughters with men of rank and high birth. Alice and her mother knew our hero's history, and doing so, they both felt apprehensions that the meeting with Mr. Marchmont might cruelly dissolve the happy dreams of the young lovers.

Arthur, now that the excitement was over, also had his misgivings as to the reception he might meet with from Mr. Marchmont, when Alice would be restored to her father, principally through his courage and perseverance ; but would that alone reconcile the wealthy merchant to give his beautiful and accomplished daughter to a man not only without fortune, but worse, actually without a name he could conscientiously lay claim to.

To drive away unpleasant thoughts, having seen that Alice had all she required, and Mary having told him she had persuaded her to take some hours' repose, he took a look at those setting up the rigging of the brig ; they were most of them English sailors, brought for that purpose from Jamaica. Though jury rigged, and hastily put up, yet the " Foam " was beginning to look shipshape ; she had a quantity of stores in her, and plenty of new sails, which, with a couple of reefs in them, would suit the jury yards tolerably well. He then proceeded to board the English schooner to spend the evening with Lieutenant Staunton ; he felt so amazed at the escape of Captain Courtney, that he could scarcely think of anything else. The lieutenant received him very kindly, for he was rather curious to hear all the particulars of the mutiny aboard

the " Foam " and the abduction of Miss Marchmont.   He had
noticed the attachment of our hero and the fair Alice ; in fact,
he thought it could scarcely be otherwise, so fascinating and
lovely did the lady appear.

Our hero, as they sat enjoying their wine and cigars, frankly
told him all their adventures from the time they left England.

Lieutenant Staunton was surprised, and so intimate and
friendly did the two young men become, that they parted late
that night with a feeling of sincere friendship.

The following morning Alice and our hero met at breakfast.
As he pressed the fair hand held out to him, and gazed fondly
into the sweet, pale, thoughtful face, he said,—

" My own Alice, I fear you have suffered more than you
choose to say.   Oh ! that I had that villain, Saunders, in my
grasp ! "

" Better as it is, dear Arthur ; better, far, that the God he
has outraged should punish him, than his blood should be on
your hands.   I have been mercifully spared ; and though a
great sufferer, I have been providentially saved from greater
evils.   Let us think no more of the past, but look hopefully
to the future.   How miraculous was Captain Courtney's pre-
servation !   Does it not show, Arthur, that even in the most
apparently helpless and desperate situation there is a hand
to save ? "

" Your father, dear Alice, will no doubt return some time
to-day, for he will hear of your rescue, either from some of
the Woolwa Indians, or the Sambos of Quamwatta.   I see the
larder of the 'Foam' requires some little dainty to be added to
it. Lieut. Staunton says he will hasten the fitting out of the brig,
so as to take advantage of this high spring tide, and get over
the bar ; so I and Joseph will take the small boat, and go up
the river and kill you a few of the blue-winged teal.   Some
time ago you said you should like to have one of those beautiful macaws.   I will catch you one if I can."

"Oh do not go ashore any more on this coast, dear Arthur ;
who can tell who may be prowling about, watching us ? "

" Depend on it, dearest, the ruffians are all dispersed, and
far away by this time.   The news of a strong party in pursuit
of them is sure to have reached and induced them to fly into
the interior."

Still Alice begged him not to mind the macaw ; so, kissing
the fair hand held out to him, he promised to obey her wishes.
Lovers' promises should never be broken ; but we will not
anticipate.

On ascending on deck with his fowling-piece, he called
Joseph, and told him to get the small boat ready, as he was
going to shoot a few teal and duck.

" I would go with you, Bolton," said Lieutenant Staunton, joining him, " but I promised Captain Courtney to inspect and hurry the work aboard the brig. He did not like to let Mr. Marchmont go without his company. It is a fine day, but there will be another storm before twenty-fours are over. You will be back to dinner ? "

" Oh, yes ; I shall only knock over a few teal; they keep farther away, now the vessels are here, than they did; they soon learn to know an enemy."

" Will you take another hand with you ? " asked the lieutenant, as our hero and Joe pushed off.

" I thank you, no ; there's plenty to do aboard. We shall float up with the tide, and come back when it turns."

Alice, from the cabin window, watched her lover, till the bold jutting promontory, half a mile up, shut him out from her view.

" It is very strange, Mary," said our heroine to her attendant, " but I feel dreadfully nervous, seeing Mr. Bolton go up the river to-day ; I have such a horror of the miscreants we so blessedly escaped from, that I think they would sacrifice life to be revenged upon him."

" Indeed, Miss Alice, I feel equally nervous ; not that I think there can be the slightest risk to Mr. Bolton whilst he stays in the boat; but he might just as well have remained aboard the brig."

" Why, you see, Mary, he is anxious to get me a few birds, as he is aware that there is nothing but salt meat aboard, and he knows I do not like it ; but I trust our uneasiness may be nothing more than a feeling caused by our past sufferings."

Alice, nevertheless, continued uneasy, and watched the turning of the tide. Still no signs of her lover's return.

Lieutenant Staunton saw that Miss Marchmont was anxious, and, with much kindness and good taste, said, " I have no doubt Mr. Bolton has gone further up the river than he intended, hoping to meet Mr. Marchmont and his party." This Alice thought very probable.

Towards sunset two boats were seen descending the river, before a strong gale which had sprung up; Lieutenant Staunton knew they were those belonging to Mr. Marchmont and Captain Courtney.

" Here comes your father, Miss Marchmont, and Captain Courtney, and no doubt Mr. Bolton is with them," said the lieutenant, " for I see a small boat towing astern." But the sun was setting behind the forest-clad hill, and those in the boats were in the shade.

Alice had not seen her father for several years ; therefore, with an anxious beating heart, she hurried on deck. It was

still light enough, when the boats came alongside, for the keen
eyes of Alice Marchmont to perceive that amongst the party
Arthur Bolton was not ; she felt her heart sinking, and her
limbs trembling under' her. But her father sprang aboard,
and, clasping her in his arms, kissed her fondly ; but as he did
so, she heard Lieutenant Staunton say to Captain Courtney,
" Did not you meet Mr. Bolton? How came you with the
dingy ? "

" Arthur Bolton ! " repeated the captain. " No ! we came
across the dingy, bottom up."

Alice heard no more ; and when her father gently lifted her
head from his shoulder, he perceived, to his great astonishment, that she had fainted. In a moment Captain Courtney
guessed the cause ; he, however, said nothing. More than
one excitement he had no doubt had caused Miss Marchmont
to faint. The anxious father carried her below, consigning
her to the care of Mary Pearson, who placed her on the sofa
in her own cabin.

In the mean time much alarm was felt by Captain Courtney
and Lieutenant Staunton.

" Where did you find the dingy, Captain Courtney? "
anxiously inquired Lieutenant Staunton. " It is now getting
dark, and there is every appearance of a heavy gale, for
already the gusts are violent."

" We picked up the boat, bottom up," said Captain Courtney. " I knew the dingy was yours, but I had no idea that
any one had been using it. We imagined it had got adrift
from you, and had been upset somehow. It's being upset does
not alarm me as to my young friend, Mr. Bolton, being
drowned ; he is a most splendid swimmer, and Joe, the lad, swims
well. We did not look ashore, for we saw this storm brewing, and pulled vigorously back. My idea is, they have
landed to shoot something, and the boat got adrift and upset.
By Jove ! it is beginning to blow tremendously, and the brig
will float next tide."

" I would send a boat up along the opposite shore," said
Lieutenant Staunton, " but no boat could make head-way
against this tide and gale, which looks as if it would increase
to a hurricane."

And so it did ; before twelve o'clock that night a furious
tempest raged from the north-west, and the night was intensely dark. So tremendously did it blow, that when the
brig floated she was carried two miles below where she first
ran a-ground, and with great difficulty was brought up ; the
guarda-costa was driven ashore, and the English schooner
narrowly escaped the same disaster.

When morning dawned, the gale continued so severe that

no boat could make head against such wind and sea. As the bar had barely sufficient water for the brig to float over, should the wind continue in the same point and the spring tides falling, Captain Courtney resolved to put to sea at once, the brig being quite ready. He would stand along the coast, he said, and anchor off Bluefields. The guarda-costa was got off and put to sea, and, deeply as it grieved him, Lieutenant Staunton was forced by his orders to keep with the brig; but Captain Courtney and Mr. Marchmont resolved to send out persons from Bluefields to traverse the country and endeavour to trace out the fate of Arthur Bolton and the boy Joseph.

CHAPTER XX.

WE have stated in one of our previous chapters that Sir Richard Morton's intention was to proceed to New York. He accordingly embarked, and after a tolerable passage of fourteen days, reached that city. Too anxious and too intent on accomplishing the object of his voyage to trouble himself with sight-seeing, the following day he was on his way to Williamsburg, having disguised himself in the simple garb of a working artisan looking out for a place to settle in. He then proceeded to Delaware, and took up his abode at a small inn. The town, built upon the broad peninsula, formed by the confluence of the Pamunky and Mattapone Rivers, which, however, at this point are called the " York River," was a place of considerable size and importance ; it would therefore not be very easy to discover where such a man as John Mason was located, and such Sir Richard found to be the case, and for several days he was baffled. Mason did not dwell in the town, of that he was soon convinced. At last he learned from a farrier, who chanced to put up with half-a-dozen horses at the same inn, that there was a man of the name of Mason, who farmed a tract of land—swampy land it was for the most part—on the banks of the Mattapone River, some fifteen miles from Delaware, and dealt largely in horses, the farrier said.

" Was he a man much liked by those who knew him? " questioned the disguised baronet.

" Well, for my part," said the farrier, " I can only say what I hear, as I don't live nigh enough to him ; I only goes for a spell at odd seasons. They do say as how they are a hard family to do with. When they came to these here parts, there was the father, mother, three sons, and two daughters. Two of the sons were very young, and so was one daughter. The eldest daughter was married——"

" Married!" interrupted the baronet, with a start, and a flush overspreading his face, which attracted the notice of the farrier, who was drinking some mint julep at the baronet's expense.

" I guess, friend, you be interested in these Masons—or an old sweetheart of the girl's perhaps."

" Yes, friend, I am," returned Sir Richard, in considerable emotion, "though not the girl's sweetheart. I knew the Masons before they came to this country, therefore I am anxious to know how they get on. I intend going to see them."

" Well, friend," returned the man, "I'm of the old country; though twenty years knocking about these here parts has made almost a native of me. I'm going to-morrow, or the day next, within five miles of Mason's farm, and can give ye a lift to the Fork; and there's a rough road from there right away through the swamp to his house."

To this the baronet agreed with many thanks; he felt as if a might weight was taken off his mind. If Mason's daughter was married, it was clearly evident that the whole confession of Jay Pearson was a fabrication.

It then occurred to Sir Richard that it would be desirable to make inquiries whether the names of the two witnesses attached to the confession were in existence, or whether they ever existed.

After half an hour's thought, he determined to consult a professional man.

Having made inquiries, he heard of a gentleman of the name of Bowen, a Welshman, who bore an exceedingly good character, and who for five and twenty years had practised his profession of attorney in Delaware, and with considerable success. Having changed his clothes, he proceeded to Mr. Bowen's residence, and had an interview with that gentleman.

Mr. Bowen was an elderly man, with very agreeable manners.

On requesting to know how he could serve his visitor, Sir Richard at once stated who he was, and that he had come from England for the express purpose of making inquiries concerning a family who had left England in the year 184—, and had settled either in Delaware or its vicinity.

Mr. Bowen was a shrewd man of business; the title and distinguished appearance of his visitor induced him to pay special attention. He therefore replied: "Most probably he could give him the information he required, as he kept a record of events, and also a book of reference, respecting every settler from the mother country who visited and took up their residence in Delaware or its immediate vicinity."

" The persons I seek are named Mason,—John Mason, the father."

"Dear me," interrupted the attorney, "I know the family quite well; they occupy a farm called the Fork, upon the banks of the Potomy. They arrived—let me see,"—and he took down a large folio with the date 184— on the back, and opened it. After turning over some pages, he read out: "John Mason and family—wife, three sons, and two daughters; wife since dead; aged about forty-eight or forty-nine."

"That's the family," interrupted Sir Richard. "Are the two daughters unmarried?"

"Well, I can tell you all about them, Sir Richard; but regret that I cannot say anything in their favour. The two sons are wild and fierce fellows, addicted to drinking and hunting more than farming. The old man breeds a good number of horses on the rich flats; but his eldest daughter made a bad match of it, having married one Jackson, a notorious horse-lifter, who was shot three years ago by the men of Maryland; and since that the old man has got into a pretty fix; he has to pay penalties of nearly £1,000, and besides, he has not paid the £1,000 due for the purchase of the meadows he holds; the interest of which he is even unable to pay. Now, you see, Sir Richard, I am employed by the owner of the land, and he has ordered me to sue for the penalties, and the fact is he will be turned out neck and crop, unless £2,000 be forthcoming before the end of September."

The baronet listened attentively and eagerly; he felt assured that all the papers he possessed were forgeries, except the marriage certificate, and that, in fact, his first wife died in childbirth, and that by some means they had contrived to deceive Jay Pearson.

"Pray, Mr. Bowen," said the baronet, "did you ever hear of a person called John Jay Pearson?"

"Yes, Sir Richard, I have; there was a person of that name came here some two or three years back in great distress and miserably ill; he, too, was inquiring for the Mason family, and John Mason assisted him; but who, or what he was, I cannot say. He died here shortly after his arrival."

The baronet remained thoughtful for a minute, and then said: "Now, Mr. Bowen, if you can spare one day so as to give me your undivided attention and advice, I will become your debtor for fifty pounds for that day, and any further business that may consequently arise shall be liberally settled for."

"You are very kind, Sir Richard," returned the solicitor; "I can only say that I will be at your service whenever you wish, and with great pleasure assist you to the utmost of my ability in unravelling any intricate matter that requires one experienced in the law to elucidate."

" Then I will make you acquainted with every particular," said the baronet, and he did so, and Mr. Bowen became perfectly well informed upon the subject of Sir Richard's first and second marriage.   He also placed in the attorney's hands several papers, amongst them Jay Pearson's confession.

Mr. Bowen read the latter document carefully.   When finished, he looked up into Sir Richard's face, saying: " This confession, Sir Richard, though exceedingly well got up, is, in my opinion, all false ; nevertheless, exceedingly likely to deceive you ; my opinion is, that Jay Pearson himself was also deceived.   May I ask you if John Mason's daughter was any way like Miss Grace Manning ? "

" Yes," returned the baronet thoughtfully, " remarkably alike when not seen together."

" Ah!" returned Mr. Bowen, " I think I see how Jay Pearson came to be deceived, especially in his then weak state, so near death, when he could scarcely be able distinctly to remark the features of the female introduced to him.   As to the signatures, they may be those of any rascals John Mason could pick up for a quart of whisky.   It can be easily proved that John Mason's daughter married Joe Jackson, who, as I told you, was shot, and the widow is at present with her father at Fork Farm.   They are a bad lot, Sir Richard, but their machinations against you, though artfully contrived, are utterly worthless."

" Well, Mr. Bowen, I am of the same opinion as yourself; still, I must have full confirmation, and not only that, but I must have it from John Mason's own hand, that the whole is a deception.   Miss Manning, my first wife, was a most amiable girl.   Her son, of course, becomes my son and heir— Lady Morton is quite reconciled to that.   The terrible blow we both apprehended, and which would have broken our peace of mind for ever in this world, once removed, we shall indeed gratefully acknowledge the goodness of Providence for the mercy we received.   Will you, therefore, accompany me, to-morrow, to Fork Farm—and be a witness to my interview with John Mason ? "

" Most certainly, Sir Richard, I will do so ; and take my chief clerk with us.   There can be no deception practised now—you will see the daughter, said to be buried, instead of your first wife—and that alone will put an end to all doubt or uncertainty."

Sir Richard then arranged to start for Fork Farm at ten o'clock on the following morning, Mr. Bowen promising that his waggon, drawn by two stout horses, should be ready at that hour ; so, shaking hands with the worthy attorney, Sir Richard returned to his inn, and sent for the farrier, who had so kindly offered him one of his horses to ride to the Fork. The man looked greatly surprised at his change of dress ; but Sir Richard, giving him a couple of dollars, told him he was going with a gentleman, on the morrow, in his waggon ; but was equally obliged to him for his offer of a horse.

The next morning, a very light, handy, spring waggon, with a cover, and drawn by a pair of handsome iron grey horses, drew up to the inn-door. Mr. Bowen was seated in it, with his clerk. The baronet soon joined them.

Two hours' drive over a very tolerable road, and through a well-cultivated and picturesque country, brought them within sight of Fork Farm. It was so called from lying near a fork of the river. The house appeared a good substantial house of one story, and surrounded by several outbuildings. The broad river ran within half a mile of the house. The land along the banks of the river was low and swampy ; but by the house, and for a mile or two to the westward, it appeared a dead level, and nearly all pasture land. There was a by-road, more than a mile long, leading up to the house ; this was in a wretched state of repair, and threatened every moment to smash the light waggon, being formed of trunks of trees, with great spaces between.

When within five hundred yards of the farmyard, they met two young men, with guns in their hands, and half a dozen fierce-looking dogs, coming towards them.

" Ah," said Mr. Bowen, " John Mason's two sons."

ʰ They came up to the waggon, keeping away the dogs, who seemed greatly inclined to attack the horses in the waggon.

" Holloa, neighbour ! " said one of the young men, a strapping youth over six feet, and not more than twenty-two or twenty-three years of age. " I guess you're trying your springs rather hard. You had better walk to the house, if it's there you're going, for the next two hundred yards the timber is taken up ; we're making a new road."

" And, I hope, a better one, Mr. William," said the attorney, who had some misgiving about his springs.

Mr William raised himself up on the shafts, and looked in.

" Ah," said he, in rather a surly tone, " it's you, Charles Bowen. I guess father don't require visits from chaps of your kidney. Who's the stranger with you ? " and both young men, very unceremoniously, got up and sat on the side of the waggon, looking with a bold stare into Sir Richard's face.

" This gentleman is from England," said the attorney, motioning with his hand to Sir Richard, who was looking earnestly into the faces of the two young men, of whom he had not the slightest recollection, for they were mere boys when their father left England.

" I guess my father don't want to see any gentleman from the old country. What's your business, stranger ?" added the eldest of the two, looking the baronet fixedly in the face.

" That I shall tell John Mason when I see him," quietly replied Sir Richard, rising up, and turning to address the attorney :—

" Mr. Bowen, I think we may walk the rest of the way."

He was preparing to get out, when the young men said, with a laugh :

" I calculate you had not better step down; those dogs of ours may like the least taste in the world of your hide—they ain't particular."

" Then, sir, get down and call them away," said the baronet haughtily. " I must see your father."

" There's no must in the case," returned the young man named William, doggedly. " What's your name—I guess you've a name ?"

" Come, this is trifling," said the baronet. " My name is Morton—Sir Richard Morton, of Morton Chase. You remember those names, young as you were when you left England. I cannot say that your manners are improved—your courtesy certainly not."

The two young men looked entirely confounded—staring with open mouth, and a bewildered look at the baronet, who was eyeing the six huge dogs sitting on their haunches, glaring up at the waggon, evidently eager for some pretence to commence hostilities.

Mr. Bowen looked rather startled. As to the clerk, there was no mistake in his appearance, for he never took his eyes off the dogs.

" You had better drive on, James," said Mr. Bowen, to the driver ; " the waggon will stand worse than this—I've tried it."

The two young men jumped down without a word, and, calling the dogs, walked rapidly towards the house, with their guns on their shoulders.

" Drive on," said Sir Richard eagerly, to the driver ; " if we break, down I will pay for a dozen waggons sooner than not get to the house as soon as those uncouth youngsters."

James gave the horses the reins, and a touch of the whip ; away they went, bumping the waggon over the trunks of trees, and making the passengers stand up and grasp the sides; but, nevertheless, they entered the large farm-yard at the same time as the two Masons. Coming out from the house, hearing the noise and the barking of the dogs, an old man and two women were seen ; the eldest of the two looked up surprised, at observing the waggon, and at the excited manner of the two young Masons, who called out :

" Go in, d—— you—go in, and shut the door !"

It was too late. Sir Richard, who was standing up in front of the waggon, had fixed his eager glance on the women ; the moment the elder female looked up, he called out :

" Thank God ! there is Eliza Mason alive and well !" and at once jumped out ; and, before any one could prevent him, or understand his motives, he caught the old man, standing at the door looking bewildered, by the arm, saying—

" John Mason, you cannot but remember me ; I am Sir Richard Morton."

As he spoke, two of the fierce dogs, seeing him grasp their master rushed furiously towards him, but the youngest daughter drove them off, the two younger Masons leaning on their guns, with a fierce troubled expression on their countenances. Two or three farm men had also come out from a large barn.

John Mason, a strong man, still hale at sixty-five, trembled in every limb, as he heard Sir Richard declare his name ; but he recollected him at the same moment. This fear only lasted a moment ; the colour rushed back to his cheeks, and, releasing his arm, he stepped back, saying, in a firm voice, " Well, Sir Richard—suppose I am John Mason ? I am in a free country, and have committed no crime against its laws."

The two females drew near their father, both gazing fixedly and most anxiously into Sir Richard's face.

" I do not accuse you, John Mason," said Sir Richard, calmly, " of anything of the kind ; let us go in. I wish to do nothing against you, whatever, although," he added, lowering his voice, so that only John Mason heard his words, " your son attempted to murder me, and left me for weeks hovering between life and death."

John Mason staggered back, pale as death, saying, " And George—he is "—the rest of the words stuck in his throat.

" He has escaped as yet," returned the baronet, " but I know nothing of him ; he stabbed me, and robbed me of five hundred pounds I intended for him ;—but come in—I again say I mean you no harm."

Then, turning to the eldest of the females, who looked very sullen, he said, " Come in with us, Mrs. Jackson, I am, you may well judge why, very happy to see you alive and well."

Mrs. Jackson's eyes flashed. She was still a very fine handsome woman of forty ; but neither her manners nor her morals had improved since her departure from England and her marriage with a notorious horse-lifter.

As she turned away and joined her two brothers, she said, with intense bitterness, " You may live yet to regret that I am alive."

"I hope not, Mrs. Jackson," returned the baronet calmly. "I mean you no ill, nor any one present." He then walked into the house, followed by Mr. Bowen and his clerk. The latter would have given a week's salary to have been back again in Delaware.

John Mason walked sullenly into a large room, evidently the great kitchen and sitting room of the family.

"Well, sir," said John Mason, as the baronet seated himself on a bench, "what do you expect to gain by this visit? You see that my daughter lives, and I suppose that satisfies your conscience."

"No," said the baronet sadly; for, as he looked into John Mason's features, the memory of the past came vividly before him, and, alas! the past had many cruel memories in it.

"I am, however," continued Sir Richard, "so far satisfied, for now I feel a great relief, being saved from committing a great wrong."

"Aigh, aigh!" fiercely broke in John Mason. "No doubt; no doubt you thought in your youth nothing of destroying a poor orphan girl. Knowing that you had me in your power, you artfully induced me to second your wicked designs. I pretended to aid you, but nevertheless I baffled you."

"Then, why, John Mason," sternly interrupted the baronet, "knowing that Grace Manning was truly my wife, did you not at once say so, and save me, twelve months after, from deserting my child?"

"I did not tell you," returned John Mason fiercely, "because Jay Pearson was as great a rascal as any in England. I took your child and put it where I knew it would be taken care of, whilst I continued my search and inquiries after Jay Pearson, who disappeared after what you supposed to be a mock ceremony. I afterwards informed your sister who the father of the child was. Had its mother lived, my plans would have been very different. But all this is useless talk. You have certainly defeated my son's project. But why he should attempt your life, is to me a mystery. What was it for?"

"Because," returned the baronet, "I attempted to take the papers he said he possessed, from him; and here they are," he continued, taking Jay Pearson's confession and others from his vest. "In the struggle we had, he dropped them on the floor, then stabbed me, and also robbed me of the very five hundred pounds I had on my library table, and which were intended for him."

"Ah!" said the old man, bitterly, "he only stabbed you in self-defence. I know he never intended to hurt a hair of your head. You only reaped what you sowed."

"Come, John Mason," said Sir Richard, "cease this bit-

terness ; let the past be, alas ! not forgotten, but let it be
looked upon with regret and repentance. My youth has been
one of sin and sorrow. On a bed of suffering for weeks, I
learned to look upon upon the errors of my youth with intense sorrow and regret, and vowed, if God spared me, to
atone for the evil I had committed.

" I did not come here to reproach you, for we are equally
guilty. I came to assure myself that I was spared the commission of a second crime, and that the remainder of my life
might not be embittered by beholding the tears and sorrows
of an amiable woman and her innocent offspring. Thank God,
from that I am spared : and now listen to me, John Mason,—
it is in my power to make you some atonement for the past.
You are in difficulties ; you will lose your lands if you do not
pay two thousand pounds before next September."

John Mason looked eagerly into Sir Richard Morton's features ; as he ended, he said, " I am involved. I became
liable to a thousand pounds penalty, from my son-in-law's acts ;
and the purchase-money for the best part of this farm is
unpaid. We shall be driven out of house and land, if these
debts remain unpaid in two months. I have no right to expect
help from you, Sir Richard, that I well know."

" Never mind that now," said the baronet ; " we have both
erred ;" and taking out his pocket-book, he took from it a blank
cheque upon a New York Bank ; looking for pen and ink, he
filled it up for three thousand pounds, saying, " I lodged this
money in the bank at New York, in case this important affair
ended amicably, which I now hope it will. I forgive the past ;
do you the same, John Mason, and accept this, it will release
you from your difficulties and leave you a thousand pounds
for future use." And the baronet handed the cheque to the
amazed and overpowered old man ; for several moments he
appeared unable to speak, his hand trembled as it held the
paper, which he put at once into a pocket-book, and the muscles
of his face worked with some internal emotion he strove to
conquer.

" But if my misguided son," said John Mason, " is
taken——"

" I will not appear against him," said the baronet. " The
accusation against him for making away with my son, which
he did, according to my wishes, though he carried that project out quite contrary to my instructions, I can easily stop.
My son is by this time in Jamaica. I shall write immediately
for his return, and establish his rights. All I ask of you is to
permit this gentleman, Mr. Bowen, who is acquainted with all
the particulars, to draw up the necessary papers to establish
his claims, and proofs of his birth and his mother's mar-

riage and death; and should your son George escape out of England, which I expect he has by this time, that you will exert your influence and prevent his ever returning there."

John Mason, relieved from a state of destitution, for Mr. Bowen had told him that the entire family would be expelled the farm, felt eager to perform every wish of the baronet's; in fact, he strove all in his power to show that he could be grateful. He sent for his two sons, but they had left the farm, and so had Mrs. Jackson, and gone, the workmen said, in their light waggon to the Fork, where they had some storehouses. However, Mr. Bowen and his clerk, delighted at the change of affairs, and being provided with materials, drew up every necessary paper to fulfil Sir Richard's wishes. These were only rough drafts. The old man engaged to come the next day to the attorney's office and sign the proper documents before responsible witnesses. The youngest daughter, Emily, a very pretty and interesting young woman, busied herself eagerly in putting the best refreshments the house afforded in a small parlour off the kitchen. The horses were taken out of the waggon and fed, and the utmost harmony apparently prevailed.

Sir Richard, whilst Mr. Bowen and his clerk were employed in the little parlour, had a long and serious conversation with his former steward. It appeared by this conversation that much of the plotting and scheming of the Mason family were concocted by the sons, George Mason especially.

The baronet having settled and arranged everything to his entire satisfaction, and Mr. Bowen having finished his labours, they prepared to return to Delaware. John Mason appeared to have regained heart and spirits; the prospect of freeing his farm and himself from the clutches of his creditors, without further plotting or crime, seemed to give him new life.

Thus all parted, exceedingly well pleased the one with the other. The baronet released from a load of bitter reflections, and with a sincere feeling of repentance for his past errors, and firmly resolved to do his duty by his first-born, no matter how trying the ordeal he would have to go through.

It was late that night when Sir Richard and his solicitor reached Delaware; the next morning he moved with his luggage into the best hotel the town afforded.

CHAPTER XXI.

JOHN MASON was punctual to time and place, and faithfully performed his part of the contract. Mr. Bowen drew up all the necessary documents to substantiate the baronet's first marriage and the birth of his son, by his first wife, had them witnessed by three highly respectable citizens and a magistrate, and then John Mason, after taking leave of Sir Richard with a good deal of apparent emotion on his part, returned to his farm.

Three days more completed the baronet's business, and settling with Mr. Bowen in a most munificent manner, he set out for Williamsburg, on his return to Europe, a happier and better man than when he left its shores.

At this period there were no railroads from Delaware to Williamsburg, only a kind of stage waggon that carried some fifteen or eighteen persons of all grades, seated promiscuously in this conveyance, which was covered with a canvas awning, and drawn by four active horses.

As Sir Richard had suffered considerably in this conveyance on reaching Delaware, he resolved to travel as far as Williamsburg on a hired horse, with a guide also mounted, his luggage being forwarded by the waggon.

The country for miles after leaving the town of Delaware was a most uninteresting flat, with here and there some very well-cultivated lands. About eight miles from Delaware the road takes a bend in the direction of Fork Farm, and enters a thick forest with a wide good road through it, formed of trunks of trees, covered with gravel. Sir Richard, as he rode along, became deeply immersed in thought ; he heeded very little either the road or the scenery around it. His guide, who was riding some fifty or sixty yards in advance, was suddenly startled by the sharp report of a rifle in his rear ; turning round, to his horror and dismay, he beheld Sir Richard Morton fall senseless from his horse, and lie motionless upon the road. For a moment he was incapable of motion ; when another report, and the whizzing of a ball close to his head, so startled the lad, that digging his spurs into his horse, he galloped without pulling in for two miles, and then stopped before a small public-house, where horse travellers often stopped to refresh their steeds.

The ill-fated Sir Richard Morton lay dead upon the road, on his back—the ball had pierced his heart.

No sooner had the guide disappeared than two men attired in waggoners' frocks and leather leggings, their faces concealed in the folds of thick handkerchiefs, came hastily forth from the thick belt of trees, and after a keen scrutiny all round, they approached the dead body of the baronet, and one kneeling down commenced searching all the pockets ; but swearing a terrible oath, he said to his companion,—

" Baulked by ——, not a paper of any kind in his pockets."

"Curse it! then we have killed him for nothing. Let us go; we have had our revenge, at all events."

The other ruffian stamped upon the ground in a savage passion, saying,—

"I cannot understand it. What can he have done with them? He told Bowen—my father heard him say it—that no inducement would cause him to put them from his person till he reaches England, and I'm —— if there's a paper to be found."

"Then, as I said, we have killed him for nothing."

"Curse it! this is a bad job," returned the other; "but take all the valuables and cash he has, and let us be off; the waggon from Williamsburg will be here in an hour or so."

Having completely rifled the baronet's pockets, the two men retreated into the wood, took up their rifles from behind a tree, and walked at a rapid pace for nearly a mile through the wood, till they came to a spot where two strong and handsome horses might be seen fastened by pegs to the ground. Without losing a moment, the two men mounted, and rode off at a rapid pace.

This cold-blooded and brutal murder was committed in broad daylight, on the main road between Delaware and Williamsburg. The two murderers rode across the country till they came to a road framed with timber, close beside a river; along this they continued, travelling very leisurely and conversing. These heartless villains were the sons of John Mason, of Fork Farm, and their vile and ungrateful father was an accomplice in the fearful act they had committed.

"There will no doubt be a rigid inquiry as to who killed the baronet," said Charles Mason to his brother William.

"Not a bit of it," returned the other; "and if there is, our plan is so well arranged that I defy detection; but curse it, where are the papers? What we have got is not worth fifty pounds; whereas, the papers would have been worth five thousand to that Arthur Bolton, who is the baronet's real heir, for without them he cannot claim either the estates or the title."

"It is a bad job, killing him," returned the other brother rather moodily. "Now there's nothing to be had for the job, I wish I had never listened to our sister's vindictive hatred of Sir Richard."

"To the devil with your qualms of conscience!" returned the elder brother—the one who fired the shot. "He has only got what he richly deserved. Didn't he wrong our family in every way—didn't he try to deceive our sister and afterwards our cousin by a false marriage? He made father his tool, and intended to cast us all off, his rightful relations, with a pitiful present of £3,000—that barely clears the Fork

Farm of its incumbrances—and then there's our brother's
life in jeopardy in England through him. Curse me, if I
regret killing him; the loss of the papers maddens me.
Confound his cunning, what could he have done with them?
Not surely sent them with his baggage to Williamsburg again.
Why did he change his place of embarcation? Why did
he not return to New York?"

"I should not wonder if that Welsh rascal Bowen put him
up to some dodge about those papers. I should like to put a
bullet through that Taffy's head," said the younger brother
savagely; "he holds the bonds against Fork Farm. First opportunity I get, he shall have one—but here's the ford—get down
and unbridle our beasts and turn them across the river into
Patten's Farm, and we can come back for them in a day or two."

The two men alighted, took off the horses' bridles—saddles
they had none—and putting the horses into the river, they
drove them across into a range of low-lying meadows, where
numerous cattle were grazing. The whole of this tract of
country was, at this period, very thinly inhabited, the farms
few and far between.   They were then only three miles from
Fork Farm, but they remained under shelter of a thick wood,
for it began to rain heavily, till quite dusk; they then crossed
the country into their own land, and gained the house without
being seen by any of the farm servants of the place, who
always retired to rest with the cessation of daylight.

The old man and the eldest daughter, Mrs. Jackson, were
the only persons up in the house. They were sitting in the
great kitchen, the old man drinking repeated tumblers of
strong whisky toddy, the daughter helping herself to a share.

"They are very late," said the old man, who, notwithstanding his potations, looked very pale and agitated; he was not
an habitual drinker, but this night he drank hard. "I wish
we hadn't agreed to do this terrible deed."

And he trembled, and rocked himself in his chair.

"Pshaw! you've grown a coward, father," said Mrs. Jackson scornfully. "You forget our wrongs. I don't believe
him, that my brother has escaped. Did he not," she
savagely continued, "deceive me? he tried to make me his
mistress till he saw Grace Manning, and then he scorned me.
I don't forget—hark!"

And she paused.

As the father and daughter listened, they heard a slight
noise at the back of the house, and then a key turn softly in
a lock.

"Ah!" she exclaimed, "they are come back."

And even she turned pale; but thoroughly contaminated by
her marriage with a desperate horse-stealer, she soon reco-

covered herself, and proceeded to the back kitchen to open the inner door.

None of the male farm servants slept in the house, but were located in a large building at the further end of the farmyard Two female servants, however, slept in the house with the family, in the east end, for it was a very long building.

Emily Mason, the youngest daughter, in every way totally different from the rest of the members of that terrible family, had retired, as was her custom, early to rest.

It will be here necessary to state that a farm adjoining the Fork Farm, but separated by the river, was occupied by a man of the name of Patten. This man was a suitor for the hand of Emily Mason, but being of a somewhat doubtful character, Emily did not very much favour his suit; her brothers hated him, for it was owing to him that Mrs. Jackson's husband was detected in one of his horse-lifting expeditions, and frequent fights and disputes took place between him and the brothers. Luke Patten was to all appearance well to do in the world, and held a very large farm.

When Mason got into trouble, Patten resumed his offer of taking Emily for a wife, and besides offered to help her father in clearing the Fork Farm. The old man was willing enough, and even partly succeeded in persuading Emily to listen to his proposals, when a violent dispute occurred between the brothers and Luke Patten, about a piece of land, and a fight took place, in which Luke Patten was the victor, and then a deadly hatred between the families took place, and all intercourse ceased. Such was the state of affairs at the time of Sir Richard Morton's visit to Fork Farm.

Mrs. Jackson having admitted her brothers, they threw off their soaked over-garments, and followed their sister in a very sulky savage humour into the kitchen.

The old man looked up, saying, in a tremulous voice,—

" Have you the papers ? "

" No ; curse it!" fiercely exclaimed William Mason, " we shot him dead ; but he had no papers about his person."

" Good Heaven !" stammered out the old man, and his hands fell powerless upon the table. " Ah," he muttered, " another crime, and no use. So he's dead ? "

And he looked up into his eldest son's face, who was helping himself to a horn of whisky in its pure state.

" Yes," he returned, putting down the horn, " dead enough."

" But how was it that you lost the papers—the papers were what you did this—this——"

" Murder for," said the son savagely, seeing his father pale and trembling.

"William, William, why do you use that word," said John Mason, shaking as if in an ague. "I am sure he had the papers concealed on his person. Did you search every part of his clothing?"

"I tried every pocket, and the linings in the breast of his coat, and his great coat, and took all he possessed, that it may be thought he was robbed for his cash and watch, for his is not the first robbery and murder that has been committed on that road."

"Did you try or feel the back of his coat?" asked the old man, with a sudden start, and grasping William Mason by the arm, and gasping almost for breath.

"Feel the back of his coat," repeated the son, with a slight change of colour, "what the deuce makes you think of that?"

"Then you did not?" said the old man, with a groan. "What a forgetful old fool I am! I now remember Sir Richard" (he shuddered, as he pronounced the name) "said 'he would have a double lining put to his coat, and the back was the best place, as the papers would be flat.' Oh, fool that I was not to recollect the observation!"

William and Charles Mason looked at each other, uttering a savage oath at their own stupidity in not turning the body of the baronet round, for he lay on his back in the middle of the road, and they contented themselves with trying all the pockets, and ripping open the lining of the breasts of the two coats. The back being an unusual repository, and the body pressing heavily on the garments, they observed nothing to attract their attention.

"Well, there's no use cursing and fretting about the matter," said Mrs. Jackson, "he's justly punished for the way he treated our family. We have the £3,000 to clear the farm, and that's something."

"Give me the pocket-book out of the desk," said the old man, trembling, and his voice hoarse, his lips blanched, though he swallowed a full horn of whisky toddy at a draught.

"What do you want with the pocket-book?" said Mrs. Jackson, with a sneer. "You are weaker than a child, and look as if the ghost of your old accomplice was standing up before you."

"Do see if the cheque is all right, we were all so confused and scared by his coming so suddenly upon us, that I took the cheque after he drew it without looking at it."

"Pooh!" interrupted the son, as Mrs. Jackson opened a massive oak chest in a corner of the room, "it's all right you may be sure, and, for fear of accident, I'll cash it to-morrow at the branch bank in Delaware."

N

Mrs. Jackson took out the pocket-book, and gave it to her father. He put on his spectacles, and with trembling hands unclosed the book and fumbled through some papers till he came to the cheque. One look, and with a groan of agony he tossed his arms up, and then his head fell heavily upon the table.

The son seized the cheque, and gazing at it, with a fearful oath, struck the table violently, saying: " By —— he neglected to sign it ; it is worthless."

The old man never stirred. Mrs. Jackson, aghast, and now trembling herself, raised her father's head, and then with a piercing shriek, let it fall back on the table, and then sank fainting in a chair. John Mason was dead.

Before night came, the inhabitants of Delaware were roused into a state of uncommon excitement. The dead body of the unfortunate Sir Richard Morton was brought into the town by the stage waggon from Williamsburg, and deposited in a chamber of the same hotel he had left in the morning in health and spirits. Mr. Bowen, who was known to be the confidential adviser of the deceased baronet, was sent for.

The consternation of the worthy attorney was overpowering ; for some moments he remained overwhelmed with grief and dismay. Then he thought of the valuable papers—papers of such consequence to the baronet's heir, that he seized his hat and rushed, late as it was, to the hotel.

In the parlour he found Mr. Baxter and Mr. Fowler, the two chief magistrates in the town.

" This is a horrible affair, Mr. Bowen," said Mr. Baxter, " an English gentleman of rank murdered and robbed within twelve miles of the town ; there has not been an act of the kind committed since Mr. George Carver was shot down and robbed by two of his own tenants, and that's nearly two years ago. You were intimately acquainted with that gentleman during his short stay here, Mr. Bowen. Have you any reason to suspect any one ? "

" Has Sir Richard Morton's coat been searched?" demanded the attorney most anxiously.

" His pockets were cleared out, I can tell you," said Mr. Fowler, " and the lining of his coat on the front had been ripped open."

" But was the back of his coat searched ? " questioned Mr. Bowen, " for I know he had a case of soft leather made to contain sheets of paper of great—of vast importance. In fact, Mr. Fowler, you yourself witnessed the signing of those papers by old John Mason, of Fork Farm—your name and two respectable citizens besides are attached to them."

" Let us proceed instantly and have the coat searched,"

said Mr. Fowler, "the body lies on its back, and no one has touched the coat or taken off any of the garments."

All three, attended by the landlord with lights, proceeded to the chamber where the body lay covered with a cloth.

Mr. Bowen shuddered as the landlord threw back the sheet and disclosed the face of the deceased baronet.

The handsome features of Sir Richard Morton still retained their beauty; there was a placid calm repose in the noble features, but little altered by the hand of the destroyer. Death, by a gunshot wound, leaves no traces of agony in the features of the dead.

"He was a very handsome man," said Mr. Baxter, "and still in his prime—not fifty I should say."

"No, not fifty," said the attorney, much affected. "Alas! what an ill-timed choice it was of his to ride to Williamsburg, and not travel in the stage waggon."

"We must have a searching inquiry into this brutal murder and robbery, Mr. Bowen, to-morrow. Just put your hand along the back of the coat, and see if the papers you speak of are there. They would be of no use to a robber."

The landlord raised the body, and Mr. Bowen searched the coat.

"Good God! they are gone," he exclaimed, turning very pale; "the lining is cut entirely away."

"Then this murder has been committed for the sake of those papers. I will have the whole family at Fork Farm arrested the first thing in the morning," said Mr. Bowen vehemently. "No human being could have had the slightest interest in those papers, except the Masons."

"Ah," said the magistrates, "they're a bad lot! the two sons and that fellow Jackson, the horse-lifter, were notorious at one time. They shall be arrested—father and sons, the first thing in the morning," said both magistrates. As they all retired from the room, Mr. Bowen shook Mr. Baxter and Mr. Fowler by the hand, saying, "I will defray all expenses incurred by the funeral, and will communicate at once with the family of Sir Richard Morton."

The following morning six armed constables with an officer of police proceeded to Fork Farm to arrest John Mason and his two sons.

They were seen approaching the house and Mrs. Jackson felt overpowered. William and Charles Mason, who had made up their minds how to act, betrayed no fear. They considered their plans so well laid as to be impossible of detection, so desiring Mrs. Jackson to go up to her sister, who was fearfully grieved at the death of their father, very coolly opened the door to the police officer and the constables.

"Well, mister," said William Mason, in a contemptuous tone, "are you come to turn us out of the farm; if you are, you're a day too late."

"I am come, Mr. Mason," said the police officer, "to arrest you, your brother, and your father on suspicion of being concerned in the murder and robbery of Sir Richard Morton."

"You don't say that the baronet has been murdered!" said both brothers, with a well-feigned start, and then with an oath; "if so, we are ruined."

"Where is your father?" said the officer, a little surprised.

William Mason threw open the door of the kitchen and walked in; the officer and constables followed, when William Mason threw off a cloth from a table, all started back, for laid out on it was the body of John Mason.

"How is this?" exclaimed the officer. "When did he die, and what the cause of death?"

"He died suddenly last night, when sitting at table; all the family were present except my youngest sister. He has for some time suffered from disease of the heart."

' Have you sent for any doctor, or have you let the coroner know?" asked the officer, "this is a sudden death."

"We have sent to both those functionaries," said the son. "I expect them every moment. You have accused us of a crime——"

"Which I saw you commit with my own eyes, William Mason," exclaimed a loud, bold voice; and then a tall, powerful young man, carrying a rifle in his hand, and who pushed through the surprised constables and entered the room, stood facing William and Charles Mason with an expression of stern, implacable hate.

The brothers fell back, pale as death, exclaiming: "Patten—Luke Patten!" and then in a burst of passion William Mason started up, and with a face purple with rage, shouted, "Liar! you are stating this lie from malice and a desire to destroy us."

"If you had been destroyed years ago," fiercely interrupted Luke Patten, "it would have been better for you than to die now steeped in crime."

What followed was the work of scarcely a minute. Both brothers were powerful, active men; with a sudden and irresistible bound they sprang amidst the constables, dashing three to the ground, and gained the door. Luke Patten never stirred to prevent them. The constables and the police officer, furious with rage, rushed after them, but the fugitives had banged to the heavy massive door of the farmhouse, and several minutes elapsed before they could open it. When they did, they saw several farm-men standing in the yard, looking stupefied and bewildered, but the brothers were nowhere to be seen. There was a thick cover at the back of the farm, and through this they had rushed. Four of the constables hotly pursued, but the brothers had snatched up two bridles off a hook, ran into the far paddock, and at once caught two strong young horses, and before the constables could come up, had mounted and galloped off at a furious pace, escaping the pistol-shots fired at them.

The noise, confusion, flight, and pursuit, had alarmed the two sisters above. Mrs. Jackson had recovered her nerve and resolution. Emily, who knew nothing of the plot between the rest of her family to destroy Sir Richard Morton, was terribly afflicted by the sudden death of her father. Mrs. Jackson ran upstairs, on seeing the constables. Pale and startled, Emily said, " What is the matter, Eliza—you look so fearfully pale ? who are those men whose voices I hear ? "

" They are constables, and a police-officer," said Mrs. Jackson, sinking into a chair.

" What can they want ? " said Emily, surprised. " Such men can have no business here. Sir Richard Morton's generosity has freed us from all fear of being turned out of the farm."

" They are not here for that," returned Mrs. Jackson sharply. " You were always different from the rest of us— not a bit like one of us. Talk of Sir Richard's generosity, indeed, after destroying our family, and, for recompense, giving our father an unsigned cheque for three thousand pounds."

" Hark ! I hear Luke Patten's voice," said Emily, starting up, and turning pale—for it was now nearly sixteen months since a complete rupture between the two families had taken place. As the two women stood listening, they heard their brothers rush out, and slam the house door, and, going to the windows, they beheld them clear the farm-yard wall, and then saw the constables in pursuit.

" Good God ! " cried Emily, " what is all this about ? Why do our brothers fly ; and why do those men pursue them ? "

Mrs. Jackson made no reply, but ran down stairs, and Emily Mason, her heart beating painfully, followed.

In the kitchen, the police-officer and Luke Patten were standing, earnestly conversing. For a moment Mrs. Jackson hesitated, whilst Emily trembled, without the power to move. Patten advanced towards Emily, and said, in a low tone, " This is a terrible affair, Miss Emily, and I regret that a sense of justice forces me to become the accuser of your two brothers, having seen them commit a fearful crime."

"You—you—Luke Patten," exclaimed Mrs. Jackson, in a tone of intense passion, and pushing her trembling and half-fainting sister aside, "and do you dare to come under this roof to gratify your hatred by uttering a monstrous lie?"

"Why did your brothers fly, then, if they were innocent?" said Luke Patten calmly.

"Well, this is quite a useless argument now," interrupted the police-officer, "and I have no time to waste. Mr. Mason is dead, and his two sons have escaped for the present, but they will be caught; and you, Mr. Luke Patten, must be ready when called upon, to give evidence as an eye-witness of this atrocious murder."

"Merciful God! what murder—who is murdered?" said Emily Mason, staggering up to Luke Patten, catching him by the arm, and looking him anxiously in his face.

"I grieve, Miss Emily, to say," said the young man, "that Sir Richard Morton, an English gentleman, was cruelly murdered, and by your brothers William and Charles."

Emily uttered a wild cry of anguish, and would have fallen on her face, but Luke Patten caught her in his arms, and placed her in a chair in the kitchen, leaving her to the care of the two terrified female attendants of the family.

In this state, we must leave not only the vicinity of Fork Farm, but the shores of the North American continent, and return to the waters of the Punza Pulka River, where we left our hero.

CHAPTER XXII.

WE left Arthur Bolton and his faithful and attached follower, Joseph, proceeding up the Punza Pulka River in the small dingy belonging to the cutter, to shoot a few duck and teal for the use of the cabin of the "Foam." In fact, Arthur thought he would have more leisure for thought during his excursion upon his approaching meeting with Alice Marchmont's father. He felt much uneasiness at this meeting, knowing how utterly without name, fortune, or friends, he stood in the world. It appeared to him, therefore, notwithstanding Mrs. Marchmont's sanguine view of his wishes and their realization, a very doubtful affair, particularly with a man of Mr. Marchmont's character and disposition.

Joe, who was looking out for game, and had nothing to think of particularly, was steering the boat as she ran up the river with a strong tide, called the attention of our hero to a large flock of the white ibis.

"Are they fit to eat, sir?" asked Joe; "faix, they are as big as a goose."

" But not half as good, Joe ; there's a large flight of teal over on the east shore ; they are on the wing at present, but they will soon light. A good shot with my double-barrel will bag a supply for two or three days. Edge the boat on, Joe."

Joe did so, but the teal took a sudden whirl and went much further up the river. Our hero could have killed several single birds, ducks and teal, but he preferred keeping his shot for the great flock.

" There will be a storm, Joe," said Arthur Bolton, " or some great change in the weather, the flocks are so exceedingly uneasy."

Just, however, as they came near the opening of the creek that led into the Tonza lagoon, he had a famous double shot into a large flock sailing out of the creek. Seventeen teal was the result, after a long chase up the creek after the wounded.

" Come, this will do," said our hero. " A few more ducks now will furnish our larder well."

" Look, sir," said Joe, " there are a dozen macaws and parrots chattering, with their young ones on the ground. I could catch one or two easily."

" Let us try," said our hero, without thinking of his promise to Alice not to land; " but let us be quick, for the tide is on the turn."

Fastening the boat, they proceeded in search of the macaws.

Arthur Bolton had not the most remote idea, that from the moment he approached the entrance of the creek he was most keenly watched from the shore by a party of men, with the most deadly intentions, creeping amongst the entangled mass of vegetation, which hid them completely from observation.

" Oh," said William Saunders, who was the leader of the party, who had been previously watching the movements of those aboard the brig and schooner, and whose intention was to board the little turtle schooner that our hero had possessed himself of, when he carried off Alice, and endeavour to get her to sea. " Oh," said William Saunders, with a ferocious oath, " if I could only get him within sure shot !"

The villain had his face bound by a band passing round his head, for the shot fired by Arthur Bolton on the night he rescued Alice had broken his jaw, and fearfully disfigured him. He was willing to sacrifice life if he could only be sure of killing Arthur Bolton.

" Maladetta !" returned one of the Mexicans. " Have patience, they will surely land ; see, they are coming into the creek."

" Ah, curse him ; I'll not shoot him, I'll give him days of torture before I finish him. Keep cautiously out of sight, do not tread even on a twig."

Thus watching, and getting within pistol-shot, the four men saw those in the dingy land. Arthur Bolton was standing under a magnificent cotton-tree, close to the bank of the creek, and Joe had just failed in catching a young macaw, when our hero received a heavy blow from the butt of a musket, from behind, which felled him, bewildered, and for the moment senseless, at the feet of Saunders. Joe had turned round, perceived the fate of his master, and, just as two of the Mexicans rushed at him to seize him, he fired his gun full in the face of the foremost, killing him on the spot, and then, dropping his gun, plunged into the creek and dived, thus escaping the shots fired at him by the furious Mexicans. Before they could again load, Joe had gained the other shore, and rushed into the dense jungle on that side.

The frantic maledictions and oaths of the ruffians thus baffled were horrible to hear. As to Saunders, he cared nothing about the dead Mexican, he stood exultingly with his foot upon the body of his victim, uttering the most savage threats. He had bound Arthur's hands and legs securely, before he had time to recover from the effects of the blow, and stood glaring at his victim as a tiger would at his prey before he tore him to pieces. Arthur Bolton had become quite conscious, and his first look into the face of his unrelenting enemy, told him mercy for him was not to be.

"What's to be done?" asked one of the Mexicans sulkily, if not savagely, glaring at Saunders, whom they all detested, but who had, in their then desperate state, gained a temporary mastery over them. "That infernal youth has killed Carlo."

"More fool Carlo to let himself be killed by such an urchin. Why didn't you shoot him? we didn't want him alive. Go and send the punt adrift, upset it, and let it go down with the tide. Those aboard the brig will think them drowned."

"What shall we do with the body of our comrade?" grumbled the others.

"Do with it?" said Saunders, with an oath, for every word he uttered gave him intense pain from his unhealed jaw. "You can't eat it, can you? Tie a heavy stone to it, and sink it in the creek."

The men growled and swore, but they proceeded to do Saunders's bidding.

"So," said that ruffian, as he saw Arthur Bolton make a desperate effort to free his hands, "you are in my power at last. Curse you, what I have suffered through you!" and taking a pistol from his belt, he pressed the muzzle against our hero's face. Stop your struggles; I could blow your infernal brains out now, but that would be a poor revenge for all that I have suffered from your —— interference."

"Villain! your own evil passions and vile nature have caused your sufferings."

"You lie!" roared the ruffian, and with a brutal cowardice he struck his helpless captive a blow across the mouth, that caused the blood to flow copiously.

Arthur Bolton felt choking with the internal emotion he experienced. He was resigned to die, but he saw that he was reserved for some terrible torture, and dark despair took possion of his soul, when the last words he heard his own Alice say occurred even in that dark moment to his memory:

"Even when hope is hopeless, there is still a hand to save; remember Captain Courtney!"

After a time the Mexicans returned, having sent the dingy adrift, and sunk the body of their comrade, Carlo. Then Saunders, putting additional cords on the wrists of his captive, cut those which bound his legs, and with an oath and a savage kick, cried:

"Get up, if you don't want me to slice you with my knife!"

Praying to God to grant him patience and resignation, Arthur Bolton stood up; his dress was covered with blood from the blow he had received in the mouth, and smarting pain in the head from the deep gash made by the brass-butted musket.

"What are you going to do with your prisoner?" asked the Mexican who spoke English.

"Put him in the pit," said Saunders, "and let him die by inches. Pity that he will only take eight or ten days to die of starvation."

"We shall not get into the lagoon to-night, there's a hurricane coming," said one Mexican.

"Then the sooner we launch the canoe the better," said Saunders; "the party in search of the girl are no doubt aboard the brig by this time. That infernal rascal Punka Bosswash shall be served out yet before we quit the country."

Driving Arthur Bolton on before them, a strong breeze roaring through the thick wood, they reached the spot where they had left their canoe.

The three Mexicans, by no means satisfied, and grumbling and swearing at the loss of their comrade, Carlo, launched the canoe, and then, as a precaution against any effort of their prisoner to escape, knowing his strength and daring, they firmly bound his legs together, thereby frustrating the very thing our hero intended to do—kick out the side of the canoe and swamp her.

They lifted him in, and all entering, they paddled across the creek up to the weather side till they came to the rapids, where they landed, and lifted our hero out and hauled up the canoe. Saunders then freed his legs, and, striking him brutally, forced him on before them, till they entered 'the same cave where our hero and Joe passed the night of the storm.

The Mexicans and Saunders were evidently not on good terms—they did not like his plans, and they said so—but they feared him, and he cursed them bitterly.

On entering the cavern the prisoner perceived that it had served for a habitation for those miscreants for several days; most likely they had taken refuge there to avoid the armed party of Mr. Marchmont when traversing the country in search of his daughter.

There were piles of wood heaped up and the remains of a fire and pieces of the manitou hanging up.

Though it was very evident that the Mexicans hated Saunders, they nevertheless all showed their vindictiveness to Arthur Bolton. One ruffian proposed to burn him alive. Saunders ferociously assented; but immediately after said:

" No! death in the pit will be ten times worse."

" Well, then, lower him down at once," said the Mexican who spoke English—saying something to his comrades in a low voice. Yellow pine torches were then lighted.

During this time the captive had struggled hard, but in vain, to free his hands. He saw the Mexican knife in Saunders belt, and thought if he could have freed his hands and seized it, he would have fought desperately to avoid the horrible doom these wretches intended him; but he knew of no pit in the cave, and he gazed all round the cavern.

To define or analyse his thoughts during this painful moment would be scarcely possible. Hope from human hands he had none—though he rejoiced at the escape of Joseph, still he knew he could get him no help, for the poor lad would be lost for hours in the wild jungle he had plunged into, and perhaps perish in it; his only chance of escape would be to swim the creek, and then endeavour to push his way along shore till opposite the vessels at anchor, and try and attract their attention,

Saunders and his comrades, having fastened two cords together, seized Arthur Bolton in their grasp, and fastened the cord round his waist; whilst one carried a torch, the other three dragged him through the cavern till they came to a second cavern, in the middle of which was a yawning gulf. Arthur Bolton could not avoid shuddering. Saunders saw that he trembled.

" Ah," said he, with a ferocious laugh, the pain of which caused him to swear fearfully. " That's a nice place, seventy feet deep, and perpendicular. How long do you think you can live down there, eh? there's not much water down there now, but enough to cool your hot temper."

"Miserable wretch," said our hero calmly, mastering every sign of fear or of emotion by a great effort. "There is an Almighty eye fixed upon you, even now. You think you triumph, but your brutal ferocious triumph will be short-lived."

"Curse ye! do you think so?" said Saunders. "No matter, you won't witness my doom, whatever it will be—and now—off with him!" and he and his comrades gave a violent jerk to the rope, and Arthur swung helpless over the awful pit, down whose depths the light of the single torch threw but a very feeble gleam, revealing that its sides were almost perpendicular, and ascent from its depths impossible. With a horrible laugh, Saunders and his comrade held him swinging over the mouth, jerking him, and pretending to let him go.

Our hero, suspecting that would be his fate, recommended his soul to his Maker, and murmuring the name of Alice, he closed his eyes. He heard the withering curse of the ruffian that he might live a week and suffer every pang hunger could inflict, and then he felt himself lowered, and roughly knocked against projecting rocks. Down he glided into the damp and suffocating hole, bruised and shaken, till suddenly the rope was let go, and he fell some feet; but he fell upright, and sank back in a cavity; for having his hands bound he had no power of resistance. Scarcely had he fallen when a fearful yell rung through the place, and immediately came a strange sound, a kind of crash as of a body striking against the sides. Instinctively he drew his body nearer the fissure of the rocks, and the next moment, with a horrible squash, something fell with terrible violence at his feet. Then a dead silence prevailed. Our hero felt an indescribable horror, he could not breathe; he was sick at heart; and for the first time in his life his stout frame shook with a tremour like an ague. He was conscious that a body had been hurled into the pit, and had he not fallen into the cavity where he stood, he would have been crushed by the miserable wretch, whom instinct told him was William Saunders. Conquering the terrible emotions he felt, and recovering his nerve, he listened—was the man dead? But the next instant, a low, scarcely audible groan issued from the bruised mass at his feet. The man, whoever he was, was not dead, still he could not bring himself to move from where he was. Not a ray of light pierced the horrible darkness of the pit, for, besides its depth, it was in a cavern where little or no light penetrated even in the broad day.

Did hope enter his breast, for suddenly Arthur Bolton recollected that if it was Saunders lying there he might still have his knife in his belt.   Heavy groans came from the body, and our hero thought words were spoken, and, kneeling down, he turned his back and groped about the body; he felt the mass heave under his touch, and as he groped, a voice said: "I'm not dead—no—I'm not dead—curse you!   I will live—live to hear you groan in your torture and despair."   These words were spoken at intervals, as if the speaker was in horrible torture.

Doubtless every bone was broken, yet the wretched miscreant lived.   Presently our hero's hand touched the knife, and he contrived to draw it from its sheath ; as he did so, he felt the grasp of a hand upon his arm; it was like a child's grasp, so feeble and impotent, but it showed that the mutilated wretch had still the power to move one arm.

"Do you want to murder me ?" gasped Saunders.   "You can't escape—my cursed comrades pushed me over,"—and then followed a string of impotent curses and awful groans, as the mass of mangled, bruised flesh strove to turn, but uselessly, for the power to do so was gone for ever.

"Wretched man," said Arthur, " make your peace with God whilst you have still life, and a perception of your terrible, awful situation.   I told you the hand of God was everywhere—His power infinite.   I feel I shall yet escape from this horrid pit."

"Never ! " shrieked the miserable wretch.   " Never !— no one ever comes here—no—never !   I shall live as long as you—curse you !—if you knew how I hate you ! "

"Yes," said Bolton bitterly, " I think I ought to know, miserable man,—what did I ever do to cause this hate ?"

For several minutes Saunders could not speak, from passion and agony.   Strange to say, though a mangled mass, no vital part was touched.   His legs and one arm were broken, his body bruised and mangled, but life still strong within him, and those few hours of life were passed in uttering fearful oaths and imprecations.   In the mean time, our hero had fixed the handle of the knife in a fissure of the rock, and then pressed and sawed the cords that bound his hands against its sharp edge, though he cut himself several times, till he freed his wrist, and then thanked God even for that relief.

Still there appeared no hope.   By feeling the sides, he soon ascertained that the pit he was in was a deep rent in a mass of rocks, the sides being perpendicular as far as he could feel ; the bottom was of small extent, and he judged from the ripling of water down the side, that in rainy seasons a torrent ran

lown the cleft. After a time Saunders seemed to gain
strength, as far as speaking went, for he kept venting imprecations and fearful denunciations against our hero.

"Don't think to escape! No, no! I'm sure of that; our
bones will rot together."

At times he seemed to rave—he uttered such strange
threats, and boasted of such horrid crimes.

"Do you know who you are?" he almost shrieked out,
after a few minutes' silence. "It will make you more miserable to know what a fine title and estate you might have had
f I had not put you into this place."

"Miserable man, cease!" said our hero, whose own
thoughts were terrible enough, though he prayed to God to
give him patience and resignation. "You cannot have long
to live."

"It's false!" interrupted Saunders; "you lie; I'll live to
hear you curse your existence. Perhaps you'll eat me to pro-
long your life. Ha, ha!—eat me—that's good!"

"So you won't believe you're a great man," again began
Saunders, "when I tell you Sir Richard Morton is your
father—your lawful father. You're not a bastard."

Our hero started; even in his terrible position, the words
uttered by the miserable Saunders attracted his attention.

"Do you hear me? Curse you! do you hear me?" muttered Saunders, groaning with the intense agony he suffered
as he strove to move his broken limbs; when he spoke, there
were at times long pauses between the words.

"Do you remember," he again began, after an interval,
" the perfumer as he called himself—George Reynolds?—his
name was Mason—do you remember his companion, the sailor,
who put you aboard the 'Foam'? Aigh, aigh! I know you do,
though you won't speak. You are kneeling close to me, I
feel your breath. You're anxious; and a horrible death
before you. I'll tell you all, for you will be more miserable;
you will never get out of this place. My bitter curses on
those Mexican rascals!" He paused, exhausted.

Arthur Bolton did feel a pang as he listened to the dying
man's words—dying he was, and that rapidly, for the tones
of his voice got weaker.

"Are you listening?" he began again; and he muttered
something, and then commenced a rambling account of his
own crimes, and after a time returned to his original subject.
" Do you know that sailor was my brother, he who helped
Reynolds—Mason, I mean—to entrap you. I knew all about
it. My brother told me, if I had an opportunity, to knock you
on the head. I would have done so at the time of the mutiny,
but for that meddling fool, the first mate—Curse you, go out

of that!—what brings you here? don't you see Jackson and
our captain standing grinning at me, and his little miserable
steward hiding behind him? Oh, you don't frighten me
grin away!—oh, gone, are you? don't come back; you'll get
nothing out of me!" He then uttered a shriek of pain, and
became still.

Arthur Bolton was horrified; we only repeat part of the
wretched man's ravings. Sometimes they were too horrible
to listen to. Our hero thought he was dead. He knelt beside him and listened. He could not hear him breathe, but
finding his hand, he felt that his pulse beat weakly. The
silence and dense darkness were horrible, and our hero prayed
that his brain might not become affected. For nearly two
hours, as well as he could judge, William Saunders lay
breathing as light as an infant—not a word escaping his lips.
Our hero placed his hand upon his face—the perspiration
poured down his wasted features. "What sufferings this man
is enduring!" he uttered aloud. "O God, have pity and
mercy upon him," and he felt the tears stealing down his
own cheeks. Suddenly he started, for a low, quiet voice
said—

"Mr. Bolton, kneel close to me; I'm dying—quick, my
time is short. You will be saved. I saw you saved in my
dream. I heard you say you pitied me, and you even prayed
to God to forgive me. I can't be forgiven—no, no—
impossible!"

"Yes, yes," said Arthur Bolton. "Yes, God's mercy is
infinite. You repent?"

"I have dreamed," said Saunders, speaking low, but distinctly, "you were saved. Hear me, put your hand on
mine."

Our hero did so; it was wet as if it had been dipped in
water.

"You thought," continued Saunders, "I was mocking
you, when I said you were Sir Richard Morton's lawful son;
but you are. Your mother was an orphan girl of good family.
Grace Manning was her name—she died." He paused; and
when he again spoke, said—"Moisten my lips with water; I
hear it running down the rock." Our hero took some in the
palm of his hand, and passed it over the dying man's lips. He
then said, "Your mother died in giving you life. Your
father, the baronet, thought you were not his lawful son, for
he believed the marriage ceremony between him and your
mother was a sham; but it wasn't—a real clergyman married
them. John Mason and his son George planned it all; hold
my hand and pray for me, and, O God, merciful God, forgive
me!"

A violent shudder and a dreadful struggle took place. Our hero felt his hand grasped with wonderful fervour ; the next moment William Saunders ceased to exist.

CHAPTER XXIII.

WHEN Joe beheld Arthur Bolton stretched at the feet of Saunders, he thought him killed ; and having shot the Mexican who endeavoured to seize him, he escaped by swimming the creek, and plunging into the dense jungle on the other side. After pushing his way into a tangled mass of vegetation, the poor lad paused, and burst into a flood of tears. The supposed death of Arthur Bolton, to whom he had become devotedly attached, made him miserable. He listened to every noise, but the rising gale drowned every sound, as it raged amongst the trees and branches above him. " They have not pursued me," thought Joe. " Perhaps my master was only stunned. I will go back to see what they do with him. Retracing his way, he kept as close to the brink of the creek as he could with safety, keeping himself concealed under a mass of tangled vegetation, from whence, though concealed himself, he could distinctly see what passed on the opposite bank. The two Mexicans were just at that time turning over the dingy, and letting her go adrift into the Punza Pulka river.

" Ah, you cursed villains ! I see you want to make believe we are drowned," muttered Joe. Seeing the two desperadoes returning upon the bank, he continued to creep along his side also of the creek ; and then, to his intense delight, he beheld his master, as he called him, alive, with his hands bound behind his back. He watched their proceedings with intense interest, and saw them put his master into the canoe, and then pull up towards the rapids. Determined to track them as far as he could, he continued cautiously to push his way through the jungle, now and then catching sight of the canoe, till they landed near the cave, and into which they went, driving Arthur Bolton before them. By this time it was nearly sunset. Another time Joseph would have felt intense horror at passing the night in the wild jungle without any weapon of defence, exposed to the attacks of wild beasts ; but so intensely anxious was he about our hero's fate, that he forgot self entirely. He lay, therefore, stretched out, dripping wet as he was, in a mass of shrubs, not more than thirty or forty yards from the mouth of the cave, which he at once recognized as the same cavern where he and Arthur Bolton passed the night of the great flood and storm. As he lay straining his eyes, and eagerly watching the men, he felt the grasp of something upon his shoulder. Horror and fear prevented him uttering a cry, for a moment he could not even turn his head; he thought he was grasped by a wild beast, and every saint in his calendar was evoked to save him. The pressure was removed, and raising his head his eyes encountered, not a wild beast, but the dark, brilliant eyes of Achupa, the Indian girl.

Greatly amazed, he murmured, "Achupa!" The Indian maid nodded her head, and put her finger to her lips. She was lying at full length close behind him, and yet he had not heard the slightest noise—not even the snapping of a twig. It was very evident that the Indian girl knew what he was watching, for she resumed her gaze upon the mouth of the cave. Joe looked at the handsome Indian maid with wonder; her fine-moulded limbs were as motionless as those of the dead; no part of her body stirred; she scarcely even breathed, so intense was her anxiety. Joe lay quiet, but it was not like the graceful statue-like composure of the child of the forest. She had a sharp iron-headed spear by her side, and at her back was her bow and quiver.

The gale howled through the jungle, and the affrighted birds and animals uttered wild cries and sought shelter for the night. Soon the darkness of night spread over the forest, but the fires in the cave threw out a bright glare. Presently the cry that Saunders uttered, when dashed into the pit by his treacherous comrades, startled the Indian girl and Joe. She sprang to her feet and drew her bow to the front. Joe was horror-struck. Could the cry come from his master? A moment of thought satisfied him. No; such a cry as they heard, Arthur Bolton would never have uttered under any circumstances. Presently they beheld the three Mexicans come to the front of the cave, and throw some wood on the fire. The Indian girl laid her hand on Joe's, and counted three of his fingers. Saunders and our hero were missing. Joe would have given all he ever possessed if he could only have made Achupa understand him; he thought to himself, " Surely she cannot be alone in the forest; there must be more Indians: the best way would be to go for help." But Achupa was a girl of intrepid courage, and the fact was, for the first time, the Indian girl loved, and Arthur Bolton was the object of her devotion. She never expected him to return her love, though Achupa, of a handsome race, was one of the most beautiful of her tribe; but she would sacrifice life to save the white man she secretly loved.

She said to herself, " They have killed him," and her eyes flashed, and her bosom heaved; " they shall die !" and drawing an arrow from her quiver, Joe, in the faint light, to his horror beheld her take her bow and creep to within fifteen paces of the mouth of the cave. Achupa fixed her arrow in the bow, and stood upright, her dark form concealed by the trunk of the tree.

The three Mexicans, after the horrid butchery of their comrade, were coolly cooking their supper at the large fire blazing near the mouth of the cave. Achupa was acknowledged by all the tribe the best shot amongst all the maidens, and even rivalled many of the best amongst the braves. She was strong of arm, and firm of heart.

Before Joe could recover from his amazement at her daring, the arrow sped, with wonderful force; almost the same instant it stuck quivering in the throat of one of the Mexicans, who rolled over on his back, kicking and struggling in the agonies of death. Joe started to his feet. But Achupa pulled him down flat beside herself, for the amazed Mexicans snatched up their muskets; and as Joe, in his awkwardness, snapped some dried branches, they levelled their muskets and fired. Had they been even on their knees, they would have received the balls in their bodies, for they crashed and scattered the twigs and leaves an inch above their heads.

Achupa kept her hand pressed upon Joe's arm, intimating to him not to stir. The Mexicans were now evidently terrified, and afraid to expose themselves: they lifted their comrade, but he was quite dead. They then began to reload their muskets, keeping as much in shelter as possible. Achupa was prepared for another shot, and Joe determined to rush at the remaining one with the spear, provided Achupa wounded another; one of the Mexicans, no doubt thinking that the fire betrayed their movements, moved out from his shelter to disperse the wood embers; as he did so, an arrow pierced him in the side: with a frantic howl of pain the man broke the shaft, and then the two fairly fled, crashing through the branches, and making for their canoe. Achupa and Joe listened, but the tempest was at its height. Neither stirred for a considerable time; but after awhile Achupa crept after the retreating Mexicans, motioning Joe to stay where he was.

She was nearly an hour away; and yet so silently and noiselessly did she return, and her dark form so mingled with the dark objects around, that, till she touched him, Joe knew not that she was beside him.

" Come," said the Indian girl—one of the words Arthur Bolton had taught her—" Come; " and she walked fearlessly towards the cave. Joe, grasping the spear, followed. They entered the cave, and Joe threw some dry wood on the fires, and then gazed anxiously round the cavern. Achupa lighted a pine torch, and then they began searching the cave for our hero and Saunders, whom the Indian girl knew must be imprisoned somewhere in the cavern, for out they did not go.

The light of the torch showed them the fissure between the rocks, and with an exclamation Achupa passed through and paused, with an emotion of terror, on the brink of the chasm. Joe's first thought was that the Mexicans had thrown his master and Saunders into the pit. Achupa thought the same, and the young girl trembled: waving her torch, she gazed down its depths, whilst Joe shouted at the top of his voice. Immediately the voice of Arthur Bolton answered from below. The joy of Achupa and Joe was in truth great; Joe jumped about like a madman, and the Indian girl's tears ran down her dark cheeks with joy.

Joe, approaching the mouth of the pit, gazed into it to see if by any possibility he could go down, but Achupa shook her head, and then began to think: but Arthur Bolton called out, tiellng Joe to make a slight rope of dried grass, full seventy feet long; that he had a strong rope below, which Joe could haul up by the grass cord, and making it fast, he would then be able to ascend; but that Saunders was lying below, and had just expired.

Joe was amazed: Achupa eagerly listened, and tried to understand from him what his master said. By signs he made her comprehend what he wanted to do. She understood him at once, and then both went into the outer cave. Joe shuddered as he looked upon the dead body of the Mexican desperado—the arrow had pierced the throat through and through. Gathering a quantity of the long jungle grass, Joe began twisting it into a thin line, and Achupa's nimble fingers assisted; between them, in an incredibly short time, they had a line ready of the requisite length, and then, fastening it to a piece of stick, they lowered it down, till the cheerful tones of our hero's voice calling out, " All right," made them pause. Having fastened the strong rope, by which he had been lowered, to the line, they drew it up. The next thing was to fasten it: this was a puzzle—for our hero called out that there was no more rope to spare. So Joe gave it a turn round his own body, and lay down, placing his feet against a projecting rock: he then called out that it was fast.

It required a strong and uncommonly active man to ascend a height of seventy feet by a single, unknotted rope, especially as the sides of the cave had few projections; but the captive was both powerful and active, and in a few minutes he stood panting upon the summit, and seeing the joy of the Indian girl, he caught her in his arms and kissed her cheek, and then rung Joe's hand till his fingers tingled.

"Thank God! thank God! for this deliverance from that fearful hole," he exclaimed, his eyes moistening as he thought of the terrible death he had escaped. He thought he could never repay Achupa, whose bright eyes sparkled with intense pleasure.

"And so, sir, that villain, Saunders, is dead, and down there?" said Joe. "How the dickens did he get there?"

"His comrades threw him in, Joe, after lowering me down, and by a most providential circumstance I escaped being crushed to death; but I think I heard the report of guns awhile back—was it so?"

"Yes, sir. I'll tell you all about it by and by. That brave girl Achupa killed one of the Mexicans with an arrow, and wounded another; they then fired at random and fled, thinking there were many Indians lying hid."

"It is very strange how she came here," said Arthur Bolton, and then he made signs with his hands to the Indian girl: she nodded, looked pleased, and then led the way into the outer cave.

"Ah!" said our hero, as the light of the fire fell upon the body of the Mexican, "she is a brave girl. Let·us carry this body, Joe, into the inner cave. It's not a pleasant sight; but what a tremendous storm is raging without!"

Achupa busied herself, whilst our hero and Joe carried the body of the Mexican away. In hunting about the cavern for food she found the birds Arthur had shot during the day, for the Mexicans had taken them out of the boat and carried them with them for their own use. Achupa, therefore, very calmly replenished the fire, and commenced feathering the teal to make a meal of them. She also found Indian corn-meal in a basket, some plantains, and a couple of gourds full of strong drink.

Neither Bolton nor Joe had tasted food since the morning, neither had Achupa. Our hero sat down beside her, and endeavoured by all manner of signs, and some words he knew of her language, to find out how she came to be alone in the woods. As well as he could make out she explained that she was not alone, that her brother was with her in the morning, but was blown across to the other side of the Punz Pulka river in their small canoe; they came to the wood to set snares for the Indian rabbit and wild ducks. After losing her brother she was making her way to the cave which the Indians frequently retired to when out hunting in those parts, and they had to pass the night there, when she caught sight of the boat with our hero and Joe coming up the creek, and then watched them.

He then contrived by a variety of signs to ask her what

became of the other two Mexicans who fled. Achupa replied by signs and words that they fled in their canoe to the other side of the creek.

"Those ruffians will surely return, Joe," said our hero, "when day breaks, to see who killed their comrade. If so, we must seize their canoe in order to regain the brig: those aboard will be amazed at our not returning ; they will think us swamped by the hurricane."

Achupa, quite happy at seeing Arthur Bolton released from a frightful death through her means, went on, with Joe's assistance, roasting the birds for their supper. Our hero strolled outside the cavern to reconnoitre, but the dense darkness of the night, and the furious storm raging, drowned every sound, save the crashing of branches and the roar of the gale through the jungle. He considered their situation, without fire-arms to defend themselves, extremely critical. The Mexicans would doubtless get help in a few hours, and return to revenge the death of their comrades, and they had no method of escaping or of regaining the ship in such a tremendous gale of wind as then blew, and one likely at that time of the year to last several days.

Even under the guidance of Achupa it would be difficult to traverse the jungle, swim the creek, and get to the Woolwa Indians. His thoughts then reverted to what he had heard from Saunders, whose recital amazed and excited him. He did not doubt the truth of his words, for his tone and his solemn, subdued, penitent manner, when his last moments approached, removed all shadow of doubt from Arthur's mind that Saunders spoke the truth. According to the dying man's declaration, he believed that he was the son of Sir Richard Morton by his first wife, and that having married again, his father wished the children of his second wife to be his only acknowledged children by the world, and it was evident that it was only lately that the baronet considered him to be his legitimate son, and having found that out had resolved to put him out of the way, at the same time giving him a chance of pushing his fortune in a different part of the world, and under another name.

Now what was he to do, presuming his notions to be correct? Was he to force his father to acknowledge him, if disinclined to do so ? Where were his proofs of birth—to whom was he to apply for them ?

One feeling, however, gave his heart joy; he felt that he was somebody, and he did not despair of getting his father to acknowledge him ; he neither coveted his title nor his wealth —simply position. Acknowledged as a member of the Morton family, he would have some hope of gaining the hand of his beloved Alice.

Retiring into the cavern he found supper ready, and the three strangely-assorted companions, notwithstanding the perilous scenes they had gone through, and might have to go through, set to with very keen appetites to enjoy it. Achupa by signs and words contrived to make Arthur Bolton understand that a watch must be kept all night, and that she would keep awake whilst he and Joe slept.

" No, no ! " said our hero, " Joe and I will watch by turns. You must be fatigued, Achupa."

The Indian maid shook her head and smiled. She could not understand his words, but she knew what he meant, and watch she would; her sense of hearing sounds in the forest was more acute than his ; besides it would be daylight in a few hours.

Arthur Bolton felt that to sleep was out of the question, but, to please Achupa, he stretched himself out by the fire ; and Joe, notwithstanding the roar of the storm without the cave, fell asleep in a few moments ; and though our hero was kept awake some time by his thoughts, just before daylight he dropped into a profound sleep.

Achupa was a study for a painter, as she paced the cave with noiseless tread, sometimes going without and listening to every sound : her tall and graceful figure became the simple attire she wore : a short petticoat, like a Highlander's kilt, of striped cotton, was fastened round the waist by a belt, ornamented with beads of pure gold ; this petticoat was in many folds, gathered to the waist, and reached nearly to the knee ; round her left shoulder she wore a scarf, which fastened to the belt round her waist ; and on her feet were a pair of very handsome mocassins, lacing up a very beautiful leg. Her skin was very little darker than a Creole's, and her hair was of a beautifully glossy black, and merely confined to the head by a band of hide, ornamented with beads and a small light scarlet feather.

Daylight had just commenced, when some sound without the cavern attracted the girl's attention, though the gale still raged unabated. Approaching the mouth of the cavern, and concealing herself by pressing against the rock, she looked out. After a time, as the light increased, something attracted her attention, for she suddenly ran back into the cavern and awoke our hero : he started up, and so did Joe.

" Come," said the Indian girl, " Mexicans," and she pointed to the mouth of the cave, and then led the way to the inner cave. As she did so, the report of a musket was heard, and, at the same moment, a ball splintered several pieces of rock from the side of the cavern, close beside where our hero stood.

" Ah," said he to Joe, " just as I thought ; those rascally

Mexicans have come back with the daylight—get behind this rock. Only one at a time can pass into the inner cave, and we are sheltered from their shot."

" Faix, it's a bad job, sir, that we have no fire-arms."

" I have Saunders' knife," said Bolton. " Run your hand over the dead Mexican ; he doubtless has a knife in his belt, and a Mexican knife is not a bad weapon at close quarters."

All three were safe within the inner cave, in which they could not be distinguished, whilst they could see distinctly anyone approaching the outward cave.

Achupa had her bow and eight arrows, as deadly a weapon, for a near shot, as a clumsy Mexican musket.

Whoever fired the first shot seemed evidently very cautious at showing himself, for several minutes passed and not a soul was to be seen near the mouth of the cavern. No doubt they were afraid that there might be many Indians concealed within it.

Half an hour passed, and not a soul was seen stirring across the entrance to the cavern. Arthur was getting impatient, when he felt Achupa lay her hand on his arm, and whisper:—

" Come, white man, come."

Her quick eyes had caught the gleam of steel, amidst the low brushwood, a few feet from the cavern's mouth. Our hero soon beheld the cause of Achupa's emotion, for cautiously coming forth from the thick jungle, he beheld five of the Mexican desperadoes and three Sambos, all armed with muskets.

" The Lord save us !" said Joe, with unconcealed alarm. " The villains will murder us all."

" Keep a stout heart, Joe," said his master, cheerfully. " Only one can pass through this opening between the two rocks, and their bullets cannot touch us. This brave girl shows no fear."

" Oh, be dad," said Joe, courageously, " I'm not afraid to fight, sir, or to die either ; the saints in glory will fight for us against such villains."

Achupa, with her bow, and an arrow on the string, stood concealed, but ready to lodge an arrow in the body of the first Mexican or Sambo that dared attempt the passage. Our hero and Joe, with their long, sharp Spanish knives, fit only for close quarters, and to that it was sure to come, also stood prepared for their enemies. Fire-arms were useless, as they left no part of their persons visible.

Evidently the enemy knew not what to do ; they saw no one to fire at in the outward cave, and the Mexicans knew to force the entrance to the inner cave would surely be the death of him who made the first rush. Still they advanced to the mouth of the cavern, and keeping as little exposed as possible, with their guns ready cocked, they gazed stealthily in. They could not tell how many Indians might be within the inner cavern, neither could they know how many might be within hearing of their muskets in the forest. But a fierce desire, a thirst for vengeance against those within the cavern, whom they readily surmised had released Arthur Bolton from the pit, induced them to risk their lives to be revenged. There-fore, urging the reluctant Sambos forward by threats, and even blows, they made a rush into the cavern, and for the cleft leading into the inner cave, when an arrow from Achupa's bow stood quivering in the breast of one of the Mexicans, who rolled over, mortally wounded, on the ground, whilst, at the same time, our hero drove Achupa's spear into a Sambo's throat, felling him headlong to the ground. Joe was not idle, for, with the thrust of a knife, he drove back another Sambo. This resistance rendered the Mexicans frantic. Retreating, they fired their muskets through the cleft, but with no result. At this moment our hero, anxious to obtain the fallen Mexican's musket and pouch, rushed out ; he had just seized them when a shot from one of the Mexican's guns struck him on the side of the head, knocking him senseless beside the dead Sambo.

CHAPTER XXIV.

WHEN recollection and perception returned to our hero, he appeared to awake as from a trance ; he felt as if a long period had elapsed, a dreamy kind of stupor overpowered him ; but at length he became conscious of surrounding objects. What he then saw were realities, not visions of a diseased brain.

Opening his eyes one day he looked around him, and be-came satisfied that he was not dreaming ; he perceived he was lying on an Indian couch, upon soft bedding, and that he was in a spacious Indian hut—it was broad daylight, but he was alone—the door of the hut was open, and a refreshing breeze blew into the room, and he felt new life as he inhaled it. At the farther end of the hut was another couch, and hanging above it was the bow and quiver, and several other articles he recognized as Achupa's. Whilst endeavouring to bring the past more distinctly to his confused brain, a shadow darkened the doorway, and then the Indian girl, with a light step entered the hut. Achupa uttered a cry of joy, as her dark eyes met those of our hero, and he exclaimed :

" Ah ! it was no vision—Achupa is alive and well ! "

The Indian maid was the next instant beside him, and

stretching out his arm he drew her towards him, kissing her cheek as a brother would. Achupa gazed at her patient with delight sparkling in her eyes, and then our hero said :—

" Where is Joe ? "

Achupa understood the word Joe; but before she could answer him, Joe himself, hearty and well, entered the hut.

Joe's joy was great, seeing his master at last sensible, and able to talk and to know those about him.

Achupa seeing him so well, and anxious to talk to Joe, left the hut to get him food, now that he seemed capable of eating some.

" How long, Joe," questioned our hero, " have I been lying here in this state ? I feel all of a sudden quite well. I am certain, for several days back, I have seen you and Achupa, and some tall woman, pass before me ; but I felt as if I was dreaming, and that you were visions."

" The Lord be praised ! sir, that your senses have come back ; Achupa said, the last few days, that you were getting round fast, and that you would soon know us again."

" How many days have I been ill, and where am I ? "

" Faix, sir, it's just twenty-one days since we came to this village."

" Twenty-one days ! " repeated our hero, amazed.

" Be dad, it is a fact, sir ; you were a week without opening your eyes, and dickens a bit did you eat ; all you took was a little liquid Achupa gave you, through a great quill. Punka Pigwash used to shake his head, and sit looking at you, smoking his pipe. ' Be gor,' says he, ' he'll never go to the hunting grounds again, he's done for, and more's the pity ;' but Achupa got angry, when he wanted some wise old woman, as thin as a herring, and with a nose like a turnspit, to doctor you her way, and faix, a queer way that was. Be dad, I was going to duck the old witch ; she wanted you to be stript and sewed up in the fresh skin of that big beast they call a manitou; and to drink its blood mixed with the oil of a fish's liver and——"

" Confound the old woman ! " interrupted Arthur Bolton ; " a nice way of curing a gun-shot wound in the head."

" Be dad, it was, if you knew the rest of the doctorings. But Achupa said she would cure you herself, and, thanks to the saints, she has, only using herbs, and washing the wound many times a day. How do you feel your head now, sir ? "

" I feel my thoughts and ideas and memory all right, but I cannot move my head without some pain, and I am tired to death lying here."

" A few days more, sir, will set you all right, I hope."

" But, Joe, what must they think aboard the Foam ; have

you sent any message there, or have they made any inquiries? But first of all, tell me how we were rescued. I remember being hit and falling senseless on the ground. What happened after that?"

"When you fell, sir, Achupa gave a great shriek, for one of those murderous Mexicans was going to run his long knife into you. We both rushed out, and Achupa drove the spear you dropt into the rascal, and then fell on your body, whilst I got a blow on the head that tumbled me over. In two minutes they would have cut all our throats, but there came such a war whoop from the jungle outside that the Mexicans were startled, and before they could escape or do anything, our old friend Bogwash and a dozen Indians rushed in, and in a twinkling they settled the remaining Mexicans, and then pitched the entire dead down the pit to rot with their old comrade Saunders. I saw it all, for though I was knocked down I was sensible enough; and, faix, the Woolwa young gentlemen made very short work of it—they hated the Mexicans so. But I'm sure I'm talking too much; you'll be tired out."

"No, no; excepting a slight heaviness in the head I feel all right. I owe that kind noble-hearted Indian girl my life."

"Faix you do, sir, for that respectable old witch would have settled you in no time. But there are letters for you from Bluefields, sir. Messengers have been sent to Bosswash to inquire after you, for the brig has sailed with all the family for Jamaica, and they have left all our things at Bluefields, with the English gentleman who resides there."

"Ah!" said our hero, a little uneasy, "I thought, when you said I had been three weeks lying here, that such would be the case. No doubt they were all anxious to quit this unhealthy and inhospitable shore. Where is the Indian chief now?"

"The whole tribe are gone on a great hunting expedition, sir; only the squaws and the children remaining."

"I will not read the letters to-day," said Arthur Bolton, "my head would not bear it; but a few days, please God, will enable me to get up."

A week elapsed, however, before he could leave his bed and take air and exercise. Joe replaced Achupa, watching him at night, and every attention the devoted girl could show him he received. He rapidly regained strength, and the wound, some small pieces of bone having worked out, became healed, so that a few days more would restore him.

Though health and strength were returning, Arthur Bolton was sad and thoughtful in mind. He had read the three letters sent to him. One of them informed him that when his residence with the Woolwa Indians became known to Mr. and Mrs. Marchmont, Captain Courtney had not entered the harbour of Bluefields with the Foam; she drew too much water, and the gales of wind off the coast were heavy. So he sailed at once for Jamaica, Mr. and Mrs. Marchmont following in a few days with their daughter in the schooner. All our hero's effects were landed from the Foam, and left under the care of Mr. Stockwell, the English resident, with a letter from Captain Courtney to be given him when he reached Bluefields.

One of the letters sent to our hero from Bluefields was from Mr. Marchmont, the other from Mrs. Marchmont, enclosing one from his beloved Alice. This last letter, which he treasured in his heart, consoled him for the somewhat unexpected one he received from Mr. Marchmont. We will give that gentleman's letter in full :—

" Bluefields, 184—.

" My DEAR SIR,—We hear with great regret that you are suffering much from a gunshot wound, inflicted by one of those miscreants from whom you rescued my youngest daughter. I would I could send a surgeon to you, but unhappily no such person is to be had here. But we understand you are going on most favourably, and we trust in a very short time that your health will be fully established. Mrs. Marchmont, myself, and daughter, beg to express our most heartfelt gratitude for your most gallant and successful undertaking, risking your life to preserve my youngest daughter. I am quite aware from Mrs. Marchmont's knowledge of your disposition and character, that an offer of pecuniary recompense would be offensive to your feelings. She has also candidly informed me that during the voyage you entertained an affection for my daughter Alice. Knowing such to be the case, and my daughter being very young, and also knowing my views respecting the future settlement of my daughters, Mrs. Marchmont has acted very imprudently and weakly in not at once checking an intimacy that could only lead to unpleasant results.

" From what I have heard of your character and conduct, I could have no possible objection to receiving you as a suitor for my daughter, provided you had a name and position in the world ; I could dispense with wealth, but never the want of birth and position. God forbid I should say this to wound your feelings in the slightest degree, for I esteem and admire your principles and your conduct. But you are young, and so slight an attachment as one contracted in a few weeks at sea may easily be conquered, and I trust your own good sense will convince you that I am not harsh or unfeeling to you. We shall return immediately to England. I shall abandon my intention of remaining in Jamaica a year or so, and I now offer you, if you are willing to accept it, one of the most lucrative situations for a young man on the island.

"You will begin with a salary of £400 a year. I will leave full instructions with my agent in Jamaica, Mr. Fitzhugh, a gentleman of high integrity and in a most responsible position. He will make you fully acquainted with the situation I trust you will accept, and I sincerely hope we shall meet in a few years without any feeling on your part that I have acted ungenerously or harshly, after the great service my family have experienced at your hands. Wishing you a speedy restoration to health, and a prosperous career,

"I remain, ever gratefully yours,
"PHILIP ARCHIBALD MARCHMONT."

Mrs. Marchmont's letter was all a noble fond mother could .write. She bade the deliverer of her child from a cruel fate never despair. She earnestly implored him to accept the situation her husband earnestly wished him to fill, and to trust to her endeavours and time to bring Mr. Marchmont round to her views. As to her daughter, though she would never disobey her father by marrying without his consent, still her heart was firmly and irrevocably his, and no other should ever possess her hand. It was a long letter, full of motherly feeling and motherly counsel, and it soothed and calmed the irritation of feeling he certainly felt on perusing Mr. Marchmont's epistle.

Alice's fond and most feeling letter he treasured in his heart of hearts. She was herself not without hope. She said her father was a most loving, kind parent, and one that would never force her inclinations, though he refused his consent to their union. Alice did not appear to wish him to accept the situation offered him in Jamaica. She wished him to exert all his energies in investigating the mystery that enveloped his origin, and this wish Arthur Bolton resolved to follow up, especially after hearing William Saunders's declaration, and get to England on the first opportunity.

As for Achupa, content at beholding Arthur Bolton's restoration to health, in accompanying him and Joseph and some of the tribe on short hunting excursions, her days passed quite happily, without bestowing a thought upon the time when the white men should leave her presence for ever.

Punka Bosswash had returned after a most successful hunting expedition, and was heartily rejoiced to see our hero restored to his former vigour.

He had concluded a peace with the Sambos of Quamwatta,

who, now that the Mexican desperadoes were exterminated, very willingly agreed to his proposals. They were no longer to be opposed when inclined to capture turtle, and no amount of shells was to be paid for permission to frequent the turtle grounds, and in return for these concessions, they were to supply the Sambos with the game of their forests—for the Sambos were but poor hunters—in exchange for other commodities.

Mr. Marchmont, before leaving Bluefields, sent Punka Bosswash many presents; amongst them a dozen excellent muskets, with a considerable amount of ammunition. To Achupa both mother and daughter sent many pretty trinkets and ornaments, so that the chief and his tribe were quite proud of the part they had played in the rescue of Mr. Marchmont's daughter, and of Arthur Bolton.

Achupa, when our hero told her of his intended departure, appeared to realize her feelings, and to feel acutely what the separation would cost her. Arthur always treated the Indian girl with most affectionate, brotherly tenderness; he had taught her, during his three months' residence with the tribe, to speak and understand many English words, and he had himself picked up almost enough of her language to ask for anything he wanted. The young Indians of the tribe looked upon him with most favourable eyes; he brought down his game with his rifle, with unerring eye; he could match the best amongst them in activity, and in strength he surpassed them. They all, therefore, looked upon his departure with exceeding regret, and half-a-dozen of the youths of the tribe were selected to take him and Joe to Bluefields; and a fine, roomy canoe having been prepared, they were to descend the Punza Pulka river and then coast it to the Bluefields lagoon.

Achupa bore the departure of her favourite with apparent fortitude; at least no one present could judge of her feelings of bitter regret by her features or manner.

She called to her aid all the wonderful fortitude and stoical indifference an Indian can command, under every trial, whether torture of body or mind.

Arthur, who twice owed his life to the courage and fidelity of the chief's daughter, felt and showed his affection and gratitude by his manner, and told the young girl that he should never forget her, and kissed and bade her farewell with all the natural affection of a brother. He had no token of remembrance to leave her, but her brother, who was to accompany him to Bluefields, he promised should bring her one. As our hero entered the canoe, and it paddled down the creek, Achupa turned away with a swelling heart and sought

he deep solitude of the forest. Of the after-fate or life of
he Indian girl we know nothing, as Arthur Bolton never set
oot on the Musquito shore again after leaving it, during the
emainder of his life.

The party reached Bluefields in safety. Mr. Stockwell
eceived our hero kindly, and offered him every hospitality in
iis power. From his private effects, Arthur selected the only
valuable article he possessed—the gold chain of his watch—
or Achupa, which he begged her brother to give her, with his
most affectionate regards. To the six Indians he gave each a
musket and pistol, which he purchased from Mr. Stockwell's
store, together with some ammunition. The delighted Indians
bade him farewell with great regret, and returned at once to
their tribe, quite proud of their presents, which they fired
several times in imitation of the English war schooner when
saluting the Governor.

By great good fortune an American brig touched at Bluefields, bound to Liverpool, and in her our hero took his passage—leaving several letters with Mr. Stockwell to forward
by the first vessel to Jamaica. In his letter to Mr. Marchmont, he thanked him for his offer of a situation, but simply
stated that circumstances had occurred which prevented his
accepting so lucrative a post, and that he was about to return
to England by the first opportunity that offered. To Mrs.
Marchmont he expressed all he felt; he declared that his
devotion to Alice would only cease with life, and that he did
not despair of proving himself worthy of her love and her
hand. He said nothing about his hopes of discovering the
mystery of his birth, or of the revelations made to him by
William Saunders ; he would not raise hopes in his beloved
Alice's heart that might never be realized. Satisfied with the
knowledge of her faith and undying love, he left his intention
unrevealed. But our hero might as well not have written, for
before his letter reached Jamaica Mr. Marchmont's family had
sailed for England.

Our hero and Joe, after a prosperous voyage, reached Liverpool on the 9th of October, just fourteen days after the landing
of the Marchmont family at Southampton. They had returned to England with Captain Courtney in the Foam.

Establishing himself at the Blue Boar Hotel, Liverpool, his
first object was to fit himself and Joe out, for their stock of
garments required replenishing. He possessed in reality but
a small sum, but he retained the order of £100 from a London
bank upon a mercantile firm in Jamaica, and he made no doubt
but that the bank would pay the amount, as it was expressly
payable to himself. Therefore, having provided himself with
suitable garments, he took the train to London. The following

day he presented himself at the banking establishment of Messrs. Freeman and James.

Requesting to see either of the partners, he was shown into a private room, where sat Mr. James, busy with his ledgers and accounts.

"I presume, sir," said our hero, after taking a chair, "you recognize this document; it was intended to be presented by me to a firm in Jamaica, but circumstances prevented my reaching that place. I suppose the order is presentable here."

Mr. James took the paper and read it over, then looking up and regarding our hero attentively for a moment, said : "I remember this order very well, sir. The sum was lodged in our hands, and we gave this order payable to Mr. Arthur Bolton to a highly respectable firm in Jamaica. You are Mr. Bolton, I presume ?" On our hero answering in the affirmative, Mr. James continued : "Can you bring any resident in London to testify to your being the proper person named in this order, for if my memory does not fail me, I saw some time back, how many months ago I cannot say, a reward offered by a superintendent of police for any information respecting the disappearance of a gentleman named Arthur Bolton from the Crown Hotel. The name struck me at the time, but as Arthur Bolton is not at all an uncommon name, I did not, after a moment's thought, connect the name with that in the order, as the person who obtained it was a gentleman of rank, wealth, and station—in fact, Sir Richard Morton, of Morton Manor, Derbyshire, who said he required it for a young man who was going out to the West Indies to fill a lucrative situation. Now, are you the Mr. Bolton advertised for? or are you the Mr. Bolton who——"

"One and the same person, Mr. James," interrupted our hero, smiling, "and the superintendent of police you mention, if in London, will at once identify me as the Arthur Bolton missing, for any information concerning whom he advertised."

"Still," said the careful Mr. James, a little mystified, "that will not make you out the Arthur Bolton to whom this order is payable. You will pardon me, I do not in the least doubt your word; still it is absolutely necessary that——"

Mr. James was interrupted by a light knock at the door, and a gentleman entered the room; he was a tall, handsome man, scarcely fifty. The moment the stranger entered, Mr. James jumped up, and as he heartily shook hands with him, he said : "You have taken me by surprise; by Jove, you look well and hearty ! I saw your arrival in the paper a few days ago. How have you left Mrs. Marchmont and your daughters ?"

Arthur Bolton gave such a start at the name of Marchmont that he upset his chair, which caused Mr. James to turn round. Looking surprised at our hero, whose agitation was perceptible, he said : " If Mr. Bolton, you——" here the worthy banker paused, for the start his friend Mr. Marchmont gave at the name of Bolton was quite as great, and his agitation was also as perceptible, as our hero's.

Mr. Marchmont, to do him justice, though a proud man, and an ambitious man, was a gentleman of highly honourable principles, and generous to a degree. He recovered himself first, and to the intense surprise of the banker advanced towards our hero, and, holding out his hand, said,—

" You must be the Mr. Arthur Bolton to whom myself and family are under such weighty obligations; my wife's description of you is too correct to be mistaken."

" This meeting is very strange, Mr. Marchmont," said our hero, much pleased with the manner and appearance of Alice's father, " for I believed you still in Jamaica. My letter, in reply to your generous proposals, I forwarded from Bluefields to Jamaica ; of course you never received it."

" No," returned Mr. Marchmont ; " we left the island before it arrived there. But all this is a mystery to you, friend James," continued Mr. Marchmont, turning to the banker.

" By Jove ! you are right, Marchmont ; but in one thing I am quite satisfied, that I now require no further proof of this gentleman's being the person he represents himself."

" Oh, I'll answer for that," said Mr. Marchmont, " though this is the first time we ever met. However, as we must not occupy your valuable time, friend James, I must beg Mr. Bolton to favour me with his company at dinner. I am at the Clarendon, all alone, for my family will remain some time at Southampton."

Our hero willingly and gladly accepted the invitation, and Mr. James, signing the order for the £100, which he told him he would receive in the office, took leave of both gentlemen, received his money, and returned well satisfied to his hotel, where he found Joseph transformed into a very smart, handsome lad, as an attendant, having had a complete outfit.

Joe was so attached to our hero, and he to him, having gone through such perilous scenes together, that he could not bear to part with him, and as he determined to share his fortunes, whether good or bad, and had neither parents nor relatives, that he knew of, our hero gladly consented.

After Arthur's departure from the banker's, Mr. James, an old and very esteemed friend of Mr. Marchmont's, said :—

" That is a remarkably fine young fellow that has just

left us. Confess, now, is there not some mystery about him? Though you seem never to have met, yet you deem yourself under great obligation to him."

"So I am," returned Mr. Marchmont. "I'll dine with you to-morrow, and tell you all about him. There is some mystery about his birth; in fact, he knows nothing respecting his parentage."

"Nevertheless," said the banker, thoughtfully, "I could give a very good guess as to who his father is."

"The deuce you can, James! How have you got a glimpse into the past history of this young man? Tell me, for though I am come on business, I feel so deep an anxiety concerning that young man, that anything you can tell me I shall be grateful for."

"Well, the fact is, friend, I believe him to be the illegitimate son of Sir Richard Morton, of Morton Manor, Derbyshire."

Mr. Marchmont's cheek flushed; he did not like this announcement. The bar-sinister was a terrible bar to jump over, if ever he entertained the prospect of bestowing his daughter's hand upon her deliverer; for Mr. Marchmont had very clearly seen that his daughter's attachment to Arthur Bolton was no evanescent feeling, to be cast off at pleasure.

"Why do you think so, James?" he demanded of the banker.

"Well, I will tell you. Our bank has large dealings with the Morton family. They are now abroad. It was only the other day I remitted them a letter on a Geneva bank. Sir Richard Morton is married to a younger daughter of the late Lord Pintire—a good match in every way—and has a son and two daughters grown up; the son and heir is about nineteen. Sir Richard came to me some months ago—faith, nearly a year ago—and told me he wanted to send a young man he took a great interest in out to Jamaica, to pursue a mercantile career, and begged me to give him a letter of introduction to a respectable merchant at Kingstown, and a letter of credit upon a banking firm there for £100, for his private purse, till he got employment. He told me he was a highly-educated youth, about twenty-two.

"Humph!" said I to myself. "Twenty-two years of age. Very likely to be his own son. Sir Richard has the character of having been wild and extravagant in his youth, and there were some queer stories afloat; I heard them myself, when in that part of the country. However, I said nothing on the subject, gave him the order on a firm you know very well, and also a letter to the principal partner, that would be sure to get his *protegé* a first-rate situation out there."

" Ah !" said Mr. Marchmont, " after all, you only surmise, or think it likely, he is Sir Richard Morton's son."

" Of course, my dear friend, I cannot speak positively, but I remember about that time an advertisement appeared in several papers, that somehow attracted my attention. The exact particulars I cannot give you, but it had reference to the singular disappearance of a young gentleman of the name of Arthur Bolton, who was known to have left the Crown Hotel, Cavendish Square, to visit some house in a low locality, near London Bridge. From the time he left the hotel nothing further was heard of him ; his trunk, &c., remained in the hotel, and for any information respecting the said Arthur Bolton a considerable reward was offered."

" This is somewhat mysterious and extraordinary," remarked Mr. Marchmont, " and quite out of our power at present to unravel. To-morrow, however, I shall be able to understand matters more clearly, for I expect to learn everything concerning him that he himself can impart."

The two gentlemen then proceeded to talk upon business matters, and after a time Mr. Marchmont took leave of his friend, the banker.

CHAPTER XXV

On arriving in London our hero avoided taking up his abode in the Crown Hotel, where he had left his luggage, and from which he had so mysteriously disappeared. He wished to remain quiet and unnoticed, and disliked becoming an object of curiosity ; at all events for the present. Full of hope and happy anticipations of the future, he proceeded to dine with Mr. Marchmont, who received him in the most cordial manner, and whose conversation during dinner was varied and agreeable, insensibly leading his young guest to speak on various subjects, and thus discovering how well he had profited by the education he had received ; and how capable he was of succeeding in any career fortune might place before him. It was not till after the meal was ended, and as they sat over their wine, that Mr. Marchmont said,—

" Before, my dear young friend, I ask you a few questions, I must inform you that since we left Jamaica my mind has been completely changed on one point. I mention it now, that hereafter, should circumstances turn out favourable to your hopes, you may not suppose me influenced by those circumstances."

Arthur listened with wrapt attention and considerable emotion as Mr. Marchmont continued,—

" When first I heard from my wife of the mutual attachment between you and Alice, I confess I was much annoyed. I gave you in my letter my reasons for feeling so; therefore it is unnecessary to repeat them. Since then I have thought much on the subject, studied my daughter's character, considered the services you had rendered her, and the likelihood of a very strong attachment arising out of the circumstances in which you both were placed; therefore I was prepared, when I encountered you so singularly at my old college friend and correspondent, Mr. James's, to feel very favourably disposed towards you, and I did intend to write to you—thinking you still in Jamaica—to that effect. My short acquaintance with you has strengthened my determination, and I now tell you, whether you succeed in ascertaining who your parents were or not, it will make no difference in my wish to consider you as my future son-in-law."

Arthur sprang from his chair; his face flushed with excitement, and his heart beating almost painfully with joy and happiness; grasping Mr. Marchmont's hand, he expressed himself so well, and painted the happiness he experienced so eloquently, that that gentleman himself became exceedingly moved, and embraced our hero with a great deal of affection in his manner.

After a few moments they became more composed, and Mr. Marchmont then requested to be told every particular connected with his infancy and manhood.

All was quickly related, and the dying declaration of William Saunders astonished Mr. Marchmont much, as he emphatically declared,—

" There must be some foundation for this man's statement; but allowing its perfect truth, there will be immense difficulties to contend with. Sir Richard Morton will, no doubt, endeavour to maintain the legality of his present wife's children's claim to the title and estates. I do not see how you can proceed without the evidence of that man Reynolds, or rather Mason. I would advise you to try and see Mr. Baldwin, the superintendent of police, to-morrow; it strikes me that he meant more in the advertisements he put in the papers at the time of your disappearance than meets the eye. In two or three days I shall be ready to accompany you into Hampshire, where all, I need not say, will be rejoiced to see you. I shall write to-morrow."

After passing one of the happiest evenings of his life, our hero bade Mr. Marchmont good night, and returned to his hotel, to indulge in golden dreams, whenever his happy anticipations of soon seeing Alice allowed him to close his eyes in sleep.

Whilst eating his breakfast the following morning he took

up a morning paper, and in turning it over carelessly his gaze
rested upon a heading of a column in large characters—as
follows:—

" Mysterious Murder of an English Baronet in
America."

The young man felt a strange feeling of dread steal over
him as he perused those words, but he read on,—

"It is with exceeding pain and regret that we have to record
the violent death of an English baronet of station and fortune,
Sir Richard Morton."

A pang shot through the reader's frame, and for a moment
a mist was before his eyes, and the hand that held the paper-
trembled as he murmured,—

"My God! my father! I know it; I feel he was my father."

Whilst he remained in a manner overpowered, the door
opened and Mr. Marchmont hastily entered the room. He,
too, was agitated, as he said, taking a chair,—

" I see you have read this dreadful news, Arthur; it is
horrible!"

" Horrible!" repeated our hero; " yes, it's a horrible
crime, and to me it's a fearful blow. I know he was my father,
be it how it may; and now I shall never feel the embrace of
a parent, and I trusted, hoped, prayed, that things would so
turn out, that at least he would acknowledge me as his son,
and give me his blessing:" and Arthur Bolton showed that he
was deeply moved.

" I feel for you, indeed, my dear Arthur," said Mr. Marchmont, taking a paper from his pocket; " it will be a terrible
blow to the bereaved Lady Morton's family. But have you
read the article? It's exceedingly strange Sir Richard Morton's going to America, and it's still more strange the terrible
events hinted at in this article, that took place before the
baronet and his family left England."

" I have not read it, my dear sir. I was so shocked
when I came to Sir Richard Morton's name that I read no
further."

" I will read the statement in this paper; it has a much
longer and apparently clearer article than the paper you were
perusing."

Mr. Marchmont then read as follows:—

" About this period last year we mentioned in our columns
an occurrence that took place in the family of Sir Richard
Morton, of Morton Chase, Derbyshire, which created considerable excitement at that time in the vicinity.

" One morning Sir Richard was found by Lady Morton in
his library, apparently bleeding to death from the stab of a

bowie knife lying on the floor beside him. Most fortunately a surgeon, coming to visit one of the servants of the family, was riding up the avenue, and most probably Sir Richard Morton's life was saved by his prompt assistance. Still he was in great peril. An eminent physician from the metropolis was sent for, and after a long and painful illness the baronet recovered. All that the public ever knew of this mysterious attempt at assassination was, that a person had requested to see Sir Richard that morning, and was shown into the library where the baronet was. An hour or so afterwards he was seen to leave the house, and Lady Morton going to the library found her husband insensible. When Sir Richard recovered sufficiently, the whole family proceeded to pass the winter in a mild climate.

"So far these circumstances were forgotten by the general public, when the startling intelligence of the unfortunate Sir Richard Morton's murder reached England. The first intimation was copied from a New York paper, but we have now authentic particulars from our own reporter. It appears that the baronet was in Delaware on business, that he visited a farm-house called the Fork, and that the owner of Fork Farm, it has been ascertained, was formerly in Sir Richard's employment as bailiff at Morton Chase. This man's name was Mason."

"Ah!" interrupted our hero. "Mason! that's the real name of the man who enticed me into the house in Thames-street, and afterwards put me on board the 'Foam.'"

"Yes," returned Mr. Marchmont, "I remember; there is some terrible mystery connected with that family of Mason. I am convinced with them lies the elucidation of the mystery of your birth. I will continue the paragraph,—

"'It seems Sir Richard Morton, and an attorney named Bowen, had an interview with Mr. Mason in Delaware, and that Mason signed some important papers and documents, which the deceased baronet wished to bring safely to England, and for that purpose carried them on his person. He left Delaware attended by a guide, both on horseback. In passing through a wood, about ten or twelve miles from Delaware, the guide, riding in advance, heard the report of a gun, and turning round beheld the unfortunate baronet fall from his horse, evidently killed, for he never stirred after reaching the ground. The guide was terrified, and whilst he hesitated, a ball whistled close to his own ear, which made him put his horse to a gallop. He fled to a small roadside inn about three miles off to procure help.

"'When Sir Richard's body was found and conveyed to Delaware, Mr. Bowen, the attorney, was sent for. He ordered that an instant investigation might be made of the deceased's garments for the papers, but neither papers, money, watch, or even the ring on the finger—a valuable one—were found; all had been abstracted before those who found the body reached the spot. I am prevented," continued the reporter, " giving you further particulars, as I have only ten minutes in which to finish my letter. By next mail I shall, I trust, be able to throw some light upon this mysterious and horrible crime.'"

"This fearful act has been committed, I feel fully satisfied," said Arthur, deeply affected, " by those Masons, to get possession of those papers—for what use or purpose I can only imagine. I will leave England for America by the very next packet, and never cease till I discover the miserable wretches who committed this crime, and bring them to justice."

"I think you are right, Arthur," replied Mr. Marchmont. " The next packet sails from Southampton on the 18th—this is the 12th. I will be ready to leave London with you on the 14th, and will see you off; before which, try and find Mr. Baldwin, the superintendent of police—he may be able to give you information that may be useful."

After some further discussion upon the late event, and the manner in which our hero would act on reaching Delaware, they separated, Arthur proceeding to the station, to inquire after the superintendent of police.

Mr. Baldwin had arrived the day before from Canterbury, and was, when our hero inquired for him, in his office.

He recognized Arthur at once, but his surprise was very great, as he sprang from his seat, and shook him warmly by the hand, saying,—

"This is a surprise, indeed! If you disappeared mysteriously, your return is quite as singular. I sincerely rejoice to see you alive and well; but this is no place for us to converse in—we shall be interrupted every moment, as I have one or two cases to dispose of."

"Well, then, my dear sir, can you make it convenient to dine with me at the Clarendon? Name your own hour; I have a great deal to say to you."

"Well, be it so," returned the superintendent. "Say seven o'clock, and I will be with you, for I have important matter to communicate."

"Seven o'clock it shall be," said our hero; and shaking hands with the kind-hearted Mr. Baldwin, he left the office.

Mr. Baldwin was punctual to the hour appointed, and they sat down to dinner, during which the conversation turned on indifferent subjects. When the wine and dessert were placed upon the table, and they were left to themselves, Mr. Baldwin, who was exceedingly anxious to hear our hero's adventures, begged him to give him a brief outline of them.

Arthur did so; the worthy superintendent listened, exceedingly astonished.

"You have been quite a hero of romance," he remarked, "and your life has been preserved in a most providential manner. Your narrative satisfies me," continued the superintendent, "that my conjectures respecting your birth were, from the beginning, nearly correct. The mysterious murder of your father, Sir Richard Morton, is a terrible blow; for I feel convinced his proceeding to America was for the express purpose of restoring you to your rightful position as his son and heir; and I am also satisfied that the Masons were the perpetrators of the horrid crime related in the papers."

"Yes," said our hero, with a sigh of deep regret, "of that I am sure; but I wish, before I leave, to gain all the information I can respecting the Masons, previous to their leaving England."

"I can give you every information you require," returned Mr. Baldwin, "and also inform you of some parts of your family history unknown to you. I daresay you have often wondered how Mrs. Morton, of Ramsgate, came to be so completely separated from all intercourse with her family?"

"Yes," replied Arthur, "I have often thought of that."

"Mrs. Morton," continued Mr. Baldwin, "was, you know, many years older than her brother, Sir Richard. During her father's life, she ran away with a man every way inferior to herself in birth and position. She got married, and went on the Continent. The man, whose name was Polson, was a low-bred adventurer, and, finding he could not make it up with your grandfather, who sternly refused to give his daughter one shilling, took to drinking and gaming, and was finally consigned to a Neapolitan prison, for swindling and stabbing a Neapolitan officer. The officer did not die, and, after a certain term of imprisonment, Polson would have been released; but before that time he, with five criminals, attempted an escape, and was shot dead by one of the jailers they had nearly murdered. It was a good riddance, however, but Mrs. Polson, broken-hearted, and feeling her degradation terribly, returned penniless to England. There she learned her father's death, and feeling no desire to visit her native place, she wrote to Sir Richard, describing her situation, and stating her determination to drop her husband's name, and return to some town in England, where, under the name of Mrs. Morton, she could live in great retirement, if a small annuity were allowed her. Sir Richard settled on her £500 a year (she in reality being entitled to the sum of £10,000), provided she continued single, and lived in retirement. After a while she settled in Ramsgate, and there she remained till her death. All this I discovered during my inquiries after you.

" When you disappeared so suddenly from the Crown Hotel, I set a most intelligent officer on your track, and also inserted an advertisement in the daily papers.

" The officer I employed tracked the two men who decoyed you to the old house in Thames Street, into Derbyshire, and with a comrade, by my permission, pursued and tracked them into the vicinity of Morton Chase ; then it was that this Reynolds or Mason attempted to assassinate Sir Richard Morton. By a concatenation of untoward circumstances, Mason and Saunders baffled the detectives, and finally got off in a vessel to America.

" I was desperately vexed, and some short time after, having a week to spare, I went myself into Derbyshire, where I was quite unknown, and took up my abode at the little inn in which my two detectives had been baffled, after actually having Mason and Saunders in their power. Sir Richard and family had at this time left the country for the Continent. Of course the recent attempt at assassination, and the escape of the criminal, formed a fertile source of conversation all over that neighbourhood. Knowing Reynolds' real name to be Mason, I began my investigations. I learned that the mother of the woman who kept the little inn had once been a servant of John Mason's when a bailiff on the estate of Morton Chase. She was then a very old woman, and was living with her son, a joiner, at Chatsworth.

" Well, I went to Chatsworth, and found James Dulford, the joiner, and the mother ; they were both very shy in answering any questions, and I despaired of gaining any information, till I found out that James Dulford was in difficulties, and was sued for a sum of £30.

" He was about to sell off all he possessed, and put his mother in the poor-house, when I stepped in and offered to pay off his debts, provided his mother would give me truthful answers to a few questions I wished to ask her. The old woman was awfully afraid of the workhouse, and she said,—

" ' I know very well what you wish to know, and I can tell things worth hundreds to the right person ; but I'm told he's dead.' "

" Well, there's the £30," said I, putting three ten-pound notes on the table, " and I promise you this, if the person you mean is not dead—and I am pretty certain he is not—you shall get well rewarded for any information you may give me.'

" Well, indeed, sir, I fear he has been made away with,"

said the old dame, "and I will tell you why I think so. I saw George Mason, not six weeks ago, and he said, in talking about him, ' He's dead by this time, at all events.' Now, why he should wish him dead, I cannot imagine."

" Do you know, my young friend," continued the super-intendent, "that I was really startled by what the old woman said, for I began to imagine Mason and his accomplice might have been excited, by any resistance you were sure to offer, to kill you, though what benefit they could gain, like the old woman, I could not imagine."

" Ah !" observed our hero, "I now see where I committed a great error. When the ' Foam ' lay-to off Ramsgate to take up passengers, I ought to have written you a line, and ex-plained how I had been carried off. Your kindness and in-terest in my affairs I can never sufficiently appreciate, and your expenses——"

" Oh, we will talk upon that subject hereafter, my dear sir ; we have some difficulties to overcome yet. If you fail to recover those most important papers, so mysteriously taken from the baronet's person at the time of his death, we shall, I fear, be baffled by the technicalities of the law. I can make it quite clear to the understanding, and to the public in general, that you are unquestionably Sir Richard Morton's eldest legitimate son ; but the law, to substantiate your claim, will require something more than assertions. Let me give you the substance of the intelligence I was able to obtain from old Dame Dulford. By her account she lived as domestic servant with the Masons several years before the late baronet came into possession of the Morton estates. It is necessary, though painful, to state that your father, before he came into possession of the estates, had actually courted, and even talked of marriage, to John Mason's eldest daughter ; whose father had great hopes of being able to entrap the young baronet, when he came of age, into a marriage ; but at this time there came on a visit to the Masons a schoolfellow, an orphan, and extremely beautiful. Miss Grace Manning, by a strange freak of nature, bore an extraordinary resemblance to old Mason's daughter. When not together, they were singularly likely to be mistaken for each other. But they were widely different in temper and disposition. The young baronet transferred his attentions and affections to Grace Manning. It was at this period that Sir Richard Morton discovered that John Mason had put his signature to a £1,000 cheque. He thus gained complete power over the Masons, and, I regret to say, he forced them to aid his designs upon Grace Manning. A false marriage was intended, but John Mason, to be revenged, to a certain extent, upon the baronet, employed a real clergyman, but a most consummate rascal, a disgrace to the cloth, and who shortly after met his deserts, was disgraced, and had to fly the country to avoid prosecution for fraud. Your poor mother, who was, Mrs. Dulford said, devotedly attached to your father, fortunately never knew the fraud her husband intended her; she died in giving you birth. The Masons knew that they had Sir Richard Morton in their power, for a year after his wife's death he married again, a lady of station and fortune, who was devotedly attached to him. Old Mrs. Dulford acknowledged to me she knew that Jay Pearson was a clergyman, and that she received ten pounds for keeping the secret. But it seems that this same Jay Pearson departed without giving them the certificate of the marriage, and before John Mason could get hold of him he had fled to America. The whole proceedings of the Masons before their departure for America was a deep-laid scheme, to hold Sir Richard Morton in perpetual terror, and by those means extort money. The only mystery I cannot well understand was the attempt to assassinate Sir Richard Morton in his library. Nor could Mrs. Dulford enlighten me on that particular subject, although she hid George Mason in her house for three days after his flight from Morton Chase, and finally aided him in escaping out of the country, by disguising him in female apparel."

"I have no doubt," remarked Arthur, "that my father proceeded to America for the sole purpose of unravelling the mystery of his first marriage, and to obtain positive information relative to my mother's death—information so important, for without such proof his second marriage became a myth, and his children illegitimate; a circumstance sufficient to break his heart, or render the remainder of his days wretched."

"Happily," remarked Mr. Baldwin, "Lady Morton and her children are saved from such an infliction, and though you would, of course, take the title and family estates, yet Lady Morton's own large fortune, settled on herself, and an estate worth £1,500 a year, left her eldest son by an uncle, leaves them not only independent, but affluent. The great question is to gain possession of the stolen papers—stolen, no doubt, for the sake of the reward that may be offered. There will be no difficulty in proving that you are the infant abandoned on the sands at Ramsgate; the chain of evidence on that point is clear and decisive."

CHAPTER XXVI.

ON the 24th of September, the fine steamer, Ocean Queen, sailed from Liverpool, bound for New York. She was to touch at Cork for passengers. On board this steamer was our hero

and his attendant, Joseph.   He had proceeded with Mr.
Marchmont to Southampton, and had spent a week with the
family, who were now located in a pleasant villa residence,
some short distance from the town.   Need we say that the
meeting of the lovers was truly one of pure happiness, though
its brightness was certainly obscured by the melancholy fate
of Sir Richard Morton ?

The eldest Miss Marchmont had also been relieved from
many painful thoughts since their arrival in England.   Intelligence had reached her that Lieutenant Singleton, the young
officer to whom she was sincerely attached, had, shortly after
his arrival in India, been appointed a captain in the —th Foot,
then in England, and by the death of an uncle had also in-
herited an estate in Scotland worth £2,000 a year, without
incumbrance.   Miss Marchmont, therefore, felt satisfied that
no opposition would now be made to her lover's proposals.
Captain Singleton was shortly expected in England.

The steamer that was to sail from Southampton had met
with an accident, and would not be fit for sea in less than a
month, and much as he enjoyed the society of his beloved
Alice, our hero felt so anxious to reach the scene of his father's
untimely death, in order that the cruel perpetrators of this
crime might be brought to justice, that he resolved to depart
by the first steamer from Liverpool.   He had made many inquiries after Lady Morton and family, but all the intelligence
he could gain was that they were on the Continent.

Alice had a tinge of melancholy, and a feeling of some unknown dread, on her mind as she fondly bade her lover farewell.   She could not divest her mind of the belief that the
object he had in view had a certain amount of danger in it.
Any dealings with the Mason family to her appeared a risk of
life, from the treacherous, scheming character of the whole
family.   Besides, the assassins of the baronet were still at
large.   The newspapers stated nothing about the death of old
John Mason, the last account simply being that "the murderers of the English baronet were positively known, but had
baffled all pursuit."

Alice tenderly implored Arthur to be careful and cautious,
and not rashly embark in a pursuit of the Masons into the
wilds of a country where any crime might be committed with
impunity.

"You broke your promise to me, dear Arthur," she said,
with her expressive eyes fixed fondly on her lover, "when
you went to shoot in the Punza Pulka river; and see to what
a terrible, awful trial you were put."

"True, my beloved," returned her lover, pressing a kiss
upon the fair girl's lips, "and I deserved the punishment I

received. But that is no excuse; for my thoughtlessness caused you, my own Alice, pain and uneasiness. But, thank God! we are, through a merciful Providence, again re-united, and I look forward with hope, and a firm reliance on Divine mercy, to be able to bring the cowardly murderers of Sir Richard Morton to justice, and recover the papers so essential to establish my rights, so that you, my own Alice, may not have to bestow this dear hand upon a nameless individual."

"Ah, my dear Arthur, you well know that my affection does not depend upon a name. Whether Arthur Bolton or Sir Arthur Morton, it makes no difference to Alice Marchmont."

Our hero received many directions and cautious advice as to how to proceed on reaching Delaware, and from Mr. and Mrs. Marchmont, and provided with ample funds, he and Joseph, who had become a general favourite, set out for Liverpool.

There were sixteen cabin passengers. Captain Spalding gave our hero a very kindly welcome. "I am really rejoiced," said he, "to have you for a passenger. Courtney gave me but a brief outline of the mutiny aboard the 'Foam;' so now I shall have a full account of that extraordinary affair, and of his most miraculous escape."

"You shall hear how it all occurred," replied our hero; "we shall have time enough on our hands. Do you expect many passengers, touching at the Cove of Cork?"

"Twenty-two in all—nine for the cabin, and the rest steerage—and probably several more since we had our agent's letter."

The Ocean Queen was a fast steamer, and the weather fine, so that in sixteen hours after their departure from Liverpool the vessel anchored in the Cove of Cork.

Arthur, during that short passage, had but little opportunity of judging whether his fellow-passengers were agreeable or otherwise, for though the weather was fine, there was a heavy swell from the south-west, which appeared to render most of the ladies uncomfortable, and two or three of the gentlemen also.

The Cove of Cork, with its noble expanse of water, the islands, and the scenery of the surrounding shores, meets the eye unexpectedly, the entrance from the sea, between two high hills, being extremely narrow.

There was no delay, the Ocean Queen was true to time; all the passengers were prepared for her arrival, and, knowing that she would remain only sufficient time to embark the mails and passengers, all came out to the vessel at once in a small steamer.

Amongst the cabin passengers, as the steamer dropped alongside the Ocean Queen, our hero was struck by the appearance of a family in deep mourning, consisting, evidently, of mother, two daughters, and son. The mother had all the appearance of a lady in high station ; in age about forty, exceedingly pale, but with very beautiful features, wearing a very sad expression. The daughters were handsome girls, and the son a young man about twenty, slightly made, but tall and elegant in his appearance and manners. There were two female attendants, with but a small amount of luggage. The whole party looked depressed, and appeared to shun observation or conversation, retiring immediately to the three state-cabins they had secured for the voyage.

Arthur Bolton was also in deep mourning, and as the luggage remained a moment on deck, had the unaccountable curiosity to read the name, feeling somewhat disappointed on reading that of Herbert, New York.

Before sunset the Ocean Queen was steering through the still waters of the Cove, and passing the lighthouse on the east shore, and then shaping her course for the old Head of Kinsale.

Our hero joined Captain Spalding on the bridge. The weather had not as pleasant a look as in the morning, and Captain Spalding remarked that they would have a breeze before morning.

"It looks like it," observed Arthur, "the heavy swell of yesterday was a sure sign of a breeze in the Atlantic. Did you remark," he continued, "the family in such deep mourning that came on board at the Cove? Their name, I see by the luggage, is Herbert."

"I did," replied the captain, "and I also observed the singular likeness young Mr. Herbert bears to you. It struck me immediately. They engaged their private cabins in Liverpool."

Arthur started.

"Like me!" he thought to himself; "it's very strange, but something of the sort flashed on my mind."

The old Head was shortly passed after the lights were visible, and then their course was shaped for Cape Clear.

"Come, Mr. Bolton," said the skipper, laying his hand on our hero's shoulder, "I have an hour or so to spare. Come to my cabin ; we will have a cigar and a glass of grog, and a little chat ; before morning we shall be pitching into a head sea, and no mistake."

Before dawn it was blowing a strong gale from the southwest, with a very heavy sea, which soon tried the sailing qualities of the cabin passengers, only five sitting down to breakfast with the captain and our hero.

None of Mrs. Herbert's family appeared, the steward stating

that they were not very unwell, but not disposed to trust their legs, for the sea was a cross sea, and the vessel rolled heavily, though she made good six knots against the gale, which increased in violence.

At dinner the passengers were reduced to three—the captain and Arthur Bolton, and a naval officer.

"Faith, captain," said the latter, a burly-looking gentleman, in years about forty, helping himself to the half of a roast fowl, "this is seasoning your passengers with a vengeance; if the wind continues like this, half the voyage will be over before the passengers come to know one another."

"It will blow itself out to-night, I think," returned the captain; "it looks for a change into the north-west. We can hardly expect gales of long duration this month. Our fair passengers will enjoy the rest of the passage, for we shall have fine weather and smooth water. Pleasure of a glass of wine, Mr. Bolton?"

As the captain uttered the word Bolton, the door of a state-room opened, and Arthur beheld the young gentleman named Herbert enter the cabin. He had evidently heard the name, for he paused, and looked earnestly into our hero's face as he raised his glass to his lips.

"I am glad to see you able to join us, Mr. Herbert," said the captain, ordering one of the stewards to screw down a chair for the young gentleman; "I hope your ladies are not suffering from this rough weather. You do not look as if you had been a victim to the perfidious sea, as our French neighbours call that noble element."

"No; my mother and sisters suffer very little sickness, captain," returned Mr. Herbert, "and I never suffer at sea; but I had a very violent headache when I came on board. It blows very hard, I suppose, judging by the various sounds, and by the motion of the ship?"

"Yes; it blows hard, but nothing unusual: only one of our equinoctial gales," answered Captain Spalding.

Young Mr. Herbert had sat down beside our hero. The bluff gentleman, whose name was Sullivan, was placed opposite. Captain Denis Sullivan, after looking earnestly, first at our hero, and then at Mr. Herbert, both of whom were in mourning, said,—

"Upon my conscience, you two gentlemen are wonderfully like each other; excuse me, but, by St. Patrick, I could fancy you were chips of the same block, only that one is called Bolton and the other Herbert."

Mr. Herbert changed colour, but made no remark, whilst Arthur Bolton replied, with a smile, looking into the handsome, ingenuous countenance of his neighbour,—

"Those chance likenesses will sometimes occur; Captain Spalding remarked our similarity the moment you came on board, Mr. Herbert."

"I must say I observed it myself," answered the young man, seeing our hero addressed his observation to him.

"By the way, Mr. Bolton," interrupted Captain Sullivan, who was skipper of one of the Canadian line of packets, "your name, though a very usual one in both Ireland and England, recalls a circumstance that occurred, some fourteen or fifteen months ago, to my mind, which created a great deal of excitement amongst us skippers, and of which I have heard nothing since. I dare say, Spalding, you remember the tragical event as well as myself—I mean the mutiny aboard the 'Foam,' a Jamaica packet ship; her captain, a brave and skilful seaman, was inhumanly murdered, and the ship afterwards wrecked, somewhere or other—where, I never heard; but I know the names of the passengers in the 'Foam' were published, and a young man named Arthur Bolton was one."

Mr. Herbert looked exceedingly pale; his eyes became fixed upon our hero, and his agitation he could scarcely control.

"By Jove, Sullivan, you have hit the nail on the right head!" replied Captain Spalding, before our hero could reply. "This is the very Mr. Bolton who was aboard the 'Foam,' and who so gallantly risked his life to save my old friend Courtney, whom I am happy to tell you is alive and well."

Mr. Herbert rose hastily from his chair, praying them to excuse him; his head felt very light, he would retire and lie down.

"Faith, I thought, sir, you were not very well these last few minutes," said Captain Sullivan. "You look very pale; better lie down; by St. Patrick, we do pitch a bit just now! but, Spalding, you amaze me. Captain Courtney not murdered? that's strange; but I rejoice to hear it, and rejoice to make your acquaintance, Mr. Bolton;" and Captain Sullivan held out his hand and shook our hero's heartily.

The dinner-things were cleared away, wine placed upon the table, and Captain Sullivan, eager to know our hero's account of the mutiny, settled himself comfortably, whilst Captain Spalding proceeded on deck.

Arthur, in his brief narrative, merely confined himself to the actual account of the mutiny, the running ashore on the Musquito coast, and the providential escape of Captain Courtney.

Whilst our hero was relating the incidents of the mutiny to Captain Sullivan, Mr. Herbert, who had retired from the cabin on the plea of returning headache, passed through his own little cabin, and into a narrow passage leading into the small but comfortable state cabin occupied by his mother and sisters. These ladies were not suffering from sea-sickness; they were dressed, and reposing on the sofas beneath their couches, talking seriously and cheering each other as much as possible ; for though each countenance bore the impress of recent grief, smiles often gleamed amidst the gloom, which proved their grief had lost its first bitterness, and could be conquered.

"Dear me, Richard," remarked the elder sister, looking up into her brother's face as he entered, "you are exceedingly pale; you must be suffering from sea-sickness, though I thought you were proof against that malady."

"No, Kate, I am not suffering from sickness," he answered, as he seated himself next his mother, whose hand he took, saying, "Do you know, dear mother, who is on board this ship as a passenger?"

The mother raised her head from the cushion with a repressed sigh, and a half-smile, as she said, "I have no idea, Richard; no one who knows us, I trust."

"No; there is no one, I am sure, that you ever saw before; but though the person I mean has no knowledge of us personally, nevertheless we are intimately connected : in fact, dear mother, my half-brother, who passes under the name of Arthur Bolton, is in this ship, and is now sitting in the cabin with another passenger."

Mother and daughters raised themselves with feelings of intense astonishment; the mother exclaiming, "How is that possible? We know he sailed in a brig called the 'Foam' for Jamaica; that the crew mutinied, murdered the captain and passengers, and was afterwards wrecked, somewhere—I forget where."

"Precisely," returned her son; "this young man—and a remarkably handsome fellow he is, as ever I saw—is the identical Arthur Bolton who embarked in the vessel called the 'Foam;' I left him, a minute since, giving an account of the mutiny, and the murder of the captain, to the passenger, who is the skipper of a large ship."

"How extraordinary !" said both mother and sisters.

"Shall we still continue under our travelling name, or shall we make ourselves known to this Mr. Bolton?" questioned the eldest daughter.

"No," returned the mother, after a few moments' thought, "I think not; it would lead to such inquiries, and create so much curiosity, as to become terribly painful to us. No; I would advise Richard to cultivate his acquaintance in a friendly way—as two young men meeting on board ship usually do—

and when we reach New York we can easily introduce ourselves, and reveal to him our near relationship. Doubtless," she added, with a heavy sigh, " he has ascertained who he is, and is now, like ourselves, hastening to Delaware to investigate the causes that led to his father's cruel and untimely fate."

As Lady Morton spoke, the tears ran down her cheeks, and she buried her face in her hands.

At the end of six-and-thirty hours the gale ceased, the sky cleared, and fair weather and a north-east wind carried the Ocean Queen rapidly on her proper route.

Mrs. Herbert, as we shall still call Lady Morton, and her daughters, for health's sake, left their cabins, and mingled with their fellow-passengers at meal-times, and walked upon the deck, as the sea was by no means unruly, and the wind fair. In three days Arthur and young Mr. Herbert had become extremely intimate ; a feeling of great partiality the one for the other sprang up between them. Mr. Herbert introduced our hero to his mother and sisters, and though Mrs. Herbert trembled, and her heart beat faster as she gazed up into features so strong in their resemblance to her deeply-lamented husband, still she mastered her emotion, and conversed with him on various subjects, charmed by his manner, and interested by his unassuming demeanour ; and so also were the two sisters ; altogether they became extremely intimate.

A continuance of fine weather brought the Ocean Queen within three days of her destination, when she encountered one of those sudden and tremendous hurricanes so often met with in that latitude, and at that particular time of year.

Her skilful commander and a most efficient crew, however, enabled her to weather the first fury of the hurricane ; but the second day the starboard paddle-wheel was struck by a tremendous sea, which washed away the entire box, and crumpled up the iron work of the wheel like hoop-iron, completely destroying the working of the starboard paddle. Close-reefed fore-and-aft sails were then set, and, with the aid of one wheel, the ship was kept head to wind.

Arthur and Capatin Sullivan remained on deck all night, to render any assistance in their power, for several of the crew had been hurt by being knocked about the ship by a sea that had swept over her decks.

During the second night of the storm, which was even more violent than the first, the gale right ahead, and the darkness intense, the boom of a heavy gun resounded above even the howling of the gale, and the crash of the breakers, as they surged against the stout sides of the ship, was heard by those on deck. At this moment Captain Spalding was standing by Arthur Bolton's side, and close beside the wheel, which required two men to manage.

"That gun, Mr. Bolton," cried Captain Spalding, "is, I imagine, fired from some ship, no doubt in distress; and by the sound can be scarcely a quarter of a mile distant. It is very probable she got a glimpse of our lights."

"There's another gun, captain," said Arthur, with some anxiety.

He had scarcely uttered the words before a succession of blue lights threw their startling gleam over the storm-tossed billows that roared and broke in foam, whirled into the air by the wild storm-blast that howled through the rigging of the ship.

In the bright gleam of the blue lights all on board the steamer caught sight of a very large ship, as she rose and fell upon the tremendous seas. She did not appear more than three hundred yards distant. She was evidently drifting towards them, as well as they could make out. But all doubt was almost immediately removed by a bright sheet of flame shooting up into the air, increasing each moment, till at last all on board the steamer could plainly see that the great ship drifting down upon them was wrapped in a blaze of fire.

What a fearful sight became revealed to the excited crew of the Ocean Queen! The fore part of the strange ship was in flames, whilst the after-deck was crowded by a mass of terrified and horror-struck people. The flames had first seized the fore rigging, and then the mast, sails, and yards, presenting a grand but fearful spectacle.

"Be steady and cool, my men," exclaimed Captain Spalding to the sailors at the wheel.

Orders were given to put on more steam, and then the course of the Ocean Queen was altered, drifting two or three points to leeward. The burning ship, quite ungovernable, was rapidly advancing under the stern of the steamer.

It was an awful sight. All the male passengers of the Ocean Queen had managed to come on deck, and stood stupified, holding on by anything they could grasp, gazing at the doomed vessel as it drifted by, the shrieks of her heart-stricken passengers and crew ringing through the storm, whilst the tremendous sea raging added to the horror of the scene; for huge waves struck the steamer as well as the burning ship, drenching their crews with the flood of water over their decks; but the flames raged the fiercer, as if in mockery of the opposing element's efforts to extinguish their fury. There were no boats evidently on board the burning ship. No doubt they had been washed away and broken by the seas that swept her decks.

" We must make an attempt, Captain Spalding, to save some of those unfortunate creatures," cried Arthur, ready and determined to risk life in the venture, and greatly excited.

" Yes," answered the captain, "but they must be volunteers ; the risk is awful in this terrible sea."

Our hero turned to the crew of seamen, shouting in his clear, manly voice, " Now, my lads, who volunteers for the boats ? We cannot see our fellow-creatures perish, and not try to save them. Who volunteers to try ? "

A hearty British cheer, " to a man," they replied, "we are ready."

" Come, then, my brave fellows," said Captain Suilivan, " Mr. Bolton will take charge of one boat, and I will take the other."

Again a cheer, that mocked the storm-gusts as they roared through the rigging, and the splash of the mighty waves as they swayed against the sides of the noble ship ; but neither the storm-gust, nor the wild broken-crested waves daunted the stout hearts of the British tars.

The Ocean Queen was kept away following the drifting ship. It was an awfully grand sight—the strange vessel was above a thousand tons burden, and by this time the fierce flames, fanned into redoubled power by the relentless force of the storm, had devoured the rigging, spars, and yards of the foremast, and was rapidly advancing aft. The heat must have been even then overpowering.

Six men were all that could be spared to each life-boat, and watching a favourable moment, both boats were skilfully got over the sides with their crews all ready, each man supplied with a life-belt, and were lowered into the boiling sea, and then with a hearty cheer they gave way for the burning ship.

As Arthur steered his boat to gain the side of the stranger, he could perceive upon her after-deck, by the lurid light of the flames, women holding up their children in frantic despair, hoping that the sight of helpless innocence would stimulate the brave hearts who already were risking their lives to save them. The sea was tremendous, and the greatest skill, watchfulness, and care was necessary to prevent the boats from being swamped by the breaking billows.

It would be scarcely possible for the boats to take in more than fifteen persons in each, though they were fine commodious boats. The great peril, however, to be feared was the fatal rush generally made by those on board ships on fire : to go alongside was out of the question ; the boats would be stove in pieces : dropping, therefore, under her stern, our hero and Captain Sullivan hailed and told those who were furiously pushing their way aft to be calm, and to throw ropes over, with any floating article attached. The crew of the ship, which was British, behaved nobly; they drew back the mad crowd, got ropes and a small hawser over the lee side of the boat, and insisted on the women and children being put over first.

Thanks to the main and mizen masts being carried away before the fire took place, the flames did not make such rapid progress aft as otherwise would have been the case; but at times a tremendous sea would strike the ship, and send her dead before the gale, and then again she would fall into the trough of the waters rolling—though a heavily-laden ship and high sides—till her bulwarks touched the seas. Just as our hero had successfully embarked six women and their children, and five men, a man on the deck of the burning ship shouted through a speaking trumpet, "Be quick, for God's sake! there are fifty barrels of gunpowder on board."

This was not pleasant information for those in the life-boats, and created such a panic that numbers threw themselves into the boats and into the sea, shouting wildly to God for help.

Still the gallant crews of the life-boats saved all they could, and with eighteen human beings in his, Arthur let go his ropes and made for the steamer: they were dangerously deep. Captain Sullivan also was full. As they moved from the ship shouts and screams of despair mingled with the furious blasts; many threw themselves over to perish by water, sooner than by fire.

"We will come back again," roared our hero, till his voice failed him. After incredible efforts, they succeeded in reaching the steamer, which was kept as close as possible to windward of the burning ship.

After putting those rescued on board, the life-boats again, with a cheer, pulled away for the wreck, when a tremendous sea struck Captain Sullivan's boat, turning her right over, and leaving her entire crew scattered amid the waves. Aided by the flames of the ship, Arthur's men rescued them from their perilous situation, but in doing so their boat became half full of water. As they drifted towards the ship, bailing out the water with buckets, a fearful explosion took place on board the doomed ship. She was rent asunder; burnt and blazing planks, spars, masts, and human beings were hurled aloft in wild and horrible medley, and the next moment the boats became enveloped in the pitch darkness of a terrible night; whilst the squalls rushed past with terrible force, and the wild seas chased each other as if in sport, dashing the gallant boat and its hardy crew into an abyss of foaming water. Just then they came against a spar, and a cry of a human voice caught their ears: several hands grasped at a man clinging to the spar, and dragged him into the boat.   The last man saved was the captain of the fated ship.

"God help the lost ones!" exclaimed our hero, as they drifted down on the Ocean Queen, where those on board were suffering a state of intense anxiety, burning blue lights, and firing a gun.

"Steady, men, steady!" said Captain Sullivan, "another sea like that and we are lost;" in fact, the boat could scarcely live, for sea after sea dashed over them, but skilfully steered and pulled she was rounded to under the lee of the steamer. Hooks and ropes were ready, and with a hearty cheer boat and men were safely deposited upon the deck of the Ocean Queen."

Drenched, and no little exhausted, Arthur leaped from the boat on to the deck amidst a crowd of excited persons, who cheered and praised them all for their gallantry.   He felt himself embraced, and a soft voice whispered: "Dear Arthur, thank God you are back safe and well!" and then the voice added, still lower and more affectionately, "It is a brother who embraces you."

Astonished, our hero turned and gazed upon the speaker; the light of a ship's lantern fell upon the pale, handsome face of young Mr. Herbert.

Delighted and amazed, he returned the brotherly embrace, saying: "Is this possible—oh! how I rejoice to feel, for the first time, the pressure of a brother's hand."

"Keep the secret for a while, dear Arthur, and now hasten and change your soaked garments; this has been a terrible night, and oh! my God, a fearful and horrible scene."

All the night, and the greater part of the next day, the storm raged with unabated violence.   It then gradually subsided, and the Ocean Queen, having temporarily repaired the damages received, pursued her course towards New York. Every possible attention was bestowed on those of the crew and passengers who had been rescued from the North Star, American packet ship.   Every solace that kind words and sympathy could give was freely bestowed; whilst praises and admiration for those who saved them fell from each lip and was felt in each heart.

CHAPTER XXVII.

WHEN Arthur met Mr. Herbert the next day, the latter gave him a brief explanation.   Our hero then knew who Mrs. Herbert and her daughters were: this discovery afforded him great satisfaction, but the young men mutually agreed to let the knowledge of their relationship remain a secret from the other passengers; but as soon as they landed in New York, it being Lady Morton's intention to proceed to Delaware, there would be no longer any necessity for keeping that relationship from any person's knowledge.

After the subsiding of the storm, Captain Webb, of the North Star, stated to his brother captain and those assembled at the supper-table, that the fire on board his ship broke out the day previous to the gale, and baffled all their efforts to subdue it; they, therefore, fastened down all the hatches and carried on all sail, still hoping against hope to be able to make land before the flames quite overpowered them. They had their boats, but in the frightful hurricane they lost them all, when just as the fire was forcing itself out through the hatches and deck, they made out the lights of the Ocean Queen. All, no doubt, would have been saved but for the terrific violence of the gale and the height of the sea.

Captain Webb became anxious, after the cessation of the gale, to ascertain who and how many of his crew and passengers were saved; they were accordingly mustered on deck, that is the male portion of them. Arthur and his half-brother were standing near, as Captain Webb, with a heavy heart and a faltering voice, called over the names. He then knew that seven passengers and nine seamen had perished, eleven of his crew saved, six first-class cabin passengers, five children, and nine steerage.

As Arthur let his eyes rest upon the faces of the male passengers he started, and a flush came into his cheek, and his eyes flashed fire with excitement. Drawing back a little out of observation, he again gazed earnestly at the two passengers who first attracted his attention; one he instantly recognized to be the villain Saunders, the associate of George Mason, who placed him in the " Foam;" the other had received a recent severe cut, that divided his upper lip, and this cut, with the piece of plaister across it, considerably altered his countenance, but the second inspection satisfied him that he beheld the possessor of the inimitable perfume, George Mason. His first impulse was to start forward and confront his enemies, who did not appear to notice him; but a moment's reflection convinced him that doing so then could lead to no good result. He, however, resolved that they should not leave the ship unknown to him: he was uncertain whether he could have them arrested on landing in New York, but he would speak to Captain Spalding on the subject, and take his advice.

" You have seen some one amongst those men, Arthur," observed Richard Herbert, " you recognize; your expression of countenance struck me—is it not so?"

"Yes, Richard, I have. The wretch who attempted to assassinate our father is now in this ship, and also his detestable associate Saunders, who helped him to inveigle me on board the 'Foam,' and whose brother, one of the mutineers, perished so fearfully in the hole they threw me into."

"Good heavens! do you say so? how extraordinary. But, on account of my mother and sisters, don't you think it better to let them remain in ignorance that you recognize them?"

"Such is my opinion, Richard; but, nevertheless, they must not escape me."

After the muster of the crew and passengers of the North Star was over, and the sailors and passengers dispersed themselves over the ship, two men seated themselves on a chest in the fore-cabin, and began conversing, as soon as they found themselves alone.

Our readers can readily surmise that these two men were George Mason and Saunders. They were known as passengers in the North Star; Mason calling himself Peters—Saunders, Brown. Arthur was mistaken in supposing he had not been recognized, for Mason had discovered his identity when he threw himself off the deck of the burning ship, striking his face against the gunnel of the boat, and splitting his lip open. Hauled up into the boat, half drowned, stunned, and bleeding from the severe cut, he had remained in the bow of the boat, unnoticed by our hero. Saunders, a cool, collected seaman, saved himself by getting into Captain Sullivan's boat.

"I wonder," observed Saunders, to his companion, "did he recognize us, when mustered upon deck? It's all up with us if he did."

"Tut," interrupted Mason, contemptuously, "what matters—but I don't think he did—and if he did, what power has he to injure us in America?—none. We baffled every attempt to arrest us in England, though we were hunted through three counties, till we finally got to Ireland. We suffered enough, curse them! But now we're safe, and will pay back some of our sufferings on the head of him who caused them. Strange that he should be aboard this ship!"

"Where do you think he is going?" questioned Saunders. "I cannot imagine how he escaped when Bill and the rest of the crew of the 'Foam' killed the captain, and threw him, and all on board, into the sea. I have never been able to learn what became of Bill and the brig."

"Why," returned Mason, "now you mention it, I saw a paper in the North Star, in which it was stated that the brig 'Foam' was driven ashore on the Musquito Coast, and all the passengers saved; so he must, by some unaccountable method have escaped Bill's knife, and got to England, and by some means or other has learnt something about himself, and is perhaps going to Delaware to hunt out my father.   My dropping the papers during the scuffle with Sir Richard Morton in the library has ruined all my prospects ; luckily I got the five hundred pounds I seized, safe and sound in my belt.   Now the baronet is quite willing to acknowledge this Arthur Bolton as the lawful son of his first wife, provided he can satisfy himself that his first wife died before he married his second."

"Well, how will he discover that ?   Blow me, I should like to throw them out !   I detest that youngster, for, somehow, it strikes me he has done for my brother Bill ; he's a cursed fiery chap."

"Patience, Jem, we have not done with him yet ; I intend to make money of him, now he has again come in my way. But as to Sir Richard finding out that his first wife died before he married his second, he can do it easy enough, by going to Delaware and finding my sister, Mrs. Jackson, in the land of the living."

"Well, let us get ashore, in New York," said Saunders, "and I will keep my eye on the movements of this youngster ; and if I find that he has taken my brother Bill's life, I'll put my knife in him with more certainty than you did yours into his father."

"Curse it ! that was a madman's act of mine," responded Mason, bitterly.   "He would never have had the papers without paying a large sum, but for that.   I was an idiot to carry them about me, and a greater fool to say so ; but there's much to be done yet ; and if he goes to Delaware and near Fork Farm, my younger brothers will soon make short work of him.   Let us keep close till we anchor ; once ashore, we are all right."

After a favourable run of three days, the Ocean Queen reached her destination, and landed all her passengers. George Mason, and his companion, Saunders, were allowed to go on shore, to their infinite pleasure, perfectly unmolested, and fully convinced they had neither been noticed nor recognized by one for whose destruction they were forming wicked devices.   The different passengers disposed of themselves according to their previous determination.   Mrs. Herbert and family, with Arthur, now acknowledged, and indeed treated as the head of the family, and as successor to the late Sir Richard Morton, remained together—her ladyship being perfectly satisfied in her own mind as to the fact of his birth, and his mother's marriage.

We must, however, for a time follow in the footsteps of George Mason, who, leaving Saunders to watch the proceedings of Arthur and the family he seemed so intimate with, set out with all speed to reach Delaware, little imagining the news that awaited his arrival.

On reaching Delaware he was forced, owing to the severity of the night, to put up at a hotel. This hotel was the same to which the unfortunate Sir Richard Morton had been carried when brought back wounded to Delaware. During the journey Mason avoided all conversation with those he came in contact with, trusting that the scar on his face had so altered him that he would not be recognized by those who formerly knew him, till he reached Fork Farm, and learned how affairs stood there.

Entering the large room appropriated to travellers, he perceived two persons sitting at the table smoking and drinking. It was a wild stormy night, and the rain came down in a deluge, or he would have proceeded to Fork Farm, even if he walked the distance, so eager was he to reach home.

He called for a pipe and a tumbler of hot whisky toddy, which the landlord himself brought in, and then George Mason got a view of the two other occupants of the room ; he started as he sat down, turning his face away from the others, who were no strangers to him. One was Luke Patten, the other, Mr. Bowen's, the solicitor, clerk—a cousin of Luke Patten's.

"It's a wild night, stranger," said the landlord, as he sat down and joined the smokers. "You don't, I calculate, think of stirring abroad till morning?"

"Well, not now, in this torrent of rain, certainly, but I wish it were better weather, for I want to get to Fork Farm."

"Fork Farm," repeated the landlord. "Well, I guess you would soon like to be back again; there's no one in Fork Farm—none but keepers. Old John Mason's dead."

"John Mason dead!" repeated George, starting from his seat, his lips parched, and his cheek deadly pale ; "then where are his sons?"

A loud call from the bar caused the landlord to leave, saying, as he departed, "there's Luke Patten, a near neighbour to the Fork, will tell you all the news. I guess it's some time since you were in these parts."

Luke Patten, one of the guests at the table, got up and approached the shocked George Mason, for disregard of family ties was not one of his crimes ; he was fond of his father, and he felt the intelligence of his death severely ; besides which, Fork Farm being in the hands of keepers confused and oppressed him terribly ; where then were his two brothers, Mrs. Jackson, and his sister Mary?

When Luke Patten approached George Mason, the latter

looked fiercely up into his face : there had always been ill-blood between them, but Luke Patten said,—

"I recognize you now, George Mason ; that scar on your lip and cheek might puzzle others—not me."

"What is it to you, Luke Patten, if I am George Mason ? there never was much friendship between us, and I do not see why there ever should."

"I must wish you good night, Luke," said James Nicol, Mr. Bowen's clerk. "It's a bad night, and my governor keeps regular hours." The young man shook hands with his cousin, nodded to Mason, and departed.

"I tell you what," said Luke Patten, seating himself by the side of the sullen George Mason, "it is better that we should be friends now, if we never were before. In the first place, I am the husband of your sister Mary."

Mason bit his lip with passion and vexation. "So," said he, "the weak fool married you at last. Where were my brothers, for I suppose it is since my father's death you obtained her ?"

"Exactly so," returned Luke. "Your brothers were accused of murdering an English baronet—Sir Richard Morton."

With a fearful oath George Mason sprang from his seat. He would have seized Luke by the throat, but his brother-in-law was a powerful, and, he well knew, a very determined man.

"Now, George," remonstrated Patten, very coolly knocking the ashes out of his pipe, "this is folly, giving way to passion with me. We can assist each other. I shall make it clear to you that I am willing to be your best friend, and that without me you are in a bad way. Fork Farm will be lost to you ; be friendly to me, and I will surely enable you to keep possession of it."

Mason was bewildered. He felt deeply his father's death, but to lose Fork Farm besides, and to be told that his brothers were accused of murdering Sir Richard Morton, appeared a thing so incredible that he remained stupified ; tossing down a tumbler of strong whisky, he sat down, saying :

"Luke, we always hated one another ; probably we do so still, but we are necessary to one another. If we are to ride in the same boat, we should pull together. Answer me one question. Is Sir Richard Morton dead ?"

"I deeply regret to say," answered Luke, "he was cruelly murdered, and by your two brothers."

Mason could scarcely contain himself—he was savage with passion.

"Murdered, and by my brothers !" he muttered : then, with

a fierce execration, he exclaimed aloud, " Did they kill their father, too ? "

" No, George, that they did not," replied Patten, calmly. " Moderate your passion and listen to particulars, and then you will understand your true position, and how we may act in concert and for our mutual benefit."

" But who accused my brothers of this murder ? " demanded George, in an excited manner.   " What brought the baronet here ? "

" To ascertain the legitimacy of his first-born son," returned Patten.   " He obtained the necessary documents from your father, and in return presented him with a cheque on a New York bank for £3,000."

" What ! " exclaimed Mason with an ironical laugh, " after receiving £3,000 my brothers murdered their benefactor ! this is incredible.   Who saw them commit the deed ? "

" I did ! " returned Luke, " and I accused them of the crime when the constables entered your father's house to arrest them on suspicion."

Mason again sprang to his feet : this time he drew a revolver from his breast coat-pocket and cocked it. Luke never stirred, but coolly replenished his tumbler, saying,—

" Put up your weapon, George, killing me will only get you hanged ; whereas, if you can bring yourself to listen quietly for ten minutes I will make all clear to you.   But if you burst into passionate fits and interrupt me, I must leave you to your own headstrong passions."

A slave to passion all his life, Mason gazed with bewildered feelings on the calm, self-possessed man before him.   Thrusting the pistol in his breast, he said,—

" Order more liquor and I'll listen to you.   You are not now, I suspect, the prosperous man I thonght you were."

" No," returned Patten, bitterly, " my folly and infatuation, and love of play, have ruined my prospects.   I would save my wife, whom I dearly love, from poverty and misery, and that's the reason Luke Patten leagues with George Mason, to—to—better his fortunes."

More liquor was brought in, and the two men then sat for some moments, each engrossed with their own thoughts. Mason, who was addicted to drink, seemed inclined to give way to it, for he drank off a couple of tumblers before he uttered a word.   Luke Patten could drink, but he rarely indeed ever gave way to intemperance.   He waited patiently till George Mason had recovered himself: at length Mason said,—

" Now let us thoroughly understand each other.   You have, you say, married my sister Mary, that my father is dead, and that my two brothers killed Sir Richard Morton, and that you, the husband of their sister, accused them of the crime."

" I was not the husband of your sister when I accused them of a crime I saw them commit. Mary had been prejudiced against me by the representations of her brothers. When they were lodged in prison I had an interview with Mary. I explained away many things, and promised if she would marry me I would get her brothers acquitted. Well, I did so, by stating I was mistaken, and refusing to swear that they were the persons I saw shoot down the baronet on his way to Williamsburg."

Patten then proceeded to explain to George Mason the manner in which he became acquainted with the commission of the murder by the brothers. As soon as he had finished that part of the narrative, George Mason said, eagerly,—

" Then what became of the papers the baronet carried about his person ? "

" Knowing where they were," returned Luke, " through the agency of my cousin, Mr. Bowen's clerk, who mentioned the circumstance to me without attributing any importance to it, I possessed myself of them."

" Ha ! " muttered George Mason between his teeth, " and so you let my brothers commit this mad and useless crime to profit by it yourself."

" No," calmly returned Patten, " I did not ; neither could I in any way prevent the deed. I could not even guess what their object was in lying concealed in the wood; I never thought of Sir Richard Morton—never saw him. Where I was hid I could see them, but could not see the Englishman till at the very moment the trigger was pulled, when the horse started forward and the baronet fell dead. I was amazed and horror-struck at the deed, but when I saw them eagerly searching the garments of the dead, the thought struck me that the murdered man was Sir Richard Morton, and that for some reason or other your brothers wished to obtain the papers that my cousin mentioned the baronet carried in a soft leather case at the back of his coat. The idea then struck me that I might possess myself of them, and so I did."

" And now that you have these papers," inquired Mason, looking ghastly and trembling with excitement, " what do you propose to do with them? Did you discover what other motive, besides to gain possession of these papers, prompted my brothers to commit this useless crime, after receiving three thousand from the man they had killed ? "

" Mrs. Jackson's vindictive hatred to Sir Richard Morton

spurred on your brothers, and their own desire to gain those papers, hoping to get a large sum of money for their restoration."

" Still I am bewildered," said Mason. " What became of the three thousand cheque, for if they possessed the means of paying off the mortgage of two thousand, why is Fork Farm in the hands of the mortgagee keepers ? "

" I will explain," replied Luke. " Either in forgetfulness or in the agitation of the baronet's interview with your father, the latter handed the cheque to the old man without signing it——"

" Idiots !" muttered Mason ; " and they, no doubt, did not perceive it."

" Neither your father, who held the cheque, nor Mr. Bowen, who was present, perceived the inadvertency, for John Mason at once locked it up in his chest ; the old man signed the requisite papers required by Sir Richard Morton, and then they parted, apparently good friends. What followed, after Sir Richard's departure, between your sister, Mrs. Jackson, and your brothers, which led to the crime perpetrated two days after, my wife, who was never trusted with any knowledge of family matters, could not tell. She says her father was subject to a disease of the heart, and all excitement added to his suffering. I believe the knowledge that his sons had killed Sir Richard, and the finding the cheque unsigned, gave him such a shock that he laid his head on the table, and when they went to rouse him they discovered he was dead."

Mason groaned, the perspiration ran down from his forehead : " Oh," said he, " had I been at home, none of this sorrow would have occurred. Not," he revengefully added, " that I feel a particle of regret for Sir Richard's fate. He deceived and abandoned my sister after many promises of marriage, and thought to destroy Grace Manning by a false marriage, but we defeated him there ; and now I swear his son by that same Grace Manning, his lawful wife, shall never inherit either the title or the estates of his father whilst I live."

" I cannot see," observed Patten, " why the sin of the father should be visited upon the son ; however, that is no business of mine. My object is to get that cheque for three thousand cashed."

" Ah, I see," returned Mason bitterly, " my brothers, I suppose, told you I was an adept in forging names ? "

" Not exactly, George ; they knew you would shortly return, and we agreed, if you did, that you were the only one who could imitate the baronet's signature. I did not expect, of course, to find you here. I came this morning to meet my cousin, to try and stave off a troublesome mortgagee, who threatens me. This cheque of the late baronet was a *bonâ fide* transaction ; it was a just payment for services rendered, and you are certainly entitled to it as your father's representative. Sign it, and I will go to New York and cash it. You shall have the two thousand, and with the other thousand I can stave off my creditors, and pull up for the past by industry and exertion."

" But how did you get the cheque from my brothers? there never was much friendship between you."

" Well," answered Luke, " I suppose they felt some gratitude for my saving them from hanging ; besides, they had not a dollar, and Mr. Hendrick put in keepers, and seized all the stock in Fork Farm. I gave them five hundred dollars, and took this unsigned cheque, not worth a cent., as security. Now you have three months given in which to redeem Fork Farm ; I know it is now worth four thousand pounds. Put the baronet's name to that, and to-morrow we will start for New York. I will run the risk of presenting it ; I know the banker, Mr. Coulston, personally."

Mason remained for some moments buried in thought ; he then looked into Patten's face, saying, as he stretched out his hand,—

" Agreed, on one condition—that we share whatever we can manage to make out of the paper you possess."

" Oh, willingly I agree to that," replied the other, clasping Mason's hand. " But, though I have the papers, I really cannot see how, without exposing ourselves to Mr. Bowen, any use can be made of them."

" I do," observed Mason ; " for at this moment there is, in New York, the identical son and heir of Sir Richard Morton—no doubt, come to this country to hunt for these very papers ; their possession would give him a title and eight thousand a year."

Patten looked astounded at this intelligence ; he was not a bad-hearted man, for he possessed considerable feeling, and would do any one a good turn if he could. He dearly loved his wife, who was a most amiable young woman—the more extraordinary, as she was reared amongst the other members of her family, who were totally without principle and moral conduct in any one way.

" Well," said Mason, seeing Luke Patten in a thoughtful mood, " has my intelligence altered your intentions in any way ? "

" No—not altered them," replied Luke ; " but recollect ; you, just a few moments ago, said that the son of Sir Richard Morton should never inherit his father's name or title whilst you lived. Now, I was considering, this son, so opportunely come into this country, would be the very individual the most likely to pay a large sum of money for those papers, and the matter could be very easily arranged."

"There's another son of Sir Richard Morton's, by his second wife," observed George Mason, "who will be disinherited should the youth, now in New York, gain possession of these important papers. I think the second son would be the most likely to pay a very large sum to see them destroyed."

"Yes," responded Patten, not looking very well pleased, "provided you knew he was a man inclined to commit so iniquitous a fraud as to deprive his lawful brother of his birthright; besides, you have the one brother on the spot, and I do not think, for many reasons, that you would like to return to England."

"How do you know that?" interrupted Mason sharply, and looking keenly into his companion's countenance.

"Well," returned the other, carelessly, "in looking over a file of old English papers, sent to me by my father's youngest sister, who is still alive and residing in Hampshire, I observed a paragraph alluding to the abduction of a young gentleman, and a robbery of his effects : this advertisement stated the young man's name to be Arthur Bolton, and that a person calling himself Reynolds, but whose real name was George Mason, was concerned in this abduction, with an accomplice named James Saunders, also under an alias. The advertiser offered a considerable reward for their apprehension, and application was to be made to the superintendent of police—I forget his name."

"Curse him and his name, too!" savagely interrupted the other. "But I baulked him and his infernal spies."

"This Arthur Bolton, then," inquired Luke, "is, I suppose, the late Sir Richard's son?"

"Yes, so far you are right, but we will talk of this matter when we get to New York, and find out what are the young man's projects. I can tell you he is a difficult subject to deal with —he is of a fierce and fiery spirit—and not easily handled ; but where is Mrs. Jackson and my brothers?"

"I am sorry to say," said Patten, "that they have leagued themselves with the well-known horse-lifters, who are known to have a retreat amid the Mattapone Swamps. I have heard that Mrs. Jackson is going to marry one Steadman, who possesses some land near there. Report says he's the chief of the gang—and a lawless, desperate lot they are."

"Then you see my brothers sometimes?"

"Yes," returned Patten; "their retreat is only twenty-four miles from here. I sincerely wish that they had not

come this way ; but they are looking out for your arrival—
and sometimes they visit my homestead after dark. I would
much rather they would not, for if they are caught, it will be
lynch law that they will get."

There was a silence for a few moments, and then Mason
said,—

" What was done with Sir Richard Morton's body, when
found ? "

" It was brought here to this inn " (Mason gave a shudder),
" and after the inquest and other formalities, Mr. Bowden ordered a lead and a mahogany coffin to be made ; the body was
placed in the lead one, and screwed down, and then enclosed
in the mahogany one. It was then placed in the vaults of St.
Mary's church. I hear that Mr. Bowen expects either Lady
Morton's family, or some member of the family, to come over
and take the body to England, to be laid in the family vault
of Morton Chase."

" Now, then," said George Mason, exultingly, " I can understand the whole ; the mystery that perplexed me is cleared
up."

" What mystery ?" inquired Patten, with some curiosity of
manner.

" I will tell you briefly," returned Mason. "I embarked
from Cork with a friend, in the North Star : this ship, when
within three days' sail of New York, took fire and blew up—
however, half the crew and passengers were saved by the crew
of the Ocean Queen. Aboard that vessel I recognized the
young man called Arthur Bolton ; he seemed deeply intimate
with a family in deep mourning—a mother, a son, and two
daughters. Somehow, whenever I got a glimpse of the two
girls' faces, I thought I had seen them before, still I could not
recall the where—now I have it—the widow is Lady Morton,
the others her son and daughters. The daughters I once saw
at Morton Chase, and I never forget a face once seen—they
are now in New York, and coming here."

" Then the sooner we set out for New York the better,"
cried Luke Patten.

" Be it so ; we will start in the morning."

CHAPTER XXVIII.

STILL retaining the name of Herbert, Lady Morton and
family, our hero included, remained for some days quietly in
their hotel in New Nork for a few days before proceeding to
Delaware.

" I wish, my dear Arthur," she said, one morning after
breakfast, "that you and Richard would go to Messrs. Coulston

and Brothers, bankers, and see how," she added, with a sigh, " your lamented father's account stands with the bankers. I am well aware he took out a large sum of money to lodge in the New York Bank, for the purpose of rewarding those terrible Masons, if they quietly acceded to his requests about certain papers necessary to prove your rights ; but it would be a cruel mockery if those fearful men should reap the reward, forfeited by their monstrous and horrid crime ; for that my unfortunate husband owed his death to their wickedness is quite certain—and God grant that justice may yet overtake them, and punish them for their crimes !"

" If the law cannot, after what has passed, touch them," returned Arthur, bitterly, " it is my firm intention to hunt them out, and take justice into my own hands."

" Ah ! my dear Arthur, better leave them to God's judgments, than risk your life seeking such miscreants."

Arthur made no reply, but shortly after he and Richard proceeded to the bank.

On requesting to see Mr. Coulston they were shown into a private apartment. The young men at once stated who they were, which much surprised the banker, who was acquainted with the late Sir Richard Morton during his stay in New York, and in whose bank the sum of three thousand, intended for John Mason, still remained.

" How very fortunate," said Mr. Coulston, " your arrival and calling here to-day."

" How so ?" exclaimed both the young men.

" I will explain, said the banker, " for I was in some perplexity how to act. Now you both can materially assist me."

" Yesterday, a Mr. Luke Patten, a highly respectable farmer in Delaware, presented a cheque drawn by your lamented father, Sir Richard Morton, on this bank, for a sum of three thousand, in favour of John Mason, of Fork Farm, also near Delaware. Now, I happened to be from home, and my brother also. Our cashier stated he could not cash the cheque till one or both his principals were consulted. Sir Richard Morton being dead, the instructions relative to that cheque were only known to them. When Mr. Patten inquired when he could see me, my cashier appointed this morning ; therefore I expect the holder of the cheque back every moment."

" Who is this Mr. Luke Patten ?" questioned Richard Herbert, " and how, I wonder, did he become possessed of a cheque given to John Mason ?"

" Luke Patten, is, I know, in difficulties," said the banker. " He married a daughter of John Mason's, and I also under-

stood that he was the accuser of the two Masons who were
arrested for the murder of the unfortunate Sir Richard ; but
he afterwards retracted his accusation, stating that he was
mistaken—that he could not swear to them."

" Ah," observed Arthur, " a somewhat doubtful character
is this Mr. Luke Patten."

The door of the room was then opened, and a clerk, putting
in his head, said,—

" Mr. Luke Patten, sir."

" Ah ! " said the banker, turning to the brothers, " if you
have no objection, we will see him here."

" I should wish to see him very much," responded Arthur,
for I strongly suspect some foul play respecting this cheque ;
the long delay in presenting it is suspicious."

" I think the same," answered the banker.

A moment or two, and the clerk ushered Mr. Patten into
the room.

The brothers looked with some curiosity at the Virginian,
who was a tall, strong man, with handsome features and good
figure.   His dark eyes rested at once upon Arthur, and
then upon his half-brother.   He held the cheque in his
hand, and mechanically handed it to the banker, who, taking
it, said,—

"Mr. Patten, these gentlemen," waving his hand towards
the brothers, " are the sons of the late Sir Richard Morton."

Luke started, and became flushed to the very temples ; but
merely bowed, and then in a moment recovered himself.
The banker, in the meantime, carefully examined the
cheque.

" Excuse me," said Richard Herbert, stepping forward, and
looking also at the cheque : " that signature is not my
father's—it is a forgery ! "

"What's that you say," interrupted Patten, somewhat
fiercely.

" I say," returned Richard Morton, firmly, " that signature was never written by my unfortunate father.   I admit
it is a facsimile of his handwriting before an attempt was made
upon his life by a villain named George Mason.   In attempting
to stay the blow the two first fingers of his right hand were
nearly severed; afterwards his signature was not the same
as before.   Here," and taking out a document from a pocket-
book, the young man handed it to the banker : " there
is my father's signature, after the maiming of his right
hand."

All present could see that the two signatures were widely
different.

" You are quite correct, sir," said the banker, " for I also possess the late baronet's signature, which is similar to yours, Mr. Richard Morton."

" You may think what you say is correct, young gentlemen," said Patten, harshly, " but I tell you, and I can bring most respectable witnesses to back my assertion—one Mr. Bowen, a lawyer, well known to you, Mr. Coulston. He saw this cheque handed by the late Sir Richard Morton to John Mason, in compensation for certain papers, signed by Mr. John Mason in Mr. Bowen's presence, and he saw the late John Mason lock it up. This cheque, after his father's death, became the son's property, and it was passed over to me for certain considerations—my wife, Mary Mason, being entitled to a certain portion. You can write to Mr. Bowen, and he will tell you the same story."

" Allowing what you say to be true," observed Arthur, quietly, " still, this cheque is not payable without John or George Mason's own signature. I know that John Mason is in this country; he landed in New York from the Ocean Queen, on board of which ship I was a passenger, and more than that, though this man attempted the life of my father, I was the means of rescuing him from a frightful death."

Patten gazed into Arthur Bolton's handsome features somewhat surprised, muttering something indistinctly, as if to himself, and then said aloud, with a slight increasing colour,—

" Then I suppose, Mr. Coulston, you refuse this cheque? All I can tell you is this ; the late baronet, Sir Richard Morton, lost most valuable papers—-they were taken from his person—and I now tell you that if this cheque is not paid by twelve o'clock to-morrow these papers will never more be heard of."

Turning on his heel, the speaker was preparing to leave the room, when his arm was grasped by Arthur, who arrested his steps. Furious with disappointment, and suspecting he had criminated himself, Luke, a strong and determined man, made a vigorous effort to free his arm ; but he had to do with one whose grasp was of iron—he was held as if in a vice.

" What do you mean, sir ? " he exclaimed, flushed with passion, and looking fiercely into Bolton's face, whilst Mr. Coulston stepped out of the room.

" I mean," replied our hero, " to arrest you on the charge of conspiracy, and of being leagued with one George Mason in attempting to obtain money by a forged cheque, and of having a guilty knowledge of the robbery of certain papers from the person of the late Sir Richard Morton, baronet."

Patten remained for a moment speechless with rage.

" Now, Mr. Patten," continued Arthur, "judging by your looks, there is something about you that predisposes me in your favour. I can scarcely believe you to be the accomplice of assassins and robbers."

Patten coloured to the temples; he appeared inclined to say something, when the banker returned, followed by two policemen, who at once advanced to the side of Mr. Patten.

Looking in our hero's face, Patten said,—

"You persist, then, in giving me in charge to these two men ?"

" I do, " returned Arthur, calmly.

" Then, Mr. Bolton, you are acting with less judgment than I gave you credit for;" and turning round he quitted the room in charge of the police-officers.

Our hero was roused from a reverie he was thrown into by the last words of Luke Patten, by Mr. Coulston saying,—

" This looks serious, gentlemen ; I fear you will find Mr. Luke Patten a very difficult person to draw anything from ; he looks a determined sort of person."

" Yes," returned Arthur, " I give him credit for that. I am greatly puzzled. He appears to me to be a very different sort of man from George Mason, and his still worse comrade William Saunders. He may be mixed up in this cheque affair, and have some knowledge of the lost papers, but I firmly believe he had neither hand nor part in the murder of my unfortunate father. His first accusation against the Masons was, without doubt, a true one. His marrying the sister possibly altered his determination in prosecuting them."

" Our criminal laws," observed Mr. Coulston, " are unfortunately but little understood, and very loosely carried out, in the Border States. It is well known that great crimes are committed, and that in nine cases out of ten the criminal escapes, to perish sometimes by lynch law afterwards."

Just as the half-brothers were taking leave of the banker the room was hastily entered by one of the clerks, who, in an agitated manner, said,—

" He has escaped, sir ! got clear off from the police. But they are in full cry after him, and think they will be sure to catch him again."

Arthur looked vexed, and his brother uttered an exclamation of astonishment, saying, " What exceeding carelessness ; four men having the care of a prisoner, and to let him escape ! "

" Bless me ! " exclaimed the banker, " how did he manage it ? "

" The police neglected to handcuff him ; but they must surely catch him."

"How did this happen, Mr. Jones—did you hear?" questioned the banker of his clerk.

"A policeman told me, sir, that just as they turned the corner of the street, a mob of rowdies, in a tumultuous rush, suddenly came against them, and bore the prisoner and the two policemen to the ground : they were all fighting, and in the confusion Mr. Patten, who is a very strong man, got away ; but they say they will catch him again."

"I doubt it very much," observed Arthur. "He will get out of the city ; and, once in the country, his capture will be difficult."

"He owns a large farm close to the Fork Farm that the Masons possessed, and not very far from the spot where your unfortunate father fell a victim to their malice. I really," continued the banker, "cannot comprehend the motive for this terrible crime. I do not see what use they could make of the papers, even if they succeeded in getting them—which they did not—for it is now very evident that this Luke Patten either has them, or knows where they are. They have lost this sum of money "—holding up the cheque—"for it is a decided forgery."

"Yes ; of that there is no doubt ; " returned Richard Morton.

"We will not detain you longer, Mr. Coulston," said our hero. "I have a half-digested plan in my head for the capture of this Luke Patten, for I am satisfied he will not be taken in New York ; he has confederates here ; that pretended mob of rowdies was in readiness for action, should his project of obtaining the cheque cashed lead him into mischief. Two notorious villains—part of the same gang—both known to me —in fact, one was George Mason himself—landed from the Ocean Queen the same time we did. They were saved, amongst others, out of the burning ship, the North Star. I did not like to arrest them, not understanding the technicalities of international laws."

"As they could have had no hand or part in the actual crime committed by the brothers Mason," said the banker, "you could scarcely bring a charge against them here. Mason, for his attempt on the late baronet's life, at Morton Chase, could have been apprehended and sent to England, to be tried on that charge."

"Perhaps I did wrong in letting them escape," said Arthur, thoughtfully. "However, I will not acknowledge myself worsted yet."

Taking leave of the friendly banker, the two young men left the house to return to their hotel. As they descended the steps and proceeded along the crowded street, a man in the garb of a common sailor, with a coloured handkerchief covering half his features, and a sou'-wester pulled low over his forehead, stepped out from a low spirit store, and, keeping his eyes fixed upon the brothers, followed their every movement, keeping himself well back, for, though pretty well disguised, very little of his features were to be seen; still, if Bolton's eyes had rested on his tall gaunt figure, he would at once have recognized Bill Saunders. He beheld them enter a yard belonging to a noted dealer in horses, and getting into a position to see and not be seen, he beheld several horses—good, bad, and indifferent—paraded by the helps before the eyes of the young men. Saunders could not hear what was said, but he judged by the notice the young men took of several of the very best horses, that they were selecting some of the lot. He then followed them till he saw them housed in their hotel.

Having left the bankers, as the two half-brothers proceeded along the street, Richard Morton said to his brother,—

"Now, how do you intend to proceed, Arthur? I begin to get staggered by the obstructions we meet; that rascal, Patten, will, I fear, give us the slip, and he evidently is possessed of the papers so material to you to obtain."

"My present idea, Richard," returned Arthur, "is to get to Williamsburg before him; but I must not enrol you in a perhaps dangerous enterprise."

"What!" exclaimed Richard Morton, with a slight flush on his cheek, "do you doubt either my courage or my affection?"

"Good heavens! not for an instant, my dear brother; but recollect you cannot possibly leave your mother and sisters to travel alone, without male protection, from this place to Delaware. They would be wretched and miserable, and imagine dangers existed. You are your dear mother's only hope. This adventure I must attempt, assisted only by Joe; the fewer the better, for force would be of no avail. I can easily judge that this Patten has, by some singular chance, got possession of the papers our father carried concealed about his person; but I do not think he had any hand in his cruel death. Patten, by what I have heard, is in difficulties; he wants to make money of these papers; and, if so, he and I can come to terms, always provided he proves to me that he had no act or part in the death of our parent. I am going to purchase a couple of horses, and Joe and I will ride post after getting to the first post-town, after leaving this city. I wish to leave no hint of my purpose, or trace of my road. We will start in two hours; I will not leave by the direct road to Williamsburg, but strike into it afterwards."

After some further conversation on the same subject, Richard

Morton allowed himself reluctantly to be convinced that his brother's mode of proceeding was the most likely to succeed; at the same time, he expressed deep regret at being compelled to remain inactive whilst his brother ran such risk.

They found, on their return from the horse-dealer's, where Arthur had selected two excellent horses, fit for the road, with saddles, bridles, and holsters, Lady Morton and her daughters preparing for their journey to Delaware. At this time there were no railroads into the interior of the Northern States. Some lines were just commenced, but none ready for traffic.

Arthur made Lady Morton acquainted with what had occurred at the banker's, which greatly startled her; but when our hero stated it was his determination to proceed as rapidly as possible to Williamsburg, and thus to Luke Patten's farm, she did all she could to dissuade him from trusting himself among such men as Patten, Mason, and his detestable associate, Saunders.

Lady Morton felt satisfied that the forgery of the late Sir Richard's name to the cheque was done by George Mason— her lamented husband had often told her, that father and son were remarkable for their skill in the imitation of signatures. But the young man felt so sanguine that he could deal with Luke Patten, and had arranged a plan in his own head to bring him to terms, that he resisted all the solicitations of mother and daughters to abandon his project; so, giving up their opposition, they wished him every success. Before two hours were expired, he and Joseph left New York, well mounted and well armed.

CHAPTER XXIX.

Before leaving New York Arthur Bolton had visited the sergeant of police, who was most interested in entrapping Luke Patten, and who felt annoyed at his escape; but he was completely baulked—he could find no trace of the fugitive; in fact, he became persuaded he had quitted the city at once, for he was certainly not amongst the rowdies and other desperate characters that infested that populous city. Our hero thought so too; he felt persuaded that Luke would fly into the country at once: his project for getting cash for the forged cheque having totally broken down, he would, therefore, hasten home, where he would be safe.

Our hero did not feel the slightest uneasiness in trusting himself with Patten—his sole object could only be to gain a large sum of money in exchange for the papers. To kill him would be defeating his own projects, for the papers would be utterly worthless to anyone else, for, Arthur disposed of,

Richard Morton would have no one to dispute his succession to his father's estates, personal effects, or title; therefore the documents substantiating his birth, &c., would become waste paper. With very little rest day or night, he and Joseph pursued their journey, leaving their horses at the first town, and hiring fresh ones from town to town, till they reached Williamsburg.

After a rest of four hours they proceeded to Delaware. Now it was scarcely possible that Patten could have reached his farm before them. It was late at night when they put up at the same hotel where the unfortunate Sir Richard Morton had been carried. This Arthur did not know, and he made no inquiries till early the next morning, when he requested to see the landlord.

"How far may it be," he asked of the long, lanky, devil-may-care looking individual that sauntered into the room, whistling a tune, and with his hands stuck deep into his breeches' pockets—"how far may it be to a farm held by a man of the name of Luke Patten, if there is such a person in these parts?"

"I just calculate there is, stranger," said the landlord, biting off a huge piece of tobacco, "and a darned good sort of fellow is Luke Patten. I guess he could tell you a trick or two. Your a Brittisher, eh, stranger! just fledged, and come out to see what kind of a devil the real Yankey is— eh, sar?"

Arthur only smiled, saying, "Oh! the Yankey is not a bad sort of fellow when you come to know him and fall into his humours; but you have forgotten my question. I am anxious to visit Luke Patten's farm and see him."

"Then, I guess you just wont, for Luke is in New York. Maybe his wife would do as well; she's as comely a lass as you do meet between here and the great city."

"Well, perhaps his wife will do," returned our hero, quietly. "I remember her family well in the old country."

"I guess, if you did, you must have been a particularly young pup, seeing that the Masons have been here nigh twenty years, and I calculate you haven't got many years to spare above that figure."

"Well," returned our hero, getting tired of the loquacious landlord, "I have little time to spare; can I walk to Patten's farm in three or four hours?"

"I calculate, to look at your legs, you can. It is a crooked bit of a road to the ferry; but I can get a lad that will show you the way for a dollar. After you cross the river you can't miss the farm, as you will see the house from the hill above the ferry."

" Thank you," returned Arthur, " pray send for the lad at once.　At the same time I wish to engage apartments in your hotel for a lady, and her family and servants, who will arrive in two or three days ; they will require five bed-rooms."

" Well," returned the landlord, " we'll talk about that when you come back ; at all events there's plenty of room if they wanted ten beds.　I'll go and get you a guide to the ferry over the Mattapone."

Leaving Joseph at the hotel, and putting a brace of double-barrelled pistols in his pocket, our hero and a stout lad, who led the way, having left the town, struck into the road to Williamsburg for about four miles, and after a fourteen or fifteen miles' walk they came to the ferry across the Mattapone. Giving the guide his fee, our hero crossed, the only individual in the boat being the ferryman.　He could see the road bending over a woody cliff, so he asked no questions, for he had discovered that when you have to ask a question of a native, they invariably ask ten before you can get any reply to your own.　Too much employed by his own thoughts, he paid little heed to the scenery he was passing through, though it was sufficiently striking to attract attention, till he reached the summit of the hill, and got to a spot that commanded a very extensive view over the flat country that lay beneath him, and through which ran the two streams of the Pamunka and Mat-tapone, whose united waters form the York river.　He stood gazing over the fine meadow-land lying on each side of the streams, and the vast number of cattle feeding on its apparently unenclosed pastures.

Whilst he stood looking down upon the placid quiet scene, and had just made out the large farm-buildings constituting Patten's homestead, two men, in the ordinary costume of a Virginian farmer, came up to the hill from the other side, apparently going towards the ferry over the Mattapone. When they beheld Arthur attired in the travelling dress of an English gentleman, they paused, and one said to the other,—

" That's a Brittisher, I calculate ; what the devil brings the like of him into these here parts, and alone ? "　Both these men were young, tall, and strongly built ; their countenances bore a strong resemblance to each other, and proclaimed a near relationship.　They, however, walked on : each carried a gun, with shot-belt slung over their shoulder.

Arthur Bolton turned, and, looking at the two men, a slight flush came on his cheek—he could not say why, but as he looked into their faces, there was something in their manner which induced him to think he had seen them before, or some one resembling them.

The two young men paused as our hero came abreast of them, saying,—

"May I inquire the nearest road to Luke Patten's farm? Yonder homestead is the house, I suppose, but here are two roads leading in the same direction nearly."

The brothers looked at one another with a very meaning look, as the elder replied,—

"I calculate you will not find Luke Patten in this part of the country just now, stranger. What's your business? Do you want to purchase horses? If you do, you will have to keep your weather-eye open, as our friend is not a chicken in horseflesh."

"I do not want to purchase horses," replied Arthur Bolton, regarding the two young men with a strange feeling of dislike. "However, I suppose either road will do;" and was preparing to walk on, when one of the young men said,—

"We are going to Patten's homestead ourselves; his wife is a sister of ours."

A shell exploding under Arthur's feet would not have caused the dismay and horror those words created in his mind. His face flushed crimson, and his limbs trembled under him with excitement and intensity of feeling.

"Luke Patten's wife your sister!" he repeated, casting a look of unmistakeable disgust upon the surprised brothers, as he added, "then you are the two younger sons of John Mason, of Fork Farm?"

"Well," returned the eldest of the brothers, dropping his gun into the hollow of his arm, and casting a fierce look at our hero—"who are you, stranger, that seems to hear and treat the name of Mason with such scornful looks? Who are you?"

"Who am I?" repeated Arthur Bolton, his chest heaving with suppressed passion: "I am the son of Sir Richard Morton, whom you so cowardly and brutally murdered."

This announcement for the moment perfectly paralysed the brothers; their harsh, thin features looked ghastly, but their fiery and revengeful natures soon recovered their natural ferocity and determination.

"You are either a fool or a madman!" exclaimed the elder brother, "to dare to make such an accusation to our faces. Have you not not heard that the accusation was a false one—that we were acquitted when unjustly tried for the Englishman's death?"

"Luke Patten swore falsely," returned Bolton, passionately; "he did not wish to see the brothers of his wife receive their due from the hangman's hands."

With a frightful imprecation, the elder brother raised his

gun, and levelled it at Arthur's breast, but before he could pull the trigger a loud shout rather startled him from his aim.

The ball grazed our hero's forehead, rasing the skin, and giving him a slight shock, but drawing his postol, he shot the elder Mason dead.   The younger brother, frantic with rage and excitement, placed his gun against our hero's side, and pulled the trigger, just as he turned round and made a grasp at his throat.   The gun hung fire, and the ball merely passed through Arthur's garment.   A deadly struggle took place, for each grasped the other, and both were powerful young men; but William Mason contrived to draw his bowie knife, and our hero received two desperate gashes in the side.   Thinking himself mortally wounded, he exerted all his great strength, and dashed his assailant to the ground, who, rolling over, received his death-wound from his own knife.

By this time the man who had shouted at the top of his voice, and who was on horseback, when he beheld the first shot fired, dug his spurs into the jaded and worn-out horse he rode.   The exhausted animal made a start forward, lost his footing, and fell, throwing his rider with strong force to the ground.   When he had picked himself up and reached the scene of contention, he stood aghast, holding a pistol in his hand, and looking first at Arthur Bolton and then at the dying William Mason.

"Luke Patten!" for he it was—"Luke Patten!" fiercely, though feebly almost screamed the dying man, "why do you stand staring like an idiot?   Shoot him dead—he has murdered us both!   Let me die avenged."

Our hero had also recognized Patten, and drew another pistol from his breast; but his sight grew dim.   He felt he was fainting, dying perhaps from loss of blood.   He strove to keep up, but his power was gone, and murmuring, "Father! I have avenged you; Alice, dear Alice!" he fell insensible beside his foe.

A wild horrid laugh burst from William Mason's lips.

"Put your pistol to his head, Patten.   Make sure of him; he's the old baronet's son!   Ah! I'm a dead man!"

Patten, horror-struck, stooped down, and attempted to raise William Mason, for he was pressing on the knife, but with a convulsive shudder he ceased to exist.

"This is horrible!" cried the farmer, wiping away the beads of perspiration that poured down his face.   "What am I to do?   Oh, crime! this is your fruit," he added, bitterly: then bending over the body of Arthur, he tore open his vest and placed his hand upon his heart.

"He lives!" he exclaimed, with a feeling of joy.   "Oh!

this scene I shall never forget; it's a fearful lesson; but if God
is willing to receive my repentance my future life shall be
different from the past."

He rose and looked about him, and perceiving a man
coming up the hill from his own farm whistling, as he drove a
light cart, he cried, " Ah! thank God, I may yet save this
young man's life ! "

When the carter reached the spot and beheld the three
bodies stretched out in their ghastly state, for the ground was
greatly stained with blood, he uttered a loud cry, jumped off
his cart, and was making the best of his way back to the farm,
when the voice of his master stayed his purpose.

"Come here, you fool!" angrily exclaimed Patten, "I want
your assistance, and you run away : " he was bathing Bolton's
face with water from a pool close by.

" Oh Lord, master ! " exclaimed the youth, " did you kill
all three ? darn it, it's murder."

" No, you fool, I killed none of them ! "

" Oh, Lord ! " it's the missus's brothers ! " And the man
shook with terror.

" This young man is not dead, Bill, and we must get him
to the house as quickly as possible, and send a cart for these
unfortunate young men ; they are dead, and no mistake."

Patten then tried to staunch the blood that flowed from
the two deep gashes made by the bowie knife in our hero's
side, by tearing his own inner garment into strips. Roused
by the water poured over his face, Arthur began rapidly to
revive. On opening his eyes he beheld Patten on his knees,
and the farm man beside him, both earnestly engaged stop-
ping the flow of blood from his wounds.

" Ah ! " said Patten, cheerfully, " you have only fainted
from loss of blood ; no vital part has been touched. Could
you bear the motion of a cart to my farm ? You need not
fear me now, Mr. Bolton ; I am a changed man. What I have
seen this day will not easily be forgotten."

" I do not fear any harm at your hands, Mr. Patten. I had
a better opinion of you than you gave me credit for. I was
going to your house, when this strange meeting with my
father's murderers took place ; they attacked me, not I them.
I killed them only in my own defence, but I do not fear
you :" and raising himself up in a sitting position, he added,
" for if you had wished to do me harm the power was
yours."

Taking a flask of brandy from his pocket, Patten requested
him to take a little ; it would revive him, and enable him to
be able to bear the motion of the cart to his farm.

Our hero did so, and then, with the stupified farm man's assistance, he was placed in the cart.

" I must for the present," said Luke Patten, " put these bodies into yonder thick brushwood, till I can send a cart for them. If possible, this terrible affair must be kept secret."

" I do not see why it should," said Arthur, in a faint voice, for he felt exceedingly weak and sick. " They would have taken my life, and I only defended myself against their murderous intentions."

" We can't wait to talk more, Mr. Bolton," said Patten, I will explain another time. Here, Bill, help me with the bodies."

Bill shuddered—he was by no means a hero ; but between them they carried the bodies, and concealed them in a dense mass of bushes and long grass, near at hand. Picking up the guns, and concealing the stains of blood by covering them with gravel and earth, the party then proceeded towards the farm, Luke supporting our hero on the cart; but before they reached the house he became again insensible, from the still continued bleeding from the wounds, the motion of the cart increasing the flow of blood.

When Arthur revived a second time, and was able to look about him, he perceived that he was lying on a bed in a tolerably large room, not furnished after the fashion of our times, but in the plain, substantial style of a farm-house in Delaware, some forty years ago. His coat and waistcoat had been taken off, his wounds washed, dressed, and bandaged, and a piece of sticking-plaister applied to the injury on his head. It was not yet dusk, but not far from sunset, for through the small leaden squares of glass that formed the window but a dull light entered the room. He was not left long to employ his thoughts, for the door opened, and Luke Patten entered the room.

" I am glad to see you come to yourself, Mr. Bolton," said Patten. " You have received some ugly gashes, though not particularly dangerous ones, I think ; but you have lost a great amount of blood, which has caused this weakness and fainting."

" I am much obliged to you, Mr. Patten, for your care of me," returned Arthur, sitting up, feeling exceedingly weak and light-headed. " As well as I remember, I think I heard you express a desire to keep this affair between me and the Masons from public attention ; but this must not be, for ——"

" Nay, Mr. Bolton, you may rest easy on that score ; I have

altered my mind, and have already sent a message to a magistrate in Delaware, and the bodies have been brought here, and
are now lying in one of my out-offices. It is better for all
parties that there should be a clear investigation of the affair.
I witnessed the encounter from beginning to end, and but for
my broken-down horse, I should probably have prevented
those misguided young men from losing their lives. They
were men of ungovernable passion, as you may well suppose. I am guilty so far as joining the Masons in endeavouring to obtain a sum of money positively given them by the
late Sir Richard Morton, but inadvertently the cheque was
given unsigned. But act or part in his melancholy death I
had none ; and though I witnessed the act, I had no earthly
power to prevent it, as I will hereafter explain. You had
better now not talk ; strip and get into bed, and take some
little nourishment, which my wife is preparing, and to-morrow you will find some of this weakness you suffer from
subside."

Arthur, although a strong and powerful young man, and
one who would not readily give way to bodily weakness, was
nevertheless forced to follow Luke Patten's advice, for even
speaking was painful ; he, therefore, with Patten's assistance,
got into bed, and remained perfectly quiet, after taking some
gruel and wine he brought him. Though his body was quiet,
his thoughts were far from being so.

The next morning when he awoke from a refreshing sleep,
on opening his eyes he perceived, to his surprise, Joseph sitting by the bedside, gazing at him with a look of devoted
affection. Seeing him awake, the faithful youth seized his
hand, and with tears in his eyes, as he pressed his lips to it,
said,—

"Ah! sir, why did you leave me behind, and you going to meet
such villains ? Sure I never failed you in danger or difficulty.
But glory to the saints, you will be nothing the worse ; only a
few days' confinement."

" My faithful friend," said Arthur, pressing his hand affectionately, how in the world have you found me out ? "

" Sure, sir, the faithful dog will track his master, and why
not the devoted servant ? When night came, and you never
came back, I got frightened. That old lanky, tobacco-
chewing landlord, laughed at me, asking me if my master
was weaned yet, that he could not stay out at night without
his nurse. Be dad, I felt inclined, tall and lanky as he is, to
send him where he would want a nurse. I could not go to
bed, sir, and before daylight I set out for the blessed ferry
over the Madpony River."

" Mattapone, Joe ? " said our hero, with a smile. " You

remember you never ceased calling that most respectable Indian, Punka Bosswash, any other name than Hogswash."

" Faix, sir, he was a dacent, respectable man entirely; if we could only have persuaded him to put on trowsers, he was fit for any society ; but, be gor, when I think I see him in his grand cocked hat and very short shirt, I'm fairly beat with laughing."

" But how did you find the way, Joe, to the ferry without a guide, for it's a crooked road ? "

" The dickens a ferry I ever found at all, sir. I got adrift somehow ; but, be dad, I found the river at all events, and, as I knew I must cross it to get to this Mr. Patten's farm, faix, I stripped, tied my clothes on top of my head, and swam across. I was not afraid, like in the Punka River, of being stopped in my passage by some monster or other. When I got to the other side, two of those blessed Yankees, and two women, with pitchforks in their hands, came running down to the bank—faix, I believe they took me for a antiphibious animal, for, says one of the women, with a giggling laugh, ' It's a man, I calculate, John.' ' I'm darned if it is not,' said the man. ' I guess you find it cold, youngster ? What made you swim across, and a ferry a mile below, eh, stranger ? ' ' I found myself too hot,' said I, dressing myself. ' Can you tell me where's one Luke Patten's farm is ? ' ' Well, stranger, you're not far out ; this is Luke Patten's farm, and yonder is the homestead.' ' Be dad,' says I, finishing my toilet, giving a look at the women, who were no beauties, ' I hit it nicely ; ' so, wishing them good morning, I left them laughing heartily at my swimming the 'Pony, and a ferry close by—but, how do you feel, sir ? Can you eat your breakfast ? You know, sir," added Joe, " when we was in those foreign parts—and for the matter of that, we're amongst a queer lot now, though they do speak English—but, as I was saying, you used to say, ' Joe, can you feel ? ' ' Yes, sir,' says I, ' and no mistake.' ' Then you are all right, Joe.' "

" Well, I can eat, Joseph," replied our hero, pleased to have his old companion, in so many a trying hour, to attend upon him.

" Then I'll go and get your breakfast, sir. Mrs. Patten, sir, is a kind and very handsome young woman, and very anxious about you, though she looks very sad and cut up, and, faix, no wonder, though the villains deserved their death ten times over. Still, sir, they were her brothers, though she lived in dread of them."

CHAPTER XXX.

ARTHUR BOLTON felt exceedingly anxious to get back to
Delaware, to await the arrival of Lady Morton and family,
who were expected in two or three days. Besides, a troublesome, painful investigation must take place : Luke Patten's
conduct puzzled him, his manners and attentions to his wants
evinced a great change in his ideas and intentions since they
parted at the banker's in New York. What had become of
George Mason and the villain Saunders? Did Patten know
of their whereabouts? Would he be induced to give up his
father's papers? These and many other questions he re-
peatedly asked himself, without being able to answer them
at all to his satisfaction.

As he was eating his breakfast, his host came in, and sitting
down by the bed-side, said,—

" I am glad to see you looking much better, Mr. Bolton."

" Thank you," returned our hero : " I feel much stronger
to-day. I bled so much before the cuts could be closed, that
I became as weak as a child. I think—indeed, I am sure—if a
mattress was put on a cart, I could bear the short journey to
Delaware, for my hurts are mere flesh wounds."

Patten was silent a moment, and then said,—

" Perhaps you could, but to-morrow would be better. You
have no need of moving to-day ; we shall have a couple of
magistrates here about mid-day."

" I hope, Patten," observed Arthur, " you will incur no
risk from that affair of the cheque ? "

" Oh, none whatever, Mr. Bolton. When I explain matters, which I will do this evening, with your permission, you
will see that any prosecution for the forgery of the late Sir
Richard Morton's signature would be unjust in one sense, and
utterly useless besides. Consequently, as the money is not
paid, there is no harm done."

" I am satisfied, returned our hero, " that no further
notice of the cheque will be taken by Lady Morton or her
son, and, unless I become possessed of certain papers, her
son succeeds to the title and estates. I never intended to
deprive my brother of the estates, even were my birth established ; but I should like to be acknowledged as the legitimate son of the late unfortunate Sir Richard Morton before I
unite my destiny to that of a most amiable lady."

" Rest contented with my assertion, Mr. Bolton," returned
Luke Patten, with a flush on his cheek, " that, when you
return to England, there will be no difficulty in your assuming
the name and title of your unfortunate father. As I said,

this evening we will have an hour's talk together: now you will excuse me.'

Joe entered the room, and Luke Patten left.

As there was a large easy chair in the room, Arthur Bolton partly dressed himself, with Joseph's assistance, and placed himself in it. Any exertion was somewhat painful, but judging by the sensations he experienced, he felt satisfied he could move into Delaware the next day.

About one o'clock two magistrates and their clerk were shown into the room, and introduced by Luke Patten as Mr. Hendrick and Mr. Sampson. We shall not weary our readers with the dry and prosy details of magisterial eloquence, the cross-questioning, and repetition of details.

After every detail of the circumstances relating to the attack on Arthur Bolton, and his own account of the affair, Luke Patten's evidence was taken down. The magistrates seemed to care or trouble very little about the matter, complimented our hero upon his courageous resistance, which had one good effect—it finished the career of two notorious characters, who it was very well known had been latterly leagued with a daring gang of horse-lifters.

" Now that we have finished the business required by law," said Mr. Hendrick, filling himself a stiff tumbler of whisky toddy, the materials being plentifully supplied and placed on the table, " may I, without being accused of undue curiosity, ask you, Mr. Bolton, some little explanation respecting your statement that you are the son of the late Sir Richard Morton? You make your depositions under the name of Arthur Bolton, and yet you accused the two Masons of having murdered the late Sir Richard Morton, your father: which accusation, according to your own statement, led to their desperate assault upon you. We are quite aware that these two Masons were tried at Delaware for the murder of Sir Richard Morton, an English gentleman ; but they were acquitted for want of evidence. Their accuser was, as you know, Luke Patten, but he stated on the trial of the brothers that he was mistaken as to their persons ; there was no other evidence whatever, and of course they were acquitted. Luke Patten was not thought ill of by his neighbours for this act, for it was very well known he courted their sister, and a young man in love is something like a man in liquor—doesn't know well what he is about."

" I can sufficiently explain this seeming inconsistency to you, Mr. Hendrick," said Arthur. " My lamented father came out here to obtain papers from the late John Mason, of Fork Farm; he was anxious to establish the facts of my birth, which, without these papers, it would be difficult, if not impossible, to do. He procured the papers, and was

returning to New York, when he was murdered, for the purpose, we must suppose, of gaining possession of those papers
which he carried concealed on his person. These documents
were taken from his body, and I have come into this country
to try and recover them. I was brought up and reared under
the name of Bolton, and unless I recover these papers I must
retain the name I have always borne."

" This is quite satisfactory," said one of the magistrates,
" and I trust you will be able to recover the papers you
require. I remember Mr. Bowen, the lawyer, being extremely anxious about them at the time of the sad murder,
and no doubt he will help you in your present search for them.
If you will summon Mr. Patten," continued Mr. Hendrick to
his clerk, " I will just ask him a question or two : after that
we will not longer disturb you, Mr. Bolton, for you must
still be rather weak and exhausted."

Luke Patten shortly afterwards entered the room, looking
serious, but not at all disturbed.

" Mr. Patten," said Mr. Hendrick, " may I ask, were you
aware that your brothers-in-law were in this part of the
country, for you know they are accused of several horse-
lifting jobs, and, if seen and caught, would undoubtedly not
have escaped this time ? "

" I did not know they were in this neighbourhood," returned Patten ; " in fact I could not know it, for the last
week I have been in New York, and was on my way to my
farm the morning on which they fell victims to their own
intemperate passions. My wife knew that they were here,
and the knowledge made her very uneasy, and anxious for
my return."

" I must ask Mrs. Patten a question or two," said Mr. Hendrick, after exchanging a few words in a low voice with his
brother magistrate. " Can Mrs. Patten oblige us with her
presence here ? "

" Oh, certainly ! " answered Luke, " I will bring her in ;"
and he retired.

Our hero felt distressed ; he was the cause of both brothers'
death—a death they richly deserved ; still, a woman must feel
a certain repugnance to being brought into the presence of
the destroyer of her brothers, let the characters of those
brothers stand ever so criminal.

In a few minutes Luke Patten re-entered the room, followed
by his wife. The clerk handed her a chair.

Arthur perceived that she was exceedingly pale, but perfectly self-possessed and calm ; for an instant she let her fine
dark eyes rest upon our hero's face, and he thought that there
was much of sadness in her expression, but neither anger nor

dislike. She was young, tall, somewhat slight, but extremely prepossessing. She was attired in deep mourning.

"Mrs. Patten," began Mr. Hendrick, politely, "I wish to ask you one or two very simple questions. Pray when did your late brothers visit your house first?"

"Two days ago, sir, I was surprised by their arrival, in the dusk of the evening. I knew it was dangerous for them to be seen in this neighbourhood, and, my husband being absent, their visit agitated me."

"Did they tell you why they came?" questioned the magistrate.

"They said they wanted to see my husband, about some property left by my father, and of which they claimed a share."

"What property was that, Mrs. Patten?" asked Mr. Sampson, "for it is well known John Mason was desperately involved; and, in fact, had not paid for his holding when he died, and the sons were unable to pay after his death."

"Such was and is the case, sir," returned Mrs. Patten, in a steady, clear voice, and looking Mr. Sampson calmly in the face.

"Then what property did your brothers expect to share?" demanded Mr. Hendrick.

"The late Sir Richard Morton," returned Mrs. Patten, "gave my deceased father, John Mason, a cheque for three thousand pounds, for the express purpose of paying off the encumbrances on Fork Farm; in return for which cheque, my late father, in the presence of Mr. Bowen, who saw it presented, gave the baronet every information respecting this gentleman's (Mr. Bolton) birth, and signed whatever papers the baronet required. My unfortunate and misguided brothers, therefore, claimed a share of the three thousand pounds given to their father."

"Was this cheque cashed, Mr. Patten?" inquired Mr. Hendrick, who, in point of fact, was the person to whom the two thousand was due for the purchase-money of Fork Farm.

"No," returned Luke Patten, firmly. "I went to the bank in New York, on which the cheque was drawn, to cash it; but the cheque was refused by the banker, because it was incorrectly filled up; and the baronet no longer existing, the sum is lost. The fact is——"

"I beg to observe," interrupted Arthur Bolton, who had listened attentively, "that, as I am now persuaded this cheque for three thousand pounds was positively given in good faith and for services rendered by the late John Mason, I will engage now, before all present, that this sum shall be paid into the hands of Mr. Luke Patten, by the present Lady Morton, who will be in Delaware in two or three days. I left her, and her son and daughters, in New York, preparing to follow me."

"Indeed!' returned Mr. Hendrick, evidently highly pleased, and anticipating the receipt of the two thousand due to himself; "then things will go straight after all. I wish I could, Mr. Bolton, aid you in any way, respecting those papers so mysteriously lost."

"Thank you, Mr. Hendrick, I do not despair of their recovery."

"Neither need you, Mr. Bolton," said Luke Patten, proceeding to an iron safe or chest, standing in a corner of the room.

All regarded his movements with great interest.

Mrs. Patten rose up, whilst her husband was unlocking the chest, saying in a slightly agitated voice, and looking at Mr. Hendrick,—

"Do you wish to question me any further, sir?"

"No, Mrs. Patten, no; we are perfectly satisfied with your straightforward answers."

Mrs. Patten then withdrew.

Her husband, in the meantime, unlocked the chest, and drew forth the leathern case the unfortunate Sir Richard had carried about his person on the day of his untimely death. Turning to our hero, Luke Patten, amid a profound silence, said, with a good deal of emotion,—

"I return to you, Mr. Bolton, untouched and uninjured, the identical papers taken from the person of the late Sir Richard Morton. How they came into my possession is not of the slightest consequence to any one. It has fallen to my lot to restore them. They will give to you your father's name, his title, and his estates, and I can only add, may you live long to enjoy that which you so richly merit!"

Arthur Bolton was not astonished, but he was greatly moved. He pressed Luke Patten's hand as he laid the case down, saying, amid the congratulations of the magistrates,—

"You have acted nobly, Mr. Patten, and I can appreciate what you have done, and, believe me, you will find me a fast friend for life."

Luke warmly returned the pressure of the hand, but spoke not.

"Well, upon my word," observed the two magistrates, "things have turned up most satisfactorily. As Mr. Patten says, it's quite immaterial where those papers came from; the fact of their being in your possession, Mr. Bolton, is quite sufficient, so permit us, in bidding you farewell, to drink your health, and wish you a speedy restoration to the station you deserve to possess, and were born to fill."

And down went two tumblers of whisky toddy.

After a few more words with Patten, the two magistrates took their leave, telling our hero that they would be most happy to see him when able to remove to Delaware, and to render him, or Lady Morton's family, any service in their power; and Arthur, tired and weakened by the sitting up during the long examination, was helped into bed by Luke and Joseph, quite overcome. The bag, with the precious documents, so unexpectedly restored, he placed under his head, only to be parted from with life.

After taking some refreshment he fell fast asleep, and Joseph, seating himself in the easy chair by the bedside, watched his master with that devotion and vigilance so strong in the heart of the faithful lad.

When our hero awoke it was night—at least it was a couple of hours after sunset. Joseph brought in a roast fowl and some light wine, and feeling greatly refreshed by his sleep, he made a tolerable meal; still, his side gave him considerable pain at times, so much so that he doubted his ability to move the next day; but he could write, and Joseph would take the letter to the hotel in Delaware, and wait for Lady Morton's arrival. Patten was anxious that a surgeon should be sent for, to examine and dress the several stabs he had received, but our hero refused, alleging they required only the attention they received, and quiet, for they looked healthy and free from any inflammation.

Late in the evening Patten came into the room, and, sitting down by the bedside, said,—

"I will now, Mr. Bolton, if you have no objection, give you (as you expressed yesterday a wish to hear it) a very short account of myself, and the motives that induced me to commit acts that were poisoning every hour of my life."

"I am very desirous to hear your tale," answered Arthur, "and I can very well imagine by the manner you have acted lately, that when you did err, you did so against the feelings of your heart. It's never too late to mend, and I feel quite sure that the atonement you have voluntarily made will rob the past of its bitterness, and render the rest of your life one of consolation and self-reliance; and in the affection and devotion of an amiable wife, who must rejoice in the moral courage you evinced in confessing your errors, and determination to make atonement for them. Depend on me—if God spares me—to free you from every difficulty, and to place you in a position of comfort and independence ——"

"You have a kind and noble heart, Mr. Bolton," returned Patten, much moved. "What I have to tell of myself will be soon said. My father came from the old country, he and

his wife, and purchased—after several years' various fortunes
—this large tract of land along the banks of the Mattapone.
There was a younger brother when they died. They left a
considerable sum of money and this farm, then well worth
nine hundred a year.

"I was very intimate with the Mason family before my
father's death, and in my early years attached to the younger
daughter; but I always had an exceeding dislike to the two
youngest sons—their unbridled tempers and savage propensi-
ties led to desperate disputes between us. Emily Mason, the
eldest daughter, became acquainted with a comrade of the two
young men, of the name of Jackson, a most notorious character—in fact, a well-known horse-lifter. I knew this character, and thinking to do a service to the family, warned Emily
not to be imposed upon by any of his specious tales of himself
and his occupations. He was a handsome, fine-looking man,
with pleasing manners, but at heart a most confounded repro-
bate. Emily Mason turned upon me like a tigress, said she
saw through my schemes, that I wanted her sister—but she
vowed I should never have her as long as she lived—and that I
was a liar and a slanderer. But not to dwell on my story,
sufficient to say she married Jackson, and finally contrived to
turn the whole family, even her sister, against me.

"You are aware that Jackson was, soon after his marriage,
tried for a daring and desperate raid he and some others, the
two younger Masons included, made along the banks of the
Mattapone, carrying off a drove of fine horses, and six of mine
amongst the lot. I collected a number of young and stout-
hearted farmers, and pursued the horse-stealers into the
swamps of the Mattapone, and finally, after some singular
escapes and encounters, we captured Jackson and three others,
and recovered eleven horses.

"As you are aware, Jackson was hung with two others—
this made the breach between me and the Masons more fierce
and deadly. Till the affair cooled down, I went to New York
to purchase some things I required, and to keep out of the
way till the furious rage of the brothers against me became
quieted. It's needless for me to say how I was induced to
enter into the dissipations of New York. I was young, possessed of a considerable sum in my bankers' hands, and being
introduced to two or three of the wildest of the New York
bloods, I was induced to frequent one of the most fashionable
of the numerous gaming-houses in the city. I did not know
I had a passion for play till induced to try my luck—then the
dormant feeling was roused and I became a gambler. In two
visits I paid to New York I lost every fraction of my available funds, and a year afterwards began mortgaging this farm,

till not an acre was left ; and then I plunged into greater excesses, but the whole time my heart and my feelings rebelled against the course I was following. I knew Mary Mason was attached to me, but she hesitated to unite her destiny to a man so reckless."

Luke went on to relate how he chanced to witness the murder of Sir Richard Morton, without its being in his power, as our readers already know, to prevent it.

"After the shot was fired," continued Luke Patten, "I guessed who the unfortunate victim was, but not till then. Neither did I imagine for what purpose they were watching, for Sir Richard Morton became visible to them before I could catch a glimpse of that part of the road. Shifting my position as they ran forward, I obtained a view of the body as it lay on its back on the road. I saw them search the pockets, and heard their bitter oaths at their disappointment. I knew where the certificates were secreted, and, after they left, I possessed myself of them, without any fixed purpose whatever. I knew that the unfortunate baronet had them, and where they were placed, for my cousin is articled to Mr. Bowen, and he heard the baronet say he would conceal them about his person, laying them unfolded in a thin leather case in the back of his coat.

"You are aware that I accused the brothers of the crime they had committed, and how they were acquitted. I then steeped myself in further guilt, to obtain Mary for my wife. Still my case was desperate—my creditors were pressing me for a settlement—my farm would shortly be taken from me, and myself and wife thrust upon the world penniless.

"In this state I agreed with George Mason, who was just returned from England, to make use of the cheque for three thousand given by the late Sir Richard Morton to the deceased John Mason. 'If I get this note cashed,' said I, 'I will restore the papers to the rightful owners ; they will be of no use to us.'

"'Not so,' answered George ; 'that sum would be a paltry remuneration for the restoration of a title and a noble inheritance to "a penniless adventurer," such as he styled you, Mr. Bolton, and described you to me as a young man without principle, and as wholly unworthy of supplanting Sir Richard Morton's son by his second wife ; that you were vicious and depraved ; that your father knew of your evil disposition, and was forced to send you from England to the West Indies to get rid of you. His proposal was to sell the papers to the son of the second wife, who would surely give three thousand pounds for them.

"I agreed to go to New York. Mason came with me. I

presented the cheque. You know the result. You gave me into custody; although you spoke harshly of my conduct, you pleaded in my favour, as the cheque was evidently intended as a gift for the late John Mason. I was prepared for a cata-strophe of the kind, and a parcel of rowdies, led by Saunders, all of them half drunk, were in readiness to set me free. I got out of New York, and fearing pursuit, rode the entire distance to my home, using three horses. Nevertheless you arrived before me. The horrible events of that morning, and the death of the two brothers, had a fearful effect on my mind. I told all to my distracted wife; stated I had never enjoyed a moment's peace from the hour I had plunged into guilt. She threw herself into my arms, and, with tears and sobs, implored me to redeem the past as far as lay in my power. ' We shall be beggars,' I exclaimed bitterly. ' Your child will be born in misery and poverty.' ' Better so, dear Luke, than born with its parents steeped in guilt.' I yielded—my own heart prompted me to the act. Mr. Bolton, you now know all. You have still two bitter and sworn enemies, but they are far away—at least I left them in New York, and neither of them will ever venture to set foot on the shores of England again."

Arthur and Patten remained conversing nearly two hours, our hero giving a brief sketch of his adventures and the suffer-ings he had endured from the vindictive villany of James Saunders's brother, and how nearly wrecked his hopes in life were by his schemes.

Luke was greatly surprised and interested.

" You have gone through and endured a great deal of per-secution and wrong, and during a very short life ; but you have all through trusted in Providence, and you have reaped the reward."

" I hope, before I leave this country, Mr. Patten, to be able to relieve you from all your difficulties, and see you and Mrs. Patten happy. By attention and industry, and a reliance on God's mercy, you will yet do well and atone for the errors of the past."

Arthur, shortly after this conversation, partook of some slight refreshment, and feeling fatigued, after the events of the day, soon fell into a refreshing sleep.

CHAPTER XXXI.

JOSEPH, when his master was asleep, trimmed the lamp ; and seeing everything in the chamber was in due order, felt a great inclination to rest himself, after two nights of wakeful watching ; he was to rest upon a mattress at the foot of his master's bed. Joe, though the most devoted of followers, was about the worst night-watcher that could be selected—provided he was permitted to sleep—for, once asleep, nothing less than a most vigorous shaking could ever awaken him. There was no necessity that night, his master was so much better, that he should keep awake, so to sleep he went, little thinking or dreaming of the manner in which he should be roused from his slumbers.

Luke Patten's land and farm extended along the fine pasture level bordering the Mattapone; for grazing it was unequalled, and great numbers of cattle were yearly fattened off those lands. The farm-house and appurtenances were extensive; the sheds for the cattle and the buildings appropriated to the male helps on the farm were situated a short distance from the house inhabited by the female portion of the establishment, consisting of six men and four women, besides Luke and his wife. The former having bidden his guest good night, returned to the large and comfortable kitchen of the house. Mrs. Patten was sitting at a table, on which was laid a light supper; she was busy sewing, but her very handsome and interesting countenance bore a very dejected look; as her husband entered she put by her work, and looking into his serious countenance, said, " You have had a long conference, Luke, with Mr. Bolton, I hope you have convinced him that you are less involved in this terrible affair than appearances would lead him to imagine."

" Oh, yes, dear; he is quite satisfied on that head, I assure you; he is a generous, noble-minded youth, and he quite agrees with me that we should do far better in England, and he has promised me every help necessary to establish us comfortably."

" Oh, Luke," exclaimed his wife, her eyes suffused with tears, " I shall never feel happy till we quit this land, and I do so rejoice that Mr. Bolton will not oppose our wishes; it is so kind of him ! Sit down, dear Luke, the women are all gone to bed ; take some refreshment, for the last three days have been ones of great excitement, and our situation is still critical."

Luke sat down and filled for himself a mug of home-brewed beer. " I do not see why you should alarm yourself, Mary. Your two brothers will be buried to-morrow; better as it is, than that they should continue to lead the life they did, and with such associates—men capable of any crime."

Mary Patten shuddered as she answered, " And yet, Luke, even with such associates Mrs. Jackson lives, and intends again to unite herself to the chief of the band. She has sworn vengeance upon you, and I never sleep at night with a quiet heart or mind."

"You let your imagination, dear Mary, torment you too much; those horse-lifters will not venture over the border here; there will be no mercy shown them if taken. I am thinking more of your brother George and that ruffian, Saunders, whom I so unfortunately mixed myself up with in New York. If I can get Mr. Bolton safe into Delaware to-morrow, I do not fear their arrival. George could not well be here before to-morrow evening, or next day; and whether he will bring that Saunders with him or not I can't say."

"God forbid George should arrive here before Mr. Bolton has left! his furious temper would be roused to madness, finding his brothers dead, and he who was the cause of their deaths an inmate of our house. Ah! Luke, I tremble to think of the consequences!"

"After all, my dear Mary, George and this Saunders are but two men. I have six attached men in my service, and they would protect Mr. Bolton and see him safe into Delaware; but, please God, I go with him myself to-morrow morning; he is anxious to leave—most anxious."

The supper-things were put away, the doors bolted and and locked, and the two dogs that were chained in their houses in the yard, let loose—this last act Luke always performed himself. The large and powerful dogs were perfectly trained, they paraded all night round and round the building, and no sound at a distance ever induced them to leave the immediate vicinity of the house; by twelve o'clock every inmate of the homestead was buried in repose.

The night was extremely dark, there were no stars, and a thin, grey vapour came up from the waters of the Mattapone, spread over the flats, and crept up to the higher land, on which stood the farm buildings. There was scarcely a perceptible breath of wind, and all was as still and free from sound as in one of the great prairies of the far west.

About this time there came up from the river twelve or fourteen men, who had landed from a large flat boat, about two miles from the homestead of Patten. They walked quickly and silently, crossing the meadows, and scaring the numerous horses and grazing colts, as they moved through the mist, without a word spoken. On they tramped till they came close up with the outhouses of the farm, in one of which the men slept. We have said that the cattle-sheds and farm buildings were some little distance from the house; so that this silent body of men might easily reach the buildings without their approach being observed, or any sound heard by the watch-dogs, especially as the buildings had a grove of trees between them and the homestead.

To account for the appearance of these men at such an hour,

we must request our readers to return with us to New York, on the evening of Luke Patten's escape from the police, aided by the rowdies—a species of gentry whose name and existence have now become well known to us in England.

Luke had arranged with George Mason and Saunders, that should he require to be rescued, he would, after his escape, meet them at a certain house in one of the worst localities in New York ; but Patten had begun to repent his conduct, and after seeing and hearing Arthur Bolton at the banker's, determined to alter his mode of life, cut all connection with the Mason family, get home, sell off stock and land, and with the remnant left turn over a new life. He therefore quitted New York and proceeded home, urging his own horse, which he had had the precaution to leave at a spirit store some two or three miles out of the city, till he broke down, and then exchanged for another, which he knocked up just as he beheld our hero and the two brothers contending on the hill above his own farm. The reason he made such desperate speed was fear of arrest, through the energy and determination of Arthur Bolton, who would, however, he thought, scarcely follow him to Delaware.

George Mason and Saunders, in a very moody temper at the failure of the cheque, waited till night for the appearance of Luke.

" I tell you what, George," said Saunders, taking his pipe from his mouth—they were drinking and smoking in a small, dirty, ill-furnished chamber of a low pothouse, frequented by the worst characters—" that brother-in-law of yours will play us false. I don't like his phiz. He looks too shy, and shirks our projects. He's only a half-and-half chap. He seems to have what he calls a conscience."

" Well, if I really thought that, Bill," said Mason, sulkily, " I wouldn't spare him. He certainly undertook to try and cash this cursed cheque, because he said he considered I was justly entitled to it ; but in any other project against that infernal youngster, Bolton, he refused to join. You see he holds those papers ; how the deuce he got them I cannot imagine, but he has them. Now they are worth five thousand to this Arthur Bolton, for they will make him a baronet, with I suppose about eight thousand a year, and without them he will only remain what he is. I guess Patten has struck off home, maybe to treat for himself with Bolton, and cut us out."

" Blow me !" cried Saunders, striking the table a terrible blow in his passion, and uttering a string of oaths, " if I only knew that, and if it is so, I'll cut both his and that cursed Bolton's throat, if I swing the next day for it !"

" If I could only finger the five thousand, you might cut their throats and welcome ; that youngster's luck has baffled every scheme of mine. But I tell you what, we must leave this place by daylight. Bolton, of course, knows we are in the city, and now that Patten has escaped, he will hunt us up. We will be off for Delaware, and ride hard to get there, and then once ahold of Patten, we shall be able, with my two brothers' assistance and the gang they are joined with, to make my brother-in-law act, or revenge ourselves upon him, and those who have outwitted him. Now that I have found out who the party at the hotel are—the late Sir Richard Merton's wife, son, and daughters—I can, I think, play a game when we get them all in Delaware, that they will find it difficult to win."

Before dawn the two plotters left New York, and hiring horses, and using good speed, they both reached Delaware on the morning of the magistrate's visit to Luke Patten's homestead. Of course the news of Mr. Bolton's encounter with the two Masons and their death was the absorbing topic of conversation in all public-houses in Delaware, then a very small place compared to its present state.

Mason and his associate did not put up at the hotel where the former first met Luke Patten, and where they concocted the project of cashing the cheque. He preferred going to one where he was not known, or, at all events—owing to time, and the scar across his cheek and lip—where he would be unrecognized. As to Saunders, who was quite a stranger to horse exercise, he was cursing Mason for his unreasonable speed, which half killed him.

As they sat smoking and drinking, both nearly knocked up, on the morning the magistrates, going to Patten's farm, with their clerks and half a dozen constables, passed by on horseback,—

" What the devil's on the time now ? " exclaimed Saunders, getting up and going to the window to look at the *cortége*.

His companion started, and changed colour as he looked out. He knew Mr. Hendrick very well ; he was the holder of the mortgage upon Fork Farm. Calling the landlord, he asked him where the magistrates and constables were going.

" I calculate then, neighbour, you have not heard the news that came last night. I guess there's been a bloody murder at Luke Patten's farm." Mason turned fearfully pale, and seemed so struck that the landlord perceived it " Maybe, mister, you know something of the Masons that was killed the other day by the Britisher, who is now lying dying at the farm."

George Mason sank back into the chair, whilst Saunders appeared half-stupefied.

With a wonderful effort the former conquered his emotion. With all his crimes, this man had a strong and fierce attachment for all his family, excepting Mary Patten—he had always shunned and disliked her.

"Well," said he, looking steadily at the landlord, "I did know these Masons years ago, and I'm shocked. I've been many years in England, and did not expect on my return to hear that my old comrades were murdered."

"I guess, mister," returned the landlord, "that you know very little about these said Masons since you left this country. Your old comrades have made hot nests for themselves. The two sons of old John Mason, of the Fork, were tried for the murder of a British baronet, and Luke Patten was their accuser; but somehow, I calculate, he did not like hanging his two intended brothers-in-law, so he shammed, and made believe he was mistaken in their persons. But you see it's a mistake to say the two Masons were murdered—it's quite the contrary; I guess they began to fight, what for I can't say; but they intended to kill this Britisher, but it seems he was too much for them, for he killed them in self-defence, though he got sliced a bit by their bowie knives. Somehow Luke Patten came up on horseback and saw them fighting, and thought to stop them, but his horse was knocked up, fell, and threw him. So when he got up the mischief was done; they were both dead, and the Englishman very little better. So Luke Patten had him carried to his farm, and there he lies, and the magistrates you saw are going to investigate matters. I must say it's a good riddance getting the Masons out of the way, for they joined those infernal horse-lifters in the Mattapone swamp. Why, it's not possible to graze a horse or a colt within ten miles of their haunts."

"Well," returned George Mason, repressing his intense anxiety and passion, "I did not know all this; when I knew them it was different."

The landlord left the room, and George Mason let his head drop upon the table, covering his face with his hands. Had remorse at last struck a chord in this man's heart? Was he repenting the error and crimes of his past life, or had twenty-five years of plotting and scheming steeled his heart against remorse? Was he acknowledging that there was an all-seeing Eye that overlooked man's works and deeds, and that could, when it pleased, strike down the criminal when he least expected the blow. He had had warning sufficient. His father was struck down in the very act of plotting mischief against his benefactor. His brothers, with innocent blood on their hands, and in the very act of committing fresh crimes, were also struck down by the hand of the son, who thus avenged his father's blood shed by them. Did all these circumstances press upon this miserable sinner, as he bent his head upon his hands, and remained without moving for several minutes?

Saunders, who did not possess one spark of human feeling in his nature, who was as reckless of crime as he was of life, gazed upon his companion with supreme contempt. He smoked his pipe, refilled his glass, and seeing Mason still in the same position, he cried out,—

"I say, my hearty, are you asleep, or are you feeling like a sick girl after a runaway lover? Is that the way you take your brothers' murders?"

"You are a fool, Saunders!" exclaimed Mason, raising his head, his eyes sparkling with passion. "I was thinking how to have revenge upon the man who killed my brother, and upon that artful, double-dealing villain, Luke Patten. I told you he was playing a double game, the villain. Now you can see it. Instead of blowing out the brains of the man he saw murder his wife's brothers—curse him! he helps him, carries him to his house, gets his wife, who always hated us all, to nurse him, and why? because Luke Patten has the papers that will give him title and estates, and he can bargain for them—no doubt feigning repentance—and be well rewarded. But he shall not—everlasting curses be on his head! This night I will burn his house about his ears, and bury him and the slayer of my brothers beneath the ruins."

"Blow me, that's your sort, George!" said Saunders. "But who'll pay the piper? We're not so flush of cash. I am just in the humour for finishing up both Patten and this Bolton, who I feel sure has somehow swamped my brother Bill; but, as I said, where's the plunder? That youngster has none about him, and I'll swear Luke Patten has none. Suppose now we carry off Bolton to the haunt of those comrades of your brothers; force him to pay a few thousands for his life, and kill him afterwards, if you like; but let us force him to pay first, now that you have lost that three thousand pounds."

"Well," returned Mason, disguising his real intentions from his comrade, "be it so, but the work must be done this night, or it will be too late. We must ride twenty-four miles and be back by midnight—so come along. I will hire two horses."

Saunders began to make objections, for he remembered the ride from New York and its fatigue; he was no horseman.

"There's no time for hesitation, Saunders," said Mason; "either follow me or remain here."

With an oath, Saunders objected to being left, and said,—
" Well, come along ; pay the score, and I'm ready."

Before an hour had expired, the two accomplices had left Delaware on horseback, for the purpose of carrying out Mason's iniquitous projects of revenge.

CHAPTER XXXII.

ABOUT four-and-twenty miles from the town of Delaware, following the banks of the Mattapone river, before it joins the Pamunka, both streams being then lost in the confluence forming the York River, the traveller would pause to gaze upon a great tract of flat land intersected by many small streams, great pools, and marsh land, dense thickets of willow and alder, and several trees that flourish in marshy land. This tract of country could not be recognized now by any travellers of forty years ago. At that time it was a wilderness, almost impossible to traverse, even by one moderately acquainted with its paths, but to a stranger quite impossible ; he would, if in the dark, be assuredly drowned in one or other of the narrow dykes or still pools. Nevertheless, numerous horses and colts were bred and fed on sundry parts of this level tract, miles in extent. On some of the most elevated banks of the stream several large log-houses had been erected, in which dwelt a mixed race of savage outlaws, who banded together and permitted themselves to be under the guidance of one of their number.

These men—and some of them had families—lived chiefly by plundering boats, &c., descending the streams ; stealing horses, which they either sold south, or, if too young, grazed them in the swamps till they were old enough to drive south and sell.

They did not plunder land travellers, for the best of all possible reasons—no travellers ever attempted to cross this vast tract either on horseback or on foot. The outlaws had large flats with which they traversed the streams and descended the rivers.

The chief of this band of horse-lifters and river-robbers was a native of New York, named Stephen Steadman. It would be quite useless to state for what crimes this man became outlawed from society—quite enough to say that a more cruel, ferocious villain scarcely ever existed ; he was a strong, massive-built man, with by no means a repulsive countenance, rather the contrary, and not more than forty or forty-two years of age. This wretch was a near relation of Jackson, the horse-lifter, a man notorious for his exploits. Nevertheless, he was captured chiefly through the courage and enterprise of Luke Patten, and hung.

Luke Patten from that period became a marked man; upwards of thirty outlaws swore to be revenged upon him for Jackson's death. They swore to serve him out, as they termed it, and put him to a more excruciating death than hanging.

The younger sons of John Mason were early acquainted with these men, probably owing to Mason's daughter having married Jackson, who was a well-looking man, and was not known at that time, to the Masons, to be the chief of the outcasts of the Swamp; but, vicious, profligate, and idle, their lands ill-cultivated, and perpetually borrowing money on the farm, their necessities soon induced them to join the outlaws in predatory excursions.

After their release from gaol, the accusation against them for the murder of Sir Richard Morton failing, and Fork Farm, together with all the cattle, implements, &c., being seized by Mr. Hendrick, till the £2,000 owing should be paid, they and their sister, Mrs. Jackson, fled to join the outlaws. She knew Stephen Steadman already, for she had often seen him with her husband before he suffered the penalty of his misdeeds, and Stephen Steadman, shortly after their residence amongst them, offered himself as a second husband, and was accepted. Mrs. Jackson was quite as guilty of the crime committed by her brothers, indeed, much more so than they were, for she instigated them to the act that in the end cost them their lives.

To this community of outlaws George Mason and James Saunders directed their course. George Mason, though never associated with them in sharing their plunder, knew both Jackson and Steadman intimately. He and his father often bought young unmarked colts from them, reared them till four years old, and then sold them at the horse fairs throughout Virginia.

After two hours' ride, the horsemen reached a lone house on a wretched bridle-road leading to a little-frequented ferry across the Pamunka river; this house was scarcely three miles from the entrance into the Swamps. Here they left their horses and proceeded on foot; a stranger could never have found the path, but George Mason knew it well, and he knew the signal to give when he should come across any of the band at the entrance of their retreat, and meet two or three he was sure to do.

" Well, blow me, George, this is boxing the compass!" said Saunders, as they proceeded through singularly intricate paths over bridges of such light construction that a couple of men

could carry them any distance. During their progress they
passed two or three men, who examined them keenly till
George Mason made certain signs, and they then took no further notice of them.

At length they reached Steadman's log-house ; it was a long
building formed simply of trunks of trees all neatly put together, and roofed with thatch made from dried flags. The
house consisted of four rooms—one large and lofty, which was
used as kitchen and general smoking and sitting-room, when a
meeting of several of the gang took place. Two coarse, slo-
venly-looking women were occupied about some domestic
affairs ; they paused and looked at the new comers with great
surprise, but as Mason and his companion approached the door,
Mrs. Steadman happened to come out. She uttered an exclamation when she recognized her brother, and embracing him,
led him into the house, saying, in a low voice,—

" Who is your companion ?"

" All right," said Mason, " he's one of the right sort.
Where's Steadman ?"

" He's not far off," said the woman ; " he is with some of
the men, collecting some colts to take to Regan fair to-
morrow."

" Then send for him, for I have something else for him to
do."

" Well, sit down both of you, and I will send for him. I
suppose you did not meet either of your brothers ? They
are gone to Luke Patten's to see how he succeeded with a
cheque they gave him. I told them they were fools to trust
that false cur, but they said it was not possible to be done
without him."

George Mason wiped the perspiration from his forehead ; he
was not particular how he wounded or tried people's feelings ;
he sat moody and silent, whilst his companion helped himself
plentifully from the whisky jar placed before him, with bread,
cheese, and meat, by Mrs. Steadman.

" You have some bad news, George," said his sister, at
length observing his gloomy countenance and abstracted manners ; " good or bad, let us hear it.

Mrs. Steadman herself was much altered. She was tall and
gaunt ; her face thin, yellow, and devoid of a healthy colour.
She was beginning to feel the influence of the swamp malaria.

" Yes," returned George, " I have bad news—news that will
stir your blood, and make you, like myself, thirst for vengeance."

Mrs. Steadman was startled.

" Don't keep me in doubt then, let me hear it—my life has
had troubles enough—I can bear a trifle."

" Well, then, your two brothers are dead!"

Mrs. Steadman staggered back, and dropped down upon a bench, gazing stupefied at her brother; but as he said the words, " your brothers are dead," Stephen Steadman entered the room. He had heard the words, for he instantly said,—

" What do you mean, George Mason? Your words drive everything else out of my head. However, you are welcome back to this country;" and he held out his hand, adding, "who is your comrade?"

" A staunch friend, that you may trust."

Steadman shook Saunders by the hand.

" Now, George, in the name of fate, what news is this you bring—did I hear you right?"

" Yes, Stephen, right enough, as far as hearing me goes. My brothers are both dead, and now lying stark and stiff in one of the out-barns of Luke Patten's farm."

" Ah!" exclaimed Mrs. Steadman, stamping her foot, and her pale face flushing with passion; " that villain Patten has been a scourge to our family! Shall we never be revenged on that traitor, and his degenerate wife?"

" You astonish me," said Stephen Steadman. " Did Patten have a hand in their death? Who killed them? How did it come about? I have sworn to have my revenge upon this cursed Luke Patten, and the time is come."

George Mason then stated all he knew about the affair, putting Luke Patten into the worst light possible; in fact, making it very evident tha the had betrayed him and Saunders, and might have prevented the death of the two brothers had he not been a traitor, and thinking to secure to himself a large sum of money by handing over to Arthur Bolton the papers he had come to America to seek.

" Then death to the traitor," said Stephen Steadman, " and this very night!" and he swore fearfully that his death should be a cruel one. " As for the Britisher," he continued, " we will bring him here, and see what torture and the fear of death will extract out of him. We have made up our minds to change our retreat; we cannot hold on here much longer, and after this night's work there will be a mustering, to hunt us out. Patten has a dozen or so of fine horses in his pasture, we will make a sweep of them. I am sending on our best cattle in an hour or so."

" Oh!" exclaimed Mrs. Steadman with intense bitterness, " that I were a man for twenty-four hours, what a terrible revenge I would have for all the wrongs inflicted on my family by the Morton family, and that wretch Patten! You may extort what you please from that man who killed my brothers, but blood for blood. I must have his life!"

" Rest easy, Eliza," said Steadman, with an oath ; " you shall be satisfied ; put more mugs upon the table, and leave us for half an hour."

Mrs. Steadman did so. The temper and frame of mind she was in made her tremble all over—she could scarcely control herself. Having placed more food and drink on the table, she left three as cruel and vicious men together as ever breathed.

Having satisfied their appetites, they took to pipes and whisky.

" How do you mean to proceed? " asked George Mason, filling a pipe ; " and how many of your men can you bring? "

" Ten and our three selves will be quite enough," said Steadman. " Patten has, I think, six men on his farm, but they all sleep in the cattle-sheds, and the stables and cow-houses are some distance from the house. I don't care for the six helps, for we can secure them and prevent an alarm ; but I know Patten keeps two large and fierce dogs, trained to keep about the house."

" Ah ! " said George Mason, " if once that Englishman is roused, he and Patten, both powerful men, and well armed, will lessen our number before we get in on them."

" Don't be uneasy ; I have a plan. There won't be a shot fired. Leave that to me. We shall go down the river in a large flat in three hours, and land within a mile or so of the homestead."

The rest of the day was passed in drinking, smoking, and plotting, till the time arrived for departure. When it became dusk, the thirteen men embarked in a long flat-bottomed boat, well armed, and ready for any wickedness their leader, Stephen Steadman, should urge them to commit.

As stated in our previous chapter they reached the farm buildings of Luke Patten, without creating any alarm to any of the inmates, or attracting the attention of the watch-dogs.

CHAPTER XXXIII.

WE have said it was an extremely dark night when these men marched up from the river, so silently and so stealthily ; but as they halted close to the building, the heavy clouds opened a little, and a breeze sprang up. One of the men carried a coil of thin, strong rope ; several had dark lanterns, and two crowbars. Approaching one of the windows of the building, which was defended by strong shutters, the men with the crowbars went skilfully and noiselessly to work ; they forced off the hinges, and removed the shutters. The window itself was merely wired across; this was also removed, and an entrance into that part of the building gained where the six men slept.

Farm servants are not easily roused from their first slumbers; in most countries they are a hard-worked race, not very well fed, and generally badly lodged. These sons of toil, whose labours rarely finish at stated hours, sleep soundly. Luke Patten's farm-helps were, however, well fed, and well and decently lodged. They worked hard, but they were contented, and were much attached to their master and mistress. They fared widely different from the same class in the small farms in South Wales, Great Britain. There they always sleep over the cattle, on straw, or musty hay—bed-clothes wholly unknown—their food, barley bread and milk, and soup guiltless of meat, skim-milk cheese, and, maybe, in some of the rather better farms, a piece of bacon in the soup, and at chance times a few potatoes; up with the light, to bed with its decline.

So soundly did Luke Patten's men sleep, that Steadman and his gang of miscreants actually stood in the room where they reposed, and flashed the lights of four lanterns upon their faces, before one of the number opened his eyes.

It was by no means a pleasing sight that awaited them when they did awake, for a rough, fierce, bearded ruffian stood with a revolver, the muzzle within a couple of inches of each man's head. Had they not been taken unawares, those six men would undoubtedly have caused the enterprise to fail, though blood would have been shed, for on hooks opposite the stretcher on which they lay hung each man's bill-hook and hatchet, formidable weapons in the hands of strong men.

"Utter a word or a cry," said Steadman, with a savage oath, "and a knife will be in your throat."

The poor fellows lay still, vexed to the heart that they were thus caught. In a singularly short time each man was firmly bound hand and foot to his bedposts.

"Now hearken to me," said Stephen Steadman, "which of you men feed and tie up the dogs of a morning? Come, no hesitation, or we'll slice one of your throats for an example. You have heard of my name, if you never saw me, I am quite certain. I'm Steadman, of the swamp; that will satisfy you I mean to do what I say."

"I do," said a young, robust, healthy-looking man; "I feed and tie them up, master lets 'em loose."

"Get up, then," and two of the men unloosed the cords, "dress yourself."

The man doggedly dressed himself, casting a longing look at the hook where his bill-hook hung.

One of the ruffians took two tempting pieces of meat from his huge pocket.

"Now, listen to me; take this meat, and give a piece to each dog."

"No, curse me if I do!" said the poor fellow; "what, poison the poor dumb beasts! Not I. Cut my throat if you like; I'm —— if we had only heard you coming you wouldn't stand there now."

Two or three of the miscreants seized the man, and after a fierce struggle threw him on the stretcher, one holding a bowie knife to his throat, whilst Steadman stamped with passion.

"Come, come," said George Mason, "let him be; we need not have his blood on our hands; he never injured us. Tie him up."

"Not I," furiously exclaimed Steadman; "the villain shall pay for his obstinacy."

"I say," exclaimed another of the men, "curse ye, ye blood-thirsty souls! I'll tie the dogs up; they will follow me as well as John Simmons; they shan't give a bark, but let my comrade be."

"Tie him up, then," said Steadman, "and let the cur feel that he's tied. Now, jump up, you brute, and mind, you have made me savage; there's a dozen more of us surrounding the house. If you attempt to escape, or the dogs bark,"—and he swore a fearful oath,—"I'll cut the throat of every man lying here, and set the farm on fire; now be quick, and come back!"

The man who had so stoutly refused to poison the dogs was cruelly tied and gagged, and the other man cast loose.

The latter dressed himself, and was let out of the barn; when once outside, he was sorely tempted to give the alarm to his master, for he felt satisfied that they came to rob the house, but he said to himself, what could master and the wounded Britisher do to defend themselves against thirteen or fourteen armed men, and more of them hid somewhere within call perhaps. As he approached the house, the two great mastiff dogs paused in their rounds, evidently they sniffed the air, but broke into no bark, and walked quietly towards the man, and rubbed their heads against his knees.

The farm man looked wishfully over the front of the house; all was dark and silent, no ray of light shone in any window of the building. The man hesitated for a moment; "dang it —it's no use," he muttered to himself, and taking the two dogs by their collars, evidently much to their surprise, for they hesitated about being taken away, and no sign of the dawn, he led them to the farm buildings, and put them into a brewhouse in the back, locking the door on them, and pitching the key into a hedge, for fear the villains watching for him might still wish to poison the poor brutes. With a dogged air of indifference, he returned to the room where he found his poor comrades quaking with fear, thinking he might be tempted to run away or give an alarm.

" Where have you put the dogs? " demanded Steadman.

" In the brewhouse, at the back of the building."

" Good," returned the horse-lifter. " Now, my lads, make him fast, and let us to work."

Whilst all this was taking place the inmates of the homestead were supposed to be buried in repose—and so they were, all but one. Although Mrs. Patten retired to rest at the same time as her husband, and endeavoured to persuade herself that she might safely sleep, as the house was faithfully guarded by their good watch-dogs, still sleep she could not; many thoughts kept her awake, though her fearless husband slept like a top, by her side—he was not a man to be kept awake through fear of anything. Mrs. Patten, though in dread and terror of her younger brothers when alone, still could not but feel and mourn over their violent deaths, knowing as she did how fearfully guilty they were. She had a still greater terror of her brother George, who always treated her from a child with exceeding harshness. She well knew his scheming, plotting, revengeful nature, and his hatred of her husband.

She was distracted when Luke Patten confessed to her, on his return from New York, of his having leagued with George to present a cheque with a forged signature at the bank, and his narrow escape from imprisonment; but he calmed her fears by solemnly swearing that from that time he would become an honest man, and make atonement where he could. Now this very promise of amending his life and shunning any further intimacy with such evil associates, though it gave her some gratification, yet filled her mind with dread, for she feared the disappointed malice of her brother and his vile associate, Saunders.

Finding she could not sleep, and being restless, she got quietly out of bed, and went to the window to look out; at this time the weather had cleared a little, and she could after a moment or two see pretty plainly as far as the little grove of evergreens, that shut out the sight of the farm buildings; she looked down for the dogs; as she did so, to her intense surprise, she beheld them rush across the court, and then, to her horror, she perceived the dark figure of a man come forward to meet them; she trembled violently, and then said to herself, " That figure going away with the dogs, and they so quiet, and neither growling nor barking, it must be one of our men;" she saw the man take the dogs with him, and walk rapidly towards the grove of trees.

"There is something wrong. Why should any of the men be up in the dead of the night?" She trembled so with agitation, that some moments elapsed before she moved, and then she went and shook her husband till she roused him.

"Holloa!" exclaimed Luke, "is it you, Mary? By Jove! I took you for a ghost. What are you dressing yourself for?"

And he sprang out of bed himself.

Mrs. Patten told him what she had seen. Luke was a little startled.

"I'll dress myself and go and see what all this is about. You are sure, Mary, you're not mistaken?"

"No, no, Luke, I am not mistaken; go to the window, you will see it's not so intensely dark as it was when we went to bed."

Luke finished dressing.

"I will get you a light, Mary, and wake one of the girls, for I see you are trembling with fright."

He went to the window and gazed steadily out, looking towards the grove of trees. As he did so after a moment, he uttered an ejaculation of surprise and rage, for he beheld coming round the trees, and standing out in the dim light, a body of men moving towards the house. Luke Patten was a man of quick apprehension and thought.

"Now be cool, Mary, don't give way to fright. We must get Mr. Bolton into our secret hiding-place. Come down into the kitchen and get a light."

Patten himself rushed down stairs, along the passage, and bursting open Arthur Bolton's door, fell full on the top of Joe, who roared murder, and strove to grasp his enemy.

"What's the matter?" demanded Arthur Bolton, starting up.

"Get up, Mr. Bolton, for Heaven's sake! The house will be beset by a pack of villains in five minutes. I have a place of safety where you can remain."

"Give me my pistols, Patten!" exclaimed our hero.

"No, it would be madness. Joe, run to my wife for a light."

"You surely will not leave Mrs. Patten?"

"Oh!" interrupted Patten, as Joe came in with a light, "they won't injure us. I am satisfied Saunders and George Mason are amongst them."

He opened the window, and fastened a sheet to the leg of a table, and threw the end out.

"This will make them think you have escaped this way.
Now, lean on me, Mr. Bolton ; you are very weak."

"Yes, or you would not be able to persuade me to seek
safety by flight ; but at present I feel I should make a poor
fight of it."

"Hark! I hear them. Don't hurry ; the doors and lower
windows will resist them for ten minutes."

They passed into the kitchen, and then they heard the men
outside preparing to force the door. One side of the large
room was framed with massive logs, neatly laid one over the
other, and polished. Pressing a knob, Luke Patten and
Joseph helped Arthur Bolton through a narrow opening that
suddenly appeared. Mrs. Patten gave Joseph a bundle of
candles, with one lighted, and Patten had just time to say,
"The passage leads to a cellar—go quick !" and as the panel
closed, a furious rush was made at the door by those without.

Arthur Bolton felt a singular reluctance in thus seeking
safety, and leaving Luke Patten and his timid wife to meet the
ruffians thundering at the door. Still, he felt he was utterly
unable to give the slightest assistance, for the least exertion
caused his severe gashes to open. He felt he was even then
bleeding. Joseph led the way, through a very narrow, short
passage, terminated by a flight of stone steps. Down these
steps—about twelve in number—they went, and then found
themselves in a large vaulted and bricked cellar, half full of
empty tubs and casks. At the farther end of the cellar there
appeared a dark, narrow passage ; but our hero felt so weak
that he sat down on a stone ledge running along the side of the
cellar. Joseph stuck the lighted candle into a broken cask,
and anxiously asked his master, " Had he not better examine
his wounds ? " for he was bleeding.

"Nothing of any consequence, Joe. My weakness proceeds
from the quantity of blood I lost when first stabbed. I should
certainly have bled to death had not Luke Patten arrived at
the time he did."

"Who are these men, sir, that are going to attack the
house—are they robbers ? "

" Luke Patten seems to think that his wife's brother, George
Mason and James Saunders, are amongst them ; if so, their
object, no doubt, would be to seize upon me and the papers I
now possess, for the first thing I did when roused was to
thrust them into my breast-pocket."

Arthur Bolton and his humble companion remained quietly
in the cellar for more than half an hour, when a strange sound
attracted their attention.

"What's that, sir ? " said Joe, starting up and listening.

They stood silent for a moment. The sound increased, and

presently a thin stream of smoke came curling down the stairs into the cellar.

"Merciful Heaven!" exclaimed our hero, "the house is on fire! It's the roar of flames we hear!" and, starting to his feet, despite his weakness, he rushed up the flight of steps, half blinded by smoke, and deafened by the roar of the devouring element—fire.

We will now return to the kitchen of Luke Patten's house, after our hero's escape from it. Luke, with his horrified wife clinging to him, had taken his gun and pistols from the rack over the chimney, and waited the entrance of the gang. With the united force of the whole band, the strong door gave way with a heavy crash, and the men, with their lanterns open, burst into the house. The crash awoke the females asleep in the room over the kitchen, who, springing from their beds, began dressing and crying out with terror.

When the leader of the gang beheld Luke Patten standing leaning on his rifle, his wife was with her head leaning on his shoulder. At one glance Luke recognized several of the intruders. He perceived George Mason and Jem Saunders, their faces flushed and their gaze fixed upon him with a most vindictive expression.

"What is the reason of this outrage, Stephen Steadman?" asked Luke Patten, looking fearlessly into the leader's face.

"So you remember me, Luke Patten?" said the leader, with a coarse laugh and an oath. "Perhaps you may remember, too, that your evidence hung my cousin Jackson? I told you then I would not easily forget you, and would pay you off some day—I am come to do so now."

"Aigh! Luke Patten," with a bitter laugh, put in George Mason and Saunders, pushing themselves forward. "You betrayed us also! Where's Bolton, and where are the papers you stole? Give them up, and we may come to terms."

"You are an unnatural villain!" said Patten, speaking fiercely. "I never betrayed you; nevertheless—and I thank God it is so—Mr. Bolton, by this time, is half way to the Ferry Inn. I saw you in time, and helped him out of his chamber-window; and he has the papers with him."

"It's a lie!" shouted Mason, savage with fear of disappointment. "Come, my lads, let us search the house; for I swear, if he has escaped, Luke Patten, we will burn your house over your head, for out of it you shall never go alive!"

"You may take what you can get, my lads," said Steadman; "but just bind this traitor first, and turn the women out."

Four men made a rush upon Patten, who stepped back and fired, just as Mason and Saunders were rushing from the room. The ball found a victim; for Saunders, with a howl of rage, fell forward, rolled over on his side, and, with a smothered execration, expired. Patten was instantly knocked down, cruelly beaten, and his insensible wife torn from his arms, and carried from the house by the women, who rushed for safety towards the farm buildings.

George Mason, though he beheld his comrade fall, struck by the ball from Patten's gun, never paused to raise him or see if he was slain, so eager was he to secure the person of Arthur Bolton, and obtain the packet he supposed him to possess. Three of the men followed him with open lanterns, and bursting into the room where our hero had slept, his first glance rested on the open window and the sheet hanging out. A savage exclamation of rage and disappointment escaped his lips. He looked at the bed, tossed over the clothes, and all the articles in the room, thinking the papers might still be found.

"No, he has escaped!" he exclaimed to his men, who were appropriating every article that suited their fancy; "but he cannot be beyond a few yards, for he is severely wounded. So, follow me, we will catch him yet. He's worth a few thousands; but set fire to this traitor's house, and let him burn in it!"

Two of the men followed Mason out of the window, scarcely ten feet from the ground, the other set fire to the curtains and bed-clothes, and then rushed out into the garden. By this time the followers of Stephen Steadman had pillaged the house of everything of value, and also set fire to the upper rooms.

"Now, my lads," cried the leader, "let us be off, there's a dozen good colts and some good brood mares to secure in the pasture—fasten up the door, and let this traitor," giving the unfortunate Patten a kick, "perish beneath the ruins of his homestead."

The flames spread with wonderful rapidity, for great part of the building was timber, and as inflammable as tinder. Patten was recovering as the savage Stephen Steadman kicked him in the side; the danger roused him into consciousness; the side walls of the kitchen were on fire, and smoke came out from the passage. He sat up, gazed wildly at the flames, and felt their scorching heat, as they approached him and almost singed his hair; he rolled himself over, tugged with fierce energy at his bonds, shouted wildly in his despair at the horrible death approaching him; over and over he rolled, and as a forked tongue scorched his garment wildly exclaimed,—

"O God, I'm doomed!" and then, his senses nearly leaving him, he uttered a fearful cry of despair. Five minutes, nay, two minutes more, and the unfortunate man would have died a fearful death, but in his struggles to break his bonds and get from the flames, he rolled over and lay beneath the secret outlet from the room. This outlet was violently burst open and split by Arthur, who thrust his body through, and, in a moment, beheld Luke Patten struggling on the floor beneath him. Half blinded by the smoke and flames, he grasped Patten by the collar, and, assisted by Joseph, dragged him through the broken panel ; there was no time to try and loose his bonds, so they dragged him along the passage, into which the flames were bursting, down the steps into the cellar, and then, exhausted and overcome by the heat and over-exertion, Arthur Bolton sank down beside his rescued host.

CHAPTER XXXIV

" Take a knife from my pocket, Joe," exclaimed Patten, as soon as he had recovered his senses, " and cut the bonds from my hands and feet. We must try to get out of this place, for when the massive roof of the house falls it will, I think, drive in the roof of this cellar."

Joseph took the knife and released Patten, who sprang to his feet unharmed, excepting that the flames had singed the hair from his head, and scorched his garments.

"Lean on me, Mr. Bolton. You have saved me from a horrible death. We must hasten away. Hark to that roar of the flames, and see, the smoke comes down in volumes that will smother us."

" Where is Mrs. Patten?" said our hero, regaining his feet, " she was nowhere in the kitchen."

" No ; thank God the villains drove all the women out after knocking me down, and kicking me till I became insensible. Joe," he continued, " keep the candle from going out, and follow me."

He led the way into the narrow passage at the further end of the cellar ; there was only room for one man at a time, but the passage was not ten yards long. Suddenly a tremendous crash was heard, the ground above them shook, and showers of stones, gravel, and earth were knocked out of the roof and sides of the passage. Joe with difficulty saved the light.

" Ah!" said Luke, " we are saved by God's mercy. The cellar must be choked up, but now we are safe."

By the feeble light of two candles he held, Joe perceived that they had entered a natural rocky cavern, of immense extent and very lofty. Down one side ran a copious stream of water, which formed a channel for itself across the rough ground, and disappeared at the further end through an opening about four feet in circumference.

"This is a most singular cavern," said Bolton, surveying its dimensions with surprise, "there's nothing artificial here. I suppose there's an outlet, besides the one by which we entered."

"No, Mr. Bolton, there is not; at least, I never could find one, and have spent many an hour looking, for this strange cavern once gave safety and shelter to a dozen or more unfortunate women, who were hunted from their homes, some sixty odd years ago, by the infatuated and bigoted savages who gloried in burning unfortunate women for witchcraft. You have read of the fierce ordeal this state of Virginia passed through; I will tell you all about it another time. I fear you are now suffering from your wounds and over-exertion."

"No," returned our hero, "I bled very little, and am gaining back my strength rapidly. I see you have had some sharp burns on the hands and arms," for Luke Patten was bathing his face, hands, and arms in the running water.

"Thank God it's no worse!" returned Patten.

"But, Mr. Patten," said Joe, rubbing his head, and looking troubled, "be dad you have frightened me!"

"How so, Joseph?"

"Faix, you said that there was no way of getting out of this place, except the way we came in, and begor the whole house is at the top of that."

"They will dig us out, my lad, before twenty-four hours are passed."

Joseph looked startled.

"Twenty-four hours!" he muttered to himself, looking at the bunch of candles Mrs. Patten had so fortunately provided them with, "be dad it's a long fast, Mr. Patten, and faix they may not think about digging us out."

"You are perplexing yourself uselessly, Joe," said Arthur with a smile; "you may depend Mrs. Patten considers that her husband escaped here along with us, and she will not rest till she gets the rubbish removed; it may be worth while seeing how far the roof of the cellar gave way. But you have not told me, Mr. Patten, the particulars of this atrocious outrage. If George Mason and Saunders were amongst the miscreants, they must have followed us into Virginia the very next day."

"I suspect so," returned Patten; "at all events, I have rid you of one unrelenting enemy. I intended to have shot Stephen Steadman, the leader of the gang, a man capable of any crime or cruelty, but somehow I missed him and shot Saunders, who was rushing along with Mason to search the house. No doubt, seeing your window open, and the sheet hanging out, they pursued you by jumping from the window.

The ruse told, for I did not see the men who went with him return to the kitchen."

"That villain, Saunders, richly deserved his fate," replied Arthur; "but your poor wife must have suffered dreadfully, seeing you so barbarously treated."

"She was carried out insensible," answered Luke, "before that savage robber, Steadman, knocked me down. She may feel some alarm at my being left in the house when they fired it, but she will still hope I succeeded in getting into the cellar. I will tell you how this secret entrance to the cellar came to be made. Some forty years ago, smuggling over the border was a favourite fancy with our Virginian farmers. My father, like others, dabbled in the pursuit. The cellar was originally entered from the kitchen, without any attempt at concealment; but he took it into his head to build a timber wall, cutting off the cellar, and made a somewhat ingeniously concealed passage into it; but after doing this he abandoned the smuggling trade, and when I came into possession I had no fancy for it, as it was dying out in this state. I kept things there, and, indeed, little cared to keep the entrance to it a secret. Several of my servants knew it; but fortunately, owing to the enmity the Masons evinced towards me, they know nothing of it. Entering the cellar one evening, I was surprised at seeing one end had given way, and a great deal of earth and stones heaped up; I then perceived a hole, and examining with my light, I was surprised to see it led into some kind of cave, so next day getting a pick-axe and shovel and two of my men, we went to work and made our way into this cavern. To my extreme astonishment, I found several rotten boxes and sundry cooking utensils of an old date, remnants of garments, and various things, which are all stowed away in yonder corner. In turning over the boxes I found some religious books, and an old Puritan bible with the name of Abraham Knox written within it, on one of the pages the names and dates of the birth of eleven children, seven girls and four boys; under this was a scrap of damp, closely written paper, but quite readable.

"Now it struck me as very strange how these things, and how the people that owned them, got into this cavern, for I could find no other outlet of any kind. There was a split somewhere in the roof, but where I can't say, for no light comes in through it, but a strong wind does when it blows hard. But now Joseph and I will go and see if we can ascertain how much of the roof of the cellar is fallen in, for perhaps it is possible we may be able to force our own way out." So placing a candle in a split of the rock, Patten and Joseph, to whom twenty-four hours' confinement without food of any kind offered by no means an inviting prospect, proceeded to inspect the cellar.

Left to himself, Arthur fell into a reverie, from which he was roused by the return of the explorers.

" We must wait to be dug out, sir," said Joseph, in a very dolorous tone ; " here we are, buried alive ; faix, sir, this is worse than our hiding in the cave from which we were rescued by that respectable Indian gentleman, Mr. Hogswash."

" What a strange name, Joe ! where did you meet that gentleman ?" inquired Luke Patten.

" He was an Indian chief," replied Arthur, laughing, " who was of great service to us when cast away on the Musquito coast.   He had a long string of names which ended with Punka Bosswash, and Joe invariably called him either Hogswash or Pigswash.   But, Mr. Patten, when you looked over those papers you found in one of the rotten boxes, did you discover who the people were that took shelter in this strange underground cavern ? "

" My wife felt interested, sir," returned Patten, "and after many an evening of careful inspection, she made out the history of the nine individuals who remained concealed here for a period of eleven months."

" Then there must be an outlet," said our hero.   "It is quite possible, that where that water runs out, some sixty years ago, there might have been a large outlet which the rocks and earth have since choked up.   What kind of a place is it outside where the water becomes visible ?"

" There is a high rocky bank behind where the house stood, now covered with a tuft of trees, and a broken picturesque heap of rocks and shrubs, about two hundred yards lower down towards the river, out of which gushes this stream. I am satisfied, of course, that there must have been a way into the cavern ; but I think when my grandfather built the house it's not improbable but that the entrance might have got filled up."

"It will pass time," said Arthur, " if you will relate all you know of these people Knox, for I suppose it was some of that family who were shut up here ?"

" Yes, there were five daughters of Abraham Knox, the mother, and three granddaughters.   The insane persecution of innocent women and young girls for witchcraft was near its end at the time of the persecution of the Knox family.   They were the last victims in Virginia.   Evidently judging by what my wife read to me, there were two families of that name, and two brothers who possessed small farms some eight or ten miles from here.   One of the elder brother's daughters was extremely beautiful, and, for the period and station in life of her father, very learned, and fond of botany and study of all kinds, spent her time in collecting plants, and was also an adept in concocting medicinal drinks for the sick. The younger brother's son fell desperately in love with his cousin Jane ; but she could not love him, for he was a low, vulgar brute, and had already distinguished himself in hunting up unfortunate women as witches. Jane Knox steadily refused to have any intercourse with a man who could so brutally join ignorant fanatics in destroying innocent women and girls.

" ' Take care,' said Reuben Knox, in a furious rage, ' that you yourself do not come under the lash of the law for sorcery, for you have bewitched me by giving me love philtres !'

" Jane started.

" ' I never gave you anything, Reuben, but simple vegetable drinks when you were laid up in illness, and you said they did you a world of good.'

" ' Oh, augh ! I guess they did,' returned the wretch. ' They cured the ague, but they bewitched me. I have never been myself since.'

" ' You are bewitched now, I can swear to that,' and she turned scornfully away.

" ' Oh !' he shouted as she left him, ' remember those words !'

" Shortly afterwards Reuben Knox was seized with fits, which lasted on and off for several days. Whenever he came to himself he would cry out, ' Jane Knox ! Jane Knox ! you have put an imp into my body—you are a witch ! If you don't conjure him out I'll have you burned !' and then he would shriek and howl, and froth at the mouth, till it was fearful to look at him.

" This story soon spread, and finally the report went out far and near that Jane Knox was a real witch. A young girl in the service of the younger Knox also had fits, and called out on Jane Knox, when in the fit, to let her alone and not be witching her. Then two cows died off, running wildly about the pastures till they dropped dead.

" At length Jane Knox was arrested as a witch, and carried into Williamsburg, where the then great witch discoverer, Philip Heartshole, held his sittings. The whole of the disgraceful trial is given in the manuscript—how Reuben Knox was brought into court in a fit, held by two men, and when the paroxysm passed off, he appeared as if taken out of a river, the drops of perspiration rolling from his forehead and face, and then he called out in a piteous tone,—

" ' Oh, Jane, Jane, unwitch me !'

" ' Reuben Knox,' said Jane, in a cold, calm tone, ' you are no more bewitched than I am. You are acting a part, and that girl whom you have ruined has been bribed by you to counterfeit fits. It's a monstrous mockery this trial for witchcraft, a thing that never existed except in the morbid imagination of the ignorant, and——'

"'Stop her mouth!' roared out Judge Heartshole; 'she blasphemes. She acknowledged that she gave Reuben Knox certain drinks; also that she said—you are bewitched now, Reuben Knox—the girl, who is now delirious, and three more witnesses, saw her gathering certain herbs, and muttering words in an unknown tongue.' Then followed a wonderful string of evidence against her, and not one person, not one of her wretched family, father, mother, or sisters, who were present, were allowed to utter one word in her favour—and this monster, Heartshole, had the horrible cruelty to condemn her to be burned alive, as a most dangerous pestilential witch— fearful to think of. The sentence was heard with frantic applause.

"It's shocking to dwell on this horrible subject," continued Patten, "when enlightened Europe set the example; when the learned judges of Geneva could condemn five hundred witches to the stake in three months, and one million perished in Germany. When the madness reached the States of America, it exceeded all belief the number that perished. Be it as it may, poor Jane Knox perished in the flames, in the marketplace of Williamsburg, and her family, some months after, were driven by the infatuated people to seek safety in flight. It appears by the manuscript that they found shelter in this cave, and that charitable people brought them food. The witch fever subsided entirely nine months afterwards; but what became of the Knox family of course the manuscript does not say. It was written by one of Jane Knox's sisters."

"Well, it is certainly wonderful," said Arthur, "to read in the history of that period, how the madness crept, or rather flew, over the world; every country in Europe became infected as if with an epidemic; men of learning, sound sense, and judgment in other matters, gave way, on the subject of witchcraft, to popular clamour and superstition. Even in the present day, in remote parts of England, Wales, and Scotland, the belief in witchcraft still survives."

CHAPTER XXXV

When the half-dressed and terrified servants of Luke Patten were driven from the house, they fled, as we have before stated, carrying their insensible mistress with them.

"Oh!" exclaimed the cook, "oh, the master, they will surely murder or burn him; see, the flames are bursting out of the windows !   But where are the men all this time ? surely they can't have cut their throats first ! and the dogs—no one heard them bark—where are they ?   Oh ! let us hasten to the barn, and get the mistress to recover ; poor thing ! she will be in a dreadful way."

When they reached the farm buildings they laid Mrs. Patten down, with her head in the cook's lap, and one of the others got some water from a trough.

By this time the fire had seized the kitchen roof, and shot up into the sky in livid masses ; a strong breeze arose, and the flames roared in their might ; then the imprisoned dogs set up a hideous howl, as if conscious that some terrible mis-chief was brewing.

" Hark to the dogs," said one of the women, " they are shut up in the brewhouse."   " Can't you get in, Martha," ex-claimed another, " and see what has happened to the men ? "

" I dare not," she replied ; " suppose I found them with their throats cut ! "

" Well, you goose," cried the cook, a strong, determined woman, " come here, and hold the mistress's head, she is re-covering fast.   I'll go—they can't eat me if their throats are cut ; something's the matter, for they could not be sleeping all this time, and the light of the flames shining in strong through the windows."

The cook found the doors locked, and no key to be seen, but the open window, and the shutters lying on the ground, attracted her.   " Ah," said she, " the villains got in here ! " She climbed in, calling out the men's names from the bottom of the stairs, and at once felt relieved, for a loud shout, and calls to come up and untie them, satisfied her that there was nothing the matter with their throats, at all events.   Ascend-ing the stairs, she entered the room, and perceived by the strong glare of the flames which partially lighted the apart-ment, that the men were cruelly tied, and each fastened to the foot of the bed ; in their struggles to free themselves they had twisted and tightened the thin cords till the skin was torn from their wrists and ankles.   " Lord save us, lads, they have trussed you up like barn-door fowls—where's a knife ? "

" Take one of the bill-hooks, Sue, and let us loose.   Curse the villains ! so they have burned the house.   Where's master and mistress ? "

" Oh, Lord help us ! I fear they have killed master, and the mistress is below, half dead."

A general lamentation ensued.   Having released one, he soon cut free the others.   " Dang it, this is awful work ! " said one of the men, as they finished dressing themselves.   " It's nigh day-light now. The country will rise after this, and give that cursed Steadman ' Lynch law.' "

"Serve him right to roast him," said the cook. " We have lost all our things, every stitch of clothes we had, and lots of money saved up, and the poor missus ruined and destroyed, and she so soon to be a mother, and her two wicked brothers dead in the out-house—it's awful times here now."

Mrs. Patten, in the mean time, had recovered her recollection ; she shuddered with horror when she beheld the sky illumined by the flames of her once happy home ; and when a terrible crash was heard, and clouds of sparks and fiery wreaths were hurled through the air by the strong wind, she nearly relapsed into insensibility, for she knew that noise proclaimed the falling-in of the great massive timber roof.

" Oh! if my poor husband has not been able to get into the cellar," she exclaimed. " Ah, he is lost, and I shall never see him again ! " and she burst into tears.

Two of the women knew of the cellar—indeed they all had perceived that Arthur Bolton and Joseph were thrust in through an opening in the wall they had no knowledge of before.

" Oh, ma'am, don't give way !" said the girls. " Master is sure to have gone into the same place where the Englishman went."

" But the roof has fallen over them," returned Mrs. Patten " we must send our men to get help from all the near farms to remove the ruins and rubbish—ah ! here are the men," and she at once directed them to proceed to the two nearest farms and to the Ferry House, and collect men and tools.

Two of the men departed on their errand for help ; the nearest farms were three miles off. By this time it was broad daylight, and all proceeded to where the house once stood. Poor Mrs. Patten clasped her hands in despair as she gazed upon the burning mass of ruins before her.

" Oh, God grant that they may have taken refuge in the cavern! if not——" She trembled. "God help me!" continued the distracted wife. " To whom am I to look for help, if poor Luke has perished ? "

But summoning all her fortitude, she set the bewildered men to work, throwing water on the burning timbers till help arrived. Before ten o'clock more than twenty men had arrived in carts, with crowbars and other tools.

Mr. Jonas M'Clure, who owned the nearest residence to Mrs. Patten's, sent plenty of provisions and drink, and Mrs. M'Clure arrived shortly after with all kinds of necessaries for the forlorn wife, who shed tears of gratitude, as the good-hearted Mrs. M'Clure covered her with one of her own comfortable cloaks. The men soon understood that in a great cellar underneath the rubbish Mrs. Patten expected her husband and two other persons had taken refuge from the fire; the real state of the case could not be explicitly explained. Nevertheless the grand point was to remove the still burning and smoking timbers, and to work they went with a will.

On the morning after the fire at Luke Patten's farm Lady Morton's family, after a tedious journey from New York, arrived in Delaware. They had stopped the previous night at Williamsburg, and came on to Delaware early. Richard Morton had been extremely anxious all the journey to hear some tidings of Arthur, and as soon as he had established his mother and sisters in comfortable apartments in the best hotel, he proceeded to find the landlord and to make inquiries. He discovered that individual in the bar, encircled by a little crowd of anxious-looking persons. News had just reached Delaware of the burning of Luke Patten's homestead, and a group of curious listeners were collecting exaggerated accounts from the lanky landlord, who felt exceedingly pleased at being able to astonish his auditors.

As Richard Morton approached, he heard one man say,— " Well, it's lucky after all that there are no children left to weep after their parents. I'm sorry for poor Luke Patten; he was a fine, hearty fellow, always willing to lend a fellow a helping hand and stand a glass at any time. I thought no good would ever come of his marriage with one of those devils of Masons, though his wife was by far the best of them."

" I suppose," said another, " the magistrates will send out the militia, or Lynch law this Steadman and his gang; it's too bad they have been let alone so long."

" Who was the Britisher as was burned in the house along with his servant ? " questioned another, tossing down a tumbler of sherry cobbler, " eh ?"

Richard Morton became alarmed as he listened to this dialogue; he knew that the Britisher and his servant could be no other than Arthur and Joseph.

" Good God !" he mentally exclaimed, " can this be a fact ? or am I mistaking what these men say ?"

As the party left the bar he, pale and agitated, accosted the landlord, who attempted some degree of civility, for Lady Morton, now travelling under her own name, was known in the hotel as the widow of the murdered baronet.

" I heard you say," began Richard, " that a Mr. Luke Patten's homestead was burnt down. Is that a fact ?"

" I calculate it's a stern reality, sar; burnt chip and block— and, worse than that, they say Luke Patten himself, and a young

Britisher who stopped here one night, and bespoke apartments for you, sar, were also burned in it."

Richard could hardly breathe. No selfish motive actuated him or caused his anxiety. Firm, unselfish love for Arthur—brotherly affection—esteem. So strangely affected did his gentle, quiet nature feel by this intelligence, that tears forced themselves into his eyes. The landlord eyed the young man, and he began to repent spreading news that was by no means confirmed. He therefore tried to get out of the scrape, which he did in by no means a skilful manner.

" I guess, sir, the news mayn't be all gospel; the farm is burnt down, but they do say that the people are digging away the rubbish, sar, and that perhaps the English gentleman and Mr. Patten may be alive in the cellar, sar."

Young Morton breathed more freely.

" How far is this farm from here ? " he anxiously inquired.

" Well, sar, some fourteen miles across the Ferry of the Mattapone."

" Then be so good as to order me a horse and guide, to proceed there at once—the gentleman supposed to be with Mr. Luke Patten is my half-brother."

The landlord looked astonished, as he replied,—

" Yes, sar, you shall have a horse and guide in less than half an hour."

Richard proceeded into the sitting-room where his sisters were busy writing. Lady Morton was writing a note to Mr. Bowen, the solicitor, requesting an interview ; she looked up into her son's face, and started, saying,—

" What has happened, Richard ? you look pale. Have you heard where your brother has gone ? "

" Yes," returned the young man, trying to disguise his agitation. " He, it seems, went to Luke Patten's farm, which, last night, was burned down to the ground ; how it occurred, I did not stop to learn."

There was a tap at the door, and the next moment the long ungainly figure of the landlord stood in the room.

" Forgot to tell you, sar," he began, greatly to the surprise of Lady Morton and daughters, " that the gentleman you said was your half-brother was lying wounded at Mr. Patten's house."

" Wounded !" repeated all his hearers. " Wounded by whom, Mr. Peasley ?"

" You see, sar, he was attacked by Mr. Patten's two brothers, John and William Mason—and he killed them both."

" Good heavens !" exclaimed Lady Morton, turning exceedingly pale. " The Masons were those——" Her ladyship hesitated; thoughts of her cruelly murdered husband rushed across her mind and brought tears to her eyes.

"Come with me, Mr. Peasley," said Richard, taking the landlord by the arm. "All this affects my mother, and brings back the memory of her loss. I thank you for your information, but we will talk it over alone."

"Yes, sar," said Mr. Peasley, "I see the lady is grieved."

In the bar parlour Richard learned all the landlord knew; he then returned and related what he had heard.

"My noble brother has avenged my father's death on his cowardly assassins, and, but for this strange man, Patten, might have died on the road side. I cannot, of course, understand everything, but in less than two hours I shall be on the spot to aid in his rescue from the ruins. I will take some dollar notes with me, to stimulate the exertions of the men employed."

"Oh, Richard, we shall be so anxious," said the sisters; "if you do not come back immediately, send back your guide, and let us be relieved from our terrible anxiety."

"This intelligence has quite overcome me," said Lady Morton; "take care of yourself, dear Richard, and do not be rash."

"Ah! mother," returned the young man, with a flush over his handsome features, "there is no fear of me; I am little better than a girl. Why did Arthur leave me behind him?"

"My dear brother," said his elder sister, throwing her arms around his neck, "why so reproach yourself? You could not leave us, surely, to travel through this country alone; but lose no time, now, and send us back word how things really are."

Kissing his sister's cheek, Richard Morton hurried down stairs; the horses were ready at the door, and the young lad, the guide, holding them. Mounting, he passed out of the town and down the same road his unfortunate sire had taken some fifteen months previously. The guide was the same who had served his father, but of that Richard was not aware, neither did the lad know that he now guided the son as he previously did the father. They rode fast, for Richard Morton was exceedingly anxious. After seven miles, just where there was another road turning off from the main, the guide suddenly pulled up on the edge of a thick wood. He pointed to a spot on the road, and said, looking up into Richard Morton's serious countenance,—

"There, sar, there's where the Masons shot down the English gentleman, and then tried a shot at me."

The listener checked his horse with a start and a painful sensation at the heart. He gazed upon the spot, and the words,—

" My poor, poor father!   Was it here, in this lonely road, in the land of the stranger, that you breathed your last sigh ? "

The young lad heard the words, and looked as if he felt for the sorrow of the son, and thought, perhaps, that he ought not to have gallopped away.

" And so it was you who acted as guide to my poor father ? "

" Yes, sar, for certain it was I ; but I could not do any-thing, sar.   A bullet whistled close to my lug, after the gen-tleman fell, and so I—I fled, sar."

" Well, my poor lad, you could render no service after the fatal shot was fired, so no blame is attached to you ; but the murderers have met their doom."

" Yes, sar ; and, thank God, they be punished."

With a sigh of bitter regret, Richard Morton pushed on. They reached the ferry, but it was blowing too hard to cross with the horse-boat ; so they passed over, the guide telling Richard Morton that he could take him a short cut by the great Quarry.   It would be scarcely then two miles to the farm.   So, following his guide, he pursued his way.

In half an hour they passed out of a thick tuft of trees and came suddenly upon the very edge of an exceedingly steep stone quarry.   The path was dangerous enough, but Richard Morton passed on, till, suddenly pausing, he called out to his guide,—

" Stop, look here!   There's a man's body lying at the bottom of this precipice ! "

The guide, for the first time, looked down ; and there, sure enough, lay the body of a man, amid a heap of small stones and gravel.

" Some unfortunate wretch," continued the Englishman, " has slipped over the edge of this dangerous path.   Let us get down ; he may not be dead."

Making a great circuit, they gained an entrance to the quarry, and Richard Morton approached the body, which was lying on its back.   One glance at the ghastly face was suffi-cient ; he started back, exclaiming,—

" Good God! it is the body of George Mason! the man rescued by my brother from the North Star, when on fire.   I recognize him by the scar on the lip."

" He's quite dead, sar," said the guide ; " but not very long, for he's scarcely cold."

" Unfortunate wretch !—how came he here ?   What a mysterious fate !   The Omnipotent Hand has one way or another hurled retribution on the whole of this terrible family of brothers.   But we must hasten on ; and we will send men to take the body out of this place."

It was about four o'clock when Richard Morton reached the scene of disaster. As he came up, he perceived a crowd of men reposing on the ground, partaking of refreshment. Three or four substantial farmers, all well mounted, were grouped together, conversing eagerly and with most vehement gestures.

Mrs. Patten was seated on a bench, wrapped in a large mantle, with two or three of her female domestics standing by her.

"That is Mrs. Luke Patten," said the guide.

Richard Morton hesitated a moment before he addressed Mrs. Patten. Rascal as George Mason undoubtedly was, he was still her brother.

His own anxiety was intense, for the sight of the still smouldering ruins roused his fears that his brother might have perished. He had already attracted the attention of the persons assembled; for his fine gentlemanly figure and English costume excited curiosity. Before speaking to Mrs. Patten, he walked up to the group of farmers, and, selecting one of their number to address, he said he had come from Delaware, and that he and his guide had taken a short cut by the side of a large quarry, and that at the bottom of the quarry they had discovered a dead body, which he instantly recognized as that of a man named George Mason.

"Why, that's the name of old John Mason's eldest son, sar! I have heard he has been in the old country some time. Are you sure, sar?"

"I am," replied the young man. "He came as passenger in the same ship with me, and was landed in New York."

"Well, stranger, if you are right, this is a new calamity for poor Luke Patten's wife; and I think it better not to tell her, till we see whether we can dig out her husband alive."

"So I think," returned Morton. "My reason for coming here is to ascertain the fate of my brother, who was in Luke Patten's house when set on fire."

"Ah, indeed!" returned the farmer, kindly. "Then, stranger, I trust you will have the satisfaction of seeing him dug out before night. We will send some men to the quarry, and have the body you mention carried to some house at the Ferry."

The men had again resumed their work as Richard Morton approached the anxious and greatly excited Mrs. Patten, saying,—

"Madam, you will pardon my addressing you at such a time as this, when I tell you I am the half-brother of Mr. Arthur Bolton. I tremble to ask you, madam—have you any hope of his safety?"

Mrs. Patten looked up into the gentle, prepossessing countenance of the questioner, with tears in her eyes, as she replied,—

" Please God, sir, there is every hope, and I will tell you why. Especially I consider your brother decidedly safe ; and God send that my dear husband is with him ! "

She then briefly explained the events of the previous night.

" Oh, madam," exclaimed Richard, " you cannot imagine the relief your words give me. My family arrived in Delaware this morning early, and hearing very vague and alarming accounts of this calamitous and daring outrage, I hurried over here to ascertain the truth."

" You see," continued Mrs. Patten, " that they have cleared away the heaviest portions of the roof, and they intend working all night till they come to the entrance of the cellar."

" I will go and encourage them in their labour," said Richard ; and he walked over, and joining the labourers, he said, attracting their attention,—

" Now, my good men, I do not doubt your honest labour and exertions ; on the contrary, I think them not only praiseworthy, but well deserving of reward. My brother is the gentleman with Mr. Patten, whom you are seeking to deliver. The moment they are rescued I will divide three hundred dollars amongst you, which will not interfere with the reward I am sure my brother, if God has spared his life, will present you."

A succession of hearty cheers followed this speech, and to work they all went with redoubled vigour. After another hour of hard labour, a confusion amongst the workmen attracted Richard Morton's attention ; they had found the body of Saunders.

Mrs. Patten, who did not know about any of the gang having been killed, nearly fainted when she heard that a body was found. The men had penetrated to the kitchen, and were clearing the steps leading down to the cellar, and not another body was to be seen. This reassured her, for all declared that the half-charred body must be one of Steadman's gang. Richard Morton could not distinguish the features ; he thought the tall gaunt figure looked like Saunders, but he could not be positive.

Night set in and fires were lighted, their red glare throwing a strong light upon the anxious group of workmen, who at length cleared the entrance and gave a hearty cheer. To their intense delight, their cheer was answered from below.

Overpowered with joy, and weakened by the long hours of ntense anxie ty passed without food, poor Mrs. Patten fainted when she heard that all were safe, and in a few minutes would be extricated.

As Richard Morton stood trembling with anxiety and expectation, Luke Patten forced his body through the mass of loose ashes and rubbish, and, bending down, extricated Arthur Bolton and Joseph. Then several hearty cheers followed; and whilst Patten rushed to the side of his insensible wife, the two brothers embraced each other with feelings of indescribable delight.

It was a scene of real heartfelt rejoicing, and no one evinced more enthusiastic delight than honest Joseph.

"You have been four-and-twenty hours, dear Arthur, under ground, and you wounded and ill. You must suffer, but still I must get you to Delaware to-night. We can get a waggon at the Ferry house on the other side."

"Joseph and I will stop at the Ferry Inn, to-night," replied Arthur, "whilst you return and relieve your mother's and sisters' anxiety. I doubt my bearing the journey farther without rest. My wounds are stiff and sore."

"I will send the guide back, then," said Richard. "I will not quit you. I will write a note on one of the leaves of my tablet."

Luke Patten here joined them, saying,—

"My men, Mr. Bolton, are putting a horse in one of my traps to take you and Mr. Morton to the Ferry Inn. I shall go for the night with my wife to Mr. M'Clure's farm. I think this will be your better plan."

"We have just settled to do so, Mr. Patten," answered Arthur.

Richard Morton then related how he had discovered the body of George Mason.

"God bless me!" exclaimed Patten, greatly amazed, "this is retribution, and no mistake. I can well imagine how this fate befell the wretched man. He was deceived by my *ruse* of fastening the sheet to the window, and in furious rage pursued, thinking to overtake you, Mr. Bolton, before you could reach the shelter of the Ferry, and in the darkness of the night and his blind rage, fell over the cliff. I must not let my wife know this for a few days. She has already received some terrible shocks."

"You are quite right in that resolve, Mr. Patten," observed our hero. "Keep away from this place for a few days, and let me see you in Delaware as soon as you can manage to put things in some order. You have now no residence, but I have one in view for you, so do not be uneasy about the future."

"I will thank you, Mr. Patten," said Richard Morton,

taking out his pocket-book, and selecting notes for three hundred dollars, "to see this sum distributed amongst the men, as I promised. They richly deserve it, for they worked like men with the heart and the will to rescue life."

" And pray add," said our hero, " that in a day or so I will forward them the same score."

" You have noble hearts," observed Luke, with much emotion. " The only bitterness that will remain in my mind is the recollection that I ever could have been induced to join such associates and act as I did."

" Do not let that recollection disturb you now," replied Arthur; " the Almighty's ends and purposes are often worked out by, to us, incomprehensible ways. Our happiness has been brought about by the very means taken to counteract it."

The two young men then got into the spring-cart with cushions, and Joseph and the guide proceeded on foot to the Ferry house, where they all, except the guide, took up their quarters for the night.

CHAPTER XXXVI.

WHILST the events recorded in our previous chapters were taking place in America, the Marchmont family had finally settled in a very beautiful property in Dorsetshire, which Mr. Marchmont had purchased. The mansion, commanding magnificent sea views, was quite a modern erection, and built with exceeding taste, not forgetting the essential necessaries for comfort. A fine lawn, bordered with grove and noble trees, led down to within three hundred yards of the sea-beach. The girls were in raptures with the situation and the beauty of the scenery; their view to the eastward was bounded by the bold outlines of the Needles and the western end of the Isle of Wight; to the west, the eye took in a long line of coast.

Alice, who, after the departure of her lover, very seldom went into society, felt immense relief when her father completed his purchase of Oakfield Manor. When comfortably settled, she felt rejoiced, for, revelling in the calm beauty of its scenery, she could wander about without fear of intruders, or any interruptions of her thoughts.

The departure of Arthur to America gave her considerable uneasiness; she knew how eager and impetuous his nature was, and how ardently he desired to bring to justice his father's assassins; that he would incur any risk to do so, she felt satisfied, and also that the men who took his father's life would feel little scruple in sacrificing him, if it insured their safety. Her thoughts at times were very painful; they had both already gone through trying and perilous sccnes, and she earnestly prayed that they might be spared further trials. Her sister's future husband was shortly expected home with the invalids of his regiment; he had gained promotion by gallant services on the burning plains of India, and all the Marchmonts felt sincere joy at his success, and the cause that led to it.

About this time Alice received her lover's first letter from New York; her cheek flushed, and her heart palpitated with pleasure. At all events, he had arrived safe. It was a long, long letter; it told of his strange meeting with his brother and sisters and Lady Morton; he spoke of them in glowing terms, and the delight he felt in winning their esteem and love. The meeting he had so dreaded was over. Most painful was it to his generous nature to think that, in recovering a name, he should inflict a pang in other hearts, and deprive a brother of a title and estates he had been reared and justly considered himself to be entitled to. All this expected misery was over ; he found the Mortons everything he could possibly have desired ; and his future conduct should show, when he came into possession, how supremely happy their love and attention had made him. "To give you, my own adored Alice, a name and station, positively my own to claim and hold, was the dearest and most ardent wish of my heart," were the words of her lover. "When this is gained, without inflicting pain upon others, and to find those I expected to be received coldly by, welcome me with open arms, and a studied affection, the brightest wish of my heart was gratified."

Arthur then told of their rescuing the crew and passengers of the North Star, and his strange recognition of George Mason and James Saunders, in two of the passengers saved from the burning ship. This part of our hero's letter, as far as Alice's peace of mind was concerned, might better have been left out, for it created uneasiness. Saunders was the man who had so brutally gagged and ill-treated her lover, when taking him to the "Foam," and it was not pleasant to her to think those two villains were once more so close to him.

Alice was reading her lover's letter in the recess of a window, whilst her mother and her sister were sitting before a cheerful fire, at some fancy needlework. Mr. Marchmont was in London.

"Now, Alice, my love, that you have read, and spelt, and learned by heart, the entire of that voluminous letter, pray let us know some of the simple details, for I suppose those

twelve pages do contain some intelligence beyond lovers' vows
and lovers' thoughts."

" I was getting them all cut and dried for you, mamma,"
replied Alice, her eyes sparkling with pleasure. " You cannot say I kept you in suspense, for I gave you the most
important part—that Arthur is. alive and well, and in New
York."

" Oh, thank you, Alice," returned her sister, laughing ;
" I, that brought you the letter, knew that before you opened
it ; for there's the star and stripes, the New York stamp, and
Arthur's handwriting—all which told the tale before breaking
the seal."

" Well, now I'll be most explicit," answered Alice, drawing
her chair to the fire—for the strong equinoctial gales were
blowing, and the squalls were, as usual in merry England,
cold and sharp. And then she told her companions the particulars, which greatly astonished as well as highly delighted
them.

" What's the date of the letter, my love ? " asked her
mother.

" The 17th of September, mamma. It has been fourteen
days coming. By this time, Arthur and the Mortons must
have reached Delaware ; they were only to stay a few days
in New York."

" I shall exceedingly like," said Mrs. Marchmont, " to make
a friendly acquaintance with Lady Morton and family; they
appear by your, or rather Arthur's account, so amiable,
loving, and disinterested. Her ladyship's visit to Delaware
will, however, be a very painful one."

" Ah, it will, indeed ! Arthur says her intentions are to
bring her unfortunate husband's remains to England to be
consigned to the family vaults in Morton Church. It will be
a melancholy voyage home, mamma."

" Yes ; it was a cruel assassination, and one I cannot understand, even supposing the wretches committed it for the sake
of obtaining the papers. Does Arthur say what time he
expects to embark for England ? "

" Alas! no, mamma ; he could not say when he should be
able to leave America, having so great an object at stake ; but
he thinks Lady Morton and family will return by the Ocean
Queen, which will be delayed in New York for three weeks,
owing to an accident in harbour. They all experienced
so much kindness and attention from the captain that they
would greatly like to return with him. Arthur moreover says,
it is not impossible but that circumstances may enable him to
return with Lady Morton. I am to expect another letter
from Delaware, and he hopes then to be able to write more

positively with respect to his chance of recovering the papers. When does the next mail from New York go out, mamma?"

"On Friday, I think, and this is Wednesday; we shall just have time to write him a letter," said the mother. "Your father will be back to-morrow; I know he wishes to write a line or two, having gained some information from Mr. Baldwin, the superintendent of police, which he considers important, should Arthur fail in regaining the lost papers."

A fortnight and more passed over, and no papers reached Oakfield from America. The mails were not so frequent from the New World as they are now; still Alice felt a little surprised, but was sure the next packet would make up for the disappointment."

The papers stated that the Ocean Queen would be the next steam mail-packet to leave New York for Southampton, and that she would sail on the 9th of November.

"Very strange," remarked Alice, as the family assembled at breakfast, on as dismal and gloomy a morning as ever ushered in a November day in our nebulous climate. It was the morning of the 18th of November. "It is very strange we got no letters by the last mail, and now the Ocean Queen is due, if she sailed on the 9th."

"Well, I dare say," said Mr. Marchmont, seeing his daughter's cheek a little paler than usual, "that unforeseen causes prevented Arthur writing in time for the last packet, and if they are coming home by the Ocean Queen, it would, of course, have been useless. She will be due at Southampton on the 19th or 20th; but we have had some heavy easterly gales and great seas ever since November set in, and now there is a shift of wind into the south-west."

"A very disagreeable time of the year, certainly, for females to cross the Atlantic," observed Mrs. Marchmont, "but in such a ship as the Ocean Queen, of 1,400 tons burthen, and so skilful a captain, there is little risk."

"I shall go to Southampton on the 20th, continued Mr. Marchmont, "and return the same night, and I hope to bring back intelligence that our friends have arrived."

That night the two sisters, who slept in the same room, were awoke by the fury of the gale, which commenced about midnight; the roar of the wind as it swept the tops of the lofty trees was like thunder; the very house had a tremulous motion as each furious blast drove with relentless force against its fron

"Good heavens, what a furious tempest!" cried Alice, trembling w th apprehension, not for her own situation, but for those who, on the ocean, were exposed to the terrible element in all its might. "Ah! if the Ocean Queen is approaching these shores, her situation is critical."

"Not with a skilful captain, a good crew, and a noble ship," answered her sister. "Do you remember how dear old Captain Hart used to say he slept more soundly—rocked to slumber by the wild waves and the roaring blast, as it gambolled over his brave ship, than ever he did in a storm when on shore."

"Ah!" observed Alice, "that was when he had a wide and open sea before, behind, aud on every side of him; not in such a narrow channel as ours, with an iron-bound coast on each quarter. Hark! oh, what a blast!"

In truth the strife of elements that night was enough to startle the stoutest heart.

The sisters early in the dawn were gazing out eagerly from their windows facing the sea. The storm had not in the least abated—perhaps at intervals it increased; the mist, haze, and foam of the breaking seas, torn from the surface and hurled through the air by the fury of the hurricane, prevented any distant object seaward or coastways being distinguished. Several huge trees torn up by the roots lay stretched and shattered across the lawn; the shrubberies looked torn to shreds. The sky presented one unbroken mass of densely packed clouds, no break or ray of light piercing its dull grey pall. Every gust shook the house, and the tall trees bent till their power of resistance appeared as nought to the might of the tempest.

"Heavens! what a gale!" said Alice shuddering. "Look at those trees; does it not strike you as incredible, when you see them thus torn from their roots, how a frail ship—frail in comparison—can resist not only the fury of the gale, but the storm-tossed billows of the ocean besides?"

"The reed yields to the tempest, whilst the sturdy oak resists," replied her sister. "I fear we shall have a sad account of wrecks."

At breakfast, when the family assembled, all having passed a very indifferent night, Mr. Marchmont declared he would proceed to Southampton. Seeing his daughter Alice looking pale and anxious, though she betrayed not the feelings of her heart, he felt she was suffering from intense anxiety. During the meal word was brought by one of the tenants that three vessels were ashore, and that not a soul was saved, as far as could be known.

"Ah!" said Alice, "just what I feared. Had any one been saved? We should exert ourselves to be of service, and render help and shelter to the poor castaways."

Mr. Marchmont left word with his domestics, should any one be picked up, to bring him at once to the house.

Being anxious himself, knowing that the Ocean Queen might have passed up channel during the night, and had to bear, in so dangerous a part of the channel, the whole fury of the gale, he posted the last twenty miles into Southampton, instead of waiting three hours for the down train from London.

By this expedient he reached Southampton by six o'clock, and proceeded at once to Lloyds' agent, whom he knew very well.

Mr. Parker soon relieved Mr. Marchmont's uneasiness. When he inquired had any intelligence been received of the New York packet ship Ocean Queen, he replied,—

"I am happy to say, Mr. Marchmont, that she is quite safe. She put in the day before yesterday into Plymouth. Passengers, &c., all well; but the ship was disabled, and her screw put out of gear in a tremendous hurricane encountered when within three days' sail of the Irish coast. She performed the rest of the voyage under canvas, and providentially got into Plymouth before this gale. This news was telegraphed to me yesterday, and this morning I received a list of the passengers, and a brief account of the voyage, for Captain Courtney is a very old esteemed friend of mine."

"Can you let me see the list of passengers, Mr. Parker?" said Mr. Marchmont, relieved of his anxiety concerning the Ocean Queen, at all events.

"Most willingly," returned the agent. "I see by this morning's letter that a large barque ran foul of them in the tremendous gale, and they thought they had sunk her, as they heard the most piercing shrieks and cries, and the sea was tremendous and the fog dense. Nevertheless, Captain Courtney says one of his passengers, a high-spirited young man, with six volunteers and the second mate, put off in one of the life-boats to rescue life if possible. The Ocean Queen was at that time disabled by loss of screw. She was forced to lie to, and burn blue lights, and at one time got a sight of the large ship, with, he thought, only one mast standing; but the gale increased to a furious hurricane, and a fog for three days was so dense that they could not see half the length of the ship; and to the captain's intense vexation—though he lay to and did all that he could—he never again sighted the ship or his own boat."

"Good God!" said Mr. Marchmont, greatly agitated, "if my surmises are true, this intelligence fills my mind with cruel forebodings. Let me see the passenger list."

"I am sorry to hear you," said Mr. Parker. "Perhaps you think you know this young man. No relation, I hope?"

"Not yet," replied Mr. Marchmont, with a sigh; "but if it is Mr. Arthur Bolton——"

" Ah ! that is the name, sure enough," said the agent, in a tone of regret.

Mr. Marchmont ran his eye along the list of passengers—saw Lady Morton's family and Arthur Bolton's name among them, with a mark to our hero's name, and also to that of the second mate and the six seamen.

" But," said Mr. Parker, " you may be alarming yourself needlessly. The ship that ran foul of the Ocean Queen evidently did not sink, and the Queen's boat, no doubt, put Mr. Bolton and his spirited crew on board. She may have made a port safely after all."

" There is hope, certainly," returned Mr. Marchmont, " but till Mr. Bolton himself lets us know of his safe arrival in England, we must remain in deep anxiety, for the name of the vessel is unknown."

The intelligence imparted to Mr. Marchmont made him extremely uneasy. He could not return that night, and when he did, the next day, he scarcely knew how to break the intelligence to his daughter. It was very possible that Lady Morton knew of Arthur Bolton's engagement to his daughter. If so, she would undoubtedly communicate with him and let him know the full particulars.

It was late the next day when he reached Oakfield Manor. By that time he had settled in his own mind what he should say.

" Well," he said, with as cheerful a manner as he could well assume, on joining the family circle, all anxiously waiting to hear what intelligence he had gained. " See what it is to have a good ship and a skilful commander. The Ocean Queen has weathered all the gales, and is now anchored in Plymouth."

" But were the Mortons and Arthur passengers in her ? " all exclaimed, Alice fixing her beautiful eyes with such a searching expression on her father's countenance, that he felt he was suspected of knowing something more than he intended telling.

He, however, replied, " Yes, the Mortons and Arthur were passengers in her. No doubt the Mortons landed at Plymouth ; but that restless lover of yours, Alice, with his chivalric gallantry, went to the assistance of some large ship, name unknown, and therefore has sought the shelter of a different harbour from the Ocean Queen."

Alice became deadly pale ; whilst her mother and sister looked anxious.

" Dear father," said Alice, with an effort to master her emotion, " do not conceal any intelligence from me, let its nature be what it may. Doubt racks the heart more cruelly than aught else.   What has Arthur done, and what have you in reality heard?"

"Precisely what I tell you, my beloved child; for the news I heard from Lloyd's agent in Southampton is very vague. Mr. Parker told me that, in a gale, the Ocean Queen either ran foul of a large ship or the ship ran foul of her.   It was a dark night and a fog, the Ocean Queen was disabled or her screw thrown out of gear, and hearing cries for help from the strange ship the life-boat was slung over the side, and Arthur, the second mate, and six seamen pulled off to the rescue.   It seems the Queen being disabled, and the fog and gale so heavy, the two ships parted company.   The Ocean Queen made Plymouth under sail; the stranger, no doubt, has taken refuge in some other port, so in a few days we may expect more explicit intelligence."

There was a dead silence for a few seconds after Mr. March-mont ceased speaking, and then Alice said, in a firm tone of voice,—

"Thank you, dear father, for all the trouble and fatigue you have undergone to bring me news of dear Arthur.   Providence is everywhere, he has been saved from many perils, and I will trust in God's mercy to save him from this—his last, I hope—on an element that has so often nearly proved fatal to him."

"Amen, my child!" said the proud father, pressing a kiss upon the pale cheek of his daughter; "let us once get hold of this adventurous lover of yours, and we will bind him in a chain he will not be inclined to break on any pretence, I feel sure and certain."

CHAPTER XXXVII.

AFTER the destruction of Luke Patten's homestead by fire, and the restoration of those buried in the cavern, the brothers passed the night in the little inn attached to the Ferry House. The next morning they proceeded to Delaware, where Lady Morton and daughters were most anxiously awaiting their arrival.   Lady Morton received our hero with all the affection of a mother.

"You are looking pale and thin, dear Arthur," said Richard Morton.   "You have not attended to your wounds, and you have fearfully overtaxed your strength.   You must send for a surgeon."

In vain our hero strove to allay her ladyship's uneasiness, though he could not deny his suffering, nor hide from her anxious eyes the symptoms of approaching fever.   Before evening he was forced to yield—go to bed—and send for a surgeon, and six or seven days elapsed before he could leave his room ; his wounds were deep and had been neglected, but now, skilfully attended and with a powerful constitution, he rapidly gained strength, and by the time a fortnight had passed he was, except being something thinner, nearly as well as ever.

After his partial recovery everything was rapidly arranged for their return to New York, so as to embark for England in the Ocean Queen. Our hero had seen Mr. Bowen, who, looking over the papers, declared they were all perfectly correct and untouched. He empowered that gentleman to pay off the £2,000 mortgage on Fork Farm, and to make out the necessary deeds, &c., for that estate to become the property of Luke Patten. When all this was done he presented the astonished and grateful Virginian with the deeds, and the remaining £1,000 of the cheque for £3,000 ; with that and the sale of his old farm he would begin the world again, a wiser and a better man.

It was determined by the magistrates and influential landowners near Delaware to disperse Stephen Steadman's atrocious gang of miscreants. Accordingly the authorities were applied to for a military force, which was granted, and the gang, after a desperate, fierce resistance, totally destroyed ; several being killed, and those caught hung on the nearest trees. Mrs. Steadman was found in the house dying of the swamp fever. She was brought to Delaware, and taken to the hospital, and after a struggle of nine weeks recovered. Mrs. Patten did all that lay in her power to soften her sufferings ; but tried in vain to soften her heart. When able, she quitted the hospital, and departed, no one ever knew where.

But long before that event took place, Lady Morton and family, with Arthur, had quitted Delaware, taking with them the remains of Sir Richard Morton. Having settled their affairs with Mr. Coulston, the banker, who congratulated our hero upon the success of his efforts, which, however, had nearly terminated his existence, they all embarked in the Ocean Queen, and sailed from New York on the 9th of October.

The weather all the passage was stormy, and the gales contrary, but when within three days' steam of the coast of Ireland, they encountered one of the heaviest gales Captain Courtney had yet experienced, accompanied by a dense fog ; every precaution was taken, lights hoisted, and neither night nor day did the captain leave the deck.

On the night of the 17th of October, when under easy steam, the sea remarkably heavy, and the fog so dense as to shut out

X

the funnel from the sight of those standing near the wheel, they were suddenly struck on the starboard quarter by a very large ship ; the shock was so tremendous, that for a moment or two Captain Courtney considered the Queen would founder, but being a new and a strong ship, only her bulwarks and a few outward planks suffered, though the shock threw the foremast, yards and all, of the strange ship right over the afterdeck of the Queen, nearly sweeping several of the sailors off her decks.

Captain Courtney and Arthur Bolton were standing near the wheel, when they both perceived the huge ship running at them. No power of man could prevent the shock; but they saved their lives, and the lives of the two men at the wheel, by pulling them down and grasping the chains stretched across the poop to strengthen the rudder, which was slightly damaged.

As the stranger fell off again after striking, even amid the roar of the gale, shrieks and frantic cries for help were heard till the ship drifted to leeward.

"Good God !" exclaimed Arthur, regaining his legs, and assisting Captain Courtney to rise, "that ship is full of women ; you could distinguish their shrieks amid the howl of the tempest."

The worthy captain's first thought was for his own ship, which he feared was cut to the water's edge; but finding it was safe, he turned his attention to the strange vessel.

"I will take the life-boat," said Arthur, addressing Captain Courtney, "we may save life."

"I will go with you," said Richard, eagerly; "this time I will not be left behind."

The second mate, also, was eager to go, and six of the seamen, including Joseph.

In the lull of the gale the life-boat was launched; but young Morton, tripping over a rope, was unable to gain the boat in time, which a heavy sea carried away from the side, snapping the bow ropes in twain.

Knowing the ship was dead to leeward of them, they pulled before the gale ; just then a light was shown, as our hero and the mate supposed, from the strange ship, but as suddenly disappeared. Just then the gale returned with redoubled violence, driving them irresistibly before it. Again lights, but of a feeble kind, were seen, but this time they perceived the lofty hull of the strange ship, just as a tremendous sea lifted the boat, and with incredible violence drove her against the bulwarks of the ship, smashing them to pieces, and crushing in the sides of the life-boat. Providentially, every one in the boat contrived to seize hold of some rope, rigging, or spar,

and gained the deck, where they found themselves amongst a
terrified crowd of persons; several women and children.
There were a few lanterns held by some of the people, therefore, as soon as our hero and the second mate, whose name
was Wilson, recovered their legs, they became anxious to
question those surrounding them, and discovered that they
were on board a transport carrying invalid soldiers and their
wives.

"But where is the captain and crew?" demanded Arthur
Bolton, amazed at the scene of confusion he witnessed; no one
answered; the howling of the terrible storm then raging,
the flapping and splitting of the sails left to the fury of the
gale, the blocks dashing wildly about, threatening to annihi-
late whoever was so unfortunate as to come in their way; the
wailing of the women and children, who kept screaming that
the ship was sinking, formed a scene of indescribable confusion
and disorder.

At length our hero and the mate found one man capable of
answering the question—"Where is the captain of this ship?"

"Dead drunk, if not mad, in his cabin, these two days."

"Where's the first, second, or third mate, and the crew?"

"The first mate and nine of the crew quitted the ship three
days ago; they said she was sinking, and if not the cholera
would kill all; the second mate and four of the crew, with
five soldiers, were washed overboard yesterday, and the rest,
after breaking into the spirit room, are dead drunk in the forecastle with the sick."

Mr. Wilson, the second mate of the Ocean Queen, uttered
an exclamation, accompanied by an oath, that such a —— set
of lubbers he never heard of.

"Who has the command of this detachment of soldiers?"
demanded Arthur.

"Captain Singleton," replied the man; "as good an
officer——"

He was proceeding to expatiate on the qualities of his captain, when our hero, in a tone of excitement, said,—

"Captain Singleton! Is it possible! Where is he?"

"In the cabin; the fore-yard, as it passed across the ship,
knocked him senseless and broke his left arm; the surgeon
was also hurt, and so was Ensign Manners; they are all
below."

"You had better," said Arthur, addressing the amazed mate
of the Ocean Queen, "with your men, get the ship before the
gale; our own vessel will surely overtake us, and see us when the
fog and gale ceases. I do not perceive that the ship is sinking.
She rides too buoyantly over the seas. I will just go below
and see Captain Singleton. I do not know him personally,

but he is a gentleman who is very dear to some friends of mine ; this is a most extraordinary case of monstrous neglect and drunkenness, Mr. Wilson."

"Well, blow me, Mr. Bolton, if ever I came across the like before ! We will see and get the ship, as you say, before the gale, and give the drunken lubbers in the forecastle a taste of a rope's end to wake them up, at all events."

Our hero then to a certain degree calmed the fears of the terrified women as to the ship's sinking, telling them they would receive help from his ship as soon as daylight dawned and the fog cleared.

He then made his way to the companion. The decks were in a fearful state—broken boats, timbers, planks, broken spars, hen-coops, casks, water-butts—all knocked to pieces, and dashed here and there by the wash of the seas ; the main and mizen masts were standing, but the sails were blown into ribbons, and the ropes and blocks flying about in wild confusion.

Descending into the cabin, he heard a loud, rough voice, swearing fearfully, and uttering the most outrageous threats. " The first —— beggar," exclaimed the voice, "that enters my cabin, I'll blow his brains out ! Yes, curse me if I don't rip him up ! How dare you lobster ruffians take the command of my ship ? I'll serve you out !"

Utterly astounded at hearing such language, Arthur approached the cabin and paused at the door, as he did so, to gaze at the strange scene before him. The cabin was large . and handsome, and lighted by a large swinging lamp. Standing in the middle of the floor was a tall, massive-built man ; his back was to our hero ; in one hand he flourished a drawn cutlass, in the other a cocked pistol. He was uttering the most fearful oaths and threats against a young man standing at the open door of a private cabin, who was in an undress uniform.

" Don't go out, Skelton," said a weak voice within ; " that wretched madman will do you mischief; wait till Hancock has finished with me."

" Ah, curse ye ! wait till you are three to one ; here's at you, you red-coated beggars !" and making a violent leap forward, he was going to cut down the young ensign, bu Arthur sprang at him and seized him, pinioned his arms, and held him in a vice. A tremendous plunge of the ship, and a violent shock of the sea, threw them both on the floor of the cabin. The mad captain—for mad he was—yelled like a fiend, and strove to free his hand that held the pistol, which went off in the struggle. The young ensign, who was also thrown to the floor, was stupefied partly from his fall and partly from astonishment at the sudden appearance of a stranger. Just then, Joseph, who was one of the men who manned the life-boat, rushed down the cabin stairs to say that the wheel was carried away and the ship quite ungovernable; but seeing his master struggling on the floor with a man who appeared to be infuriated, he threw himself upon him and wrenched the cutlass out of his hand.

"Tie his hands and feet!" exclaimed another individual, coming out of the inner cabin, "he's stark, staring mad now and must be bound, or he will do mischief."

The captain was now foaming and bleeding from the mouth and nostrils, and seemingly getting exhausted. The ensign and the surgeon furnished leather straps, and finally they bound the miserable man fast.

Then it was that the two officers looked into Arthur's face.

"Who are you?" they exclaimed: "you do not belong to this ship?"

"No, thank God! I do not: but nevertheless it's fortunate I came here. Where is Captain Singleton? And what is to be done with this miserable man? he will die."

"Die," repeated the surgeon, "well for us if he had died five weeks ago; he is mad. He has had three attacks of *delirium tremens*. This last will finish him. Just put him into his crib, and I will give him a dose of opium, that will either kill or cure him. But are you come from the ship we ran foul of awhile ago?"

"Yes," returned our hero, "I am; and I am amazed to find this vessel in the state she is. I am known to Captain Singleton by name, and should like to see him."

"Excuse me," returned the surgeon, "if I have erred in addressing you, but we have suffered so cruelly for the last three weeks. What between pestilence, a drunken mad captain, and a besotted, frightened, miserable crew that I scarcely know what I am doing or saying. Captain Singleton is in his cabin, his arm unfortunately is broken, and his head contused, but he is reviving, and I trust, as I have set his arm and bound up his head, that he will do. But the ship is rolling fearfully. Have you brought any men with you? and is your ship near? We have lost thirty-eight men with cholera and fever; the first mate and most of the crew quitted us in the long-boat, stored with provisions, when off Madeira; the rest of the rascals broke into the spirit stores, and have been dead drunk with liquor and fright; whilst the now invalid soldiers, between illness, fright, and the distraction of their wives, are worthless."

This catalogue of disasters was listened to with amazement by Arthur. He was not a man, however, to be frightened by either pestilence or mutiny. He therefore said,—

" Be so kind as to mention my name, Arthur Bolton, to Captain Singleton, and I will go on deck, and see what can be done, whilst you order the captain to be carried into his own cabin, and give him a powerful dose of opium."

As Arthur Bolton came on deck he encountered Mr. Wilson, the second mate of the Ocean Queen.

" Here's the devil to pay, Mr. Bolton, and no pitch-pot! We're in a precious mess! The lubbers below won't move an inch ; they are beastly drunk. There are six or seven soldiers down with the cholera, and the rest with fright and debility are mere live lumber. The gale is increasing. One consolation, however, the sails are blown to ribbons ; there's not a blue light to be had, so, unless we set the old hull on fire, those aboard the Queen will have no notion where we are."

" But it may clear with the dawn," said our hero.

" Not a bit of it, Mr. Bolton. We're, you see, not far from the coast of Ireland, where the fogs and the gales last like a cat with nine lives this time of the year."

" At all events," returned our hero, " with daylight we shall see what state the craft is in, and perhaps when the men get sober they will stir themselves."

" Hark ! " exclaimed the mate, " did you hear that ? that was a gun from our ship ; she is a long way off, and we have nothing to blaze away with in return."

Just then the surgeon came up from the cabin, and seeing the group of men about our hero, he joined them. The roar of the tempest at this time was terrific, and the ship lay broadside to the seas. She rolled fearfully.

" What do you propose doing, Mr. Bolton ? " asked the surgeon. " Captain Singleton is most anxious to see you. We shall scarcely survive this hurricane, in the state we are in."

" Well, blow me," said Mr. Wilson (as good a sailor as ever lived, but rough in manner), " if I can make out what the dickens you are all after, in this here ship ! Curse me if I ever saw a red-coat worth his broth at sea, except when fighting ; that they can do, and no mistake."

" You do not know what we have endured," replied the surgeon. " Soldiers are not intended to be sailors. However, if we know nothing, we can endure much. I must go and look after my sick."

With great difficulty he made his way to the forecastle, whilst Mr. Wilson and his comrades, with three of the least invalided of the soldiers, got up the hemp cable, and after some difficulty and no little risk, veered it away aft, and after a time succeeded in getting the ship dead before the tempest. She was a very large vessel, nearly sixteen hundred tons' burden, and once before the wind went comparatively steady. Our hero began to think the chances of regaining his own ship very small. He thought it not impossible that the Ocean Queen might be disabled by the shock she had received. They were going under bare poles full ten knots; thus, if the Queen lay-to, before daylight there would be many miles between them, for the gale was an adverse gale for the shores of Great Britain, and in the stray ship they were running back in their course.

"Come below, Mr. Wilson," said our hero; "I will see Captain Singleton. At all events we shall get some refreshment, though unfortunately I understand that the steward and cook both died of the disease now in this ship."

"Died of fright, the lubbers. But we must see and get our comrades some grog and some grub," said the mate.

Descending the cabin stairs they perceived Ensign Manners rummaging the steward's pantry. He turned round, and seeing it was our hero, who had most probably saved his life when the mad captain rushed at him with pistol and cutlass, he said,—

"Very likely, sir, like myself, you would like some refreshment. Our mad commander is in a stupor; ten to one if he recovers."

"Well, I'm blest if he will be much loss if he doesn't!" answered Mr. Wilson, his gaze resting on a bottle of Hollands in a hole on a shelf. "I'll just take a pull at this, Mr. Bolton," said the mate, taking a tumbler and the bottle.

"You will find some cold meat and bread in that cupboard," replied the ensign, eyeing the jolly-faced mate of the Ocean Queen.

"Blow me! that's your sort, Mr. Soldier," returned the mate, loading himself with eatables, and following Ensign Manners and our hero into the cabin.

"The ship appears steadier, though the roar of the gale is even greater," remarked the ensign.

"We have got her before the storm," answered Arthur, helping himself to a glass of Hollands, for he was soaked through before reaching the ship."

"Ha!" said Mr. Wilson, swallowing a half tumbler, "I'm not a drunkard, but a glass of grog at the proper time is better than a knock over the head. With your leave I'll just physic our fine fellows on deck with a glass a-piece, they have earned it;" and upon deck went Mr. Wilson, with the ample bottle under his wing.

CHAPTER XXXVIII.

ARTHUR BOLTON, having taken some refreshment, was shown into Captain Singleton's cabin by Ensign Manners. The wounded officer was lying in his berth, with his left arm in splinters, and his head bandaged, and in the light of the lamp swinging from a beam his face looked very pale and thin. He held out his hand as Arthur entered, saying,—

" This is a strange way and place for us to meet in for the first time, Mr Bolton, but, believe me, I am very happy to see you and make your acquaintance. I have heard all about your former adventures in the ' Foam ' from Miss Marchmont, and now I fear you are going to endure some further trials in this most unfortunate ship."

" I rejoice to meet you, Captain Singleton, though deeply grieved to see you a sufferer," returned our hero, sitting down by the side of the berth.

" Has the storm slackened, Mr. Bolton ?—we do not roll as we did a while ago."

" We are now sailing before the wind," replied Arthur ; " that renders us less susceptible to the heavy seas. But your ship, Captain Singleton, is in a strange and fearful state. Everything seems to have gone to wreck and ruin."

" Ah ! " said the captain, with an exclamation of disgust and vexation, " I know it. I strove hard against a brutal, drunken skipper, a miserable incompetent crew; and a fearful disease —cholera—has nearly destroyed us."

" But is not the vessel a Government transport? " inquired our hero.

" Unfortunately, no. Our own transport got ashore just as we were going to embark, and we were for many reasons—sickness, &c.—shipped in this vessel, the Ben Nevis, a fine ship, and carrying a most valuable cargo. The cholera was raging amongst the troops at Calcutta, and it was thought better to embark us in this ship at once than wait for the transport to be got off and repaired. It was not known that the captain and crew were utterly incapable of taking charge of such a vessel as the Ben Nevis. The captain and mate who brought her out from Liverpool were carried off by the cholera, and her crew, from some reason or other, left her and shipped in other vessels. So Captain Keaney was appointed her commander, and it seems he was permitted to pick up a crew how and where he could. But another time I will give you fuller particulars—now speaking affects my head. I will just ask you how the Marchmonts are, and where you saw them ? "

"I saw them last in Southampton," answered our hero; "they were all well and happy, and Miss Marchmont was expecting your speedy return to Europe. You had better now seek repose. I do not think at present that there is any danger to be apprehended, and daylight will give us a better idea how things are," and pressing Captain Singleton's hand in a friendly clasp, he bade him good night.

When morning dawned Mr. Wilson and our hero held a consultation. Four out of the crew of the Ben Nevis were willing to work ; three had been attacked with cholera ; and the rest were sullen and dejected. The soldiers, though sad invalids, were ready to do all they could. With this small number the men from the Ocean Queen set to work to get the ship in some order, and clear the decks. She was a remarkably fine ship, and six hours' work at the pumps cleared her of the water that had so frightened the crew and caused them to imagine she was sinking.

The gale and fog still continued, and the mate very well knew, as the tempest was from the east, that they were running away from the coast of Great Britain ; but before sunset, by diligent hard work, they had repaired the rudder and got her to steer tolerably well ; and having hauled up some sails from the hold, a new main topsail was bent. The following day, the gale abating considerably, soon after sail was set, and the ship hove to. The second evening the skipper died and two of the crew, and three more of the soldiers took the disease. It was not till the fourth day that the sky cleared and the gale completely moderated.

Mr. Wilson, who was a thorough good sailor and navigator, calculated that they were about six days' sailing from the north coast of Ireland, having been driven more than three hundred miles to the north-west. As the ship was very un-manageable without head sail, and they had no spar to erect into a jury mast, our hero proposed to take out the mizen and ship it in the place of the foremast ; this, after twenty-four hours' labour, they managed to do, and the ship, with a fine breeze on her quarter, lay her course and steered well. Light winds and calms succeeded ; but the disease and fever seemed, after the death of the skipper and two more victims, to sud-denly cease ; no new case occurred, and the sick began rapidly to recover. Still their progress, from contrary winds and short gales, was slow ; and not till twenty-one days after their separation from the Ocean Queen did they make the land, which proved to be the north coast of Ireland.

Arthur Bolton and Mr. Wilson, after a consultation with Captain Singleton, agreed rather than risk the navigation of the narrow channel to Liverpool, to run into Lough Foyle. Accordingly before sunset, on the 2nd of December, the Ben Nevis, with a leading wind, ran through the narrow strait forming the entrance into the magnificent sheet of water known as Lough Foyle, and forming the harbour of London-derry.

Excepting that he still carried his arm in a sling, Captain Singleton was quite recovered. He and Arthur Bolton, during the short time they passed together, formed a sincere friend-ship, which was soon, they hoped, to be cemented by a stronger tie—their marriage with the two daughters of Mr. Marchmont.

About five days after the arrival of the Ben Nevis in Lough Foyle, the family of the Marchmonts were assembled as usual at the breakfast-table, but a visible change had come over all since we saw them last. Both daughters looked thin and serious. Mr. Marchmont himself appeared extremely anxious, for, some few days after his return from Southampton, a para-graph in one of the papers had attracted his attention, which announced the arrival of the Bencoolen transport, with the remainder of the — Regiment of Foot. This vessel was de-layed, the paper stated, by getting on shore, but that the in-valided portion of the regiment had sailed some time before, having on board Captain Singleton, Ensign Manners, Sergeant Smith, and fifty-six rank and file, with their wives and chil-dren. The name of the ship in which they had sailed was the Ben Nevis, which vessel had not yet reached any British port.

"This is very extraordinary," said Mr. Marchmont, some-what sadly, seeing how the intelligence affected his eldest daughter, and indeed all.

"How singular it would be," said Alice, with a sigh, " should this missing ship, the Ben Nevis, be the one that ran foul of the Ocean Queen. You know when Captain Courtney was here, he said the vessel that struck him was a large high ship, with a number of women in her, and he felt quite confi-dent she did not founder, for he must have been the greater sufferer of the two by the shock, as the strange ship struck him with her stem. I do not despair but that, by God's mercy, all our friends will arrive in safety."

Thus hope kept the two charming sisters patient and re-signed, though serious, and at times almost despondent.

On the 7th of December, therefore, when they all met at breakfast, each face expressed anxiety—of course time had rendered hope less buoyant. It was a dreary day, blowing, snowing, and raining alternately, and this did not add to the cheerfulness of the party, when the servant entered the room with the morning papers. Mr. Marchmont eagerly took up the *Shipping Gazette*, broke the cover, and at once began reading the arrivals, &c. Suddenly he dropped the paper, uttering an exclamation of pleasure.

"Thank God!" he exclaimed, as Alice snatched up the paper, "one of our truants has arrived at last."

Alice's eye instantly rested on the heading of a long article, in large letters, "Safe arrival of the ship Ben Nevis in the port of Londonderry."

There was a glittering tear in Miss Marchmont's eyes as she put her hand in those of her sister, who eagerly read on, and then, clasping her sister round the neck, exclaimed,—

"A merciful Providence has saved them all; Arthur and Frederick Singleton are in the same ship."

Mr. and Mrs. Marchmont were for a moment speechless with the excitement of joy; they had done all in their power to hide their anxiety from their children. It would have been a fearful breaking up of their future felicity had their intended sons-in-law both perished.

They had received several most kind and reassuring letters from Lady Morton, expressing the most intense anxiety concerning Arthur, and stating that her son Richard had all the papers, so essential to Mr. Marchmont's intended son-in-law's restoration to name and title.

Mr. Marchmont had answered these kind letters in the same tone : still, at times, he felt heavy forebodings. Now all dark clouds had cleared away, joy given place to sorrow, and the morning, so bleak and desolate, with its snow, sleet, and storm, actually, as a gleam of watery sunshine entered the room, looked bright and cheering. The good things on the breakfast-table were untouched—great joy acts for a time like sorrow.

"Now let me see the paragraph, Alice," said her father; "you have all read it a dozen times over, and I have heard no more than the first line—'Arrival of the Ben Nevis.'"

"Oh! let me read it to you, dear papa," said Alice, her sweet face lighted up by the grateful spirit that made her loving heart beat with a quicker pulsation.

"It is with great satisfaction," began Alice, reading the paragraph, "that we are able to state with certainty the arrival of the missing vessel, the Ben Nevis, in the port of Londonderry. The ship, it appears, suffered most severely from storms and casualties. She had on board, as we before stated, three officers and fifty-six rank and file, of the ——— regiment. The Ben Nevis was, unfortunately, commanded by a man quite incapable of performing his duty, and the crew were equally so. Cholera broke out amongst the soldiers shortly after her departure from port, and in a few days carried off several of the soldiers, and three or four of the crew, whilst heavy gales added to their miseries. Their captain drank to excess, and became subject to attacks of *delirium tremens*, during which he acted like a madman. In vain Captain Singleton, and Ensign Manners, and Surgeon Penhurst strove to counteract his mad conduct,—the soldiers became terror struck as the terrible pestilence increased its devastation. The vessel in a gale sprang a leak ; the first mate and nine of the crew deserted her in the night, when supposed to be near the island of Madeira. Others were washed overboard, all their boats were knocked to pieces, and finally, in a night of tremendous storm, she ran foul of some large ship or steamer, since ascertained to have been the Ocean Queen. A gallant young man of the name of Bolton, already well known for his gallant conduct and sufferings, from a mutiny that occurred on board the ' Foam ' some time since, volunteered to board the strange ship ; the second mate and six seamen accompanied him in a whale-boat. This boat was stove to pieces against the sides of the Ben Nevis ; nevertheless they all scrambled on deck and found the Ben Nevis in a fearful state, her captain raging mad, and Captain Singleton confined to his berth by an accident ; the remainder of the crew had broken into the spirit stores, and were lying insensible with drink and terror.   Mr. Bolton and his companions just arrived in time to prevent the mad captain, in one of his furious fits, from murdering Ensign Manners and Captain Singleton, who was lying in his private cabin, incapable of resistance. The captain died two days after, and the vessel, after a variety of fortune—being without a foremast, and otherwise disabled—was brought into Lough Foyle by the skill and seamanship of Mr. Bolton, Mr. Wilson, second mate of the Ocean Queen, and their six spirited followers. We understand that the Ben Nevis carries a very valuable cargo, which will, of course, pay those gallant fellows who brought her safely into port a just and handsome recompense. The Ben Nevis belongs to the wealthy shipowners, Messsrs. Temple, Wilkins, and Burgh, of Liverpool."

" Well, upon my word," said Mr. Marchmont, with a pleased smile, " our friend Arthur has wound up his adventures on the ocean and on shipboard in a most creditable manner. I dare say, my little Alice, you will consider any further addition to his fame in that line unnecessary? "

" Quite, dear papa," replied Alice, with a glow on her before pale cheek, and a look of perfect happiness lighting up her charming features with all the brightness of other days.

The following day letters from our hero and Captain Singleton reached the family, and before a week had expired the two fair daughters of Oakfield Manor were made happy by the arrival of their equally happy and delighted lovers.

Arthur Bolton, after landing, had not stopped anywhere, but having seen his beloved Alice, and passed one night under the same roof, left immediately for Morton Chase.

His reception there need not be described, for all vied in showing affection and attention to one they loved, and who fairly merited the affection shown him. Lady Morton insisted upon his immediately asserting his claims to the title and inheritance of his father.

The papers were accordingly placed in the hands of an eminent lawyer; we need only state, where every facility was shown by the Morton family to substantiate his claim, and every document and witness brought forward clear and irresistible, the forms of law were soon gone through, and, to the surprise of many who knew and were connected with the Morton family, Arthur Bolton was declared to be the lawful heir of the late Sir Richard Morton.

Lady Morton insisted upon surrendering Morton Chase to him after his marriage with the beautiful Alice, which took place at Oakfield Manor: at the same time Miss Marchmont bestowed her hand upon Captain Singleton. One of the most honoured guests at the double wedding, and rejoicings on the occasion, was Superintendent Baldwin, of the Metropolitan Police.

Sir Arthur Morton, on his half-brother attaining his majority, presented him with the title-deeds of the Arlington Estate—a property yielding a rental of £2,000 a year—thus fulfilling his early determination of dividing the Morton Chase estate with Richard.

Before his marriage, Sir Arthur Morton proceeded to Canterbury, and made inquiries concerning the Skeltons. He would at once have visited his early school abode, but he feared his old schoolmaster would look upon his visit as one of triumph, and, judging by his knowledge of his heart, Mr. Skelton no doubt would do so.

Though only three years had elapsed since his departure,

misfortune had been busy with the family of the schoolmaster. In one of his ungovernable fits of passion Mr. Skelton so severely injured one of his pupils that the spine became affected ; the enraged father brought an action against the schoolmaster that ruined him. The heavy damages swept away the savings of years, and he lost all his scholars.

When Sir Arthur visited Canterbury the family were still in the same house, but suffering every privation. Mr. Skelton himself was dying of a pulmonic affection and a broken heart. For him all that Sir Arthur could do was to relieve him from every kind of privation, and render his last moments easy respecting the future of his family.

Fanny Skelton he found in an aristocratic family, as far as fortune entitled them to that distinction, toiling through a weary life as an accomplished governess to two young girls, on the salary of the head housemaid, and infinitely below that of the cook.

The joy of the poor girl when she beheld her favourite companion of early years, one whom she loved as a dear brother, was indeed great. She became a welcome visitor at Oakfield Manor for many a long month after her father's death—who died blessing the name of the man whose character in early life he had so little appreciated, and whom he had so harshly treated—then, assisted by her mother, she opened a ladies' seminary in Southampton, having the most ample means to do so supplied by the grateful generosity of Sir Arthur Morton.

Mr. Wilson, the second mate of the Ocean Queen, and his six companions, received a most munificent salvage for their courage and skill in bringing the Ben Nevis safely into port.

Gratitude is not confined to class. Mr. Wilson and the seamen had a beautifully executed silver cup made in Liverpool, with appropriate designs, relative to the collision of the Ocean Queen and the Ben Nevis, and engraved on the cup was a handsome inscription, stating that to the courage, perseverance, and example of Sir Arthur Morton, who first proposed to succour the helpless people on board the Ben Nevis, and who gallantly risked life to do so, was owing the chief success in saving the ship.

Joseph never quitted his personal attendance on his master. He was a privileged person in both families, and when the young scions of the house of Morton grew into comely, high-spirited boys, there was no living without Joseph ; he was their *beau-idéal* of a sailor ; they had boats made and rigged after his fashion ; they would stir nowhere without him. He made ships, cannons, and told them wonderful stories of wonderful animals in foreign parts, where he had rode on the back of a prodigious monster, who plunged into the sea with him. But what most delighted the children during the winter nights was his stories of the Indians, and particularly of their father's residence with the renowned chief, Punka Bosswash, with his scanty garments and his fine cocked hat, and his beautiful daughter, Miss Punka Bosswash, who would have died a thousand deaths to serve his master, and who performed such wonderful exploits to save them from the Mexican pirates.

THE END.

Woodfall and Kinder, Printers, Mil.ord Lane, Strand, W S.